BREWING TEMPTATION

NOMADIC RHODES
BOOK 2

SYDNE BARNETT

FLAME AND FICTION LLC

To the Noels of the world: *You ARE worthy. I see you. Keep fighting for what you know in your heart of hearts you deserve. Your Jameson is waiting.*

The Rhodes family is made up of twelve rowdy siblings, many many cousins and a handful of 'pseudo-siblings'.

*For simplicity's sake, I've **only** listed those mentioned in **this** book.*

MILO RHODES
Dad, captain of the *Rhodes Away*

JUNIPER RHODES
Mom, keeper of the chaos, deliverer of epic hugs and warm food.

I. JEANNE
Eldest sister, world-traveling surgeon, divorced, location unknown. Spontaneously appears on family text thread, usually around the holidays.

II. RHYETT
Eldest brother, entrepreneur, in a relationship with Brexley Snows, current location St. Pete, Florida. Adorably—some would say obnoxiously—optimistic.

III. JAMESON
Fisherman, next in line to captain the family boat, single, located in Mistyvale, AK. Bestower of sardonic witticisms and tough love.

IV. ELORA
Traveling life coach and public speaker, single, currently in Mistyvale, AK. Designated family know-it-all and planner of events.

V. AXEL
Fisherman, single, currently in Mistyvale, AK but travels for the winter. Equal parts sunshine and sarcasm.

VI. PAXTON
Pro quarterback for the Windy City Wolves in Chicago, single. Gazelle-like focus on his career, hates the cold.

VII. HADLEE

Travel blogger and influencer, single, location unknown. Aka, Hurricane Hadlee due to a propensity for chaos.

VIII. ALESSANDRA

Aka. "Alice", career TBD, currently in Mistyvale, AK. Jameson's favorite sister, because she's quiet and observant.

IX. FINNEGAN

Aka. "Finn", digital nomad, we think he's still in Philadelphia? Unsure. Quietest of the twelve.

X. LEIGHTON

Twins with Kaia, student and waitress, currently in Mistyvale, AK. Doesn't really know who she is yet—will report back.

XI. KAIA

Twins with Leighton, student and waitress, currently in Mistyvale, AK. Lover of all things beautiful, family makeup artist.

XII. MAVERICK

Fisherman, single, Mistyvale, AK. Bogarts the good tunes, sympathy crier.

"PSEUDO-SIBLINGS"

Broderick Allen—Best friends with Rhyett and Jameson, Philosophy Professor, single, collector of nice things, Mistyvale, AK.

Max—Best friends with Elora, Hadlee and Alice, mystery career— we think it's tech related?—travels as much as an authentic Rhodes, single, impeccable taste in both clothes and booze, currently in Mistyvale, AK.

COUSINS

Charlie—Town Sheriff, widower, two kids, June (9) and Sterling (5).
Jake—Fisherman, single, Mistyvale, AK

AUTHOR'S NOTE

Well, helloooo there darling! Thank you so much for joining Jameson and Noel for their story. I feel like every couple will steal a little piece of my heart, but there's just something so special about these two. I'm not sure how I'll get out of my Jameson hangover.

Brewing Temptation can be read as a stand alone, or after the first book, *South of The Skyway*.

As always, your mental health matters!
<u>Here are Brewing Temptation's content disclosures:</u>

Domestic violence/emotional and financial abuse (not between the two main characters), mention of cheating (not between two main characters), stalking, violence, explicit language, and explicit on page sexual content.

PROLOGUE

NOEL

The black varnish of Brexley's front door stared back at me expectantly. Waiting. Watching the lunatic that had been pacing in circles for the better half of the last hour, no doubt. I lifted my hand for what had to be the tenth time, heart pounding in my chest like the beat of a runaway train.

This was it.

This was the moment that would determine whether I could break free from the suffocating grip of fear and reclaim my own damn life. Down to my bones, that fact rang true.

"Come on, Noel," I whispered to myself, the words barely audible over the cacophony of nerves. "You can do this. Just knock on the damn door and ask for help." Taking a deep breath, my optimism warring with the knot of anxiety and betrayal in my gut, I moved within an inch before the oxygen left me in a rush. My fist fell away from the door and I whirled for the front steps, puffing air into my cheeks. A stress laugh bubbled up my throat, co-mingling with a sob that lodged itself in my chest. My feet didn't falter as I dropped down her front steps, only to screech to a halt, eyes sliding closed as they burned, shoulders falling.

"*Fuck that*. Turn. Around." My aching cheekbone seemed to throb in affirmation. Like my body was demanding I follow through. Life felt surreal, like a crossover between a morbid comedy and a horror movie. I was stuck somewhere in no man's land, armed with only four shots of espresso, a heavy hand of sarcasm...and a desperate need to remember what it felt like to be *safe*.

The problem was, with each second, my courage shrunk like an erratic accordion playing an indecisive melody–notes of hope swallowed by squawks of regret.

What if Brexley wasn't home? Okay, yes, their cars were out front, but what if they'd gone out on a date? Rhyett seemed like a 'take an Uber if you're drinking' kind of guy. What if they couldn't help me? What if...what if they judged me...or worse, *pitied* me? Would they ask me the same ten million questions I'd been asking myself? Questions that danced in my head, like demons threatening to devour any remnants of hope I had left.

Brexley and Rhyett had only been together for a handful of months, but in that short time, her boyfriend had won over our entire friend group. He was the second of *twelve* children and seemed willing to share that big brother vibe with all of us who needed it. In a matter of weeks, he'd swept my workaholic best friend right the hell off her feet and perpetually went out of his way to make sure our loyal companions felt welcome in their home, becoming one of my best friends in the process.

But he'd seen it.

He'd known, somehow, what Eric–who was *supposed* to be my loving boyfriend–was under those fitted suits and polished shoes. Must have sensed it when he came to the hospital after my 'car accident' that left my collarbone fractured. One look at my bruised face, and the man stood taller, nerves blatantly bristling. Like he couldn't put his finger on it but knew it was no accident.

Was the shocked betrayal painted so plainly in my eyes that a virtual stranger could read the words my own family couldn't? Could he see the confusion warring in my head? The wrestling match between asking what I'd done wrong, and the white-hot trepidation that overcame me when Eric's eyes disconnected as if a wall had dropped between us? Like he couldn't even see *me*. Couldn't remember that he loved me, or that we'd made declarations of forever. All he could see at that moment was that he couldn't control me anymore, and his outraged threats and manipulative undercuts were no longer yielding results.

Did Rhyett somehow know that it had been Eric's hands that ripped the wheel sideways so quickly we'd gone careening off the vacant country road into the light post? *Lucky to be alive*–that's what the officer said. *Lucky. Ha!* And because he was the damn devil incarnate, Eric walked away without a scratch across his damnably beautiful face.

Feeling trapped and terrified, he'd temporarily calmed me with what were now clearly hollow declarations of change and tearful, trembling apologies poured like honey into bitter liquid, hiding the acid beneath. He'd get help, he said. Losing me would devastate him, he said. As I stared down the black paint, embarrassment flushed my cheeks. How could I have been so stupid to swallow his poison and believe for the best?

My current fears were entirely irrational. *Of course, they would help.* Of course, Brexley would move heaven and earth for me. We'd been best friends since childhood, built our business from the ground up, *and* made it a staple in the city. And she'd found her soulmate in Rhyett Rhodes. There had been plenty of times when she'd leaned on me...and it was time I sucked it up and admitted I needed her to lend me her strength. To be *my* haven in this storm. I knew I couldn't continue to let fear dictate my future. Not this time. Not anymore.

Because what in the hell would have happened if I hadn't gotten out of that damn house?

"Come on, Noel."

Logically, I knew I was worth more than this, even as I bounced on the balls of my feet, muttering like a crazy person. Worth more than trembling with anxiety in my own house. Worth more than living in fear of constant scrutiny, of always–*always*–being inadequate. Worth more than a whiskey-laced-tongue slinging insults and an alcohol-fueled fist that finally collided with my face instead of the drywall.

Inevitable, that breaking point. Allowing my determination to see the good in everyone kept me hanging on, hoping he would heal... change...be who I knew he *could* be instead of accepting who he continually showed me he was. But logic meant little where love was concerned. It really was blind, justifying the most heinous behaviors as I clung to the idea of who I'd fallen in love with instead of the reality of him. Scared? Yes. Desperately grasping for control? Yes. Justified...?

My tongue subconsciously jutted out to taste the copper on my lip. This was it.

Now or never.

Summoning every ounce of determination, I mustered a half-hearted smile—more for *my* reassurance than anything else—and my trembling hand connected with the door. The weight of uncertainty pressed back against my aching knuckles, and I sucked down a breath as feet shifted somewhere inside. Voices glittered. It was time to face the darkness head-on, armed with nothing but a glimmer of hope, two of my best friends, and a little resilience. Squaring my shoulders, I decided to emerge stronger from whatever was behind that door. Like hell would Eric fucking Connely dim an ounce of my fire.

At least, that's what I told myself right until I turned to bolt a few seconds too late. Brexley's voice halted me at the edge of the top step. "Noel?" Her voice dripped with skepticism, like she'd tied her anxiety to my own.

Slowly, I turned back toward her, struggling to lift my chin or meet her eyes as shame coursed through my veins. The shattering of her glass jerked my attention as what could only have been her favorite merlot poured over the concrete like blood. "*Noel?!*" She screeched, lunging forward, eyes rounding when I held up a hand, wanting anything but to be touched right now. The damn thing trembled as I shook my head, eyes dropping to the ground, where the burgundy slowly crept towards my bare feet. I'd sprinted here without shoes, for God's sake.

Oh good. I must have looked as good as I felt. Suddenly, the dull throb in my cheek and lips crept past the fortifying wall of adrenaline.

"Is Rhyett home?"

His presence was irrefutable as he stepped into the door frame, only to leap past me, looking around for a threat too smart to be caught dead on his doorstep. Satisfied there wasn't an immediate danger, they ushered me inside and to the couch, where Brexley handed me a fresh glass of water and Rhyett supplied an ice pack. I cleared my throat. When I lifted my face, eyes burning, Rhyett sucked down a breath and tears trailed down Brexley's face.

"I need your help."

ONE

NOEL

"Who on earth decided that boob prisons were a good idea?"

"I don't know, but I hope they're enjoying their one-bedroom suite in hell." Laughing, I discarded my bra onto the burnt orange brocade comforter as Brexley did the same before we both sighed in relief. Rubbing at the angry ring of skin where the band had been, I watched as she wandered to the window to look out at the Anchorage skyline...if it qualified as a 'skyline'. We certainly weren't in Tampa anymore, and my heart ached as I watched her. Only Brexley would have my back as I started a new life from scratch. Our other friends were amazing for moral support, if you could count fantasizing about how my now ex-boyfriend would come to a fortunate end and supplying me with no shortage of daily affirmations. But Brexley rearranged everything to make sure she could be here, staring out at a city barely big enough to be called a city. After high school, neither of us had ever been farther west than Texas, which, let's face it, is basically just a bigger, dryer, hotter Florida sans the white sand beaches. We'd been too busy with school and building The Cracked Corset–our combination coffee shop and romance-niche bookstore–together to worry about traveling in our early twenties. And with good reason, because the last sixteen hours of busy airports, delayed flights, and rideshares were only mostly tolerable because I was in good company.

"Seriously," I grumbled, "what is so freaking offensive about the female body?"

"Nothing." Rhyett's low voice accompanied the dull squeak of the metal hotel room door as he shoved it aside, sliding a bronze trolly over the clunky threshold with his other hand. "Absolutely fucking nothing."

He didn't even attempt to conceal his adoration for Brexley, those steel-blue eyes scraping over her from head to toe as he shoved our absurd pile of luggage into the room. Rhyett Rhodes was the kind of man every girl wanted for their best friend. That radiant smile of his showered over her like early morning light despite the curtain of darkness enveloping the city. He abandoned his self-appointed adventure as our personal bellhop in exchange for a nauseatingly passionate embrace, threading his fingers through Brex's blonde waves and angling her just to his liking so he could practically eat her face. I couldn't help but wonder if all Rhodes men kissed like that. Like the world was ending, and the only way to save humanity was a passionate embrace that left no eyeballs wondering who their woman belonged to. I mean, with that many children, I had to think that at the very least, he'd learned that kind of unabashed affection from his father.

The Rhodes family hailed from a tiny fishing village called Mistyvale, Alaska, planted on a rugged island about an hour's flight from the mainland. It was their influence in town that made it such a perfect place to start over. Rhyett needed someone to manage his coffee shop while his full-time wingwoman, Brinleigh, was on maternity leave. I needed something familiar as I overhauled my life and figured out who I was and where I was going in a world without Eric.

Honestly, if it had been anyone but her, I'd have labeled this kind of make-out overboard. But if any woman deserved a man that devoured her that thoroughly, it was Brexley Snows. The girl was more likely to work herself to death than take a break to have some fun...at least until *fun* had arrived in our favorite Florida bar in the form of six feet and two inches of gold skin, blonde hair, muscle, and ink. Despite her most stubborn attempts to resist *Prince Charming*, my lifelong best friend fell hard and fast, with me contentedly planted on Team-Rhyett. Even more so after he dropped everything when I showed up on their doorstep, asking for help to escape the hellhole that was my domestic life. Never had I seen a man as charged with anger than when I was sitting across from Rhyett as I iced my cheek and told him my story. Judging by the clench of his fists and the way that livid vein had popped out in his neck when we got back to my house, Eric had just been lucky the police arrived on the scene before Rhyett did. Not that he deserved any form of luck.

Alright, the tongue action was a bit overkill. "*Ohhhhkay* you two, get a room."

Chuckling, Rhyett peeled away. "Oh wait," he quipped back, "we just did, Red."

Wrinkling my nose, I griped, "Eww," and reached into my personal *Mary Poppins* bag, fishing around until fleece kissed my fingertips, at which point I clamped on and pulled the new hoodie free. "It's freezing here," I noted, yanking it on.

The man chuckled, shaking his head and turning to offload the cart. In his defense, Captain Dreamboat over there genuinely had attempted to warn me multiple times, though the current predicament that was my life left little room in the way of logic. But damn, he had not undersold the gray. Or the mist. Or the way the chill seemed to penetrate my body—not in the way that would no doubt leave me smiley and satisfied as I drifted off to sleep. No, this was the kind of cold that relentlessly reached through your clothes, carving the meat from your bones until it wrapped its nebulous, invisible talons around your marrow.

"Isn't it supposed to be spring?" Brex asked as she popped through her own Seattle hoodie and scooped her hair back into a sleek ponytail.

"Last leg, ladies, just hold yourselves together for one more day and then we can relax." They had delayed our first flight from Anchorage to Mistyvale *four* times, amounting to a grand total of four hours, only to fly around the island for an additional two, unable to land due to—*no shock*—fog. Finally, calling it a lost cause, they'd turned tail and dropped us back off on the mainland. As Rhyett turned from the bag cart, he spotted our matching hoodies and shook his head. "Don't let my brother see you in those. All hell will break loose."

"Which one?" I teased. "Aren't there like a million of them?"

"Five, last time I counted. But if anyone could pull a bonus child out of a hat, it would be Juniper."

It had always struck me as both endearing and odd that Rhyett referred to his mom by her first name. Evidently, Juniper's dozen children had never been an adequate drain on her love, because she seemed to step into the role of mother for any who needed it–friends, orphans, or random travelers. Rhyett's stories all included cousins and bonus 'pseudo-siblings' in one capacity or another.

"Right," Brex said, eyes promising trouble. "So, *like a million*."

"Regardless, I'd hide those away from all of them. Pax would take it personally," he said like it should have been obvious.

His younger brother, Paxton, was a pro quarterback for the Windy City Wolves in Chicago. A fact my friend Josie had lost her damn mind about, after drooling over the man for the last three consecutive years. "Jameson treats disloyalty as a criminal offense, Mav would play the devil's advocate, and Axel and Finn would seize the opportunity to turn you."

"Into pumpkins?" I quipped back. *Turn me.* Turn me into what?

"Redcoats are more like it."

"Has anyone told you that you're a tad dramatic?" Brex planted a kiss on the end of his nose, but Rhyett only shrugged.

"Don't claim I didn't warn you." When his mouth returned to hers, I took my cue to leave.

"*Okay*," I muttered. "Imma go find tea." It was entirely unsurprising that the only response was a hum of approval from Brexley as I snatched what was unofficially being dubbed *my* keycard off the desk where Rhyett had set all three of them and headed for the door. As the latch snicked shut behind me, I collapsed back into the ugly, generic hotel wallpaper and pulled my headphones from the front pocket of my jeans, popping them into place for good measure.

Okay, I may have turned on my sad playlist, letting Cigarettes After Sex strip the mask of strength off my face, allowing the layer of ache concealed behind cosmetics and smiles to surface.

There weren't two better human beings to endure this transition with, but Brexley was a helicopter mom without ever having had her own children. If my anxiety made itself known, she'd spring into obnoxiously-concerned-best-friend mode and hover me to death. Well-meaning, but suffocating. Sighing, I kicked off the wall and headed for the lobby. What was it with hotels and the creepy, infinite hallways? This was no doubt the nicest airport hotel available—Rhyett wouldn't have it any other way—but the eerie stretching walls and tacky patterns were the same in every generic building.

When the bone-deep cold of a spring Anchorage evening sent tingles across my skin, I sucked a breath of invigorating air down, praying it could steady me. That damp chill of The Last Frontier was undoubtedly going to take some adapting to. I'd traveled a bit growing up, but primarily, I'd grown accustomed to the sun-soaked, balmy, forever eighty-degree weather of Florida's Gulf Coast. This was...different. Brisk. Like a slap to the face, my eyes instantly prickling. I hoped the fresh start it represented would be equally abrasive. A new beginning. A new beginning, somewhere *he* couldn't touch. Somewhere there were no memories of smooth words and slick suits and promises of a better future. No bench ads with his father's smug, insufferable face staring back at me, reminding me to vote or donate to one cause or another.

There were mistakes, like poor relationships or a Pageboy haircut, and then there were self-sabotaging catastrophes. Eric had been the latter. I'd known. Deep down, the first time he'd set 'ground rules' for my friends, or the first time he physically stepped between me and the exit, that little voice that knew better croaked a warning. But he was full of sexy promises and logical justifications, and I'd let myself get swept up in smooth words and the allure of a man like that noticing...*me*.

It had been two weeks since Eric decided he would best remedy my 'disobedience' with the backside of his hand, followed by a fist that cracked my lip open.

Two weeks since I chose myself and shattered every inch of the life that I'd fought so fucking hard to build. Two weeks since police cuffed the man I thought was the love of my life–placing his hands in front of him–and covering his restraints with his suit jacket as though they owed him some kind of respect beyond the common criminal because of his last name and job title. Eric's family had been in politics for three damn generations, and apparently, that meant more than the dignity of his victim.

The stars winked down at me despite the light pollution, and I stared back. It was that prickle of awareness up my back that alerted me to Rhyett as he approached.

"You okay?"

"Hmm?" I dragged my eyes away from the deep onyx of a midnight sky, aware of the ache of fatigue climbing into my bones. Rhyett was like the big brother I never had but always wanted. The little wrinkle beside his eyes was shining with care only a big brother could possess as he gave me a knowing smile. "Um, yeah, just needed a breather. How's Brex?"

"Passed out as soon as she laid down."

"Travel has always tuckered her out," I supplied affectionately.

"Too many people," he accurately deduced. "Too many things out of her control."

"It's like you *know her* or something." Brexley had always been the organization to my chaos, the focus to my fun, the numbers and strategy to my adoration of people. She lived by a color-coded planner and lists of to-do's, whereas I preferred a...*spontaneous,* sticky-notes-everywhere approach to my life.

He chuckled, but I felt that same intense focus he'd had when all of this started back in that hospital room. "Answer the question, Noel."

I sighed, some mix of endearment and irritation forcing my eyes to his expectant face. "I'm alright. Tired, mostly. Sad. Angry. It's a whole blender full of emotions in here right now. Mostly, I'm just... nervous, I guess."

"That's only natural. You're starting over, five-thousand miles from home. You sure about this?"

For the first time since college, I wished I had something to smoke—a cigarette, a joint, it didn't really matter what, as long as it silenced the incessant squeaking hamster wheel of thoughts spinning circles in my brain—something to do with my hands, to force myself to breathe. It wasn't Rhyett's question.

As hard as it was to walk away from our business and our lifelong friends, it was harder turning every corner and having my mind bombard me with memories and questions I would never have answers for. Was it ever real? Did I imagine the way Eric cared for me in the beginning? Was it always a play for control? Why was it that men in fitted suits with fat wallets and prominent families could do whatever the hell they wanted and walk away from it unscathed?

"Yeah," I answered, no trace of hesitation in my tone. The Rhodes practically ruled Mistyvale by the sounds of it. They knew everyone, and the few they didn't know would at least know *of them.* However, according to Rhyett, that could go either way, depending on which brother had made the impression in the first place. The sisters, he'd affectionately informed me, were all safe. "Yeah, I am. I really appreciate this, Rhyett. The job, the rental. Hell, getting us there. Everything."

Rhyett *The Connector* Rhodes had lined up a position as an interim manager for me at his island coffee shop, the Grizzly Grind, the temporary opening a perfect fit for my who-the-fuck-knows life plan. As if that wasn't enough, he insisted I 'watch' his damn house, so it 'didn't go to waste'. Did I mention his gorgeous truck needed somebody to drive it so the battery didn't die? The man was an angel, and not just for Brex.

"Of course. We'll get you in, introduce you to the family, and ensure you're settled before we go home. My brothers and Broderick will watch out for you, make sure you have what you need, alright?"

My stomach turned, sweat pricking at my spine. "Rhyett?"

"Yeah?"

Steadying myself, I ran through all the reasons I wanted this to be a clean break, primarily the freedom to become this new, liberated version of myself. Noel, the remix, the 2.0, the great reclamation. With one last calming breath, I said, "I want this to be a fresh start. No guys. No new business ventures bogging me down. No expectations, or people tiptoeing around my baggage." If I had to watch my mother or siblings stare at me like I was as likely to detonate as say hello for even one more day, I might implode. It was time, not pity, that my soul craved. "Just me, figuring out what in the hell that looks like. It would mean a lot to me if what happened in Florida, stays in Florida."

He watched me—this new, too kind for his own good, pseudo-big-brother figure—with a solemn understanding before he finally nodded, sending relief trickling through my veins. This could work.

TWO

JAMESON

There was something eternally comforting about finally spotting the abrupt jagged teeth that rose out of the sea. With the engine rumbling the deck underfoot, my eyes devoured the rolling emerald hills and mountaintops covered in towering spruce and pine trees.

"You excited to see him?" Maverick, the youngest of my brothers, asked as he nonchalantly leaned onto the edge of the wheelhouse, braced on his forearm. He still had that long, lanky build of adolescence, but there wasn't a chance it would remain after the summer. It never did.

The summer spent on the *Rhodes Away* was an initiation for us boys. We all spent our years as deckhands from about fifteen on, but it wasn't until we were seventeen or so that our dad, the renowned Captain Milo Rhodes, really put us to work. Mav, the spoiled baby that he was, had gotten it easy last year. But this was my year, and that bullshit was about to end. This was the year Milo would hand over the reins, while he still stayed aboard to make sure this transition would be smooth.

I wanted to believe Dad was excited to step away, and that the prospect of my mother sipping margaritas while watching her useless highland cows graze in The Sunshine State would be more appealing than freezing his balls off for another winter next year. But as I stared at our rocky Alaskan island, inching closer by the minute, I realized—not for the first time—that he would miss this. The exhausting hustle of it. The simultaneous peace, and the way even the calm days left our bones singing. He might not talk about it while mom poured through paint samples and handed insurance investigators their asses when her Florida project started over after a highly-suspect fire, but he would.

And with Rhyett in town, naturally, all those warm, squishy conversations were bound to rear their ugly heads. I love my brother. To the end of the earth, I do. But the man is a damn flower child if I've ever seen one. So freaking happy all the time–a complete and total *Pollyanna*. I'd never understood it. Despite his insistence on finding the bright side of things best left in the dark, I fucking loved him. It was fucked up to pick favorites as one of a dirty dozen siblings, but if I had to, it would be the sunshiny bastard.

"Yeah," I finally said, realizing I likely hesitated one heartbeat too long. Mav either didn't notice or didn't mind, because he just bobbed his head to a beat nobody else could hear. "They should be at the house tonight for dinner. Rhyett said something about a new tenant for his place before they leave."

"He's renting the house?"

"Yeah."

"So, things really are serious with him and Brex?"

I scoffed, tossing him the flippant side-eye that remark earned. "Please. Like you didn't see them together in Florida. They were already oozing thirty-thousand-dollar reception, open bar, whatever-dress-she-likes, salmon or prime rib bells."

"He seems happy," Mav pointed out, although curiosity danced in his eyes, inevitably at my tone.

"It's *Rhyett*. Give the man a cup of tea and a pretty sunset and he's happy."

An indignant snort cut off my salty diatribe. I was excited for my brother. Honestly, I was. But a dirty bathroom one-night-stand that blew him off in the name of *fate deciding*, only to end up head over fucking heels infatuated? That shit didn't happen in real life. Not for anyone else, at least.

I turned towards the offending scoff, although it didn't take a rocket scientist to guess that Axel was walking up beside us.

Where Mav, Paxton, and Finn were the spitting image of, well, *me*—dark, unruly hair and accompanying salted scruff and pale skin —Axel was Rhyett, duplicated. A little rougher around the edges, a little broader in the shoulders, but just as blonde and just as tan. It was the Rhodes family eyes that gave us all away though, and a second set of those steely-blues locked on me. Axel braced himself on the rail to my opposite side, watching as the island drew closer.

"Someone's on the wrong side of the boat today."

"Just tired," I said. Though to be convincing, I likely needed to at least attempt to not growl like a feral dog when I spoke. Palming my face, I added, "Nothing a few fingers of scotch and a night with the boys won't fix." It wasn't that I didn't want to see him—*them*—it was just the idea of *more* bodies cramming inside the main house.

I know everything in life is cheaper by the fucking dozen, but twelve kids, three annoyingly omnipresent best friends, two parents, two dogs, a cat, and a plethora of cousins was plenty of ruckus, thank you very much.

When our oldest sister, Jeanne, got married, it didn't feel like anything changed. But that was because Link had been around for most of our lives. He was already a part of the house. Honestly, I missed the fucker when I remembered he still existed somewhere out there, saving lives as far away from my stubborn sister as he could get. They'd gone their separate ways, torn apart by grief, and never reconciled. She could put on a brave face, but Jeanne would always belong to Link, just like Mom would always belong to our dad. I just hoped she'd realize it in time to get her happy ending. I didn't believe in that tacky romantic shit, but some people just...clicked.

Kinda like Rhyett and Brexley, though I loathed to admit my brother was likely lost to the rest of us.

You know the way your stomach drops when you lose balance too close to a cliff face? That same precarious drop had settled in my gut. Like Rhyett was just the first domino, the impenetrable line of Rhodes siblings about to crash one-by-one into monotonous monogamy.

Which would make our already full family gatherings seem... insane. We'd need a barn. Or church hall. Perhaps a wedding venue for Sunday family dinners.

Yeah, Rhyett and Brex, plus whatever mystery friend was coming with them, would require a strong cup of coffee. Or liquor. Maybe both.

"Hell yeah, I forgot that's tonight. Home just in time," Mav said, grinning. Honestly, the little shit was probably just still pumped he was old enough to join in.

As Milo smoothly brought us into the dock, Axel and I both dismounted over the rail in a synchronized, highly inadvisable leap. I couldn't help that some part of me was still a rebellious adolescent, the bark of Milo's disapproval settling like satisfaction in my chest. It was a move we'd seen in an animated movie as kids and implemented ourselves, much to our father's outrage.

Ropes in hand, we both hit the decking, locking gazes only to find the emotion mirrored back. Tied off, exhausted, and so fucking thankful to be back on almost solid land, I headed up through the harbor towards my truck.

"I FOLD."

Smirking at Maverick, I drawled, "Of course you do, princess." I tapped my cards against the table as he set his down in surrender. Staring down Rhyett, I leaned back in my chair, channeling a bit of pent-up energy into the simple rock and sway of it. Our monthly *guys' night* had become a thing when half of us were still in high school. Our numbers might've dwindled some as we all took our turns in college and our younger brother, Paxton, rode off to live my freaking dream life playing for the NFL.

It was almost the two of us, a couple of years apart, both local legends on the field. But when a torn ACL brought my Seattle football career to an abrupt end during my sophomore year in college, I dropped out. The only reason I'd endured classes in the first place was because they were required to play. My GPA was more of a reflection of collegiate league requirements than my actual potential. You had to give a shit to do any better. I simply didn't.

But these guys right here—my brothers, our best friends, Broderick and Max, and two of our cousins, Charlie and Jake—were the real fucking deal. The hell and high-water crew. The bastards you called to bury a body. Hell, Charlie was the town sheriff, newly appointed this year. Not a bad accomplishment at thirty.

But if we were all in town, Monday nights were for the boys. Football on the television in the fall. Whatever was on ESPN the rest of the year. Didn't matter how dirty or grime-coated the day had been, this was where we planted our asses before the daylight faded. It was exactly what I needed.

This was where my superior ability to pretend I gave no fucks won me the pot more often than not. But Rhyett—Rhyett *usually* had my number. The corner of his lips quirked, convincing me he had me. *He had me*, and I couldn't show him. Judging by the way his eyes narrowed, he knew it.

"I call," Rhyett said simply.

Cocksucker. I didn't let myself eye the pot, didn't let my posture shift from where I'd laced my fingers behind my head. Axel was practically vibrating out of his seat next to me, and Broderick knew me about as well as Rhyett, which meant he was also kicked back in his chair, arms crossed as he watched me and held his breath like a sniper.

Fold or bluff? Fold or bluff? If I folded, Rhyett walked away victorious. If I bluffed, there was a chance—equivalent to finding a four-leaf clover in a field—that he'd buy it, and I could still take the pot home. My best friend, Broderick, had even tossed in his classy brand-name watch. I mean, it might be fun to see what that felt like for an hour or two before returning it, so it didn't get wasted on boat life. None of us were dumb enough to take a trinket from the town philosopher—our trades would destroy the damn thing in a day.

Slowly, I eyed the table before sliding my gaze back up to my brother's cocky face, drawing up a slow smile. Broderick shifted in his seat, his focus nearly as acute as Axel's, like he knew. Like he knew and wasn't sure what he wanted to see play out.

"All in." I slid my pile into the center, refusing to react to Axel as he rocked in his seat and sucked down a breath that puffed his cheeks out, our ridiculous baby brother as he choked on either spit or a bite of chip, or Broderick as the tiniest curl played on his lips.

Mostly, I refused to react to Rhyett as he clenched his jaw and drilled holes in my skull like he'd developed laser vision in Florida.

This was the difference between the two of us. We might have been close, but growing up, Rhyett was all golden boy, to my rebel-without-a-clue. Not that he wouldn't get his hands dirty or throw down if he needed to, because he would. He always had our backs, end of story. But I was the unhinged one of the two of us. The one that thrived on it. The one people were nervous around because they just weren't ever sure what to expect. We'd collectively decided to let them keep being nervous when we were kids; we thought it might come in handy someday.

Which meant the shit-eating grin on my face equated to one of two things. Trouble. Or victory. His job at this table was to decide which one he was looking at. Mine was to make him question himself.

Rhyett discreetly peeked at his cards against the table before rolling his lip between his teeth. *Oh shit, no way in hell.*

I knew that tell.

"I fold." He sighed, resigned to his decision as he leaned back in the chair, jaw working as he narrowed his eyes on me expectantly.

Goddamn, that was close. Every single muscle in my body relaxed, disbelief tangling with the win. There were few things as satisfying as winning on a bluff. I mean, winning on pocket aces was generally more enjoyable and didn't tie my innards into a knot.

He turned over his cards to reveal a straight flush, and I tried not to have a coronary as I cleared my throat and collected my winnings. What the hell did he think I was sitting on? What were the odds of my brother having a straight flush and *me* getting a royal flush in one sitting? Fucker had been in Florida for too long.

"What did you have?"

I shook my head, pursing my lips as I pulled the chips across the green felt, their subtle clink and clatter music to my ears. Un-freaking-real.

"Come on man," Rhyett insisted. "You know I hate it when you do that. What did you have?"

"That's for me to know and you not to find out."

"Son of a bitch," he grumbled, tonguing a back molar as Axel and Maverick both headed for the ice chest and Broderick let out a long, breathy *phew*.

"Welp, I'm out of here before fists start flying," Max said as he stood. He was one of the 'bonus siblings' we'd gained somewhere along the way. He was best friends with my younger sisters, Hadlee and Elora, eventually scooping up Alice too, electively making him a permanent addition to our already-too-damn-busy household. Proudly half-Japanese, the man hit the genetic goldmine and hadn't aged since we were in high school. With his dark hair expertly styled and designer jeans tucked over leather shoes, he looked like he'd walked off some chic magazine shoot. He squirreled his cash away into investments like they were going out of style and loved whatever nebulous career none of us could explain if we had a gun to our heads. All I knew was it involved an ungodly amount of conference calls at odd hours, and he could type at least a hundred words per minute. Max would absolutely not be partaking in any violence, but he loved us all enough to at least show up and bail us out. He'd say it was for the girls, but we knew better.

"Good to see you," Rhyett said, standing and pulling him in for a hug as Broderick and I did the same, passing him down the line.

"Same," Max said with a grin. "How long you in town?"

"Two weeks is all. Here for the festival, but we'll fly out when the season starts." The small talk and farewells continued as everyone shuffled around gathering jackets, exchanging hugs, and heading out the door.

When the townhouse was finally empty, save for Rhyett, I sighed a breath of relief. The week had been long, and it was just getting started. Couldn't shake the feeling in my chest like a shoe was about to drop, which was never a good sign this close to summer. My brother, the eternal boy scout, was already busying himself with cleanup, cards and chips already back in their places on the table, and he was halfway through rolling the tops down on the chip bags before clipping them closed.

Smirking, I demanded, "What in God's name did you think I had?"

Rhyett shook his head, lips quirking.

"Finally get a girl and let your brain fall out or something?"

He chuckled, grumbling, "Give me a break, my head wasn't in it."

"Welp, you made my entire month, so whatever Brex is doing to you, I'll pay her to keep doing it."

"Jealous?"

"Not even a little. The pretty ones are always more trouble than they're worth." That lesson had been learned the hard way, and there was no need for a repeat.

I made my way to the tower of dirty dishes, rolling my sleeves up and staring out at the soft glow of evening as it filled the gaps in the woods. Exhaustion competed with the awareness I should at least attempt to make conversation.

"Well, what's Brex think of Mistyvale?" This was the first time he'd brought his new lady home to meet everyone–hell, it was the first time he'd brought *any* woman home.

"She's thrilled. To her, it's all easily romanticized, you know?"

I snorted. "The magic is in *not* existing in the gray nine months out of the year."

"Exactly. She says she's been ready for a change for ages, so it's refreshing." Rhyett came to lean against the counter beside me, crossing his arms over his chest with a furrow on his face. I could've pinched a damn dime between his eyebrows. He cleared his throat as though he didn't already have my attention. "Listen, Jameson, there's something else I need to talk to you about."

The edge in his voice made my stomach tighten. I nodded briskly, wishing he'd just get on with it.

"We brought a friend to town; she's getting a fresh start. I need you to look out for her, alright?"

"Alright. She okay? You sound weird."

"Yeah, she's just going to see if she likes the small-town life."

"Alright," I said, relaxing and returning my focus to the dinner platter still clutched in my hand, sponging it off. "I'll swing by and say hi."

"Thanks. I should head home to Brex. She was super wiped out." He bumped my shoulder as he stepped by. "Love you, man."

"You too. See you soon."

My brother saw himself out as I wrapped up dishes, then wrestled the trash bag free of the can. Forehead throbbing with the beginning of a tension headache, I slipped into my loosely laced, well-worn work boots and headed out back. The chilly night air greeted me as the evening gray began to chameleon into the blue light, promising midnight.

Rhyett and I had purchased one half-acre lot and split it down the center so we could build houses side-by-side a few years back. A fence would only have interfered with family football games. So the gap between us was unhindered, our trash cans gathered between the two in the hopes of reducing the temptation for bears to pillage their goods, which was fine until I had to walk the fifty yards lugging four bags of beer bottles.

The trash can lid flipped open with a plastic clap, and I was halfway to hefting the bulging bag in when movement caught my attention. Heat assaulted my chest. I should mind my business, drop the trash and scuttle inside like the bottom feeder I was.

But I was frozen. Frozen...watching the most goddamned beautiful creature I had ever set eyes on, the faint hint of her voice trailing through Rhyett's cracked bathroom window as it gathered fog from the running shower. *Frozen*, as she tossed her dress straps off either shoulder, revealing the full, creamy length of her naked back. The window frame cut her off right where her spine curved before what I could only presume was a perfect ass. Because the rest of her was perfect. Lean. Not like an athlete, but in the way women were when they never held still. And I...couldn't peel my eyes away. Knew I should. Knew this was wrong. But she inexplicably captivated me. My body pulled towards her like there was a magnet between us.

Chest heaving, pulse pounding, blood heading south, I watched her arch her back, arms stretching up to pull pins out of her hair, freeing it from the cute little bun. I'd have to tell Rhyett to buy a damn curtain for the bathroom. The idea of some unsuspecting creep catching an eyeful of this—*fuck*, some creep *like me*.

Jesus, I'd turned back into a teenager.

Go inside, asshole. You shouldn't have seen this much.

The woman turned around; her breasts both perky, mouthwatering globes adorned with rose-colored nipples. She was fucking exquisite. Face relaxed as she basked in the shower's steam. Some figment plucked out of an ethereal dream. When her eyes fell open—directly on me—they went Disney princess doe-eye wide and the lyrics stopped pouring from her lips, which parted in surprise.

I snapped my mouth shut, bowing my head and—like an imbecile—raising my hand in the assholiest of all assholes kind of casual, neighborly greeting as I rushed to dump the damn bag in the damn can and slam the damn lid closed. There was a yelp, a curse, and then a great crash that made me wince. Had she just *fallen over?* Oh shit, what if she hit her head? I was going to hell. I likely had an engraved plate on the door to my three-bedroom suite.

Should I go make sure she was okay?!

Despite the press of curiosity, I didn't dare look back. Felt like a slimy fucking prick as it was. I did the only thing any sensible, thirty-three-year-old man who still had some semblance of survival instincts could: I bolted. But retreating like a coward didn't erase the perfect image of that body. My dick was still at attention, the bastard not catching the hint, as I booked it back towards the porch. Adjusting myself did absolutely nothing. A cold shower was in store. Or two.

Oh sweet Jesus, *she* was the *friend* I was supposed to look out for, wasn't she? Had to be. Welp, this was off to a swimmingly fantastic start. Oh hell, she was going to tell Rhyett, and Rhyett was going to promptly beat me to death. *Au revoir*, solid food. *Adios*, once-attractive face.

Halfway through the beeline for my back door, a pissed-off, beautifully feminine voice sliced through the gray night.

THREE

NOEL

"Hey!" I barked, tightening the knot on the adorably fluffy robe Rhyett had hung in the guest bathroom. The creep either didn't hear me or wanted to pretend he hadn't, no doubt still blinded by my never-seen-the-sun boobs. Where Brex and Rhyett both had delicious caramel Florida tans, I had the complexion of a survivalist's flashlight. A flashlight bedazzled in many, *many* freckles.

"*Hey!*" This time it came out with a bit more force as anger heated my neck. "Peeping Tom!"

It wasn't technically possible, but I swore I heard him sigh as he froze in the doorway, shoulders slumping. *That's right, asshole, you can't skate your way around this one.* Not only had he been gawking through the window between houses, but I'd freaking fallen *into* the shower when my deer-in-headlights delayed instincts finally faded and I lunged—okay, *tumbled*—for the plush safety of the bathrobe. I was fairly certain my knee was bleeding, but I was too mad to slow down and check.

I kept my focus on the man's broad shoulders as he slowly, pointedly, turned until we were face-to-face, one hand tugging at the back of his neck. Okay, maybe I hadn't meant to climb right up into his personal space, but for one outraged moment, I forgot what boundaries even were. The man smelled better than he looked, and that was freaking saying something. Dark lashes framed intense eyes, below a gorgeous head of thick, nearly black hair. The arm he'd waved in the most patronizing salute known to man was covered in dark ink I would have loved on any other day.

But that was beside the point. *Mad, Noel. We're big mad.* I jabbed a blush-painted nail into his chest–not that it went far since the man was as solid as the rock Mistyvale was founded on. Sweet baby cheeses, he was built like a brick house.

"What. The. *Hell*?" I demanded, crossing my arms over my chest. Not that it mattered at this point, he'd already gotten an eyeful, right down main street. Honestly, I was thanking all that was holy it came out mad and not breathless.

"What do you mean 'what the hell'?" he whisper-growled with all the tact of someone hushing a child, making my cheeks flame hotter. The man held his ground, a furrow in his brow as he stared me down. "*You're the one* waking the neighbors at a quarter to midnight."

I glowered up at the still-bright sky. For fucks sake, was it really *midnight*? It was just getting dark out. Hearing about the Land of Midnight Sun and seeing it were two disconcertingly different things. *Focus, Noel.*

Straightening my spine and lifting my chin, I barked back, "*You're* the one being a *freaking creep* in the middle of the night." I didn't bother to lower my voice. If the scowling incarnation of Ivar Ragnarsson didn't want to disturb the neighborhood, he should start by avoiding loitering outside bathroom windows. "What the hell are you even doing here?"

"I *live* here." He deadpanned and tapped on the doorframe like I needed clarification. Of course he did. First week on this island, and I already had someone to avoid.

"No," I snapped, pointing back to Rhyett's still-lit, but now vacant, bathroom window next door. "*There* here. What were you doing with front-row seats to our freaking bathroom? Strip club closed tonight, thought you'd improvise?"

"Look, I was just taking out the trash," he sighed, bringing up a thumb and forefinger to pinch the bridge of his nose, eyes sliding closed. "Wasn't looking for a peepshow."

"Well, you certainly weren't shy about it when you got one."

"I looked away as quick as I could. Didn't even see anything worth noting."

"Bullshit." He'd undoubtedly gotten a full frontal. And insulted me in the process of denying it. If I was lucky, the window cut above the waist, but I wasn't entirely sure of his angle, as I was too busy panicking and then trying not to die as I nearly strangled myself with the shower curtain. Either way, the girls had been on full display in all their pale, size-A glory. I could have been the chairman of the itty bitty titty committee. That fact hadn't kept this gorgeous asshole from taking a long look though.

Tightening my hold around my chest, I snarled, "Haven't you ever heard of *privacy?*" That made his eyes snap open, one brow pointedly hiked.

"Haven't you ever heard of *curtains?*" he snarled back, dropping his hand to his side and glaring down at me. "It's called a *window.* They're generally see-through."

"Oh, so this is *my* fault?"

"You said it. Must be true." He shrugged nonchalantly as I tried to wrestle down a breath. "I'll accept your apology whenever you're ready."

"Oh, you have *got* to be kidding me."

"I am not."

"That's rich. You leer at *me* naked and *I'm* the one who needs to apologize."

"That sums it up." The corner of his mouth quirked, no doubt some stroke of male genius. "Sexual harassment, that's what it's called. I didn't consent to being flashed."

"Jesus," I muttered, narrowing my eyes and praying for patience. And for this ridiculously precarious, warm liquid feeling in my chest to subside. Okay, yeah, he was abominably gorgeous. Keyword: *abominably.*

I could be pissed, mortified, out for revenge, and also not so naïve to pretend I was blind.

Angry, Noel. We're angry. Focus.

"Now, if you don't mind, you're dripping on my shoes."

I looked down to where the water I'd collected on my catastrophic nosedive into the shower was pooling on his door frame. Glaring back at him, I bit out, "You're a real piece of work."

As I turned to stomp off his porch, the wood creaked behind me a beat before a warm, rough hand closed around my wrist, freezing my ribs mid-expansion and throat mid-swallow.

"Wait." His tone commanded that I freeze in that one word, and heat bloomed where his skin touched mine. He might have been a creepy fucking asshole, but holy stars, that touch was *electrifying.* My eyes fell to where his calloused thumb gave my arm one solid sweep before he released his grip. He sucked down a breath. "I didn't mean to...'leer' at you, and I'm sorry." He dipped his head, locking our gazes together. I hadn't actually realized my shoulders had caved in until he forced me to meet his eyes. "*I'm sorry,*" he repeated. "You're safe here. I swear on my life. I'm not some psycho." A cheeky little smile popped dimples into existence under his dark stubble. "I mean...not usually. I'll *buy you* the damn curtains, alright?"

Fully incapable of performing speech, I nodded and turned for my new home.

JAMESON

"SON OF A BITCH!" Of its own volition, my hand came up to soothe the spot I'd just smacked on the back of my head. Fucking spring prep. Fucking boat. Fucking weird metal corner in a cramped-ass part of the engine room.

"I'd recommend using a hammer next time," Axel quipped, earning a middle finger and grumbled curses. He burst into unapologetic laughter.

There was a myriad of rituals that came with our industry, the first of which was spring prep before salmon season. Our boat was hauled out of the water and dry docked, repairs were itemized and delegated, deep-cleaning was implemented, and the whole damn thing got a fresh paint job and seal before we set out for the peak of our year. The irony was it was nearly impossible to actually check off the punch list because there was inevitably some bullshit patch job in the hull, or minute task in the engine room, that sucked up most of the day.

From about twelve on, Milo drug us along with him. I'd resented it in junior high, learned to use it like a personal reprieve in high school, and come to count the days until Dad and the boys all piled onto the damn thing to bring her back to life, only to curse myself for volunteering on an annual basis. The work was exhausting and the pay nonexistent. Just part of being the captain's kid.

"Piss off," I barked, sitting back on my heels to wait for the stars to stop popping in my vision.

"Where's your brain today, James?" Mav's voice was light with suppressed laughter.

"Certainly not here," Axel answered as he wiped another wrench clean.

"I've checked off twice as many boxes as either of you."

"You've also had to bandage your thumb, your arm went numb when you smashed your elbow, and now you're using your thick skull in place of civilized tools. Maybe slow down and I won't have to follow you around with a bucket to mop your blood off my clean floors."

I didn't respond. *Couldn't* when the asshole wasn't actually wrong. It had been one of those days where I couldn't seem to make it more than a few minutes before injuring myself in some manner. The aftertaste of shame was a bitter fucking concoction. The anger on my new neighbor's face was permanently imprinted on my eyelids, and I couldn't even blame her. My lame-ass mumbled excuses had done nothing to diffuse her temper, and I'd barely slept as a result.

Worse yet, that decadent little body and beautiful pixie's face was just as vivid. She was a fucking dream brought to life. Feminine little features, a pointed chin, and fair, freckled skin. All topped off with the most appealing just-fucked red curls. I couldn't erase the image of her lifting her chin to look up at me, or her ability to plaster on a scowl that promised retribution.

"I'm fine," I bit back. "Just tired." Tired of my life. Tired of spring cleaning. Tired of kicking myself for not at least giving her my name and groveling like any half-decent asshole would.

My phone vibrated against my thigh for what had to be the twentieth time since I'd climbed into this little cubby. My siblings were nothing if not persistent.

"You see this?" Mav asked, the grin in his voice evident. On a long-suffering sigh, I fell back onto my ass, glutes and lower back aching from being curled over so long. I yanked the filthy, once-white towel off my shoulder to rub the oil from my hands as he rotated his cell towards me, and Axel leaned in to see.

The top picture was Rhyett, helping to move Miss McCarthy into her new house, carrying a dresser between his bulky arms. Growing up in Rhyett's shadow was a bit like attempting to fill vacant shoes left by the one and only *Clark Kent.* Impossible. He was always up to something, which apparently included getting tackled by McCarthy's enormous Bernese Mountain dog, Mack. Okay, knowing his relentless good deeds had earned him a face full of slobber made me chuckle.

Begrudgingly, I pulled my damn electronic leash from my jean pocket, tapping in the passcode to catch up on the Bible-length string of correspondence. The constant expectation of access to my brain space was like an omnipresent noose around my neck.

ELORA

I hope Brex made you shower after that.

PAXTON

I see Mack is in good spirits.

RHYETT

She helped soap me down.

HADLEE

Ewwwww, Rhyett. Nobody needs to picture your soapy bits.

RHYETT

Brexley doesn't seem to mind.

ELORA

I'll book her a therapy session while I'm home.

LEIGHTON

Kaia wants to know if McCarthy still needs her to pick her up on Friday for Salmon Fest.

HADLEE

Aweee, I miss that ball of fluff. He gives the best greetings. Say hi please.

JAMESON

To the dog, or McCarthy?

HADLEE

Both. But mostly Mack. Somebody squish his ears for me.

ALESSANDRA

Hey, since we're all here, can somebody pick me up before the festival on Saturday?

AXEL

Can't you just take the truck?

ELORA

I'll be home Friday night, and I need the truck.

FINN

Why?

ELORA

Nice of you to pop in, little brother.

I'm helping Max with the parade.

FINN

Miss you guys. Wish I could be there.

JAMESON

Ahh. How is our maxi pad?

HADLEE

Oh my god, James. Stop calling him that.

ALESSANDRA

Seriously, will you ever grow up?

JAMESON

No intention to, actually.

ELORA

Okay, Peter Pan. But seriously, he's a grown man. Be nice.

AXEL

I can snag you, Alice.

ELORA

And Maximus is good. He just got promoted.

ALESSANDRA

Thanks, Axel!

Miss you too Finny. How's New York?

MAVERICK

What in the hell does Max do, anyway?

ATTEMPTING to keep up with our family text thread was a feat of impossible proportions. I shook my head at the ridiculous reality that I was sitting in the engine room with two of my brothers and we were all staring at our palms. Technology was going to turn us into androids. Empty shells of what humanity had once been, incapable of holding a real-life conversation.

"I.T.?" Axel said, a furrow between his brows as he stared at his phone, perplexed.

"Acquisitions?" I guessed, trying to wrack my brain. Max worked remotely, traveling nearly as often as an authentic Rhodes, and raking in a disproportionate amount of money, which was necessary for his obsession with Armani, despite living on the dreariest, least fashion-forward island on the planet.

"Coding?" Mav canted his head before shaking away the curiosity. The three of us slid our phones away together.

"Alright," I grumbled, wiping the remaining grease off on my jeans. "That's lunch."

"It's only noon," Axel pointed out.

"And we've already knocked out ninety percent of Milo's list for the week. I think we can take a minute to eat. Besides, I could use a cup of coffee."

"Oooh, yes, I wonder if Brinleigh has popped yet," Mav said affectionately, entirely oblivious to my darkening mood and smiling like every expectant mother enjoyed being described as a fucking balloon.

I scowled at him. "She's not due for a month, kid."

"Damn, really? She was *huge* when we left last week."

"Yes, be sure to tell her that, will you?" Axel said, smirking over the toothpick he always had tucked into the side of his mouth. "I'll record it to send into this year's season of *Dumb Ways To Die*."

"You know what I mean," Mav complained.

"No. We don't," Axel and I said together. I couldn't help my smile. The best part of growing up in a town as small as Mistyvale was that everybody knew everybody. Coincidentally, that was also the worst part of existing here. But Brinleigh had known my order since she took over Rhyett's coffee shop, Grizzly Grind, years ago—had likely memorized it back in high school as we ditched class to fool around or get into trouble.

She knew what pastries to stash on days we were coming back into the harbor or working in town so I could inhale my week's worth of neglected calories at the table by the window. And she offered the promise of a tight embrace and welcome home that I relished despite myself. Anywhere else, it might have been weird to develop a platonic friendship with the woman who'd first let me finger her during a drunken adolescent round of truth or dare, but she'd stood by me through the last decade and a half, no questions asked. And I was the 'man of honor' at her fucking wedding. How's *that* for small-town dynamics?

My breath left in a whoosh the moment the familiar sweet scent of coffee cake and apple pie hit me, the warmth of the bakery the equivalent of four instant layers of clothing on my skin, blotting out the spring cold. There was nothing quite like home.

"Brin?" I barked, taking off my beanie and running my fingers through my hair as the bell rang behind me. One of my brothers caught up—likely Axel, although Mav was never one to turn down a pastry. "Brin, where you at?"

"One minute!" An innately feminine voice hollered from the back. Either the baby was up in her ribcage today, or she'd gone up an octave or two. I turned, pulling my ass up on the front counter and finding both my idiot brothers had wandered in after me. Leaning around the casing, I searched for what would inevitably be waiting.

"Bingo," I muttered, snatching the brown paper bag from under the pastry case and leaning back up to set it on my knee, ready to tear into whatever she'd left me, but my enthusiasm was cut off by a human-esque bleating noise.

"Uh-excuse me, *canIhelpyou?*" I blinked twice, attempting to make sense of the words so rapidly squashed together they were nearly unintelligible. There was something eerily familiar about that voice. Feet firmly planted back on the ground, I slowly turned to find disapproving, round brown eyes where I wanted green, and a sexy, tousled mess of dark red curls where I wanted blonde. Fuck. Me.

"*Not* Brin," I said, not bothering to hide my embarrassment. Tugging at the back of my neck, I narrowed my eyes on the object of my current nightmares. And by nightmares, I mean unwilling fantasies. "I'm sorry, *neighbor*, are you lost?"

She blinked, pointedly glaring at the counter between us. "I could ask you the same thing."

Fuck, she was pretty, even pissy. Her short hair gave the woman that chic, devil-may-care thing only cropped curls could accomplish, shy of actual sex hair. All her features were pretty and petite—doll-like, even—save for animated princess eyes that blinked back at me pointedly, like she could force me to say something. Subtle curves in all the right places made my hands buzz, even as I snapped my eyes to her face. It didn't matter; I already knew the prize beneath her explosion of colorful clothes. She was the kind of woman that would settle in my palms, not overtly feminine, but not a stick. That sexy red hair ended just below her jaw, exposing the long, creamy line of her neck, freckles sprinkled everywhere. *Goddamn.*

One look at her trendy sage crop top beneath a warm yellow sweater that hung off toned shoulders, and distressed high-top jeans told me all I needed to know. *Distressed jeans.* Whose fucking idea was it to look poor on purpose? Where I came from, you earned those scuffs and tears. You didn't pay triple the price to buy 'em off the rack that way. Colorful gems hung off her slender neck, and equally bright bracelets jingled as she shifted.

The not-so-subtle snap of her fingers brought my eyes back to hers. "Eyes are up here, *Wolverine*."

Wolverine? The smile was involuntary. If it was just the two of us, I could apologize again. I could grovel like I should have the first time. But with my brothers in tow, that would only bring about questions that would magnify her embarrassment if she still felt any.

"Boys," I said, motioning them forward. It was the first time the little bombshell's body stiffened. Didn't much care for that. "New girl, this is Axel—" I gestured to him, smirking when he gave her a nod, still spinning that damn toothpick. When I glanced back at her, there was a thoughtful little furrow in her brow, like she was focused. "And Mav." Maverick's goofy, dimpled smile popped out as he gave her a lazy wave. "Call me James."

"Hi, *James*." My name was dropped with so much pointed disapproval, it was obvious I did *not* impress her with my apology. "With all due respect, keep your ass off my counter. It's a health code violation."

"*Your* counter?" I balked. "Where's Brin?" I pulled open my pastry bag, shaking it in her direction so she could see my name written on the side.

"Who?"

"Brin. Brinleigh. Brinleigh *Wright*. Queen of this establishment."

"Home for the night."

I scowled back at her. "She never leaves early."

"Welp, she does when she's nine months along and has help."

"Does *help* have a name?"

"Sure do."

"Gonna share it?"

"Mmmm, that's a solid nope, big guy. Can I get you something? Most of our customers aren't quite so prepared and pay for their refreshments."

I jostled the bag, pulling out the generous wedge of coffee cake, my mouth instantly watering at the cinnamon smell of the crumble. With a groan, I mumbled, "Fucking *angel*."

"Fresh out of celestial entities, but I've got coffee and tea." The tempting little woman popped a hip, staring back at me expectantly. Somebody had her armor on today. Couldn't exactly blame her.

"So," I hedged, curiosity getting the better of my common sense. Ignoring her question was likely in the same ballpark as poking a bear, but I couldn't help myself. "You're friends with Brex?" When she just blinked back at me, I asked, "I assume you're the friend Rhyett told me about. You two meet in school?" This was the moment of truth.

"Yeah, when we were little kids. She's been my ride-or-die since kindergarten."

I chuckled, nodding as reality set in. Well, fuck me. She was *eight* years younger than me. Hell, she was younger than my baby sisters, Hadlee and Alessandra, who'd felt a *lifetime* away growing up. Not all of us could toss aside our morals when we spotted long legs and a pretty smile. Shame. Axel would have better odds.

"Certainly explains the fashion choices."

"What's that supposed to mean?" She quirked her head, tousled curls bouncing and begging for a man to run his fingers through them.

Seven years ago, you could have called her jailbait, you nimrod.

"Did you borrow that outfit from a mannequin?"

She glanced down at her clothes before scowling back up at me. "Aren't you *just charming*? Did you get off the boat and take a crash course in fashion?"

"I don't need a crash course to recognize a walking billboard for some overpriced city-slicker brand."

"There is nothing wrong with my outfit." She deadpanned.

Of course not. Not in Tampa, not somewhere about forty degrees warmer with a longboard on a college campus. Not if she was five or six years older, and that incessant buzzing in my hands could actually be satisfied when I slipped them under that skimpy scrap of fabric. As she lifted her chin, I swear to God her nipples hardened when I looked her over.

"Your little tube tops don't exactly scream practical in *Mistyvale*, now do they?"

"Please, at least I'm not afraid to embrace the times. Show a little personality instead of marching around like an unfrosted Pop-Tart. You look like the Bounty paper towel guy but with less flavor. Don't you know flannel shirts went out of style last century?"

I chuckled when Axel did, holding her gaze. If Brexley was Rhyett's 'firecracker', this woman was the whole damn box of dynamite. The sparks were right there as she quirked her head, cocky expectation in her eyes.

Okay, yeah, I liked shit simple. Simple black Henley's or T-shirts.

Simple flannel. Simple rain gear. Practical layers for a life spent on the harbor. So what?

"Flannel has character. Your clothes look like you swallowed a rainbow."

The woman burst out laughing, those long lashes batting as her eyes lazily roamed the length of me. "Let me guess, *Wolverine.* Your favorite color is grayscale?"

"What's wrong with that, *Skittles*? It's classic," I countered as Maverick choked on what I could only assume was a laugh.

"Classic? If you say so. Exciting? Not so much. I prefer some vibrancy to my world. Keeps it interesting."

"You look like a *kaleidoscope.* I bet you leave a trail of neon chaos in your wake."

She held her ground but shifted the turquoise bracelet on her wrist like she couldn't help but touch an example. "Better than blending into the background."

"I prefer to let my actions speak louder than my wardrobe choices."

"Actions might speak louder, but your *aesthetic* speaks volumes. And I'd rather be a fashionista with a personality than some rude, tasteless enigma."

Goddamn it, she was cute. I actually liked her colors, as ridiculous as they were. And this was by far the most nonsensical debate on record, and there wasn't really a rational plan of retreat. Thank God for good siblings. Axel nudged me out of the way, pulling his glove off to extend a hand to Sex Hair With An Attitude.

"Sorry about him, he's got a stick up his ass, hates change, and he and Brin are friends with benefits."

Brown eyes widened, that concern line between them deepening.

"Christ," I muttered. *Way to confuse the new girl, Axel.* I sure as shit wasn't sleeping with my barista–our 'benefits' were strictly professional...well, these days.

"That doesn't explain why you were sitting in what I assume were fish-gut coveralls on my previously clean counter." Every word was punctuated with her irritation, and despite knowing better, she was fun to mess with.

"More likely to be motor oil. Now. Why are *you* here?"

"I'm filling in for *Queen Wright* while she's on maternity leave. And for future reference, I don't care whose bed you climb in, please don't scoot your dirty pants across my counter. We have standards to maintain."

My brothers snickered beside me as I shook my head. "It's not like that."

Skittles actually did a once-over, arching a skeptical brow as she scanned me from top to bottom. Did she just linger on my crotch? Fuck, judging by that bratty little smirk, she totally did. I guess I owed her that much.

"Sure, it's not."

"We have a gutter-cleaning, roof-fixing, pest control in exchange for an eternal supply of pastries and espresso arrangement," I insisted. She didn't need to know it didn't start that way.

Axel, evidently satisfied with himself, flashed her that obnoxiously bright smile he shared with our big brother.

"I'm Axel Rhodes, pleased to meet you."

Madam Sass perked up, her eyes sparkling. "*Rhodes?* Any relation to *Rhyett* Rhodes?"

"Yes, ma'am. He's our oldest brother."

She smiled at the fucker. Actually smiled. I bit back the desire to shove him out of the way. The return question was written all over his too-eager face.

"He makes a hell of an impression," she offered before he could ask. "Quite the shoes to fill there."

"Don't I know it."

"Jesus," I growled again, wanting to move past pleasantries and into the realm of stimulants I could survive the day with, and then get the hell out of here. Mav snickered beside me.

Axel ran his fingers through his long blonde waves. "Gotta say, Red, you're a sight for sore eyes. What's your name?"

When the woman laughed, those brown eyes glinting, something heated in my chest. *Absolutely fucking not.*

"Well, if the hair, eyes, and smile didn't give away that you're brothers, the nickname might've."

"He beat me to Red?" Axel quirked his head. "Bastard," he said with mock disappointment.

"To be fair, it's not exactly groundbreaking."

Axel smirked as he asked, "You know what would be?"

"No," she said with a giggle. "*What?*"

"Your name."

She laughed again, cheeks flushing a delicious shade of pink. Those painted lips parted and closed twice, her feet shifting subtly before she answered. "Elizabeth. Nice to meet you, Axel. You said this is Mav?"

"Maverick," he corrected, stepping forward to replace Axel's hand with his own.

"I've heard your name!" She chirped, happily leaning back on her heels. "You're the baby of the family?"

"You and Rhyett got to know each other, I see," Mav said with a laugh. It would have taken much more control than I currently had to suppress my eye roll. Of course they did. Rhyett gets to know *everybody*.

"Like I said, some men know how to make an impression." It was with pointed expectation that Skittles looked back at me.

FOUR

NOEL

"You gave them your *middle name?*"

"Listen. Not my brightest moment, and I should have thought it through ahead of time, but I just realized if I'm reinventing myself—starting over—and trying to stay as far off Eric's radar as possible, why not keep my name off the grid in the process?"

"So you went for *Elizabeth?*" Brexley sipped on her third cup of coffee, sitting in Rhyett's T-shirt like a nightgown as the morning light cut through the space, soaking her skin in buttery warmth. I couldn't remember the last time we'd leisurely laid about, sipping coffee as the sun rose. College, maybe? "I thought you hated your middle name."

"It's not my favorite. So, that's going to be fun. But hey, at least there's no trace of Noel McShane to follow."

Rhyett cleared his throat from behind the business section of the newspaper. "Aside from plane tickets."

"Jesus, is that public record?" I said, panic bleating through me as I jerked my gaze back to Brexley.

"To civilians? No." She grimaced. "But to a politician with no moral compass and greasy friends?"

"Dammit." I sighed, leaning my head back against the wall of the bench-style banquette. They were right. "Okay, so maybe I'll book a ticket somewhere else? Make it look like I just visited?"

"I mean, if you don't get on it, it would be canceled, and he'd see that, too."

"So, you're telling me we should have driven?"

"Through Canada?! Trying to go dark, eh?"

"Hilarious."

"I try." She tossed her sleep-mussed blonde sheet of hair over a shoulder. "But honestly, Noel, how dark do you want things to go here? We were just discussing that Rhyett and his parents have some contacts around the island that could help us if you're actually scared."

Scared.

I hated that word. I wasn't one to run scared. Wasn't one to spook easily. But that bravado had kept me in a toxic hole of a house with the hope of things getting better, of convincing him to love me right, to take care of his own mental health...until in one split second, Eric took away the option of *not* being scared.

A rich, husky baritone carried through the house as the front door slammed closed. "Got any breakfast?"

I scowled at the intruding voice, demanding, "Who the hell is that?"

Rhyett beamed and set his cup down on the counter before vanishing into the hallway. Their voices trailed back to us as Brex and I exchanged curious, bemused glances. Simultaneously, we took long drinks of coffee, and I prayed the magic bean juice would somehow fortify my composure.

Florida had been home my entire life, even college, and while starting fresh was the right idea, it was...well, there were growing pains. I already missed my teal water, the bustling city, the rush of people. I missed our girls, Wren and Holland who were now both active managers at our bookstore, The Cracked Corset. Without them, there's no way we could have pulled off this little escapade. Those book-lined walls had been our home for the bulk of our early twenties. But this was good. *Change* was good. Not having to face memories everywhere I went would be good.

In the two shifts I'd had in Rhyett's shop, I'd already made some friends. The second day had brought about my first experience with regulars remembering my face—though the Rhodes brothers had been the first to ask my name. Hopefully, I'd at least feel like I knew a few people around the island by the time Brex had to go home.

"We've got coffee, bacon, and toast if you want some." Rhyett's voice was exuberant, giving me the impression of profound sincerity.

"Florida tan looks good on you, man." The distinct sound of slapping backs brought to mind that weird bro-hug thing guys always did.

"End of semester looks...exhausting."

"*Phew*, you're telling me."

"That bad, huh?"

Brexley set her ceramic mug down with a soft little clink as she slunk off her chair. "I'm, uh, going to go add some pants to this ensemble."

"Probably a good idea," I stage-whispered, stifling my laugh as I sipped my own black coffee and watched her retreat out the opposite archway. Despite my confusion, I was a bit relieved for a brief reprieve.

Rhyett's house was a mix of gray and cream, with gorgeous vaulted ceilings and towering windows that filled the space with decadent light. Subtle signs of wealth dripped from the thick black marble counters and stainless steel appliances. Not overtly cocky, but he certainly didn't scrimp on the details. Thirty-five, three careers and two and half businesses in, I suppose that was par for the course. I couldn't help but wonder if his brother next door shared his exquisite taste. Then promptly reprimanded myself for my ridiculous curiosity. He was a prick. Why did I care?

The hallway Brex had just absconded down led to both the formal dining and den, as well as Rhyett's room. He'd offered me the master once they were gone, but I had no interest in sleeping in my best friend's boyfriend's bed, regardless of him being thousands of miles away. Well, at least not *his* bed. Because the guest suite was still technically inhabited by Rhyett's mattress and solid wood bed frame and matching dresser. But like, the one he *did things in* would be weird. Right?

My inapplicable panic spiral was interrupted by a beaming Rhyett returning beside a stunning black man with a warm umber complexion in a fitted onyx suit, his curls cropped tight. A thin, precise smattering of facial hair framed the kind of bright smile that would have made me go weak at the knees if only I could forget that men were pigs and I hated them. But Jesus, it was as blinding as Rhyett's, if only a bit more reserved.

"Hey, uh—" Rhyett seemed to catch himself mid-introduction, evidently not having heard the name I'd given his brothers at the coffee shop, and opting instead for an affectionate, "*Red*, this is Broderick, one of our bonus brothers."

Said bonus brother rolled his eyes as he supplied, "Because every freaking football team needs at least two subs."

I tried to laugh, although Josie would have gotten the joke way better than I did. Broderick stepped forward, extending a hand embellished with a sophisticated brushed gold watch and ring. I accepted, returning his friendly smile, giving him a firm shake, and offering a quick, "I'm Elizabeth."

Woah, that was weird and would take some getting used to. Evidently, Mr. Rhodes thought the same thing, as noticeable relief settled on his features. The energy shifted in the room, like the static before a storm, making it difficult to focus. "It's very nice to meet you."

"Welcome to Mistyvale, Elizabeth. Don't let these two give you too much grief." He hooked a thumb towards our still-grinning companion, and I slunk around the opposite side of the enormous island. Lest my lady parts forget we were on a boycott. Only to spot Jameson, where he was leaning in the doorframe, tugging his hand against the back of his neck. Broderick's comment suddenly made much more sense, as Rhyett didn't seem the kind of man to give anyone grief.

The walking storm cloud lifted his chin, gave me a subdued little wave and matching smile—and *fuck me*, he was cute. For the second time in as many minutes, I found myself filled with the butterfly wings of attraction.

Pigs, Noel. Men are pigs.

GETTING ready for work when the girls were sending messages so incessantly my cell's vibrations were tiptoeing the line of an erratic adult toy was *impossible*. It was a little surreal for them to be awake enough to chatter in rapid-fire when I was just now heading to open the coffee shop. If I was honest with myself, the four-hour time difference was not my favorite. I missed talking to them when we were all wide awake and not running between meetings. We'd all been friends for years, and the thing I would inevitably miss the most about Florida was our bi-monthly girl's nights at our favorite pub. Vallie and Josie were popular brainiacs two years ahead of me and Brex when we got to college, and when we all collided at the third party in as many days, Val decided they were in need of two extra wing women. Naturally, they were demanding every single nitty-gritty detail of my new job, digs, and companions.

NOEL

Okay, aside from Jameson, the siblings are all just as
hot and sweet as Rhyett. Even the 'adopted' ones.

BREXLEY

She's only saying that because he pissed her off.
Jameson is hot too, but he's kind of crusty.

VALLIE

Picture?

JOSIE

Yes. Picture?

BREXLEY

Please hold.

I SWORE when the image came in; Jameson with his brothers, his flannel open and revealing the lick-able washboard of muscle beneath. Fair skin was sprinkled with dark curls, and the image gave us just a peek at the ink over his chest as the guys threw the ball around. The girls, unsurprisingly, lost their damn minds.

VALLIE

I give it two weeks, max. You'll jump that man's bones.

JOSIE

Three. Plus, she was always a secret glutton for the
bad boy.

NOEL

Absolutely not. No men, remember? Maybe I'll follow
Vallie's lead and give women a try.

JOSIE

I don't think it works like that.

BREXLEY

Would be nice if it did tho.

Just wake up one day and swing the opposite way.
Guys are assholes.

JOSIE

The worst.

BREXLEY

Total pigs.

VALLIE

Says the woman who landed a ten out of ten.

BREXLEY

Rhyett doesn't count. I'm actually not convinced he's
human.

NOEL

Judging from the sounds I hear at night, he's plenty of
man for you.

BREXLEY

blushing emoji eww. Come on, I bought you noise-
canceling headphones.

VALLIE

LMFAO

JOSIE

It's about damn time. Brex is no longer the reigning
champ of the dry spell.

WHAT I WAS MOST grateful for in all of this was the way they all
refused to treat me any differently after Eric. There had been a few
initial days of concern, helping me navigate the legal process of
getting a restraining order and pressing charges. Then, Vallie
stepped up to take on the case when his slimy family bailed him out.
Josie leapt into action, compiling a spreadsheet of different online
therapists and who took what kind of insurance, insisting I'd need
somewhere safe to talk through all the shit he put me through. But
when the bruises faded, so did the kid gloves, mercifully pretending
everything was business as usual. No walking on eggshells like my
family. No pity in their eyes like our regulars at The Cracked Corset.
I fucking loved them all the more for it.

VALLIE

SO.

Tell us about the Rhodes. I need the dirty deets.

NOEL

They're insanely welcoming.

Again, save for Jameson. He's a dick. He put his fish
ass on my clean counter.

VALLIE

That bastard.

JOSIE

Fish. Ass?

NOEL

Apparently he's friends with benefits with the manager
I'm filling in for, so he put his grimy, fresh-off-the-boat
coveralled ass right up on the counter to reach in and
get 'benefit pastries' I didn't know existed.

VALLIE

Rat bastard.

JOSIE

Oh jeez, so the man has a history and we're mad
about it?

NOEL

He called me a kaleidoscope. And then Skittles.

JOSIE

That's why he's a dick? Come on, Noel, who are you
kidding? *lip biting emoji*

VALLIE

Jesus, do you see those abs? Hell, I'll be his
kaleidoscope.

BREXLEY

Still no luck with Wrenly?

NOEL

Oh, yes. Isn't your deadline coming up?

VALLIE

Shhhhh

SEEING Brex bring up Wrenly made me smile. She was our coffee
shop manager back home, and a total boss babe. Curvy and beautiful,
Vallie had her eyes on her for the last few years, but they never
seemed to be single at the same time. When they finally were, she

always had an excuse—she didn't want to be the rebound, she wanted Wren to come to her, the list was endless. We'd finally put the screws to her on our last girls' night in Florida, setting a deadline for her to make her damn move, or one of us would do it for her.

JOSIE

Oh, hell yeah! Dibs on setting up that date.

VALLIE

I said shush.

BREXLEY

Hell no. It's time, Val.

JOSIE

Amos says to shit or get off the pot.

I CACKLED as I slid my phone back in my pocket. Amos was Josie's older brother, and not too fond of any kind of ongoing deliberation. *Ineloquent?* Absolutely. But he wasn't wrong. The unspoken dance between two of our closest friends needed to come to an end. Or rather, a beginning.

STRAY BITS of gravel ground beneath my boots as I hauled my bag out of the passenger seat and over a shoulder. Grizzly Grind was a cute little coffee shop, the mascot paying tribute to the inevitable island bear. Only, this one was cute and animated and wearing a yellow rain hat.

When I got to the front step, there was a jar of polished sea glass sitting on the mat. Every color imaginable was stacked inside, from teal, to pink, to clear. Like warped marbles, they pressed against the rim of the container, begging for my fingers to turn them over in my palm. I happily obliged before eyeing the torn piece of paper and messy scrawl that sat below it.

Lizzy. Sorry about your boobs.
Never taking the trash out again.

These are some of my favorites, collected over the years. Thought you might like them more than I do.

"SORRY ABOUT YOUR BOOBS?" Brinleigh asked over my shoulder. Hell, I was more perplexed by his use of *Lizzy*. When I turned to face her, pushing open the front door, her brows were furrowed with concern. "What's happening to your boobs? Are you okay?"

How in the hell did he beat me down here? And if he was going to leave obscure apology gifts, why wouldn't he just set them on the front step of the house instead of coming clear down to the harbor? The answer was obvious, I supposed. He didn't want me to tell Brex and Rhyett what he'd done. I laughed, more to myself than her questions, shaking my head. "Nothing, and I'm fine."

"Mmkay. That's pretty weird, as far as admirers' notes go."

Snickering, I folded up the paper and stuffed it in my pocket. "Definitely just a please-don't-hate-me note."

"Do I wanna know?"

"Probably not."

"Then what are you smiling about?" Brinleigh asked. The moment she was in the door, she knelt to pick up a box of mugs I'd abandoned in my haste to get out of there yesterday. I certainly hadn't meant to offload it to her plate.

"Oh, let me get that!"

Her brow furrowed as she stood, nonchalantly sliding the damn box of tableware onto the counter. "I'm incubating a tiny person, I'm not an invalid."

"Obviously," I said, grinning. "Rhyett doesn't hire no two-trip bitches."

She laughed then, raising a pale hand to rest on her round belly. When I locked on those vivid jade irises, I finally took her in. I'd known she was pretty, but somehow evaluating her now, after my interaction with the Rhodes boys, set her in a whole different light. Skin so fair she looked like she'd powdered it, just the right touch of pink to her cheeks, a few dozen freckles sprinkled across her nose. But it was those vivid eyes under light mascara-less lashes and blonde hair that struck me. I bet that's what hooked Jameson. He was so...*intense*, so evaluative.

"Speaking of, I hear there's *tea* that needs spilled?"

"Tea?"

"What's the deal with you and Jameson Rhodes?"

Brinleigh laughed, affection playing in her eyes as she rubbed her belly, setting a hand on her lower back. "Not much to tell, honestly. He's an old friend—you met him when he came for his end-of-week pastries?"

"That really is a thing? Axel claimed you're friends with benefits, but—" I nodded at the hand on her belly, where a beautiful cushion cut diamond ring sat, proudly announcing her status. "He certainly doesn't have one of those."

"Axel has a fat mouth. Don't listen to him. Actually, rule of thumb: Mistyvale locals have fat mouths, don't listen to any of them. This town eats gossip three meals a day."

"So you don't have some, you know—" I raised my brows, "*arrangement* with a Rhodes?"

"Nah, James and I haven't been like that in ages."

So they had, in fact, been some kind of something at some point. My interest was notably piqued as she continued. "It's our little inside joke—barista benefits. He always comes in before they head out on the water, gives me a hug goodbye, bids farewell to our team, and snags a few donuts and danishes to tide him over. Then, he's back as soon as the boat touches the docks. If it's early enough in the day, or he has to deal with the whole family, he'll grab coffee with his calories." She turned and pressed the button on the espresso bean hopper, grinning as she explained, "In exchange, he vanquishes all unwelcome critters when my hubby is out of town and does the maintenance Paul has never had a hand for." She smiled in that knowing way that only long-standing partners could. "My man is amazing, but he's a white-collar guy when it comes down to it. James wanted to look after me for free, of course."

"And that's not...I don't know...odd?"

"Should it be?" She asked, shrugging. "It's a small town. You gotta get comfortable with everybody knowing everything about everybody. I insisted, of course, on some sort of barter. The stinker picked something where his brother foots the damn bill anyways—all he's getting is my time. Why are you asking?" Some blend of mischief and curiosity poured through her question. I shrugged.

"That's not the version of him I met."

"Uh oh."

"I don't get it. You're so sweet. I mean, Axel and Mav are great.

Rhyett's a gold knight in shining armor. I haven't met the others. He's just..."

"Gorgeous?"

Obviously. That was beyond the point. "Aggravating."

She laughed, the sound airy with what could only be described as familiar ease. "He's...different. Always has been. But it's Jameson you call if shit hits the fan. Rhyett is great for the legalities and fielding local gossip, the girls are like the town's built-in cheer squad—always there to lift your spirits. Pax isn't really ever home these days. Finn's the quiet one. Even when he's on the island, you hardly notice. Mav is a sweetie—sympathy crier, that one. But, it's always Jameson to come in with his hair on fire to get shit done and set it right." Brinleigh's laugh shook her little baby bump. "Wait, *that's* why you're smiling?" Her belly grazing ceased suddenly, eyes going wide. I scowled, shaking my head as I doubled down.

"Absolutely not."

THE BELL CLANGED, and my eyes snagged on unruly blonde waves over steel-blue eyes. Axel, shortly followed by a grinning Maverick, waved exuberantly before stripping back his dripping hood. There was something in the water in this damn town, both brothers were unfairly good-looking. Maverick had that gangly, adorable, coming-of-age thing going for him, like a puppy whose paws were still disproportionately big. But Axel? He was all man, just like his brothers. My stomach tightened, that sense of being watched intensifying with only one answer available.

When I found his set, stubbled jaw and hard eyes, my belly clenched in a sensation uncomfortably close to arousal. The Rhodes gene pool was spectacular—honestly, top freaking tier—but Jameson was hands down the stunner of the brothers. As much as it pained me to admit that. Slap that man on any ad spread, and you'd be raking it in in hours. He could sell snow to an arctic penguin.

No. No, Noel. He's a creeping prick, and we're not doing men. We're not dating men.

I forced a professional little smile on my face as the Rhodes brothers made themselves at home at a corner table. Jameson didn't bother to avert his gaze as all three of them wandered up to the counter to order.

"Afternoon gentlemen! What can I get you today?" I said in my best impression of an animated sunflower.

"Hey, Red," Axel said affectionately, adopting Rhyett's little nickname. "How are you, beautiful?" He said it sincerely, but so casually it was like butter spread over toast. A compliment freely given to any it applied to. It wasn't the kind of verbal decoration bestowed by someone announcing an attraction.

"Great, thanks. You?"

"Couldn't be better. You still got black coffee back there?"

"You bet. What size, handsome?" I shuffled over to the paper to-go cups, focusing on Axel. But if I wasn't kidding myself, Jameson's jaw seemed unnaturally tense.

"Biggest cup you have."

"You got it," I said, snagging the twenty-ounce and shifting to grab the half-full pot from its burner. Over my shoulder, I asked, "What about you, Mav?"

"Craving something sweet. You wanna surprise me?"

"Sure, cutie. Should it still taste like coffee or more akin to dessert?"

"Let's do the second."

"Diabetes for your ancestors—on it!"

Maverick's laugh was endearing, but my mind was distracted by the tangible weight of Jameson's stare. It was only as I slid both cups over the counter that I looked up to meet his glower, right as another set of guys from the docks walked in. All three men wore caps under their hoods and rain boots that came up to their knees. Walton —*Wally*—Lingman, Kevin Smith, and Marvin Lowe, if my brain was doing its job of remembering our regulars properly. It had only been a week, but it would be worth the effort.

"Afternoon, gentlemen, I'll be right with you."

"Take your time, sweetheart," Wally said back, heaving an enormous white box up onto the counter. "The crew all thought you'd appreciate a local catch to fill your freezer."

I blinked, surveying the sheer size of the thing as he stripped his jacket and shook it off over the rug in front of the register. "Wally, that's way too much!"

"Nonsense. Wouldn't be very Mistyvale of us to not give you a proper welcome."

Gingerly sliding the box back toward him, I shook my head. "I know I'm new to town, but even I know how valuable a gift like this—"

"Packed full of local favorites and not packaged for resale, so it'll be on your porch whether or not you want it."

Cheeks flushing, I smiled as I swallowed my nerves down. Hell, could I eat that much fish in a *year*?! "Well, then, I guess…thank you."

"Anything for you, sweet stuff." A rough throat clearing cut off our conversation. "Oh, Rhodes! My bad. You get your order in. Just wanted to set that down."

Wally stepped back into line, motioning Jameson forward. Okay, now I *knew* I wasn't imagining it. When my eyes came back to Jameson, his tongue was running over his teeth with a special kind of irritation, shooting daggers at Wally. What was his freaking problem? I was just doing my job, and judging by the overflowing glass jar and the box of filets, I was doing it damn well.

"Everything okay over there?" I asked, brows hiking.

Jameson shrugged one of his broad shoulders. "Yep. Lived here my whole damn life, and never got a fifteen-hundred-dollar tip before."

I sighed, rolling my eyes and shoving the box over toward the other register. Not like I'd asked for it. Leveling him with a glare, I said, "What can I get for you, Rhodes?"

His cheek twitched, but he wouldn't grant me a smile, instead opting for a nondescript nod of acknowledgment. "Large black coffee, please."

"Well. I could have guessed that one," I said, smiling sweetly as I snagged another to-go cup.

"What's that supposed to mean?"

"Oh, nothing." I smiled, pouring the steaming brew into his cup. "Axel's drink of choice; just makes sense that you'd like it too."

"S'pose."

"Anything else?"

"Actually, I think I'll take it for here, Lizzy."

"Of course. But it's *Elizabeth*," I corrected, cursing the way my stomach flipped when the corner of his lip twitched. The sensation of attempting to parallel park while people watched washed over me, like I would suddenly be incapable of running the point of sale or pulling shots.

"I'll take a menu, too."

I glanced pointedly at the enormous chalkboard over my shoulder but reached for the laminated menus, anyway. "Doesn't your *brother* own this place?"

"That he does."

"But you still need a menu?"

"Thought I'd try something new."

"What are you in the mood for? Maybe I'll have a suggestion."

Brinleigh drew both of our attention as she came in the back door, radiant in that sweaty but sexy way expectant moms were so famous for. If my sister hadn't already gone through it, I'd still think it was a beautiful maternal glow. Behind her, the rain pattered against the asphalt alleyway.

"Hey, boss," I said just as the Rhodes all echoed a chorus of, "Hey Brin!"

"Wow! Full house," she said, beaming and batting those fair lashes as she stripped her jacket. It seems that Alaskans are morally opposed to umbrellas. "You all taken care of?"

"Just waitin' on a menu," Jameson grumped back, glaring in my direction like I'd been withholding it.

Brin canted her head, blonde brow arching skeptically as she tucked a loose strand of hair behind her ear. *Hah.* I wasn't the only one who thought the request was stiff and out of sorts. Take that, *Wolverine.*

"I've got him handled."

She smirked, insinuation thick in her eyes as she rotated to the men waiting patiently behind him. "What'll it be, Wally? The usual?"

"Yes, ma'am." Wally shifted to show his new allegiance to Brinleigh. Which was fair, I supposed, as Jameson Rhodes currently manipulated my attention. Their chatter faded beside me as Jameson's lips pulled up in a slow, agonizing smile that popped his dimples into existence. Dammit, those were cute.

"So," he said, leisurely leaning over the counter toward me as I poured his coffee. "You think you can *handle* me? I'm notoriously difficult."

"Please. I've had worse customers than you." I pointedly surveyed him from head to toe. Fitted dark jeans accentuated strong thighs, and I didn't even want to think about what they'd look like from behind. *Too late.* Geez, I was so bad at this single thing. They were tucked into knee-high waders, which seemed par for the course here. Another plaid shirt open at the neck. "At least you're easy on the eyes."

Those stubbled cheeks quirked sideways before he laced his reply with disbelief. "Was that a *compliment?*"

"I'm *smart*, not blind."

"*Ouch*," Maverick said with mock discretion as he choked on a laugh.

I handed Jameson the obsolete, but requested, menu before offering the coffee. A flinch accompanied his hiss of displeasure as he shifted the cup, the lid visibly leaking scalding fresh brew onto his hand.

"Oh, shit, I'm sorry. Here, let me help!" I reached forward without thinking.

Jameson, naturally, argued, "I got it."

"Here, give me one," I said, deliberating between the drink and the menu before opting for the cup. The stupid, *flimsy* paper cup which, in turn, exploded in a steaming splash down his front, the ridiculous farce of a lid popping off and landing on the counter with a dull plastic clunk.

"*Jesus!*" He barked. If there had never been a highlight reel of expletives, there certainly was now as they ran through my head in rapid succession, lips pursed so tightly I thought I might actually bite through them.

"Oh my god, I'm sorry." I fumbled for the napkins, finally freeing the busted cup from his hands, and pointedly ignoring the spark of something that trailed from where his fingers grazed mine.

"That never would have happened if you'd just listened to me and poured a cup for *here*."

"I'm sorry," I said, turning back to face him, blotting up the coffee on his arm and handing him a wad of napkins, patting at the mess down his jacket and stopping in precarious proximity to the zipper of his freaking jeans. *Phew. That was close.* "I'll pour you a new one."

Axel's snicker of amusement caught my attention as Jameson ground his teeth. "If you can manage to finish without soaking me this time, that would be great."

"Said no man ever." It was only when his eyes darkened I realized I'd said it out loud. "Oh, my god. I—*oh my god*—I'm sorry. I didn't mean to say that. *I'm fired.* I'm quitting, I swear." Something like amusement tugged on his lips, but as my eyes fell in embarrassment, I saw the red, raised skin on the back of his hands. One week on the job, and I'd scalded the owner's *brother*. Scarred the most beautiful man I'd ever damn seen. Both of our eyes flicked over to Brin as she barked her dismay.

"*Like hell* you are. I need you. And if Jameson didn't grip everything like he was trying to strangle it, that never would have happened. Stick to ceramic for *Hulk* hands over there." She snatched what looked to be a handmade mug from the open shelving behind her, tossing it my way and grinning when I caught it. That could have been a very messy overestimation on her part. "Unless Rhyett wants this kid walking out of my nether regions in the storage room, you're staying put, McShane."

"*Eww*, Brin," Mav complained, wrinkling his nose, oblivious to the fact that my stomach was turning.

I did my best to hide my wince, having decided with Brexley to keep my last name off the radar. Well, so much for that theory. As long as nobody was posting photos or anything, it would be fine. Right? The idea of Eric showing up with his buttery vocabulary and suits that screamed generational money made my skin crawl. In large part because the idea of facing him made all of this nearly unpalatable, but some small piece of me hated the look of judgment I knew would accompany his evaluation of my new home, my new job. It shouldn't matter. I *knew* that. But somehow, that glare that said I brought him shame was imprinted on my mind.

"Hey," Jameson had lowered his voice, as if he could sense the shift in my energy. And while it was deeper than his older brother's, it had that same delicious, rich timbre that drove Brex into madness. How I hadn't seen the similarities that first night was beyond me. "It's *just* coffee, Lizzy. I'm fine."

Great. Now the grump was *comforting* me after our kerfuffle. I needed to scramble and recover. "Good thing you wore your waterproof pants today, right?"

He glanced down under arched brows, glaring at his denim. "Certainly will from here on out, Skittles."

"Not that again," I groaned, carefully sliding the fresh cup his way. His eyes zeroed in on my now-shaking fingers, and I cursed my nerves. At least, right until he set that calloused palm against the back of my hand, making heat course through my veins.

"I'm fine. *You're* fine." He mistook the reason for my tremble, but that didn't change the eerie familiarity of his touch, or the way it put me at ease. Warning bells rang in my mind, emergency lights flashing. *Danger Noel McShane. Danger.*

I took pride in being unfailingly honest with myself, which meant the initial justification that it was just because he was Rhyett's brother was quickly stuffed aside. *No, ma'am, that there is pure, undiluted physical chemistry, goddamn it.* Forcing myself to stay steady, I smiled up at him.

"Anything else for you, *sir?*"

The way his shoulders tensed, eyes darkened, and jaw set told me everything I needed to know about the man in front of me. He liked that. He liked that *a lot.*

Oh man, I'd always wanted a partner who liked that kind of play. I'd only ever read about them. The storm cloud would like that dynamic in the bedroom, wouldn't he? *Dear GOD, why am I thinking about that?*

"Just a lifetime of patience so I can deal with you until Brin comes back," he jabbed, tone thick with humor. I didn't miss the smirk that slid onto his face as he spotted the jar of sea glass on the counter.

"Oh, honey," I admonished, patting his hand. "You're gonna need a hell of a lot more than that."

FIVE

NOEL

By late afternoon, my phone started buzzing incessantly in my pocket. Fishing it out, I found two missed calls from Brexley and five texts on the group thread—because apparently, in addition to living within blocks of each other, the Rhodes needed to be in constant communication. Rhyett had, naturally, seen fit to stick me on the Mistyvale chat and programmed his entire family into my phone before our plane even touched down in Anchorage.

Oh boy.

BREXLEY

Can anybody pick up Red?

ELORA

Red?

BREXLEY

My best friend, she's at work on the harbor and Rhyett's truck won't start.

RHYETT

She's taking over Brin's position for maternity leave.

AXEL

When's she off?

NOEL

Aren't we only a few miles from the house?

RHYETT

It's pouring rain. She's off at 4:00, Ax.

NOEL

Like I said, it's a few miles, NBD.

ALESSANDRA

I'm so sorry guys, I have this certification test, but I
could be there after if you just want to hang out at the
shop.

LEIGHTON

I just started work, so sorry, Red.

KAIA

face palm emoji I'm clear up on the summit. We were
camping, but I can trek back if I'm the best option.

NOEL

Absolutely not.

KAIA

It's okay, I don't want you walking back alone.

NOEL

This is Mistyvale. I'll be fine, I swear. You are
absolutely not packing up camp in the rain to come
get me. Honestly. I haven't exercised since we came
here, it'll be good for me to move my body.

RHYETT

Axel? Jameson?? Maverick?

NOEL

Rhyott, it's fine. Take care of your truck

OKAY, so Mistyvale rain and Tampa rain were two entirely different species. Florida has this fantastic habit of dumping several inches of shower-warm rain in about forty minutes, then blowing away the clouds like puffs of smoke. But when Alaska rains, it...drizzles? *Piddles*. Whatever you call this pathetic, dreary gray *blah*. This was precipitation with commitment issues. Invested enough to darken your doorstep but not enough to deliver the goods.

In my frustration, I nearly kicked a puddle, only to realize that my sad, mucky tennis shoes were in no way waterproof. Swearing internally, I ventured on, clinging to my jar of sea glass as my teeth chattered, my back aching. Rallying my courage, the pep talk began.

Kaia would not be right. I was going to get home and be able to look at Rhyett and, with my pride intact, tell him this was, in fact, no big deal. I grew up battling one-hundred percent humidity and mosquitos that put *Jumanji* to shame. A little nebulous precipitation was not about to ruin my day, dammit.

A gunmetal Chevy pickup rolled down the center of the road only to slow considerably, creeping towards the right shoulder. Was the driver *drunk*? High? Could he see the lines through this mess? I eyeballed the sharp decline of the bank. It was steep but not so severe I couldn't trust my feet to scale it quickly if I needed to. My larger concern was the fact that I was invariably alone with this stranger, not a car in sight, just the puffing towers of smoke from the neighboring homes. Could I get to one of the doors if I needed to? Hands flexing at my sides, brain scrambling to make sense as the vehicle pulled clear to the yellow line and slowed to a crawl, my entire being relaxed when Jameson Rhodes swung out of the driver's side door and waved me over.

Frustration clashed with the desire to get the hell out of this freezing drizzle. I peered through the gray to the hill ahead, knowing beyond that, it was only another block and then about a football field down to Rhyett's house. Having already made it this far, I was certainly not about to put myself one foot away from the irritatingly attractive man who'd seen me naked, insulted my taste, and now, no doubt, bared the burn blisters courtesy of my clumsiness. *Nope. No way. Hard pass, thank you very much.*

Waving in a manner that I hoped was a friendly refusal, I stepped around his tailgate.

"Lizzy! Come on, I'll take you home!" he barked.

Oh, will you now? Certainly news to me. I shook my head. "I'm fine."

"Oh, sweet Jesus. Get in the truck."

"I said I'm fine, Jameson. Thanks though."

"For fucks sake," he grumbled. Even over the engine, I could hear his frustration a beat before the door slammed shut. As my toes protested the disgusting, chilly squish of rain-sodden socks inside saturated tennis shoes, I huffed a sigh; the Gemini in me thoroughly divided between logic and pride. Logic shoving me toward the warm cab beside the sexy fisherman, while pride clung to the fact that said sinfully tempting mountain man had done nothing but insult me.

Curiosity might've killed the cat, but pure stubborn willpower might very well put an end to me, because the latter won out, and I kept right along, marching down the road. It was the subtle clink and rattle of *his* jar of sea glass clutched against my chest and the simultaneous protest of my aching feet that made me realize exactly how stupid I was being.

Window humming down as the truck crawled up the road, Jameson barked, "You'll catch your death. Get in the damn truck."

Welp, I could only stick to my guns at this point, right? "No."

"Why the fuck not?"

I leveled him with a glare, wishing my frozen feet could move faster over the rocky asphalt. *Come on, Noel. Keep some ounce of integrity intact.* I tried to remember the look on his face as he creeped through my damn window, but it did nothing to aid my crumbling resolve. Why couldn't I bring myself to be mad about that?

Grinding my teeth as my mind debated the merits and pitfalls of stubborn willpower, I added, "See you around, *neighbor.*"

"Jesus." He romped on the accelerator, engine rumbling to life, but my momentary tango between relief and disappointment was short-lived, as the truck cut off onto the shoulder, blocking my path. Jameson flew out of the driver's side door, stomping his way towards me through the gray. "Look, Skittles, I'm literally driving to the house *next to yours*. I know I'm a real prick. You don't have to like me. But I can't let you freeze to death, or Brexley will execute me by a thousand cuts. You don't even have to *talk to me*. Just...come warm up."

Pointedly, I glared at his chest before eyeing the truck like it was a venomous snake rather than a perfectly acceptable mode of transportation. It was sexy as fuck, that's what it was. Just like its dang owner. Lifted just enough to tell me he put time into it— probably used it for work— but not so much I needed to worry about his manhood. *Dammit.* When my reservation still spoke volumes, he threw back his hood, freeing loose curls that begged to be touched, dropping his head to force me to look at him.

"This is *ridiculous*. You could get hit in a downpour like this." When I kept my face directed toward the road, I swore he growled. Like a bear. Or a werewolf. I mean, it would be fitting in this climate for the creatures of nightmares to be alive and well. However, *insulting me* certainly wasn't about to entice me into being captive in his cab. Although...maybe he had a point. Seeming to spot the fissure in my resolve, he said, "It's freezing and about to get worse. Get. In. The. Truck. Or I'm *putting you* in the truck. Either way, I'm getting you home safe."

"You wouldn't *dare*," I bit out, glaring in his direction while simultaneously trying to decide if he was bluffing. Jameson's face gave away nothing as he chuckled darkly, the sound doing something wild to my insides. Thick, round water droplets began dripping off his hair onto his dark lashes, only stoking the churning in my core. Why'd he have to be so freaking beautiful? The bossy bastard.

"I have *six* sisters," he said, smirking as he added, "and at least as many cousins. You wouldn't be the first. And certainly won't be the last." Narrowing my eyes in challenge, not buying his bullshit for a moment, I harrumphed and moved to sidestep him. I didn't make it a foot before he sighed, "Have it your way," and snagged my wrist, turning me back to face him.

"Hey!" I barked, but the protest came to a screeching halt as he bent down and, in one quick motion, *threw me* over his shoulder like a freaking rag doll. "*Jameson!*" I yelped, my jar of sea glass tumbling out of my hands as they flew to wrap around his solid body, desperate for purchase. My stomach flipped in loops. A deep chuckle rumbled through his ribs, his grip moving to tighten on my upper thigh, the touch sending blood rushing to my cheeks. Nothing about my predicament should be erotic, but the rush of sensations in my body said otherwise. Embarrassment and some deeply messed up sense of anticipation collided in my chest. My therapist was going to have a field day with this.

Coming face-to-face with a delectable, denim-clad ass, I squawked, "*Put me down!*" He said nothing, shoulder barely jostling as he moved for the truck like I weighed nothing. What the hell did he *do* on that boat!? Water trickled precariously close to my nostrils, the world bouncing by in a blur of evergreen and gray. For a moment, I seriously debated the merit of biting into that perfect butt in retaliation but opted instead to slam my hands against him, snarling, "*Jameson!* Are you *serious*?!" The world flipped again as he bowed low and plopped me into the cab, gingerly shifting my legs inside to make sure they were clear.

"Stay put," he demanded, slamming the door closed to punctuate the order. Shaking his head, amusement tugged the corner of his lips up as he turned from the window.

"Screw you," I muttered. But the cab was *warm,* my feet were screaming, and the rain seemed to hammer down harder in response. There was no doubt in my mind that if I made a break for it, he would catch me and bring me right back. But, God, it *smelled* like him in here. Panting to catch my breath, I turned to glare at him as

Jameson's door swung wide. He settled into the driver's seat, arm jutting in my direction as he set the wet jar of stones back in my lap, and wordlessly threw the truck into gear. But there was a smile playing on his lips, and despite my better sensibilities, I didn't freaking hate it like I should've.

I'd tried repeatedly to convince myself it had just been imagined, my body picking up on the tension, but there it was again. That... heat. That *draw*. I'd never felt that with Eric. Not with any of the men before him, although the list wasn't particularly notable. A few fun flings. Even fewer boyfriends.

Our silence lasted all of one minute in the cab, and then he was glowering at me, planting a violent war between my tongue's desire to demand '*what*', and my mind's absurd dedication to being a petulant child.

Jameson caved first. "What the hell are you wearing?"

"Oh, for Pete's sake, not this again. *I'm from Florida*. We like color. Sue me."

"Where the hell are your boots?"

"Boots?" I balked, looking down at my expensive, name-brand tennis shoes. Expensive, name-brand tennis shoes that were positively soiled, caked in onyx mud, maybe even beyond repair.

"For fucks sake, Lizzy. Rhyett didn't make you get boots?"

"Some men don't feel the need to *make* women do things."

His displeasure rumbled in his ribs, and then he was flipping a U-turn as I yelped. "What in the hell are you doing? We're two minutes from home."

"You need boots." He eyed me pointedly but seemed to skip my general breast-age area. Were they that bad? Geez Louise. Tiny boobs are still boobs. "And a real fucking jacket."

"Rhodes, if I solemnly swear to find myself Alaska-approved attire, will you please just take me home? I'm exhausted. I don't have any money on me."

The man's ensuing eye roll could put Brexley's to shame. Which was saying something. He jerked his head over his shoulder. "Back seat."

"Excuse me?"

"There's a thermos full of coffee in the back seat. Your teeth are chattering."

"That happens when your psycho-neighbor kidnaps you a block from stripping down for a hot bath." My cheeks heated as I realized what I'd just said, instantly remembering his focused eyes, the way my skin ignited under them as they heated with what could only be described as hunger. The tiny quirk in his smile seemed to say he had too. *Well, shit.* "*Oh*, shut up."

The bastard drug his bottom lip between his teeth. On the list of things that made my ovaries weep, that deft little move was right at the top. Right up there with a man settling his hand around the collar of his shirt, that fictional book boyfriend doorframe lean, and the moment they scoop their fingers into my hair to angle my head for a kiss. *Le swoon.* All of which I assumed he would be spectacular at. At least, right until I remembered Jameson was the peeping Tom I was speculating about.

Jameson, the peeping Tom...who'd just kidnapped me for rain boots and was headed in the opposite direction of the only big box store in town. I was not about to ask him where we were going, and absolutely didn't need to because before I knew it, we'd pulled onto the black dirt road that led to the Rhodes property. Brex and Rhy had brought me here twice—once for introductions, and again for a barbeque with Rhyett's parents, Milo and Juniper.

Nonplussed, I let the jar of sea glass settle in my lap and turned for the thermos. Okay, so when that steam hit my face and the warm cup settled in my palms, I was a little grateful he'd told me it was there for the taking.

He'd barely shifted his truck into park when Jameson threw open his door. The man moved like there was a freaking fire to put out. He rounded the car to mine and didn't seem to care that I was shaking my head as he looped a hand under my elbow and pulled me out into the mist he'd vowed to help me avoid.

"Come on," he muttered, waltzing right up and entering the code to the garage. Warmth immediately seeped into my bones, the smell of home-cooked food greeting us. Was that chicken soup? Of course, it was chicken freaking soup on a day like this. Juniper was absolutely the kind of woman who would make it from scratch.

As if no further explanation was needed, Jameson waved his arm at a wall of meticulously organized boots and rain gear with a game show host's flourish. Overladen coat hooks sat to either side, boots of every color and size laid out on the shelves and ground below it. It looked like the entire town had turned up for supper.

"*What?*" I asked, blinking, equal parts confused and flustered. Was he telling me to steal gear from his family? Rather than responding like a human being, he grumbled something unintelligible and took a step back to eyeball my now soaked and frozen feet. On the tail end of a sigh—as though *I* had drug *him* away from his plans for a warm bath and bowl of whatever the hell could be scrounged out of the fridge after work—he stepped up to the shelf and snagged a knee-high pair of rubber rain boots that had a white and blue fish pattern on the inside. He flipped one over in his hand, scowled like they'd offended him, and returned it to the shelf before swiping another one. This one had coral-pink turtles inside. With a curt nod, he snatched its mate before passing them both back to me.

I stood there dumbfounded, physically aware of the ache forming between my brows in my confusion as he pulled a basket off the shelf, fishing a few pairs of clipped-together gloves out before eyeing my hands and tossing all but one set back. He huffed. Shifted. Scanned the wall. Dove in and came up with a hot pink jacket in one hand and a deep maroon in the other. Both were way cuter than anticipated.

Jameson shook the neon one, making sure he had my attention. "This one is for hiking or if you're on the water. You like pink. Plus, we can see brighter colors if you fall in, or if you cross paths with a hunter—which you will." I did like pink, and dammit, there were little flowers on the lining. He shifted to hoist the deep red one up. "This one's for town." When I didn't immediately react, his brows hiked up expectantly.

"I can't take your family's stuff, *you're* being ridiculous."

"None of the prior owners will ever notice, even if they do come home. They've been abandoned, I swear."

"Jameson."

"Lizzy," he growled back. "I mean it. Personally, I would prefer to take you down to see Luca and have him set you up with your own fitted sets, but you seem as likely to scream kidnapper as accept the gesture." Okay, he had a point. He shoved the pile into my chest, and I scrambled to catch everything when he let go. "Here, take these. One more thing."

"What? No. Hey—*Jameson!*" But he was gone, vanishing through the door into the house. Did I...did I follow him? Where was a girl to go when she was being forcefully gifted hand-me-downs? When he reappeared, he looked smug, which was somehow adorable and terrifying.

Pigs, Noel. Men are pigs.

"Sit," he ordered with one of those bossy little jutted chin moves he seemed so fond of. I glanced toward the bench he indicated, and deciding it wasn't worth the effort of arguing, sat. On command. *Like a dog.* The man knelt on the concrete, and if I hadn't been shivering from the cold, and confused as hell by his dedication to saving me, the sight of him there, strong hands moving for my legs, might have been the sexiest moment of my damn life. Jameson's smoldering gaze locked on mine, holding it, as he popped my sodden tennis shoes off and set them on the step to the house, handing me rolled-up cozy socks.

"Swap."

Scowling, I peeled my own sopping set off, replacing them with the pair he handed me. My face relaxed, a desperate little moan escaping my chest as my frozen feet were hugged in the warm embrace of what had to be the comfiest socks known to man. One of Jameson's brows shot up at the sound, my attention snagging on a tiny scar slicing through the end, even as his mouth slanted endearingly.

"*Good lord,*" I groaned with every ounce of deserved enthusiasm, "are these made of freaking *alpaca?* They're *so* dang cozy."

"Something like that," he said, chuckling, and for the first time, I noticed something like affection in his eyes, one arm braced under the other as he rested a fist against his lips, watching as I begrudgingly stepped into the boots. Thick rubber rain boots that were an irritatingly perfect fit. My gaze landed on his as surprise melted my shoulders down my back. How in the hell had he guessed my size?

Next, I slipped into the maroon jacket, and then yelped as Jameson abruptly yanked a purple beanie onto my head, then set his hands over the sides like he was making sure it covered my ears. It did. As did his big palms, which softened in sync with his eyes as he studied me like he'd possibly forgotten something. He'd thought of *everything.* Why did that make my chest ache? Hot, calloused skin rubbed across my cheekbone where he cradled my face, wiping away a stray bead of rain as it slipped from my hair, halting my ribs mid-inhale. My gaze fell to his mouth before jerking back to safer territory.

"There," he said, quiet, yet triumphant, and evidently oblivious to the way he'd just sent my pulse sprinting. "Won't be as worried about you freezing to death now."

Nearly choking on a laugh, I wrestled my smirk into obedience. "*You* were worried about *me?*"

"Shut up," he grouched, tone teasing, amusement glittering in his eyes. I could just peek those dimples as he led me back out to the truck.

When I got home—with a to-go container of Rhodes' family soup in hand—there was a still-starched pair of eggshell blue curtains hanging from my bathroom window. Behind that wall of steel, was Jameson Rhodes actually hiding a heart of gold?

SIX

JAMESON

It was the last weekend of dry-dock, which was a horribly inaccurate name this year as we hadn't had a single dry day during season prep, making painting the damn thing impossible. Regardless of the less-than-stellar conditions, we were all feeling the buzz before the busy season. The harbor was gradually packing with expectant vessels. American flags swayed lazily in the wind as the omnipresent drizzle cast its veil over our town—the same gray they had named the place for. Mistyvale. Because that said: *Come on over and settle down. It's cheery here, I promise.*

A throat cleared, jerking my attention from the spreadsheet in front of me. I hated spreadsheets. Actually, anything numbers-related bored me to tears. This had been Rhyett's portion of the annual boat prep. But *nooo*, the fucker had to start his own ventures and abandon us to tackle all of it without him.

My internal rant ended abruptly when I found Lizzy standing over my table with the pot of coffee glued to her slender, freckled hand. We'd fallen into an odd, unspoken truce after I'd fished her out of the rain and forced her into hand-me-downs. Maybe I was an asshole. But at least I was an asshole that slept well, knowing his new too-damn-beautiful neighbor wasn't freezing to the bone out of stubbornness. With six sisters, I knew stubborn pride when I saw it. It just wasn't usually so damn endearing. What I'd *wanted* to do was kiss that scowl off her face, but thoughts like that were fucking dangerous, and I'd settled for making sure I prepared her for the cosmic joke of Mistyvale weather.

"You need to smile more," she said, quirking her head in silent question.

"Why?"

"You have a serious case of resting brood face, and while I'm relieved to see it's not reserved for just me, it's scaring off my customers."

I chuckled, shaking my head as I looked around at her very full house of patrons. Another set of black and gray jackets came in the open front door. Despite the rain, they'd propped the damn thing open to keep the air fresh, or some shit. Seemed perfectly fine to me.

"Is that supposed to be an insult?"

"Just an observation. But don't worry, girls like broody."

Like I gave a damn about what girls thought about my face. I'd certainly never lacked a willing partner on the occasion that I actually wanted one. My rules were simple: I was designed to be a one-hit wonder. Condoms were a man's best friend. Women were to be treated with respect in public and shown a damn good time behind closed doors. And one of us would always be gone before breakfast.

Juniper and Milo Rhodes set an impossible standard, and until that leggy little blonde had sunk her claws into him, Rhyett had shared a very similar philosophy. Our younger brothers spent too much time on sports teams to inherit our attitude toward women, prone to letting their dicks dictate their life choices. Ridiculous. My give-a-damn would remain firmly, contentedly busted. At least that's what I told myself whenever the image of Lizzy in that damn window tried to sneak past my defenses this week. *Nope.* There was no room for a woman in my life, much less a goodie two shoes like my town-infiltrating neighbor. Under absolutely no circumstances would I be jerking off to the memory of Lizzy McShane. Tight, pale, perfect Lizzy McShane.

Goddammit.

A red pickup pulled up across the street, parking along the harbor fence in one of the few open spots and saving me from myself. Kenny, off the *Tide Turner,* hopped out and around, leaning over the tailgate to fetch out supplies. It was comforting, the monotony of this town, some things never changing. I ran my palm over my hair and glanced up at Lizzy as her eyes also pulled from the man with the armful of net. They rounded when they landed on me, and I realized I was smiling to myself, still stuck on what she'd said.

"Well now, don't look so smug. It'll take more than playing the mysterious grouch to catch a good one."

I scoffed. "And what would *you* know about a good catch?"

"Of fish? Next to nothing. A good woman? *Plenty*."

Why did everything she say have to sound like an insinuation? *Too young, too young, too young*, I chanted internally.

Never mind that I'd stopped in for a snack and a cup of coffee every day this week after our unspoken truce, or that my gut did an abysmal nosedive whenever she wasn't behind the counter.

"Careful, Lizzy, don't want to give a man the wrong impression."

"You're entirely responsible for wherever the hell your brain just went," she said with a giggle, pink flushing her pretty cheeks. The draw to this woman was insufferable. "Besides, don't you ever have a little fun?"

"I have fun killing fish for a living."

She wrinkled her nose. "Well, if that was my idea of fun, my face would be stuck like that, too."

"Alright, leave my face alone."

"Got something better to discuss?"

"You coming to Salmon Fest?"

"According to your sisters, it's a rite of passage."

"They're not wrong," I admitted with a smile. We'd been coming to the annual spring festival every year for as long as I could remember. If you could really call forty degrees and rainy 'spring' just because it was May. Milo and Juniper had been attending even longer.

"Hey, Bill!" A man boisterously exclaimed as he came in the door. I hated when people acted like everyone needed to be privy to their conversation, but when my eyes locked on Rodger Whalen, I let it go. That man had been a staple in the community since before my time.

Lizzy smirked as I came back to her. "So, what's a must-see?"

"Vendors," I said simply.

"Very helpful," she said with a roll of her eyes. "Got anything specific?"

"Nope. It's kinda cliche—exactly what you'd expect."

"Way to *sell it*, James," Elora's voice just about made me wince. Was it Friday already? I loved my sister—obviously—but she had this air about her that made me feel like I was always falling short. She was larger than life, traveling the country, speaking on stage, helping people and shit. And I lived for my days off so I could go hike...*alone*.

"Hey!" Lizzy preened, reaching for her like the oldest of friends. "Elora, right? Rhyett has told me so much that I feel like I already know you. It's nice to finally meet in person!"

"Hey!" Elora chirped happily, her gray eyes lighting up with recognition. She'd undoubtedly already befriended all of Brexley's known associates, their families, dogs, and employers. You couldn't take the woman to a grocery store in bum fuck Kansas without her either running into someone she met somewhere in the world or befriending the stock boy on aisle twelve who looked like he could use a hug.

We'd gone down to see Rhyett's progress on mom's retirement house, and, subsequently, meet his girl. Elora never—and I mean never—left a stone unturned. Especially not if someone had any intention of joining the ranks of our family. Or, *tribe*, as she said.

"You're Brexley's Red!"

"Elizabeth," she corrected, jerking her head back toward the counter. Elora blinked like she was confused before schooling her face back into a warm, receptive smile. "Welcome home! Let's get you something toasty to warm up with."

And just like that, my sister stole my sunbeam for herself. Being overshadowed by siblings should be something you adapted to, especially being sandwiched between two rays of fucking sunshine, but it never stopped irritating me. We weren't all saints.

To my dismay, when Lizzy's shift ended, she left the shop arm-in-arm with Elora, like they were the oldest and dearest of friends. Matching short, choppy haircuts and lean frames, they were nearly the same height. El was leggier, but that was about it. Where Lizzy boasted a crown of dark red mixed with copper, Elora was the genetic winner of a mousy brown somewhere between our parent's palettes. With narrowed eyes, I stared after them as they pulled hoods up over their curls and waves and vanished into the gray.

"*Subtle*, James."

Snapping my focus up to Brin, I leaned back in my chair. "Like we needed two of them."

"The world always needs more Eloras," she argued.

"Does it, though?" I grumbled back. "Bossy little know-it-alls, who befriend anything with a pulse?"

"Perspective-sharing geniuses who love big enough to save the population? Yeah. I think we can use as many as we can find."

"Suit yourself."

Her laugh felt like the first glimpse at Mistyvale mountains after weeks on the water. I'd always loved Brinleigh. For a while there, I thought it would be something special, but even as it evolved into a bizarre platonic adaptation of what had started, she was like a walking hug. A lot like Lizzy, I suppose. Rhyett, Axel, and I had run off the shit bags and lowlifes, until she met her now-husband, Paul. Great guy. Built like a two-by-four, but a great guy. And he treats her right, in a way I sure as shit never could. She was happy. And that's all I wanted.

"She could suit you, you know," she said sagely. "Balance you out."

"Take a hike."

"That could induce labor."

"So, *don't*, then."

"I just need you to come with me so you can carry my ass back down the trail if I get contractions."

I laughed, shaking my head. "Where's your husband? Isn't that what those are for?"

"Like Paul would let me hike in this condition."

"*Let you?*" I scoffed.

"I know," she said, shifting on her feet and slinking into the chair I shoved out with a boot, her shoulders relaxing as she settled. "Crazy man has this wild idea that he can force me to take care of myself and follow the doctor's orders."

"Blasphemous."

She chuckled, shrugging. "Kinda sweet."

"If you say so."

"I do. Speaking of sweet, how's Mistyvale's most eligible bachelor?"

"Axel's wrapping up the last of dry dock to-do's."

"Very funny."

"Is that not who you were asking about?"

"So you are—at least occasionally—humble."

"Don't spread that around—you'll ruin my reputation."

Her rubber rain boot thunked into my shin and I fought back the wince. "I like her."

"Who?" When Brin glared at me before jerking her head towards the door, I gave her my best mock-surprise. "Oh, Lizzy? Good. I'm glad she's an asset. Rhyett will be happy to hear it." Not about to let her insinuate anything more, I snatched the folder off the table, stuffing my papers inside and clipping it closed with my pen.

"Jesus, James," she muttered with an eye roll. "You're so stubborn you put mules to shame."

I waggled my brows as I stood, making a beeline for the front door. "Gotta run, gonna be late."

"Hey! We're not done here," Brin barked as I slipped out the propped open door and ventured out into the brisk spring air.

THE INCESSANT BUZZ of my cell on the bedside table replaced an alarm clock, and I groaned, palming my face. Fishing meant we only had a half dozen mornings to sleep in during the summer, and waking a man up just after dawn on one of those last days was punishable by banishment in my book. Sighing, I grabbed my phone.

ELORA

Happy Salmon Festival guys!

RHYETT

Happy Salmon Festival! Are we trailer hopping?

EVERY YEAR, part of the spring festival was the gathering of food trucks and trailers along with artists and vendors. We spent three whole days refusing to step foot in our own kitchen as we gorged on tacos and deep-fried bread dough, and whatever the hell else they thought to whip up, roll in sugar, and slap an Alaska-approved name on. *Bread buoys. Bear claws. Crab pots.* The creativity was at least in full force, if nothing else. None of us were much for heart attacks on a plate, but Salmon Fest was an annual exception, right up there with Christmas and Thanksgiving.

I wondered what Lizzy would think of all the fish fare, then hated myself for giving a shit. She'd been so damn beautiful in one of our *Rhodes Away* hoodies last night, nose and cheeks flushed with the chill in the air. She and Brex had humored my insane family and their need for tradition, joining in for the annual boat launch.

To my dismay, Axel had gotten awfully cozy with Brexley's little sunspot, and my skin had tried to forcibly crawl off my bones watching them for most of the launch last night. But it was better. Axel was only four years older than she was. Had infinitely more patience for colors, rainbows, and bubbly bullshit. The sooner she realized he had that same damn optimism she shared with everyone but me, and that I was the asshole, the better. Not that she'd expressed interest in either of us. Or any of the men on the island.

Hell, the other day she just ignored me when I tried to catch her attention outside Grizzly Grind.

Wally hadn't been the only boatman to take a liking to little Lizzy, and he certainly wouldn't be the last. But I hadn't seen her so much as engage with any of them beyond her role as their barista. She worked. She came home. She put up with the Rhodes clan's bullshit on behalf of Brexley and Rhyett. How she tolerated freezing on that damn boat with a smile on her pretty little face, I still didn't know. She and Brex fit right in for the annual family tradition of riding the *Rhodes Away* from the boatyard to the harbor, not even complaining when she shivered head to toe.

My treasonous body had wanted to warm her up, wrap her in my arms and keep her close.

My phone buzzed again.

ALESSANDRA

Well, we better make it count. I have news.

FINN

You got the job, didn't you?

MAVERICK

Of course she did. They'd be idiots if they didn't see what she has to offer.

KAIA

Alice!! Did you hear back already?

ALICE HAD BEEN in a weird interim, hanging out in Mistyvale as she got her feet under her. When that fancy, framed degree didn't immediately equate to a position that paid the bills, she came home. Regrouped. Evaluated. She'd just gotten certified in some kind of first aid something or other—the dozenth certificate she'd added to her collection since arriving to reassure herself of her worthiness, more than persuade an employer to see it—and had an interview the day I pulled Lizzy out of the rain.

.   .   .

RHYETT

Come on sis, you're killing us. What's the update?

ALESSANDRA

This could be my last Salmon Fest for quite a while, so
let's all enjoy it.

JAMESON

What the fuck does that mean, Alice? Spit it out.

HADLEE

eye roll emoji Don't be a dick.

ELORA

Jesus, Jameson, at least pretend to be excited for her.

JAMESON

I'll be excited when there's something to be excited
about. What's the consensus, Alice?

HADLEE

clock ticking gif

LEIGHTON

Let's go, big sister!!

KAIA

If you locked something in somewhere warmer, I will
shop, cook and clean in exchange for sleeping on
your couch.

ALESSANDRA

Remember that marketing position I applied for that I
thought I'd never get? They called me back; I did a
second interview and I'm headed to San Diego!!!!

ELORA

Confetti emojis Yayy! Congrats, Alice! You're gonna
knock them dead.

HADLEE

Surfing gif Yayyy!!! I'll come visit this winter!

LEIGHTON

Us too!

ALESSANDRA

I get full benefits right out the gate, and everything.

I BLEW OUT A HEAVY BREATH, clashing walls of pride and grief twisting in my chest like colliding seas. Yeah, I was excited she'd spread her pretty little wings and go on an adventure. Alice was brilliant, beautiful, clever, and quiet—my favorite quality in a sibling, if I was honest. She liked to watch and observe. It's what made her a talented student.

But...it meant another Rhodes would be out of the nest. Another Rhodes on the road, wandering very far from home. Not Rhyett far, or Finn far—if he hadn't ventured off to somewhere new, the bastard was still back East—but still. Somewhere I could do nothing, and knew no one, if she needed something. If it took me three goddamned planes and a rideshare to get there in an emergency, it was too damn far.

"WORST SALMON FEST EVER," Kaia said, wrinkling her nose. Misty haze saturated the air. Cold metal benches were lined in neat rows and covered by a canopy of pop-up tents. But we had about half the vendors we were used to. An entire parking lot that was usually overflowing was entirely vacant.

"Yeah," Leighton agreed. "Sorry, you guys. It's usually busier than this."

"Think the crappy weather scared everybody off."

"Eh, more for us," Maverick said, sliding over a stacked plate of tacos. The girls weren't wrong, but it didn't keep any of them from showing Lizzy and Brexley every single damn booth on the way in. Rhyett couldn't have been happier about it. That or his face had actually frozen in the shape of a fishhook, one side curled up all crooked.

"I think it's cute!" Lizzy said cheerfully before taking another bite of a deep-fried ball of bread dough. "It's just fun to see so much of the town out and about."

"Honestly, the markets in Tampa are three or four times this size," Brexley added with a smile.

"Yikes," Alice said, wincing. "Yeah, sorry, guys."

"No! I hate how busy it is back home. You can't even think, let alone find somewhere to breathe. This is cute. Festive and fun, but palatable." Brexley disagreed. How Rhyett was taking her back to that swampy, sand pit hell hole when she liked it about as much as I did was beyond me. The mountains were the only place my soul felt at peace.

"Oh," Kaia said, giggling. "Well, you're welcome, then." The girls all joined her laughter then, bringing a smile to my face, and warmth to my chest that had absolutely nothing to do with the coffee I'd just chugged.

"What about you?" Lizzy asked. It took me a minute to realize her focus was on me as my siblings all sucked down platefuls of festival food like animated Hoover vacuums.

"What about me?" I echoed back.

"You have a favorite festival food? Vendor? Game?"

I shrugged, simply supplying, "A little of everything."

"And is this, in fact, the worst Salmon Festival *ever*?"

"I w—" My response was cut off by an ass with a wallet outline worn onto the denim back pocket. My *brother's* ass. Axel slid between us, setting a tray down with two kabobs of Filipino barbecue beside dipped ice cream cones and sliding them over to the Florida girls. He shook out his hands.

"Man! The lines were long, but you gotta try the classics."

"Nice," Maverick agreed as the girls tentatively hoisted their skewers in cheers. I smiled, dropping my eyes back to the cup of coffee in my hands. They reacted as expected—with a great deal of enthusiasm the siblings all loved—but it was Lizzy's moan that snapped my attention back to her face. Her cheeks pinked, and that insufferable draw to her stirred. *Goddammit.* Suddenly grateful for the buffer of Axel's bulky shoulders, I opted to talk to Brexley.

"Well?"

"So good! Honestly, it's just been fun to see all the places Rhyett talks about." She glanced down at the second sample offered. "A little eccentric to eat ice cream in this weather, don't you think, Axel?"

"I think it's just quirky enough," Lizzy negotiated, snatching the chocolate-encased cone up. The smug bastard smiled, obviously pleased with himself, and I had to fight down the desire to shove him off the bench just to wipe it off his face.

Jesus, what the fuck?

I'd just resolved to remove myself from the situation, palming my face and scooting back when a phone buzzed. Lizzy's, naturally, appeared in her palm, only for all that delicious color to drain out of her fair face. What in the fuck was that about? What the hell could she be so goddamned scared of?

There wasn't an inch of my body that was okay with the fear in those brown eyes, every muscle suddenly alert. She forced a smile on her face. It was wrong. *Stiff.* Not the one the guys from the docks came up to drool over like lovesick puppies.

"Excuse me, I need to take this." And then to Brexley, "It's Val."

A little line appeared between Brexley's brows as she nodded, her lips echoing the concern in my gut. When Lizzy was gone, I asked, "Who's Val?"

Brexley shook her head, handing her cone to Rhyett, who took it quickly, turning his face up to snag a kiss. She responded without seeming to think about it, stepping over the bench. "A friend from Florida. We'll be right back."

The moment she was out of earshot, I scowled at my big brother. "What's that about?"

"They're old friends with Vallie. *So,* Alice, when do you fly out?"

She blinked before clearing her throat. "I start in three weeks, so I'd like to be there in two. Get unpacked before my first day. Find the good sushi. I'm going to miss ours." She told us all about the job, the company she'd be working at, the stretch of the city she was hoping to get an apartment in, but my focus rotated between Rhyett, who was pointedly not meeting my gaze, and the girls where they hovered just beyond the tents on the edge of the docks, looking tense.

Brexley wrapped one arm around her ribs, bracing the opposite elbow so she could cover her mouth with a gloved palm. The rest of them returned to their chatter, even Axel. Although at least he had the awareness to glance in their direction a few times. He was a good man, but as I noted his eyes stray to Lizzy, shoulders broadening like he sensed the same threat I did, I decided it would be a fucking problem if it was *him* that made her feel safe, and not me. He'd just scooted the bench back when I set a hand on his shoulder, keeping him on it.

"I got it," I said under my breath, aware both Rhyett and Elora watched intently as I left. Was it just a big sibling thing—the knowing that something was wrong? The younger half of our lineup seemed entirely oblivious.

The sweet temptation of kettle corn wafted through the air right as Brexley patted Lizzy on the back, turning back and locking on me. She leaned over and said something. I wasn't a lip reader, and that fact had never annoyed me until now. Whatever came out of her mouth had her friend glancing my way, offering another stiff smile as lively as my *unfrosted Pop-Tart* of a wardrobe, and then turned to walk off. Brex met me in the bustling crowd on her way back.

"Everything okay?" I asked, cutting straight to it.

"Yeah, just some personal business. She'll be fine."

"She need anything?"

"Space for a second, Jameson."

I blinked, a bit taken aback. She said it like an order. *Yeah, she'll fit right in.* The thought alone made me smile down at her. "Alright," I said, like I fucking agreed with her. For the record, I absolutely did not. "Imma hit the head."

"Okay. I think Rhyett said something about churros?"

"Jesus, Snows, take it easy. You're gonna make yourself sick."

"Speak for yourself. I learned to eat at the Tampa Fair in one-hundred-degree heat and humidity. This is what we trained for."

"Be ready to eat those *words* in a minute."

"Bet."

Shaking my head, I backed away from her with a big old grin on my face. "Tell Rhyett to get ready for Scallywags." Scallywags was a pirate-themed restaurant in town that set up a food truck every Salmon Festival, specializing in all things artery-clogging. Once a year, we all indulged together. But Brexley would shock me if she touched more than a few samples of fries and onion rings.

"Why do I feel like you're going to enjoy this too much?"

"Because I love being right. Just like you do." Come to think of it, Brexley and I shared a long list of characteristics, and I would try not to think too hard about that little fact. She grinned before tossing that long blonde hair over a shoulder and strutting back to my brother, whose smile could thaw out the entire island when he spotted her. He pulled her onto his lap before scooping her face up in his hands and laying one on her. Something like jealousy burrowed into my gut.

Partially because I wasn't actually a liar, and partly because I'd drank two cups of coffee and a pint of beer, I did, in fact, dip into the portable John before heading to track down Lizzy. It didn't take long, like I had a homing beacon on her. The red hair certainly helped. She was in front of a tent, staring vacantly at it like she wasn't really here. Like her head was still on that phone call.

"Lizzy!" I called, cocking my head when she didn't respond. "Hey, Elizabeth!"

SEVEN

NOEL

"What do you mean the case is closed?!" I demanded, trying desperately not to hyperventilate. Eric's picture-perfect smile stared back at me from the website Vallie had sent me. But where I'd once seen charisma, I now saw deceit. Where confidence used to emanate, there was now a hollow ego that needed stroking. I wanted to take a razor to that perfectly coiffed dark hair. Crack him across the face and see how *he* sported those bruises. "They can't just do that. That's not...that's not how things are supposed to work."

How was it that a man could be legally charged with domestic abuse, and some cash greasing the right palms could make the case fucking vanish?! Worse yet, where the original news article had been posted, there was now a replacement throwing around words like 'false allegations', and 'malicious prosecution,' intermingled with promises for justice and a whole slew of lovely comments insinuating I was a gold-digging whore. The comments were irritating, but what had me most concerned was how quickly it connected to our business. The Cracked Corset appeared in multiple posts and comments, and bile climbed up my throat. Brex put everything she had into that shop, and then some. I'd done the same. Hell, at one point, when I was still naïve to his true nature, Eric had handed me cash and told me to expand, and like an ignorant dog, I'd listened, offering it up to Brex's marketing efforts.

At least in the beginning, he seemed sincere. At least in the beginning...I thought he cared for me.

"Martinez is a fucking shark, Noel. I need you to know I'm doing everything I can," Vallie said, livid anger lacing her professional tone and pulling me back into the moment. Martinez was a ruthless attorney who had represented the Connely family in any litigation they'd been drug into since my parents were in college. Eric's father once boasted that the man had helped a defendant walk after killing his wife 'in a crime of passion'.

Apple doesn't fall far from the tree, I guess.

"I know, Val."

"I mean it, babe." Her facade cracked, her voice along with it, and my heart broke for dragging them all into this. "I'm your friend first and your attorney second. This is absolute bullshit. I've already scheduled a meeting with our partner at the firm as soon as he's out of court tomorrow."

"What about *the shop*, Val? We put everything we have into that place. If they come after us, we don't have a way to fight it. The Corset means the entire world to Brex, if this comes back on her—"

"Noel, babe, breathe. There's no way he's getting away with this. We have proof. And we'll make this as ugly as they want it to be."

"Val, I can't pay for a lengthy—"

"I'm going to pretend you didn't just insult me by insinuating I'd take a fucking penny from you."

"Vallie, this is your—"

"*Choice*. This is my choice. That's what you were about to say, right?"

I swallowed, the motion aching. Nope. Job. I was going to say *job*. But arguing with Vallie would be the equivalent of walking into a five-star restaurant and offering the chef advice. Foolish and a waste of both our time. "Okay, what do I do from a PR perspective for the shop?"

"First up, you loop in Brex. That's her zone of expertise. Second, Wren is right here, and Josie is already pulling in her team. We've got your back, sweetie." Wrenly had been our coffee shop manager for years—and would be Brexley's new right hand in my absence. Jos worked with a prestigious literary agency called *Charmain's*, and her public relations team was absolutely legendary. If Jos was looping them in, the girls had already pulled out all the stops. Tears pricked, clouding my vision.

"Jesus," I said, swallowing the ache stinging at my eyes. "I'm so sorry, you guys."

"Don't you dare apologize for the hellfire he put you in."

Nodding, I added, "Thanks, Val. Now, on to more important things. Did you just say you're *with* Wren?"

She cleared her throat. "I might have said something along those lines."

Grinning, I asked, "Like...you're at The Corset or like—"

"We're at Richard's, in a booth in the back."

"Ohmygod. Vallie, *get off the phone.* I love you so much, but this can wait."

"Bitches before—well—bitches." The soft sound of Wrenly snickering broadened my smile. "But the point stands. We're here for you. Don't think you have to go all *Jack Reacher* and deal with shit yourself." God, if she only knew how badly I would love to go all *Jack Reacher*, if I had the balls to do it. Some things were unforgivable. Some hearts, unredeemable. Eric's was as black as they came.

"You enjoy dinner. Say 'hi' for me."

"Will do."

"Hey, Val?" I blurted before she could hang up.

"Yeah?"

"First up—I require receipts." Her breathy laugh was worth every ounce of stress the call had just poured into my chest. "Second, I'm proud of you. You deserve this. And I love you."

"You forgot how to count somewhere along the way there."

"I did."

"I appreciate it."

"Love you."

"You too, boo."

With Vallie gone, my phone still clutched between white-knuckled fingers, I stared into the cute bohemian tent I'd been dying to see since we'd passed it earlier. Brushed gold jewelry, handmade cards, gorgeous woven rugs, and beach towels were all arranged in beautiful tiny displays inside their tent. But I wasn't shopping as I stared inside, my heart rate catching up with the information she'd just funneled into my unwilling brain like motor oil. Necessary, but a little sloppy going down.

My ribs ached, free fingers coming to trace the place on my cheek where the fresh little scar had formed. It blended in fine if you didn't know what you were looking for; but to me? It was a daily reminder of that betrayal. A prickle of awareness caressed my spine as the chatter of the crowd suddenly faded miles away. Words, laughter, and music blaring together into one big collage of white noise.

Worthless.

Scatter-brained.

Too-skinny.

You know, a talented surgeon would make you look more feminine.

Nobody else will ever want you, so know you're lucky I even think you're cute.

Goddammit, Noel, why don't you ever learn anything? You'd lose your head if it wasn't attached. This is why you need me, *baby.*

Eyes burning, I blinked into the tent, forcing a swallow down as all the thoughts I'd so diligently been avoiding flooded my mind. Absently, I brought my fingers up to my sternum, tapping like the counselor had taught me as I fought down a rasp of air.

I am worthy, I am worthy, I am worthy.

I brought my fingers to my forehead and closed my eyes, not giving a shit if the vendor noticed me and was studying intently.

I am safe, I am safe, I am safe.

My therapist's tapping routine was complete before I forced myself to engage with my surroundings.

Damn you, Eric, you piece of shit. I love people, and parties, and traditions. Do you know what combines all of those into one big event that I soak up like toast under melted butter? Festivals. He got two years of my energy and like hell would I allow him to take any more of my power.

Yes, Vallie was one of my dearest friends. She might have been young, but she was already a badass attorney with a track record that practically promised her one of those hideously heavy judge robes if she wanted one. Val was born for this and would figure it out. And if she didn't, karma certainly would. The idea of a backup plan might have some merit to it, though.

A warm palm wrapped around my bicep, radiating heat that thawed out my frozen body, an instant before a solid mountain of man chest cut off my view of the tent. I looked up until I found Jameson's beard and scowling face.

"Hey," he grumped, voice equal parts concern and frustration. "You okay?" He glanced over a shoulder before looking around over my head for some apparent threat.

"Fine."

"You look like you saw a ghost."

Ha! If he only knew how accurate his assessment was. Certainly couldn't let that happen, or it would go straight to his head. "Just thinking too hard, that's all."

"You got a second?"

I blinked, willing my feet to shuffle backwards, to put a little distance between us so I could stop soaking up the overtly masculine scent of Jameson Rhodes. The man was mouth-watering—literally. But apparently, I'd been fastened to the pavement with tar or superglue, because my rain boots stayed firmly planted. Why my body responded to him the same way it did a platter of chocolate cake, I would never understand. What the hell did he want a second for? And why on God's green earth did it make me anxious under the unruly anticipation?

Glancing around for an out or an ally and coming up empty, I finally sighed and said, "Um, yeah, sure."

"Great," he said curtly, giving me a nod of equal enthusiasm before turning me towards the end of the row and dropping his hold from my arm. Somehow, simultaneous relief and loathing washed over me at the absence.

Well, okay then. I guess we're walking.

Jameson led me down and around the row of tents, strolling us out towards the docks. When he had a decent buffer between us and the festivities, he rounded on me, concern carved between his brows.

"I need you to be honest with me."

My stomach twisted, throat aching as I fought to swallow. I nodded, trying not to cower under the intensity of his gaze.

"Who are you?"

I blinked before scowling up at him and crossing my arms. When in doubt, sports were generally enough to shake a man off a trail, which led me to blurt out, "Is this a trick question, Jorge? Because I'm lost."

"*Jorge?*"

"The giant." Jorge González–*God rest his soul*–had been my younger brother's absolute obsession when we were growing up. He'd played basketball before becoming the WWE's tallest wrestler of all time, inspiring Alex's admiration way past the man's untimely death.

He gave an indignant snort. "I'm not *that* tall."

"But you play basketball."

"Not like Jorge."

Honestly, I was a little surprised that he'd gotten the reference, although his knowledge of sports legends was probably drastically larger than mine.

"You say tomato, I say—"

"Don't finish that sentence. Focus, Red." Had he ever called me Red? I wasn't sure he'd ever called me anything other than *Lizzy* or kaleidoscope, or Skittles, or perhaps, spawn of demons.

"What am I focused on?"

"Look. I know you're not who you've told us you are. This is my town. My family. If there's trouble, like hell am I not doing some research." If he wasn't pestering me about something I absolutely had no intention of talking about in a public setting, it might have been cute—this protective side under all the gruff responses.

"Are you high?" I narrowed my eyes up at him.

"Funny."

"I don't mean *distance to the earth*."

"I knew what you meant," he bit out.

"If you say so, Andre."

He wrestled that scowl into three pointed blinks. "Roussimoff?"

"Points for a surprising trivia arsenal. Do you play down at Bailey's on Saturdays?" The town had been buzzing about the weekly trivia night, and something about that was endlessly endearing. Maybe I'd met my match for random, useless facts that could never apply to life outside it.

"Milo loves *The Princess Bride*. Though your reference was topical, at best."

"Ahh," I said, bobbing my head. "That tracks, oddly enough." Tucking my hair behind an ear, I made to sidestep him. "Well, there's a bear claw calling my name. Do you want me to grab you one or—"

Jameson set a broad, warm palm on my shoulder, halting my brief glimpse at freedom and a festival treat covered in confectioners' sugar. I'd known these conversations were coming—known, and yet, was still entirely unprepared and unsure of how to redirect him or explain the mess that was my life. Hell, I'd barely been willing to think about or acknowledge the shitshow I'd left behind, kinda hoping the momentary sanctuary of Mistyvale could last forever.

"Look. If you're in some sort of trouble, we have resources." Jameson slid his hand down the line of my arm to where my cardigan was rolled at the elbow, and I became acutely aware of how freaking good his skin felt on mine, nearly missing what he said next. "Contacts. We could help."

"Trouble?"

Thumb absentmindedly stroking my forearm where he still held onto me, Jameson said, "You spelled it from the moment you stepped into Grizzly Grind."

"You know, I think you're the first person to ever say that to me." Aside from my brother and Brexley, there likely had been no one that used the words *trouble* and *Noel* in the same sentence. Even then. Alex was always into mischief, and my existing and most likely being a little narc, had earned the jab more than once. Brexley just needed to bitch about being dragged out of her comfort zone, even though I was fairly convinced that deep down, she liked that I brought her with me.

I was a good girl. Always had been. Good grades, good student-teacher conferences—save for the semi-annual note I talked too much—good athletic performances. The principal and I had always been on a first-name basis, but it was because I thoroughly enjoyed running things, volunteered for everything, and wasn't remotely conflicted about reporting things that concerned me.

Never had it been *accusatory*. When my gaze fell to his gentle grip on my arm, he seemed to notice what he was doing, pulling away and stuffing his hand in his pocket. Clearing his throat, his features shifted to frustration, although I wasn't sure if it was directed at me or himself.

"The faster you learn that I'm rarely wrong, the faster we'll get this over with. Name. Spit it out."

"Elizabeth."

"Bullshit," Jameson sneered, furrowing his brows.

Guilt washed through me, but I still managed to gasp, feigning innocence. "Excuse me?"

"You know, I hollered for you last week when you were walking out of the Grind. You didn't respond. I let it go, brushed it off. But, just now—*three feet from you*—I said your name so many times the attendant thought I'd lost my mind. Nothing. Not a freaking blink, not a flinch."

"Did it ever occur to you that perhaps it's because you insist on utilizing that abhorrent nickname, *Lizzy*? Who wants to sound like a freaking lizard? They're cute back home, but certainly not something I'd like a moniker from." I crossed my arms, refusing to shift my weight, to grant my desperate need to either sink my teeth into him or put several steps between us. Come to think of it, I knew a lot of amazing Lizzys and now felt like a judgmental jerk. Alas, I'd dug my grave and now had to lie in it. "For the last time, Mr. Rhodes, it's Elizabeth."

"Come on, Red. Get real."

"You get real," I retorted weakly, my resolve wavering at the concern in his eyes, voice giving way to the precarious edge of tears I was tiptoeing down. Lying to this family was a mistake. Maybe I'd known it, but the illusion of freedom and a true fresh start had been way too tempting.

Jameson crossed those built arms over his chest, the movement stretching the fabric way too tightly over his pecs. And *fuck me*. He had glorious tendons and veins in his forearms, his long black sleeves pushed back to reveal a few solid inches of ink and muscle. I wanted to fill the lines of his gorgeous tattoos with watercolors. The man made me stupid. I should have been grasping at strategies, should have focused on the very real conspiracy he'd so elegantly presented in his gruff grunts and growls. Why did he have to care? Why did I fucking *want* him to?

"Look. I would have fallen for Kate. Maybe Nikki. But you are, sure as shit, not an *Elizabeth*."

I blinked. Nobody else had ever questioned it, but before this whole freaking psycho-ex, fleeing to Mistyvale fiasco, I'd never identified well with my middle name. Deciding it meant nothing that he'd come to the same conclusion, I said, "Look, *Terry*, I don't know what you hit your head on in the engine room today, but you're obviously confused. I'll call Rhyett for you. He can take you home."

"First of all, nobody is taking *me* anywhere. Second, Terry? Bradshaw?"

I had no idea who that was, so I snickered, shaking my head. "Bollea."

"*Hulk Hogan?* Seriously? I get it, I'm tall. I'm not *that* tall."

Wrinkling my nose, I said, "Dammit, I thought I'd have you with that one. Were you into wrestling in high school or something?"

"Were *you?*" he retorted. *Touché, Rhodes. Touché.*

"What are you? Six-three?"

"Six-four. You know what? *Doesn't matter*. Your relentless deflections are just confirming what I'm asking."

"*Which is?*"

Jameson was suddenly right up in my space, concern etched in his features. My breath hitched, heart pounded. Palms did their best impression of a water slide. Lady bits ached. Dammit, he smelled *so good*.

"You're not who you say you are. I will find out what you're hiding, so you might as well tell me what's going on. There is nothing on this planet I value above my family. Nothing. The closest second is this *damn* town and its *damn* people and their *damn* well-being. And if you're in some kind of trouble—"

"You'll make me walk the plank?" I balked, staggering to put a step between us. Between attraction and irritation, attraction was undoubtedly winning. And while the foundation of this fake fresh start was crumbling beneath me—my pathetic attempts at deflection not shaking him off for a second—I didn't have the slightest clue what I could tell him at this point. I'd been lying to all of them about who I was and why I was here for weeks.

How was I supposed to backpedal out of that?

For the first time since this whole thing started, guilt twisted in my stomach. Because somewhere along the way, what this man thought began to matter. And lying to him made me nauseous. Nauseous enough that my breathing had picked up tempo, head spinning as what could only be a panic attack began creeping into my body. I wasn't ready for this. Wanted to vanish. Wanted to start over—start fresh. Five thousand miles and it still wasn't enough.

His voice dropped as he tightened his self-control. "I need you to tell me the truth—"

"Jameson! They're ready for the Blessing of The Fleet. We gotta get down to the boat." Axel said as he loped up beside us, Maverick and their cousins beside him. Saved by the little brother. I didn't know what the hell a Blessing of the Fleet was, but hopefully it bought me time to think. A perplexed little sound rumbled from Axel as his eyes flicked between me and his brother. "Everything alright here?"

"Peachy," Jameson and I answered in unison, his as a growl and mine more of an anxiety-ridden, bird-like chirp.

EIGHT

JAMESON

"Is that *all* holy water?" Maverick snickered, walking up beside me and crossing his arms. I granted him an amused scoff. Maybe stupid traditions weren't the result of an obnoxiously involved family, but a town with a love of theatrics. Some years, the priest stood at the end of the channel flicking holy water off the dock, and some years—this being one of them—he showed up with a freaking hose. The idea was a formal prayer and ongoing blessing of all the boats about to head out for the season. When fishing made up the bulk of the local economy, everyone turned out to support us before summer, as we paraded through the channel between islands.

"Whatever they say, I guess," I said, glowering up at the dwindling crowd. Yeah, the priest passing off the city water for the supposed blessing was irritating enough. I wasn't exactly a religious man, but at least *attempt* to try, for pity's sake. More aggravating than that was that not-Lizzy was standing between my sisters, with Brexley and Rhyett on the other side, all grinning and waving down at us. Only, she wouldn't look at me, just occasionally Axel or Mav, as Milo stayed securely locked in the wheelhouse. It was pissing me off. And confirming exactly what my instincts were telling me.

It didn't matter what she or Axel said, I couldn't shake the knowing in my gut that she was lying to my face, keeping secrets from our family. And that didn't spell *good news* in my mind. She might have been cute as sin, but there were few things I loathed more than a liar. Especially one that had already infiltrated my line of soft-hearted sisters. *Especially* one that had her damn claws in me. I wasn't a sucker. The first time I could shrug off, but there were only three feet between us today and she didn't give me a single response. Not in that squirrelly way girls would if they were playing deaf because they didn't wanna talk to me. Skittles—because what the hell else could I call her?—didn't shift her feet, her cheeks didn't pink up, there was no nervous lip biting. She actually hadn't realized I was talking to her until I got up in her face.

Worse yet, when I tried to tell her I wanted to help, she thought so fucking little of me, she assumed I was mad she was here. I *was* mad. Pissed, actually. The reasoning was just different than she'd so *graciously* assumed.

My anger derived from three things. One: she, Brex, and my brother were obviously in this together. Two: my gut was convinced she'd lied to us—to me, to *my parents*, who had been nothing but welcoming to her. Three: fear hid under her bubbly exterior. And that pissed me off. Because what the fuck was she running from in this 'fresh start' of hers? My instincts were screaming to protect her against whatever threat had those big brown eyes so desolate when she was on that call.

Maybe it should have been obvious. What color-loving, crop top wearing sun beam traded Florida for Alaska? Willingly. My brother was lovable, but he wasn't *that* lovable, and had certainly never been one to ride the unholy tricycle. Hell, not even I had pushed that boundary, and that was certainly statistically more likely. Which meant she was here for a reason, and I highly doubted it was to give Brin a maternity leave. Rhy could've had Alice or the twins step in with way less hassle.

Moving her into his house. Jesus Christ, I was dumb as rocks. Skittles was in trouble. And I was damn well going to find out how hot that water was.

<hr>

THE STEADY *THUD, thud, thud, swoosh* sounded like coming home. Yeah, I smiled, and I didn't give a shit that I looked like some idiot kid coming downstairs Christmas morning as my engine cut off and boots met pavement. All thoughts of trouble wandered to the back burner as I watched Rhyett move, the motions still practiced all these years later. *Thud, thud, thud, swoosh.*

My brothers and I grew up shooting hoops on that driveway. Hell, Rhyett would play at all hours of the night, the steady, predictable pattern served as the background to many a lullaby as mom got the younger kids to bed. Music cranking, we'd run drills until the last light faded during the summer. Sometimes on school nights, too. As he pivoted to find me watching, Rhyett broke out that signature grin of his before tossing me the ball. It was firm and rough, obviously new. He must've picked it up when he got into town.

Dribble, dribble, dribble, shoot. Net. Victory.

Our high-five was an easy muscle memory. Wordlessly, we moved back into old habits. Ancient habits. Hell, I think Milo bought that hoop when we were twelve. The back was missing; the top had long since rusted, and the hole in the net was almost—*almost*—big enough for the ball to fall through. When we finally paused for a water break, Rhyett jerked his chin over towards his truck, the tailgate down. He coasted a palm over his sweaty forehead, snagged the case of water from the bed of the pickup, and tossed me one.

"What's on your mind?" He asked, finally taking the Bluetooth headphones out of his ears, placing them in their case after wiping them clean, and setting them beside his water.

"Nothing," I breathed, deflecting. For a beat, I just wanted to play. Clear my head. Not think about sexy little sunbeams and their baggage.

"Right," he muttered before taking another drag of water.

"*Should there* be something on my mind?" I hedged. Rhyett puckered his mouth, shaking his head before taking one last swig of water.

"Nope. Guess not. You up for another round?"

"I could do this all day."

"Oh, I remember," he said, grinning as we both put the lids back on our bottles. It wasn't an exaggeration. We'd played ourselves half to death out here. Right as we both wandered back onto the court, Axel's white pickup turned down the long drive and, judging by the tunes emanating from the cab, he had Maverick in tow. They were out of the truck and heading our way in ten seconds flat.

"Hey, old men! Wanna learn a thing or two?" Mav taunted as he came down the drive. Rhyett and Axel both laughed as I scowled in his direction.

"In your dreams, kid," Rhyett said back, peeling his sweaty shirt from his body. The idea had merit. The sun was blessedly shining, and something about the Alaska sun was warmer. Maybe it was just because we had such a stark comparison in mind, but fifty up here felt like sixty or seventy degrees in the lower forty-eight. Mimicking the motion and tucking it through a belt loop, I glanced Rhyett's way.

"Well, this should be fun."

It wasn't until we were all dripping sweat, and Elora came out to hound us about helping with dinner, that any of us were willing to slow down. With Mav anywhere-bound in a matter of months, and Rhyett days away from flying home, these moments were fucking sacred. Yeah, growing up in a big ass family was loud. And overwhelming. And sent my anxiety through the roof because nobody could hold still long enough to keep track of, or make sure they were safe. But I fucking loved having five brothers. The six of us couldn't have been a more eclectic gathering, but it worked. And this was what I missed the most about all being on the island.

"Told you to keep your mouth shut," Axel griped as he and Mav headed inside to shower off their loss before reporting to the kitchen for an assignment. We might've crossed that third-decade line, but we weren't too rusty. I might have even enjoyed his playful shove that sent Mav's arm flailing for purchase on the garage wall.

Rhyett hocked a towel in my direction before turning to rifle through his gym bag. "So. You ready to talk?" Fuck, he was always so good at that. Waiting for me to come to him.

"Yeah," I grunted, sliding my ass up on his tailgate before I wiped the sweat off my brow and set the towel around my shoulders. Might as well cut straight to it. Didn't really know how to do that frilly ass, beat around the bush dance people seemed so inclined towards. "What aren't you telling me about McShane?"

Rhyett shook his head, but only once before his eyes narrowed, the movement halting. "What are you fishing for?"

"What's her *name*, Rhyett." It wasn't a question. They'd lied to me. To us. And I was about to make it make sense.

"Remember what I told you?"

"And *here we go*," I griped.

"She's been through some shit. She's starting over. Give the woman a chance to do so. Her name is whatever the fuck she wants it to be."

"Look, Rhy. I know I've been shit at showing I care, but I need to know if she's in trouble. Should I be concerned?"

"Define *concerned*."

"Is she in danger? What's she running from?"

"That's her story, not—"

"Bullshit."

"*Jameson.*"

"I mean it. She's been here for *weeks*. She's running your shop, living in your house. I don't see Brexley being the kind of woman that would welcome a third party into bed, so there's something you're not telling me."

Rhyett deadpanned. "That's what you're basing this on?"

"Her name sure as shit isn't. Lizzy. *Elizabeth*. Whatever."

He pursed his lips before something caught his attention, drawing both our focus to the garden boxes behind our greenhouse, where mom was tromping around in brown knee-high rain boots and an oversized floppy yellow hat, showing Brex and the embodied sunshine her plots, inevitably filling their heads with tales of all things green and leafy.

The former was sporting boots that matched Juniper's, but the latter's were mint green with bumblebees on them. Jesus, even her new rain gear was colorful. That's what was confusing. By all other means, the woman seemed unapologetically herself—untethered from expectations of age or appearance—showing up exactly as she wanted to. Her wardrobe mimicked a busted bag of Skittles in a climate where the palette was all muted grays, blues, and greens. She wore her gorgeous curls wherever they fell, like taming them would offend her. And mid-twenties or not, she liked the bumblebee boots my niece would probably pick out. I hadn't verified, but had the striking suspicion her bag would contain at least one paint set, or maybe those glittery ass gel pens the girls had loved when they were younger. Zero shits to give to the opinions of others, which was, I'd wager, why everyone and their dog had fallen in love with her. It was cute as hell.

So, what wasn't she telling us?

"Earn her trust." Rhyett's voice tugged me back to the tailgate. Christ, the man was *exhausting*. I loved his loyalty when it applied to our family, but this was enough to drive me mad.

"Stop running me in circles, man."

He shook his head. "You man the fuck up and talk to her yourself. There she is, James. Go get her. If she wants to share, she will. If I feel like shit's headed in the wrong direction, I'll let you know."

"So, she *is* in trouble?"

"Does she look like she's in trouble?"

With no further fucking explanation, Rhyett hopped off the

truck and headed for his girl. What the hell did that mean? I didn't have time to contemplate though, because Skittles was now watching me intently, and that focus gave me the need to go to her. To demand she tell me everything. To demand she let us fix it together. And that didn't make a lick of fucking sense.

NINE

NOEL

Juniper's garden plots were absolutely beautiful. When we'd ducked back inside to pull dinner out of the oven, the Rhodes sisters had ushered me to a corner chair, where I dove into the series my Florida girls had begged me to read. I wasn't big on long series, thick books, or slow-burns, and this was...literally all three. When things finally got steamy, I felt the blood rush to my face, butterflies dancing when they *finally* did the damn deed. Happily, I closed my e-reader case, swapping it for my phone.

NOEL

FINALLY. Respectful dick.

VALLIE

Spitting out water gif

JOSIE

Wait, irl respectful dick?

VALLIE

What would disrespectful dick be?

JOSIE

Two pump chump?

BREXLEY

No, she finally got to book five.

VALLIE

Jesus, that was slow.

NOEL

That's what I'M saying.

And absolutely not. No more real-life dicks,
remember?

BREXLEY

Not the slow burn, the reading speed. The slow burn
was exquisite.

JOSIE

OH. FINALLY. Good lord, I've been dying to talk about
that scene. You're like halfway done? Ish.

NOEL

There better be more spice.

BREXLEY

grimacing emojis

NOEL

So help me, I will hunt you down if I just waited five
books for one scene with a tattooed grump.

BREXLEY

I mean…

JOSIE

People don't read this one for the spice.

VALLIE

Look. I think it's hot. Keep going. Or I'll put down that
Rom Com you sent me that compares his dick to a
weapon.

NOEL

Fine. But you all owe me a thriller.

SMIRKING AND SHAKING MY HEAD, I slid my phone into my
pocket and E-reader into my purse. Looking up and out the window
as laughter spilled from the kitchen behind me, I found more Rhodes
wandering down the driveway for their weekly Sunday night
gathering, which I'd somehow been invited to despite not actually
being family.

Mom had always been big on family dinners growing up. Eric

was never one for joining, his resistance to all things McShane a flagrant red flag that I dutifully ignored in the name of honoring his *boundaries* as the son of a public figure.

As I watched the Rhodes 'kids' file into the house Sunday night, the familiar routine wrapped around my heart like a freaking hug. Somehow, all at once, it felt like home and my heart ached for my family's faces and voices. Heck, I even missed my little brother, Alex.

"But, that doesn't make any sense. If she'd just been honest from the start, the entire situation could have been avoided." The words made my stomach bottom out for a beat before I realized Leighton was debating with Kaia, who was quick to rebuke her theory over whatever movie they'd gone to see today.

"What would be the point of the movie?"

"A love story," Leighton drawled back. The room was full of chatter and my focus wandered to Elora as she buzzed between the dining room and kitchen, setting bowls down on the oversized lazy Susan perched on the center of the enormous round table. It was clearly the result of the shabby-chic movement a few years back, coated in white chalk paint with scuffed edges and rounded legs.

"So, I'm flying back into Seattle next week for the conference, and then to Salt Lake after that. Then it's Denver, and I'll be home." Elora neatly placed the garden salad and a bowl full of black olives side-by-side as Juniper set down a cheesy-looking pasta casserole that required both of her hot-mittened hands. The matriarch's hair was swept back into an elegant claw clip, loose pieces of salty blonde hanging around her face and swaying as she nodded.

"Good, okay. Hopefully, it times out and the boys can be back in the harbor so you can at least see them."

"I'll be here for about two weeks, so I assume our paths will cross at some point," Elora reassured as they turned back for the door to the kitchen. The inside of the main house wasn't nearly as daunting as the exterior. In reality, the finishes were seventies yellows and greens, worn from years of too many hands and a tribe of angsty teenagers. The carpet was worn, and they covered the walls with eclectic collections of art and family photos. But it was warm, homey, and welcoming. Just like the humans that inhabited the frequently scuffed walls.

"Come, come!" It was Alice's hand on my elbow that jerked my gaze her way.

"Oh! Me? What can I do to help?"

"Nothing, silly. Come sit. You're our guest!" She snaked her arm around my waist, guiding me in. This family was barely contained chaos. A constant cacophony of voices and movements. And despite the overwhelming nature of it, I kinda loved it.

Brexley and Rhyett had told me to show up at six for family dinner—attendance mandatory the Sunday before the guys would roll out for the season. Oddly enough, it coincided with the two of them leaving, so it was a bit of a bon voyage for everyone. I wasn't sure how to feel about that.

Juniper, who had just made her way through the swinging white door to the kitchen, stained with kick marks around the bronze plate on the bottom, tsked her tongue in our direction.

"She's family," she sing-songed. "If she's Brexley's sister, she's part of the family," she boldly declared. Glad to see the unwavering faith in Brex and Rhyett was shared with his mom, I laughed.

"I mean, soul sister," I allowed. Juniper smiled in that motherly way only a matriarch can.

"Family doesn't mean blood where I come from. It means the people you know you can depend on, come hell or high water. Does that or doesn't that describe the two of you?"

"It does."

"Then you're our family now, too. Come on in. Do you need anything? Water? Wine or bourbon? Coffee?"

"Notice how she just slides the alcohol right under the radar," Elora quipped, a sly smirk on her face as she gingerly placed a bowl of roasted Brussels sprouts, followed by a basket full of rolls onto the center of the table.

"Uh, thanks for the offer but I have to be at work at five tomorrow morning, so no sleep or a hangover both seem like a bad idea. If you point me in the right direction, I'd love some water, though."

"I've got a pitcherful on the table," Juniper said, pointing toward it with a soft maternal smile.

Nodding, I followed Alice's lead, looking around for Brex. Rhyett and the guys had all vanished to shower off their basketball sweat, but I'd lost track of her somewhere between the garden and washing our hands for dinner.

"My favorite discussions every year always stem from the complexities and paradoxes of clashing philosophical theories. Anyway, this wicked smart little sophomore essentially told me it's a never-ending loop of intellectual confusion." The husky warmth of Broderick's voice trailed up the hallway, growing closer by the beat.

Everyone else continued their work, but I didn't miss the way Elora's eyes widened, or the way she rushed to set her plate down, freeing her hands to comb frantically through her hair and smooth her skirt before straightening. Broderick's voice abruptly halted, and the energy of the room shifted. I didn't have to look away from Alice, who was telling me about the new position she'd accepted at great length, to know Jameson had entered the space. The man had this force field around him. Like a palpable presence, I could reach out and touch if I knew how to.

Elora's face cracked into a honeyed smile as she turned on a heel to face them and marched back towards the kitchen. "You'd think by now you would have chosen a less perplexing hobby."

As I absolutely refused to look up, heat climbing up my spine at the mere awareness of his companion, all I could do was listen to Broderick's throaty laugh, followed by, "What do you have in mind, El? Juggling?"

I didn't catch whatever retort she threw over her shoulder that had Broderick laughing and following her. Alice began buzzing with conversation again, but the chaotic room around me seemed to fade into the background as I grew more acutely aware of the fact that he was here. That his focus was directed toward me. If my spidey-senses were correct, Jameson remained embedded into the threshold, his attention like a physical weight against my skin. I tried to keep my focus on Alice's excitement, vaguely aware the room was dripping in laughter, like a summer jar of lemon blossom honey: sweet, light, and full of smiles. But it was the man leaning against the doorframe watching us without uttering a word that sent my skin prickling, his focus as good as any touch.

Heat stirred in my belly like melted chocolate, bubbling and churning as nerves kicked up. Refusing to grant his curiosity my focus, I nodded as though I'd been paying attention, and tried to concentrate on sweet Alice. *What in God's name is she saying?*

"Anyway, I just put in an application for this apartment, and it would be a freaking dream come true. It's an old Victorian house repurposed as individual units, with original hardwood floors and great enormous windows."

Mirroring her dreamy, adorable smile, I said, "I bet the details are incredible." She was so excited, I actually felt bad for being so wrapped up in her beautiful brother and his mere ability to inhale.

Alice groaned as I forced myself to sip the water she'd slid my direction. "Stunning. When the light hits, the whole place glows. It's to die for–" As she told me the details, the weight of his presence became way too freaking much, heat creeping up my neck and chest. Would alcohol hurt or help?

Setting down my glass, I quickly said, "I'm so sorry, Alice. I need the restroom. Please hold that thought."

"Second door on the left!" She chirped, pointing at the hallway before snatching up her wineglass. I thanked all that was holy that it was the one opposite of the stormy presence in the corner and scooted my chair back in before bolting for my shot at freedom.

Family pictures lined the walls here, any previously blank slab of drywall decorated in their story, right down to the small spots between doorways. There was the distinct possibility I was actually recognizing what tiny, adorable cherub face belonged to which sibling, but I didn't want to risk running into Jameson enough to linger. Zipping into the second door to the left, I sighed as I hid like the coward I was, only to fly out of my skin when someone sucked down a breath behind me. Whirling, I looked down to find Brexley sitting with her back against the wall, tears streaming down her cheeks, knees tucked against her chest.

"Brex?" I knelt beside her. "Honey, what's wrong?"

Watery baby blues blinked up at me, her chest rising faster and harder than was probably healthy. Was she hyperventilating in here?!

"I can't do this."

"Sweetie, *do what?*"

She gave an indignant little squeak like I ought to know exactly what she was talking about. "This wasn't supposed to happen. Not yet."

"You gotta give me more than that." That dumpster fire of a family had left my bestie with a tremendous amount of baggage. Not the *wheel it behind you and stuff it in the overhead bin* kind of baggage, the *one hundred dollar penalty to check it in cargo kind of baggage*. Namely, an intense fear of commitment. She'd almost run off when she and Rhyett got serious, because of some ridiculous inferiority complex. Thank all that was holy, Rhyett has the patience of a god and gave her the space and time to think. "We already talked about Rhyett and the family, Brex. None of that has changed."

Brexley's legs slipped out from under her like she'd suddenly lost control of them. I was about to sit beside her when I spotted the little white and pink stick in her hands.

"Oh," I said, the word coming out in a whoosh. "*Brex?*"

She held it up, sliding a second one out from behind it, both showing me little blue positive signs.

"I'm gonna be an auntie?" I said, fighting back tears as she nodded at me, eyes glossy. "Oh Brex, that's amazing. What do you mean you can't do this? You were born for this!"

"How do you know?"

"Because I know."

"Very reassuring. What if I end up like—"

"If you say your mother, I'm going to have a conniption. You are nothing like that deadbeat bitch, Brex. Not on your *worst* days." Her nervous laugh brought a smile to my face. "And look around you, honey. Forget the fact that I will be a freaking helicopter for you and a cool auntie for her. Do you honestly think a single one of those siblings out there will let you feel alone or overwhelmed for even a minute? You have an army, sweetheart. Rhyett gave you that."

She sniffled as she nodded, eyes jerking up when someone knocked on the door. My heart did a somersault. Hell, it did an entire Olympics-worthy gymnastics routine. Jameson Rhodes was leaning against the threshold, concern furrowing his brows.

JAMESON

There are few things I loathed more than a woman crying—not the woman *for* crying, but that something or someone could *do something* that would *make* a woman cry. Then the ensuing helplessness that made my palms sweat. So, finding Brexley and Skittles in a heap on the floor, both glassy-eyed or with tears streaming, was like a nightmare given life. They both jerked around when I knocked on the doorframe.

"Uh, everything alright in here?"

"Yeah," they said in unison, although my latest temptation seemed sincere while Brex's lip trembled. *Awe, hell.* I really didn't feel like kicking Rhyett's ass but if he fucked this up…

"Something I can help with?"

"Where's your brother?" Skittles asked, too sweetly. I didn't have time to be suspicious or make a joke, because I knew who she was looking for and I valued my balls attached. If one crying woman was bad, the best friend of said crying woman was *terrifying.* Women went feral for each other. Once, when Elora was being picked on, Alice—who is by far the quietest and sweetest of the six—busted a teenage boy's foot, kneed him in the balls, and broke his nose. You don't mess with sisters or best friends. Ever. It's against the code.

"I think he was heading out to take a phone call."

She nodded, looking back at Brexley. In a devastatingly maternal move, she reached over to wipe Brexley's face with her sleeves, and my chest warmed. *Jesus. That wins points now? For fucks sake.*

I shifted on my feet, deeply regretting coming to look for my unfortunate recent obsession. What's the proper protocol for these situations? *Run? Help? Fuck off before one of them kills you? Blurt out the first damn offer that would accomplish two of those objectives at once?*

"Want me to grab him?" Option D was, evidently, incorrect. At least, judging by the way Brexley's tears started all over again. "Wait. Oh, God, please don't do that." She sniffled loudly, lip quivering. "I can't deal with it when you guys cry. It makes me crazy. Tell me what I can do for you, Brex." Skittles' brows skyrocketed as Brexley gave me a little sob.

"You were right." Well, yes. I was quite good at being right, kinda chapped that everyone still acted surprised. "At the festival, you made a joke about Rhyett and me." Well, *shit*, I'd made several. It was all good-natured ribbing, but my brain was panicking, trying to think of what would be worth crying over days later. But it was her watery six words that brought me to my knees. "You ready to be an uncle?"

Ten million things ran through my head, but I couldn't put a single damn one into words.

Mouth dry.

Palms—buzzing.

Back—sweating.

I studied my brother's girl for a beat before she held up two positive tests. "Awe, Brex, where the hell is Rhyett?"

She choked on her laugh. "You just said he's outside."

"I should've run to get him. You—you're—"

"Pregnant," she finished.

Not going to lie. The fear in her eyes made it harder to breathe than I wanted to admit. But I wrapped her little face in my hands to force her chin up. "Listen. I might give my brother shit, but he's undoubtedly the best man I know if we take Milo out of the equation. And he has exceptional taste in everything. I mean, *everything*." I wiped my thumbs over her cheek, soaking up the tears there. "I'm not sure if you know this, but he has never—not once—

brought a woman home to meet this family. Which tells me a few things about you. You are something special. He loves you more than I think you can even comprehend. And this family—blood or not, in name or not—takes care of our own. What do you need?" And now they were both crying as I pulled my hands away. *Fuck me.* Skittles dabbed at her eyes with the sleeve of her sweater. Jesus, could I hug them *both?*

"I suppose I should tell the father," Brex said, her voice rough and hesitant. She glanced back at her best friend, giving me a beat to suck down a breath. "You mean it? You think I can do this?"

"Of course you can," she said without hesitating.

I nodded. "Brexley, *of course* you can. And this family is good at nothing if not taking care of kiddos. I'm sure Elora and Juniper will have a rotation scheduled before Rhyett remembers how to speak."

"That's the most words I've heard you string together since I got here, Jameson." Not-Lizzy blinked at me, those little painted lips quirking up in a smirk I wanted to kiss off her.

"I mean it, smartass."

"I didn't say you didn't. You're just…"

"A man of few words," Brexley supplied over a shaky smile. Apparently, crossing my arms and making a little *hmph* noise only confirmed what they were saying, because they both burst out giggling.

"Alright. The mother of my nephew shouldn't be sitting on a bathroom floor." I stood up, reaching down for her and finding her eyes wide and round like little blue saucers.

"You think it's a boy?"

"It's totally going to be a girl," Skittles grumbled with an eye roll.

"Fifty-fifty shot. I'll take my chances." She grinned and grasped my hands, all of us rising before I ushered them through the door. The girls snaked their arms around each other as soon as we were in the hallway, and I blew out a breath, stepping ahead of them to lead them through the living room to the front porch. Sure as shit, Rhyett stood at the end of the driveway, towering spruce to either side. He spotted us in a heartbeat, his great big smile giving way to concern as he surveyed his girl. I didn't have to be within earshot to know that the phone call just ended. Skittles and I stayed back, letting Brexley go do what she needed to do. Neither of us bothered to retreat inside, staying around for the show or moral support or some combination of the two.

"That was really kind of you," she whispered. I blew out a heavy breath, just relieved they were both done crying. Rhyett had always been infuriatingly good at everything. He was the best with our little siblings and cousins, and Charlie's kids loved him but called me the scary uncle until they were three and seven. Rhyett would be an incredible father, and an incredible partner or husband or whatever label they slapped on their relationship. What I hadn't told Brexley was that my brother had shown me a ring this afternoon, hoping to take her on a walk after dinner and ask her to become an official Rhodes. And I'd put money down that with the news of impending parenthood, he wouldn't make it to the beach before popping the question.

"Meant it," I said simply.

"Back to grunts of acknowledgment, I see."

"Yeah."

"Still...*kind*."

"Better," I allowed jokingly. I couldn't stifle my smile, and she chuckled quietly, both of us rapt as Brexley made her way down the drive towards my brother as he slid his phone into his pocket. "We do. We take care of our own. Always have."

"Obviously. Side effect of there being *a million* of you. I meant the stuff you said about Brex being special—about Rhyett being a good man and her being the only woman he's brought home."

"It's true."

"What?" she chirped, blinking.

I shrugged. "Why bring somebody around if they're not sticking? Just complicates things. Plus. With sisters who love everybody, it would be like inviting the future you to deal with your future ex."

"Hmm," she hummed thoughtfully. "You share the philosophy?"

"We came up with it together the first time Hadlee insisted on hanging out with my high school girlfriend after she'd dumped me to sleep her way through my team. It was the same summer we agreed not to mess around with any of our sisters' best friends, or *any* of our best friends' sisters."

"Yikes," she said with a sympathetic grimace.

"That summarizes it."

Rhyett took Brexley's hands, stepping wide and lowering his eyes to be on her level. God, she looked so small next to him. Was Skittles even more petite? No wonder she acted like I was a giant. "What's she saying?"

"Hold on, I'll whip out my bionic ears and keep you posted."

"Smartass."

"Shh, my secret agent fly is getting close."

"*Jesus.*" Fighting laughter had become a part-time job with her in our lives.

She dug around in her back pocket. "Oooh, magic amplification gummy bears."

"Are you done yet?" I deadpanned.

"Hold on, I'm consulting my divination ball."

"Okay, I get it." I threw my hands up in surrender. "*Dumb question.*"

"Thank you," she said, smirking as she turned back to the free show.

It seemed like smiling around this woman was involuntary. But she was freaking funny. *Annoying.* But funny. Every single inch of my body froze when her hand jutted out and wrapped around my wrist. I'd never had a woman send heat into my blood the way she did. Never had anyone commanded my lust so goddamned easily, images of those hands in a very different location flitting through my mind. Why did she have to be so damn young?

"*Oh, oh!* Here we go." She squeezed me tighter, and while I wanted to see his reaction to this particular bomb, I couldn't peel my eyes from where her fingers set against my skin. Traced up the length of her toned arm, studied those painted pink lips and her freckled face. Sucked down a breath when I found her eyes on me. She pulled away, bringing that fair hand to settle against her throat right as it bobbed. Something about the visual of the two did very unwelcome things to my body.

"Yeah," I breathed, forcing my eyes back to Rhyett and Brexley right as he gave some sort of exclamation and scooped her tiny body up against his.

He was spinning her in a circle when my unfortunate fixation said, "Noel."

"For a niece?"

She laughed airily. "I mean, I would certainly be honored."

When her meaning clicked, I looked away from a now excitedly making-out Rhyett and Brexley to study her instead.

"*My name* is Noel."

Fuck, that actually fit. I smiled. "Now, *that* makes sense."

TEN

NOEL

"Oh goodie, I get to grow dark hair on my chin, and if I'm lucky, I'll get whiskers."

Shaking my head at Brex's perpetual state of worry, I pointed out, "But you'll get to glow! We can buy pretty things for a nursery."

"I'll swell up like a beach ball."

"And pick names and watch Rhyett fret over making sure your entire existence is perfect."

"Oh God, and then I have to squeeze a watermelon out of a grape."

I burst out laughing. That did it, right there. Sometimes Brexley's cynicism was tiring, but other times, it was ridiculously hilarious. We were sitting in her room at Rhyett's as she packed up their clothing in precise little piles. Hell, I'd never been this organized, let alone for a trip across the country. Time blindness made me prone to unwitting procrastination, followed by running around like a chicken with my head cut off, stuffing random odds and ends into my suitcase hours before leaving for the airport. Jealous of the fact that the two of them got to go home to my sweet cat, Chloe, and Brexley's golden retriever, Royal, but otherwise just anxious that I was going to be up here alone, I was slowly helping her through her drawers. Not that it took a lot, as they were already folded properly.

"I think the grape is built to stretch," I reassured, handing her a stack of crisp-edged denim leggings.

"Did you know Juniper had all of her babies without an epidural? *Oh god,* I don't think I can do that."

"And you don't have to. There's not a trophy for finishing one way or another. Healthy and happy is all that matters."

"Oh, Jesus, I have so much to learn."

"And you will, *in time*." I handed over a rolled-up hoodie, and she gingerly placed it into the suitcase. "How do we eat an elephant?"

"A bite at a time."

"There you go."

"And I have Rhyett."

"Yeah," I said, smiling as the stack of shirts settled on limp hands in my lap. Warmth grew in my chest. "You have Rhyett."

"Okay," she said, blowing out a breath. "Let's talk about literally anything else. The girls will drive me crazy in no time. Oh god, *the girls.*"

"Will expect the details on everything."

"I don't want them planning the wedding."

I cackled despite myself. Rhyett had—in true Rhyett form—proposed when he remembered how to set Brexley on her own two feet. According to Jameson, he'd had the whole thing planned out, but tossed the elaborate beach proposal to the wind when she told him the news. The family had lost their minds. There was toasting, and crying and celebrating, and baby books whipped out of thin air full of cute, naked rolly butts, and filthy kitchens, and tiny gremlins more mud than child. Much to Broderick's chagrin, he made appearances in a few of those, and Max showed up a handful of pages later. To his immense satisfaction, his photos were all clothed. Even the bonus brothers were teary and emotional over Rhyett and Brexley's bun in the oven.

"So, don't let them. It doesn't have to be fit for royalty. Do it your way, and then they'll feel extra grateful when I make them organize mine someday."

She laughed, setting her half-folded jacket in her lap so she could look at me. "On a scale of calling me 'twat' for six months to burning my house down, how angry would they be if we eloped?"

My throat went tight, hand hovering awkwardly halfway to her case. "Eloped?"

She nodded enthusiastically. "We could bump our flights out a few days, go hike back to those fields of purple lupine so the photos are pretty, and get married here, where Rhy grew up."

I looked out the window at the omnipresent misty gray, only sporadically broken apart by sunlight. It could work. "*Now?!*" My voice was definitely not supposed to crack like that. Still, everything about the way they met and then the impulsive driveway proposal, and now a potential mountainside elopement was so far from the precisely planned calendar and mile-long to-do list Brexley was known for.

"Yeah, I mean, you're the only family I have. So many Rhodes are here right now—we could call Pax, Finn, Hadlee, and Jeanne and see if they could get up here. But, worst case, we have the bulk of who we want already," she said with a gentle little shrug. Brexley had always been afraid to ask for what she wanted. This was good—her knowing, her *wanting*. I loved it.

"I say we do it."

"Oh, thank god, because I have to ask for a favor."

"Oh, boy."

She laughed nervously. "Will you somehow give me away *and* be my maid of honor?"

My heart stuttered, tears immediately pricking my eyes. "Of course, sweetie. Oh my god, Brex! That means the *world* to me." She threw her arms around me as I did with her, and we both rocked and somehow simultaneously giggled and cried together, leaning awkwardly over her suitcase. I released her to straighten my back and was dabbing at my eyes when Rhyett and Jameson appeared in the doorway.

"Oh, Jesus," Jameson muttered, immediately vanishing, earning a trill of laughter from both of us and a wry smile from Rhyett, who, evidently, didn't share Jameson's aversion to emotion.

"Hey ladies, we're throwing lunch on the grill. Who wants steak, and who wants chicken?"

"One of each, please?" I asked. "I'll take one for lunch tomorrow over salad."

"Roger. Brex?"

"I'm feeling steak today!"

"Good deal, beautiful. Ready in fifteen."

And then we were alone. Brexley commenced her packing as I handed her things from the open drawers. "So," she eventually hedged. "What's the deal with you and Jameson?"

"What do you mean?"

"Seemed like you two warmed up a bit last night."

"He momentarily forgot to be an asshole, and I might have liked it." It turned out Jameson could be exceptionally kind, albeit still quiet and gruff in his delivery. But between Max, Broderick, and the

Rhodes boys, dinner had been one ongoing standup comedy routine. For the first time since arriving on this mist-shrouded rock, it felt like home.

"He called you Noel when we were leaving."

"He did."

"How much does he know?"

"The bare bones of it." It was true. I'd told him I was running from poor choices and an ex I didn't want to talk about, and thought a fresh name for my fresh start would be fitting.

"Ahh, okay. So, does he know why you're here?"

"Vaguely."

"Enough that I don't have to feel like you're five thousand miles away with nobody watching your back, or...?"

"I'm watching my own back. He knows I have a shitty ex I don't feel like talking about."

"Good. You should tell the boys, at least. They'll watch out for you."

"Rhyett keeps telling me that." You know, only a dozen times a day. Once for every sibling. Okay, that might have been an exaggeration, but still, it was a lot of pressure to dump my baggage on their doorstep. Although, more often than not, it was Jameson he encouraged me to open up to.

"Maybe you should listen."

"Maybe," I allowed, shifting uneasily and hoping to redirect her focus as quickly as possible. "I need coffee. You want something?"

"I could use some peppermint tea. Trying to cut the caffeine, you know?"

Hesitating in the doorway, I glanced over my shoulder. "Hey, Brex?"

"Yeah?"

"You're already a wonderful mom."

THERE WERE ABSOLUTELY no objections when Rhyett and Brexley announced their plan to elope on the Alaskan mountainside when they got back from applying for their marriage license. As a matter of fact, Elora and Alice whisked us away to their room so quickly my head spun, pulling out all of their cocktail dresses and accessories and displaying them in neat little pods on their beds. If they kept showering her with compliments and suggestions, Brexley's face might permanently stain salmon pink. But it was fun to see the way they welcomed her. She needed that.

"Okay, so we'll go down to the spa at two for mani-pedis and facials, over to the salon at three for deep conditioning, split ends, and a blowout, and then come back here to prep heatless curls and food for tomorrow." Elora was freaking adorable, like befriending a bumblebee, happily buzzing from one task to another and never ceasing her efforts. She was most elated she happened to be in town for this. It was all...so easy. Freakishly easy. I wasn't willing to point it out to Brexley in case she freaked out and thought it was a jinx.

Milo was the officiant and deeply honored they asked. Juniper's best friend was the local florist. Alice loved few things in life as much as baking, and had already whipped together muffins and sugar cookies frosted black with their initials in white icing, and was going to make a small cake, too. Leighton and Kaia were either future cosmetologists or were seriously wasting their talents. They'd done two trial looks for Brex in the following days, both of which were exquisite...and true to her.

Rhyett and Jameson spent the afternoon before the wedding building a beautiful wood arch they could easily assemble on top of the mountain. Axel's latest date owned the local cafe and had a banquet room in the back with the Rhodes name blocking out the day. Maverick was—obviously—in charge of music for the evening.

It was seamless. Too seamless, even for me, so I was just spontaneously knocking on wood with every new excited proclamation, like a highly caffeinated woodpecker. It was of absolutely no surprise when I got a text from Brin that brought my momentum to a screeching halt.

BRINLEIGH

Um. So. My water just broke.

NOEL

Of course, it did.

BRINLEIGH

grimacing emoji

Can you come in tonight? I don't trust anyone else to make sure everything is set up and schedules are shuffled accordingly.

NOEL

Already slipping into boots.

BRINLEIGH

God bless you.

THE GUYS WERE STILL STAINING the arch when I got into the garage. Both men hesitated mid-brushstroke.

"What's up, Red?" Rhyett was, naturally, the one to break the silence.

"Brin's water just broke."

"Awe, hell," Jameson groaned, falling back on his ass and pulling out his phone.

Rhyett palmed his face. "Okay. This is fine. Worst case, we close tomorrow, no big deal."

"I'll make it work," I promised. "I'll call all our best girls."

"Aren't there only three?" Jameson pointed out, his phone already pressed to his ear.

"Plenty. Like I said, I'll make it work." I stepped out into the crisp afternoon air as Rhyett hollered after me.

"Be safe!!"

JAMESON

"Where in the hell is Red?" I blustered, pacing back and forth in front of the truck. Rhyett and Brex had already headed up the mountain, the forecasted rain blessedly holding off. She was either late—one of my most hated things in a family perpetually behind—or something had happened to her. Much to my dismay, I was praying it was the former. My brain, of course, had already conceived a million horrible ways she could have been hurt or killed. Fallen off the docks. Slipped on a hike. Mauled by a bear. The idea of anything marring that cute little face was enough to make me ralph on my ridiculous leather dress boots.

"She'll be here," Axel said with a little too much endearing confidence for my fucking liking.

"That doesn't answer the question."

"She's looking out for Brin, the Grind, *and* Brex. So she's got her hands full," Maverick added.

"Chill, James. It's only ten past. She'll be here." Broderick reassured me, but the incessant way he kept shifting from one foot to the other, crossing the opposite over an ankle as he leaned against the hood, wasn't entirely convincing. Hands in pockets, hands out of pockets. Arms crossed, uncrossed. Fingers raked through tightly cropped curls. Frantically patting at his hair like he'd fucked it up. He might have hidden it better than me, but he was getting squirrelly, too.

"Rhyett told her she could just close the damn shop. What the hell is she doing?" I demanded. The garage door opened behind us, bringing all four men to attention as if awaiting orders from a General. Mousy brown hair emerged, nicely curled and decorated with purple flowers; the owner of said curls was about as intimidating to most men as a freaking war hero.

"Okay, food will be ready at five, cake and pastries are in place, and music is good to go," Elora said into the Bluetooth earpiece as she listed things out on her fingers, ducking under the door and turning for the keypad. "Leighton and Kaia have the flowers in their car, just out of the fridge and Red is on her way." She was born for this shit. Either running lives or events, she was always corralling something. We'd given her buckets of shit for being bossy when we were kids, but damn if she didn't own every inch now. Regardless of the source, relief washed over me just knowing she'd been in touch with Noel. *Noel*, whose real name had been playing on a loop in my mind ever since she'd shared it.

Expelling a vigorous exhale, my shoulders relaxed. "Great. Everybody get in the truck."

"Shouldn't we ”

I cut off Elora's question with a jerk of my chin. No. We were not all waiting. We were already behind schedule, and I loathed being late. Everyone would be ready. Noel could leap into the car—moving, if she didn't pick up her damn pace—and tag along when she deigned to get here. Axel's snort of amusement caught my attention, his brows winging up skeptically.

"What?" I barked.

"Nothing."

"You scoffed."

"Dude, you're just...really bad at this."

"Weddings? No shit, man. I belong on the water, and we're heading out late for the season so we can do this shindig, and now we gotta do the whole tulle and lace and frosting shit."

"Not weddings, dipshit. No man with his testicles intact could be good at *weddings*. I'm talking about *women*."

"I object on behalf of Max," Broderick quipped, before ducking away from the glare I sent his direction. Maverick and Elora wisely skirted around to the other side of my silver truck, and I followed their lead to the driver's side as Broderick slid into the passenger seat.

"Are you *high?*" I demanded, ignoring Broderick in favor of Axel's comment and closing my door with a bit more strength than necessary. It was a good truck, it didn't deserve my frustrations.

"On life," Mav interjected dumbly, closing his with the proper amount of enthusiasm.

"You've got a thing for Red," Axel declared for the entire fucking world to hear.

"Nope," I said, popping the 'p' for emphasis.

"You're in love with Brexley's best friend," Elora taunted, reverting from traveling public speaker to childhood antics in two seconds flat. I blamed the rest of these idiots. Their stupidity was clearly contagious.

"I barely *know* Brexley's best friend," I countered.

"Not saying you're gonna pull a Rhyett and fall in love," Axel argued. "But you definitely wanna do her."

"Dude, not even with *your* dick." Alright. That was too far, the jab sour on my tongue. I shifted uncomfortably in my seat, not about to give him the satisfaction of admitting how violently my mind was fighting itself. Hell, despite every ounce of logic pointing in the opposite direction, I'd barely stopped thinking about how much I enjoyed her company—yes, even her incessant chatter—or how badly I wanted her wrapped around my cock. Mouth, pussy, hands, it didn't seem to matter. My mind conjured images of them all any time I got some shut-eye. I wanted to taste her. To serve her pleasure until the only word she could remember was my fucking name.

But she was twenty-five. And I was...not.

"*Eww!*" Elora protested, slapping my shoulder as Axel and Mav both laughed. Her face wrinkled up where I could see her in my rearview mirror. "*Jameson Atlas Rhodes*, that is wrong on so many levels."

"Harsh, man," Broderick said, suppressing a smile as he shook his head and buckled in.

"What?" I balked. "She's *eight* years younger than me. That's way outta bounds."

"Oh, please," Axel drawled from the back seat. "Since when are you one for formalities or societal expectations?"

"Technically speaking, women have always married or been married off to older men," Elora countered. I made a mental note to take back all the good things I'd just been thinking about her.

"Plus, Rhyett's got more than a year and a half on you, and he and Brex are legit," Mav pushed. Jesus, these guys were like dogs with one big bone, playing tug of war while they gnawed me to death. Starting the truck, satisfied with the way it rumbled to life, I turned to Broderick, silently pleading for some backup.

"Come on, Professor. Weigh in here. Would it or would it not be philosophically appropriate for a man eight years older than a woman—who is obviously fleeing her old life—to pursue her?"

"Way to give him a level playing field to work with," Axel grumbled.

"Well shit, when you say it that way," Maverick concurred.

"What other way is there to say it?" I barked back. "That's the long and short of it. Tell me I'm wrong." Deep brown eyes focused on me as Broderick thought, nudging his canine with his tongue. He shifted on his seat, resting a hand on the oh-shit handle.

"Well—"

"*Here we go,*" Elora stage-whispered in the back seat like she'd just settled in for a movie with popcorn.

Broderick continued, unhindered. "Generally speaking, when society frowns on an older man with a younger woman, it comes down to a handful of factors. We all jump to life experience, but the root of that issue is summarized with two concepts: power imbalance and developmental differences. With eight extra years under your belt, it is a reasonable expectation that you have more financial stability and social influence, which may or may not create that imbalance. I don't think any of us are worried about a maturity gap as she's already well established and successful on her own, was kind enough to uproot and come help Rhyett out after knowing him for a few months, and you're, well, *you.*" He chuckled as he ducked my halfhearted attempt to smack him. "You've never been one to give a shit about societal stigma, and judging by her free-spirited nature, I doubt that would be an issue for the younger party either. The future is a little concerning, as the life expectancy for men is already so much shorter than that of women. Adding that to her being eight years younger—you're planning for a decent portion of her life to be spent as a widow. Does she move on? Stay loyal? Can you financially prepare aggressively enough to sustain her lifestyle for the years or decades she has to continue after you die?"

Jesus, it was worse than even I thought. Had Rhyett heard this entire schpiel?

"*Boo!*" Elora heckled from the back row. Broderick turned in his seat, propping his left leg on his right so he could turn to face us both.

"I wasn't done."

"By all means, continue," she demanded, clearly fishing for more favorable perspectives.

"He just proved my point," I murmured, wishing she'd just fucking get here already so they could all stop talking about this.

"On the opposite side of thought, we're not looking at twenty or thirty years here, we're looking at eight. That's a second or third-grader, not something world-shattering. Hell, from the outside—not that either of you would give a shit—you look like the same age demographic, and share a generation, so core memories of childhood will at least overlap. If we consider personal freedom, you're both of age, so long as both parties were consenting, you have the right to make choices in pursuit of your personal happiness."

Maverick yawned pointedly. "*Come on, man,* I need a double shot of espresso to get to this damn point."

Unbothered, Broderick continued, rubbing a palm over his jaw. "With that in mind, we're really talking about emotional compatibility and shared values and interests. This train of thought would argue that your intellectual, spiritual, and emotional resonance should hold more weight than something as superficial as age. She seems rather unapologetically herself, and you've never particularly cared about the expectations of others, so you'd be a perfect candidate to intentionally challenge social norms, which encourages society to reevaluate its biases—"

"*Hell,* man," I muttered, leaning forward to set my head on the wheel. Nobody on the planet could run in philosophical circles as well as Broderick. The man had given himself stomach ulcers over his freaking dissertation because he couldn't decide if he wanted to argue for or against doctor-assisted suicide. He'd eventually negotiated his professor into a cold sweat, and they agreed he could present both sides of the argument without bias.

"Can this *never-ending loop of intellectual confusion* conclude at some point? What's the consensus, Captain Morality?" Elora asked, her tone playful. Broderick chuckled.

"In conclusion, under these specific circumstances, I see

absolutely no qualms with Mr. Rhodes pursuing a relationship with Ms. McShane." The three idiots in the back seat all burst into a ruckus of celebratory stupidity while I leveled Broderick with a glower. He chuckled, those warm, dark eyes sparkling with some sort of mischief or intent. "As your *best friend*, the consensus is you're a fucking dumbass if you let a girl get under your skin like she does, and you don't make a move. Age difference be damned. Life is way too short to not chase what sets our soul on fire. I certainly hope you'd tell me the same thing if I was being as bullheaded as you are."

I was vaguely aware there was a disproportionate weight to his words, but my focus had drifted elsewhere. To the redhead walking up in my rearview, wearing a pink dress that fanned out at her subtle hips like an old fifties housewife. A classy black leather jacket wrapped around her shoulders. She had nude little heels on, a navy tie around her waist, and a matching band in her hair. When she knocked on Broderick's window, I noticed delicate coordinating earrings hanging between dark red curls. And then she beamed in greeting, the sun ray of it striking me square in the chest.

Noel McShane was fucking adorable. And, Broderick-approved or not, I could never let myself ruin her.

ELEVEN

NOEL

My best friend got married. My best friend got married, and I did not turn into a blubbering puddle of a woman on the Mistyvale mountaintop meadow Rhyett drug our asses up to. Aside from making a snarky remark about the impracticality of heels on the back of a four-wheeler as Jameson held out a hand to steady my climb onto the damn thing, he'd been uncharacteristically quiet the entire time, save for his toast to Rhyett. When the family all offered stories, one-for-one with my memories of Brexley—did I mention it's actually exhausting to compete with an *entire family* for memories?—Jameson leaned back in his chair at the restaurant, arms crossed and eyes suddenly fascinated with the denim straining over the muscles in his legs. He was unfairly gorgeous in his gunmetal button-up, black tie, and black peacoat. Broderick and Elora had debated a childhood memory with a passionate Axel over dessert, right until the happy couple hugged their goodbyes to head to the hotel in town.

"I'll get her home," Jameson insisted, waving them off. The *her* in question was me, his offer making my throat thicken. "You lovebirds go enjoy yourselves."

Milo, arms wrapped around his oldest son, eyes glistening with pride, said, "God, I'm just so grateful I got to be here for this. I didn't know if I'd live long enough to see you happily walk down the aisle unless your mother arranged it."

Under any other circumstance, with any other family, his sudden vulnerability would have felt like I was intruding on a private moment; but The Rhodes had absorbed me like family. Their patriarch's intimate confession making me rock on my feet as I fought back a disproportionate level of emotion for the amount of time I'd known him, my chest constricting. I leaned into Brex's free shoulder as she blinked back tears, worrying her lower lip.

"Jesus, Dad," Rhyett—who looked like a magazine advertisement in his button-up and suit jacket over dark jeans—said with a laugh. "You act like you're dying."

"Never know these days."

"You're the picture of health," Rhyett argued.

"And freak accidents happen all the time." His wife came up and wrapped her arms around Milo's chest, resting her face on his shoulder. "My point is, I'm glad I got to see you marry the love of your life. You found your Juniper, son."

My face ached as Milo patted his eldest boy on the cheek, and Rhyett's jaw feathered as he nodded. But it was the glimmer in Jameson's eyes that sent tears pouring down.

"Dammit, you guys. I almost made it." I protested pressing my fingers into my eyeballs like I'd physically fight the tears back. A round of laughs punctuated the end of the perfect day. But as I glanced at my watch, anxiety sent my heart racing, because I had to be at work in seven hours and still had to dissolve the pound of cosmetics on my face, and was fairly certain this hairstyle would stay on like a helmet once I pulled the pins out, requiring at least an hour-long soak and condition.

When Broderick, Elora, Axel, and the twins headed out for drinks, Maverick half-heartedly drug himself into his parents' car, grumbling about the great injustice of being the baby in the family. Jameson and I were suddenly standing alone in the parking lot, staring at the taillights of their black SUV.

"So—" I'd just opened my mouth to suggest we get headed out when his warm hands were on my shoulders, sliding his peacoat over my jacket and simultaneously robbing the oxygen from my lungs.

"Got chilly," he said gruffly, jerking his head towards his truck with nothing more in the way of an explanation.

"Um, thank you," I said, my voice attempting to drop an anchor in my throat. He didn't answer, but I was fairly certain his cheek rounded with a smile he certainly wasn't sharing with me. Why the hell did that warm my chest? Jameson wordlessly led me to his truck, opened the passenger door, and stepped back for me to climb in. As I set a kitten heel on the stepside, a broad hand extended to me, his other settling at the low of my back. If my heart had been racing before, it was a freaking full-steam-ahead locomotive when he touched me. I glanced back to find his eyes firmly locked on the ground below me as I accepted the offering, steadying myself as I climbed up into his gorgeous, lifted pickup.

Once my skirt was safely tucked under my legs, he offered a small smile and an equally small nod before carefully closing my door. My mouth went dry, eyes locked firmly on the car parked beside us to avoid looking at his face as he rounded the hood. I blew out a long, steadying breath, beating the flame of arousal to death as quickly as I could. Simple chivalry was not enough to undo my resolve. Especially not for Jameson—*the grouch*—Rhodes. If I sucked down a breath and then held it when he turned on the heat in the cab, would that save me from having to smell him? Because Lord knows pheromones and basic masculine kindness could not be combined without an implosion of my willpower. Because that's all that was. Basic, human—

"You alright?"

I cleared my throat, forcing myself to meet his concerned eyes as he hovered precariously in his door. "Yeah, just tired."

He nodded, as though that was a perfectly adequate explanation as he took his place in the truck. When the engine rumbled to life, it was accompanied by Blake Shelton and Gwen Stefani's "Nobody But You", and I quirked my head.

"Not a country fan?" He asked, hand halfway to the radio dial like he'd change it if it irritated me. Hell, Eric never even bothered to ask.

"No, I am. I just…didn't think you'd be that kind of guy."

"What kind of guy is that?"

"Homegrown hero, hound dog on the front porch, little pregnant, barefoot blonde in the kitchen kinda guy."

He laughed, turning the song up, throwing the truck in reverse, and stretching his arm behind the back of my seat. The bastard had rolled his sleeves up, just below the elbow, freeing his gloriously inked skin. Like Rhyett, the tattoos on Jameson all spoke stories of the sea and mountains—stories of Mistyvale, I realized now. Unlike his brother, his ink came clear down to his wrist. Those gorgeously corded forearms, the scent of him filling the cab, the casual ease in his body as he maneuvered his truck…any one part of Jameson was enough to make the best woman question her sensibilities. Combining them? For crying out loud, I needed to get the hell out of this truck. Riding in the back would be wiser, if I wasn't going to freeze to death between the restaurant and the house. Sex appeal was not enough to outweigh the fact that we drove each other absolutely crazy. *Was it? Of course not. Wait, was it?*

Jesus, Noel.

He cleared his throat. "And if I told you I had been exactly that kind of man?"

"I'd emphasize the past tense and ask for an explanation."

"Hmmph." He scowled out the front window, removing his hand from behind my head to shift, and then having the fudging audacity to put it back. Like he didn't know, or planned to exploit, the effect that had on my body.

"Got more than a grunt in there on that one?"

"Nope."

"You're the one that brought it up."

"Hypothetical."

"Mine wasn't." I tried to picture natural disasters, tried to remember that this man had basically done nothing but insult my taste since I'd arrived on the island. But my very lonely lady parts were feeling things they absolutely shouldn't feel around anything remotely resembling a bad boy or black sheep. That would be a drastic over-correction to the posh and polished dick weasel next-in-line to a family empire I'd just escaped. "Come on, Jameson. Why was it past tense?"

"Things change."

"Things like...?" I fished, but he just deadpanned, as though it was ridiculous to ask, and turned up the music. He had clearly baited me with that, and for what? Irritation poked my traitorous vagina in a sharp reminder of the level of hell-no we should feel around Jameson Rhodes, the whiplash-inducing yoyo of the dirty dozen. If Axel rolled up the windows and cranked the heater with a good country song, would my blood thrum for him, too? Or was I damned to be attracted to the *Grinch's* of the world?

I was still mentally berating my terrible taste in men when Jameson pulled onto our black gravel road, the crunch under our tires oddly satisfying as he eased toward the house, his scowl still firmly in place.

So, I was a little startled when he turned the music down and blurted out, "Her name was Stephanie."

I blinked, turning toward him fast enough it shot a stab of pain up my neck. Wincing, I closed my eyes and rubbed at my spine, then jaw, opening them to see amusement playing on his mouth. Listen, in no world should I drink tequila and champagne and then stare at Jameson's mouth.

"What?"

"The reason for the past tense."

"Was named Stephanie?"

"My pregnant blonde in the kitchen fantasy."

"What happened?" I asked as he pulled into his driveway.

"My entire football team."

"What?" My eyebrows and hairline may or may not have kissed, secondhand humiliation burning my cheeks.

"My high school sweetheart wasn't the only one I wasn't enough for. We were twenty-one. Apparently, one dick doesn't satisfy my kind of woman."

"Ew," I said, wrinkling my nose and earning a dark chuckle that did not help in the between-the-thighs department. Laughter should not be a turn-on. And yet...

"I seem to break them, or something. Anyway. I walked in on her in *our* bed with *my* quarterback behind her and my tight end—*ahh, the irony*—in front." He tongued a molar as he shifted the truck into park. "I was so distracted I got hurt in the next game and never got to play again. Turns out, she'd fucked her way through the roster, some two or three at a time. Out went football. Out went the barefoot blonde."

"Geez, Jameson, I'm so sorry."

"Don't be. Better off on my own."

"That's a pretty jaded way to look at it."

He shrugged. "Two loves in my life, both cheats, the only common denominator was me. Ask my brothers. I'm good at breaking beautiful things. Can't always explain it."

"You have to see why this doesn't make sense. That's not your fault."

"Still. Easy enough just...being me. If somebody needs a good time, they know where to find me. And let's face it, I'm no Paxton. I was born for the sea." Conversation, obviously, abruptly over, he slid out of his truck onto the pavement, beelining around the front and hauling the door open before offering me a hand down. When I swallowed, it was hard—*audible*—but I accepted, this time mesmerized as he held my stare. Finding my feet, Jameson kept his hand on my elbow, but he didn't budge, all kinds of up in my space. The feel of his body against mine, his hand still wrapped around my bicep, the heat of his breath on my face. I could only stumble rigidly through the motions of breathing.

"Smart girls know when to keep their distance."

"Do you think I'm smart?" I asked back, the words breathless. Jeez Louise, how was I supposed to even think with him that close, let alone as those stone eyes tried to light me on fire? One dimple threatened to make an appearance as the corner of his lips twitched. A girl could only be *smart* for so long. Especially as his pupils dilated, gaze darkening as it fell to my mouth. It didn't help that my old pal tequila had very, *very* different plans in mind.

"I hope so." And then he was backing up, sending some asshole cousin of rejection cooling my desire with way too much ruthless enthusiasm. He motioned across his yard to Rhyett's adjoining one. Eyes still locked, I sucked in a breath, skirting past him and towards the house as my heart attempted to tunnel out of my body. I kept my eyes on the grass, where they were safe, until I got to the door and fumbled with my key, hands shaking enough that finding the damn keyhole was comical.

"Cold?"

Jumping like a freaking cat, I whirled on him. "Shit, Jameson, what the hell?"

He blew out a breath, laughter hidden somewhere in the sound. "I've been with you the whole time. Not my fault if you're not observant."

"Sweet baby cheeses."

"You gonna let yourself in?"

"Yes," I snapped. "What are you doing?"

"Making sure you're home safe."

"You're enough to give a girl whiplash, you know that?"

"Hence. Distance."

"Jiminy Cricket." Rolling my eyes, I turned back for the door, hands still shaking with some combination of misplaced adrenaline, mind-boggling confusion, and cold. His broad palm encircled my hand as he steadied me, the hard—and I do mean *hard*—heat of him suddenly flush with my ass, chest to my back, free hand hovering over my waist as he guided the key into the slot. When the front door fell open into Rhyett's meticulous, dimly lit hallway, I could *feel* his freaking smile against my hair before he stepped away, leaving me achingly cold before I had the chance to turn in his arms.

"Goodnight, Noel."

My mouth was too confused and stunned to respond.

. . .

THERE WASN'T a world in the universe where I could climb into bed smelling like Jameson Rhodes and not reach for every girl's little pink best friend in my nightstand. So, after chiseling away the layers of makeup, I hopped into the shower instead, washing three times to ensure the biohazard that was a shell of hairspray had been properly dissolved before conditioning.

One touch. One touch of his hand against mine, his palm on my back as I stepped into his truck, and my senses had scrambled like three eggs in a bowl of seasonings and milk. Palms slick with lemon soap, I ran them over my body, massaging aching calf muscles, running over the curves of my breasts. My breath came faster, and I thought for a moment, head spinning. I repeated the motion, sighing as sudsy palms slid smoothly over my sensitive nipples. Jesus, the man had my body buzzing, and he'd never so much as said he was interested. I repeated the motion again, the jolt of pleasure enough for my lips to fall open.

Steel-blue eyes flashed in my memory; that oh-so-rare, knock-your-knees-out smile burned in my vision. The feel of his body pressed into mine for the half a freaking second he'd been there to steady me. Some tiny part of my mind was yelling that this was a horrible idea, another screaming that he'd basically insulted me for wanting him, but they were both held down and drowned ruthlessly by the image of his face as he caught me naked in *this very window.* My clit throbbed.

Oh, holy shit.

I couldn't remember the last time my blood felt electrified like this. Couldn't remember a time when every piece of me thrummed to life. Distance from the past. *That's why I came here.* And hell, if it wasn't working.

Gliding one hand over my breasts, stretching a pinky to one and thumb to the other, I massaged the sensitive tissue as my other hand slid down and settled between my thighs. Oh, *holy shit.* Alert, pulsing, and needy, I pictured him flush against me, his dick hard where it pressed into my low back, remembering the warmth of his hand around mine. Stupid? Desperate? Self-destructive? Maybe. But I let myself massage my breasts and stimulate my clit and pictured Jameson Rhodes.

As moans climbed up my throat and tremors rocked my legs, I bowed against the tile wall of the shower as near-scalding streams raced across my skin. Faster and harder, I demanded pleasure from my body, some buried piece of me coming back online after months of feeling dead to the world. Because I had been.

I had died in that house.

Had died to me, to what I loved.

To this. This raw, primal need to *feel*.

When Eric fucked me, it felt like I was an inflatable. Disposable. Easy to pull out when he needed something, and stuff to the side the moment it was less convenient. There for his use, a sloppy kiss before he collapsed afterward if I was lucky, and an 'it's faster if you let me watch'. This wasn't the sexy, I-want to-see-you-orgasm kind of dirty talk, either. It was an I-don't-give-a-shit-to-try kind of demoralizing entitlement.

I deserved more.

It was the Noel before him that was awakening now. The one that lived to dance and sing and be free. The one that loved sex—that *really* loved sex—and craved that carnal release for a body I'd learned to love, that stirred now. I'd forgotten. I'd let him make me forget. Make me feel shame where there once was none.

No more. Never again would I feel shame over being a sexual woman. For being *alive*. No more questioning what I deserved, or diminishing my needs because I was asking 'too much'.

The bar for the bare fucking minimum had officially been raised.

My breath came out in a desperate little moan as my orgasm raced forward. And for a beat, I pictured Jameson. *Jameson*, who promised women a good time, if nothing else, and imagined it was his broad palm driving me home—

"Holy shit!" I cried out, a sob tearing up my throat as pleasure nearly buckled my knees. *Steel-blue eyes, that wry, satisfied smile, that big, broad, tattooed body.* Panting, shaking, and somehow satiated and simultaneously starving, I stood under the water, letting it wash away the last of that broken shell I'd inhabited back in Florida.

Little did I know there was no washing away a past like mine.

"HEY, GIRL!" Kara sang when I came in the door to Grizzly Grind the next day. Kara was sweet, young, and epically competent. I trusted the seventeen-year-old to open on Sundays above most of my twenty-somethings. The place was nearly empty—save one customer waiting at the end of the bar, and another waiting at a high-top table

—but disorganized with the lingering touch of the first morning rush. Grinds littered the counter, catch cups lined up beneath the machine, our drip coffee basket still lined, filled, and waiting.

"How are you today?" she chirped.

"Great, thanks!" I was. Despite being entirely confused by the *what-the-fuck* that was alone time with Jameson, that freaking orgasm had done something to me.

Freed me.

I felt like I was walking taller, all on my own. *Suck it, Eric. I don't need no man.*

Brex and Rhyett were on the first flight out to Anchorage this morning, heading back for a home-honeymoon back in their own bed in Florida. I offered Kara a bright smile, and asked, "How are *you*?"

"Tips were epic for opening shift, so I'm a happy little clam."

"Good!"

"How's Brin?" she asked as she snatched the coffee bin to slide it into place.

Purse stashed below the counter, I turned on the sink to wash my hands. "She sent a picture with Giddy!"

"Yay! Oh, I'm so glad they're finally safe. Sheesh, that was a long labor."

Brin had valiantly labored for over forty hours to bring baby boy Gideon into the world, and we'd breathed a collective sigh of relief when her husband, Paul, texted the group chat.

"Well, she has a lifetime to hold it over his head," I pointed out, earning a giggle as she poured water into the machine.

"Make sure to tell her that."

"I'll do just that. Can I help you with anything?"

"Nope," she said, holding up a to-go cup. Kara's dirty blonde hair swept into a cute fishtail braid down her back, the tips gold with a beautiful balayage. Drip coffee now in hand, her hazel eyes glittered as she smiled, her heart-shaped face pinking as she handed the drink over to a very attractive young man in a Coast Guard uniform. "Oh. There was a man that was looking for you."

My stomach flopped like a half-cooked pancake. "Uh, *Jameson*?"

She looked at me like I'd grown two heads. "I would've said that, silly. No, he's not local. Or at least, I don't know him, and seeing as I was born in the same hospital Giddy just was, I know everybody." It's true. She did. It was part of what made her good behind Rhyett's counter. But her words were vaguely muffled under the demanding drum pounding a rhythm in my ears.

There was no way. There was no way, and yet the twist in my gut begged to differ. The world froze over. Hell and heaven could have, too. I didn't actually know, I was too busy attempting to avoid cardiac arrest. My heart seemed to slow, breath coming in frantic, shallow little gulps. I forced down a lungful. Another.

Scrambling for my composure, I asked, "He said he was looking for Lizzy?"

"Nah, it was super sus. He's handsome, I don't know, maybe six feet but he had those fancy shoes with heels on 'em. But he just slid your photo over the counter and asked if I knew you."

"And you told him...?"

"Hadn't seen 'ya."

A trickle of relief danced through me as I pulled out my phone. "Good. Okay, thanks." I hit speed dial number five, watching Brexley's grin pop up as it connected. To Kara, I asked, "Do you know where he went?"

"No, he left about half an hour ago." She gently pushed the to-go cup into the drink carrier and slid all four across the counter to the burly guy in a rain slicker who smiled as he slid off his stool and gratefully took it before heading for the door, leaving us alone in the tiny space.

"Did he happen to say his name?" It was irrelevant. I knew exactly who came poking around in slick shoes. Brexley's phone went straight to voicemail, and I tapped Rhyett's face next.

"Introduced himself as Mr. Connely."

I was going to puke all over the shop's currently spotless floor. I was going to puke all over *my* cute new rain boots, the lone silver lining being that the damn things were waterproof. Rhyett's voicemail picked up, and I swore as my breath came faster. Who did I call next? Jameson, Axel, and Maverick were all heading for the water with Milo. It was mid-day back home, so Vallie was likely in court. Josie would be writing, or editing, or on calls or with the kids.

Kara's tentative voice cracked my stream of consciousness. "You okay, sweets? You're kinda pale."

"Uhh, no," I blurted, mind-numbing terror ripping the truth from my mouth. "Not really."

"I didn't tell him anything," she reassured me, stepping up beside me so she could set a hand on my elbow. "You in trouble or something?"

I hit Jameson's empty contact icon, a simple JR popping up like a freaking bat signal. "Something," I muttered back as the world started spinning around me. "Please pick up. Please, *please* pick up." When he didn't, I immediately clicked 'call' again. *Please don't be on the boat. Please. God, if you love me, Jameson and Axel Rhodes will not be on the boat yet.* Slowly, afraid I'd lose my balance, I turned to face the windows. But it had been a mistake. Because my shitty cocksucker of an ex-boyfriend, Eric Connely, wearing some name-brand jacket over designer slacks, stood outside on the sidewalk with his arms crossed and eyes locked on me. His chocolate hair was gelled meticulously into place, as it always was when he needed to make an impression. Skin glowing with a fresh facial. Shoes newly shined.

My skin crawled, stomach rioting at him even being within twenty yards of me. Freeing one arm from where he crossed them over his chest, he gave me a two-finger summons. Something like shame heated my face as I realized he fully expected I'd respond. *What the hell?* So much for a fucking restraining order.

"Kara, call Charlie." There. *Words.* Words were good. Jameson had introduced me to their cousin Charlie at Rhyett and Brex's wedding. Until then, I'd known him as the town Sheriff, as he and his partner dropped in for coffee a few days a week, always in uniform. In a town this small, with a family that big, it seemed relatives were *everywhere.*

I'd never been more grateful for that fact than I was as I debated frantically between dashing forward and locking the door, or ducking out the back, in hopes he'd leave the building alone. But I couldn't leave Kara unattended. I didn't want to believe he'd become that unhinged, that he'd pull a stunt in public. But there weren't any customers in the shop, which made both of us fair game. I eyed the blacked-out SUV up the street, parked behind all the other cars, obviously unbothered by blocking them in, like he didn't expect to be here for long, then lunged for the lock.

Eric beat me to it, yanking the door open before I could bolt it closed, and grabbing my arm. I jerked away from him, scowling as I fought to control my breathing, and glanced around for anyone. Of all the times for the street to be deserted.

"Noel, *honey,* we've all been so worried about you."

Sure you have, you fucking psychopath. "You *can't be here,*" I ground out.

Nonplussed, he sweetly asked, "Where have you been?"

"Took a vacation."

He crowded into my space and I staggered backward into the

shop, heart pounding, some phantom bruise on my face throbbing. Silky, saccharine words of concern spilled through his lips. "Where's your phone, babe?"

"Broke." *When I ran it over with my car.* He'd been using the damn thing to track me, showing up without notice whenever I wasn't home when he wanted.

"Hello again," he said to Kara before his eyes scraped over me, sending a chill down my spine. "I see she found you, after all. Knew I'd track her down if I just scoped out the coffee shops. My girl here loves her local watering holes." Full lips slanted in a trained, endearing smirk. Fuck, he was convincing. For a blink, I could remember. I could remember what it felt like when his smile showered over me, the way his touch had sent my pulse racing, the way his laugh had filled my chest, and what kind of dim sum we ate Saturday nights.

...The moment that wall came down between us—the second he snapped, his need for control overruling all of that.

I watched as Kara blinked in confusion, his overly friendly delivery conflicting with what I could see her instincts were telling her. *Run, Kara. Please. Run and tell someone. Anyone. But get yourself out of here.*

"Babe, I'm so sorry things got tough back home, but you can't just *vanish.* Everyone has been scared for you."

"Bullshit," I said, hating that it came out quieter than it should have. *What the hell? Was his voice always so smarmy?* How had I fallen for this guy in the first place?

"Excuse me?"

When his anger flickered behind those navy eyes, my throat constricted. I had to get out of this.

"We need to talk, sweetheart. I have so much I need to tell you. It will all make sense, I promise. I'll bring her back when we're done," he casually added to Kara before pulling me onto the sidewalk.

TWELVE

JAMESON

"Jesus fucking Christ, answer your phone." Something was wrong. Like, pit in my stomach, pine branch to the face, knife to my balls kind of wrong. Noel had called me twice in a sixty-second period, but when I'd answered, there'd been muffled voices for a second before the line went dead.

"Probably just a butt dial, dude," Maverick insisted for the tenth time.

"Bullshit," I growled, patting my fishing blades where they were strapped to my body. Axel had been oddly quiet as I called her on repeat. His blond hair was tied into a low bun, but his signature smile was nowhere to be found.

"Ax?" I demanded.

"I don't know, man, it might just be that you're freaking the hell out, but I'm kinda anxious."

"Fucking *fuck*," I groaned. That was all I needed. Just one confirmation: this wasn't in my head. Something was wrong. I leapt over the rail onto the dock and bolted as quickly as I could in boots and all my gear. Clunky fucking things. I needed a new goddamned profession. Some rational part of my brain was reminding me I didn't really know this girl. That she'd fallen into my lap because my big brother had a big mouth. But my instincts were dominant motherfuckers, and they were out for blood.

The thud-thud of my brothers following me made me thank every deity man had ever known that my parents screwed like bunnies, because if something happened to one of our girls, we sure as shit would bring hell with us.

Noel was one of our girls.

Brexley's. *Mine.* Whether or not she even knew it. I wanted the little kaleidoscope that brought color to the dreariest island known to man. Maybe that was fucked up. Maybe it would put us in one of Broderick's never-ending moral circles. Maybe it was booking me a one-way ticket to hell for being sick in the head, for wanting what I shouldn't. Broderick's words had looped in my mind all day yesterday, through the wedding and car ride home. *You're a fucking dumbass if you let a girl get under your skin like she does, and you don't make a move. Age difference be damned. Life is way too short to not chase what sets our souls on fire.*

Maybe I didn't know what it felt like for anything—or anyone—to set my soul on fire. Okay, yes, I would've kissed her last night if she'd just been sober. And that left me with the sinking feeling that I'd regret it indefinitely if I didn't say something. I'd almost gone for it, almost spun her around in my arms and kissed her breathless last night on Rhyett's damn porch. But if I let myself kiss her, I'd need to touch her. And if I allowed myself to touch Noel McShane, there would be absolutely no stopping. Not unless she told me no. And I would take and ravish until she was screaming my name into her pillow. But then sense had returned, reminding me of all the risks: of alienating my new sister by screwing things up with her best friend, of inevitably adding more weight to the baggage she was carrying when we went our separate ways. I didn't want to hurt her or make her question herself in this new life she was building.

I'd never cared what society would think. I cared what I would think. I cared about what *she* would think.

But as the idea of something happening to her crossed my mind, I realized I no longer cared about risk. I cared about *her*. The embodied Skittles bag, with her color explosion, her quick tongue, and her apparent inability to arrive in a timely manner.

My phone had barely buzzed in my palm when I flipped the answer button and pulled it to my ear. "*Noel?*"

"Mr. Rhodes?"

I blinked, disoriented with who was on the other end. "Yes, who is this?"

"Kara at The Grizzly Grind, Rhyett told me to call you after I call Charlie in an emergency."

Jesus. Kara Bronson. She was Rhyett's kid barista, the one Noel and Brin both liked so much. "Yeah?"

"Well, I don't know if it's an emergency or not, but I think you'd like to know what just went down, and Rhyett is in airplane mode."

"Cut to it, Kara. What's going on?"

"A man just came into the shop and wanted time with Elizabeth."

"Yeah?" I ground between my teeth, fear and impatience both bidding for space in my brain.

"She didn't seem like she wanted to go, and he kinda snatched her, anyway. He seemed nice at first, but he was super aggressive about getting to talk, and I don't know, I might be crazy, but she seemed scared, which isn't like her."

"No, it's not. How long ago was that?"

"Just now."

"Give me a physical description."

"Um, dark hair, not super tall."

I palmed my face as frustration lit my blood on fire. Anger threatened to wind into my tone, but I kept it at bay in an attempt to not alarm the teenage girl who had the brass to call me. "Kara, I'm gonna need specifics."

"Maybe six feet at most, but I think less. He's tan, handsome, dark blue eyes. Real well dressed—like those fancy catalog models my mom—"

"You called Charlie?" I cut in, not needing to know what kind of magazines Carlene Bronson had in her house. Our cousin Charlie was the local sheriff, and while I'd thought he was a sellout for years, I'd never been more grateful.

As I crested the end of the dock, my adrenaline jolted to life. Because Noel was being led up the sidewalk by said city dude with his hand around her wrist, her head on a freaking swivel like she was looking for help. Or an escape route. Either way, the compulsion to smash his face into the nearest brick wall slammed through me.

"Thanks, Kara. I'll be there before Charlie."

Making a beeline for them, I heard Axel fall in step behind me with an, "Awe, hell."

Noel jerked her hand away, putting space between her and the man I'd like to paint the building with.

"Play it cool, James," Axel barked. "At least make him swing first." I cracked my neck, red creeping into my vision as the man stepped after her. Noel stumbled into a table, circling it as quickly as she could, putting it between them before she gripped the edges. She was fucking terrified, and I was supposed to *play it cool*? I should feed this douche his testicles with a silver freaking spoon just for making her feel uncomfortable and refusing to be man enough to take the hint. Suddenly her nerves made sense—the fear in her eyes when her phone rang, the vague descriptions about a shitty ex and a fresh start. Noel *was* running. Running from *him*.

That didn't negate the fact that Axel was right. The Rhodes name meant something in this town, and I couldn't just waylay this motherfucker before I knew he'd earned it beyond pissing me off. Charlie could only do so much if I got looped in on an assault charge.

Altering course by a few degrees, we could come up directly behind him. The boys fell into line without a word.

God, I loved my brothers.

Noel glanced past him, gaze locking on me. Those beautiful brown eyes were round, her face even more pale than usual.

Lifting my voice when we were about fifteen yards out, I barked, "Hey! Is there a problem?"

The man didn't flinch or startle, which was concerning in and of itself. But he turned over his shoulder like he couldn't be bothered, and I bit back every curse anyone on land or sea had ever uttered. We closed the distance in a rush.

"Nope, just sitting down to chat." He canted his head when those navy eyes fell on me. "Do I know you?"

"God, no."

Affronted, one brow hiking, he calmly drawled, "*God, no?*"

"Well, if you did, you'd certainly never be caught dead with my girl cornered against a wall looking like she's about to cry." The bastard reeked of snake oil, and I vaguely remembered Rhyett using those words before. Awe, hell, this was the 'dick weasel' from the hospital after Noel's accident. His eyes widened at my claim, and I pointedly stepped around him, relieved when Noel moved for me, too. She tucked right under my arm, and despite the mind-numbingly alarming circumstances, I couldn't help but notice how perfectly her little frame fit mine. I gave her a reassuring squeeze. *Safe.* "You okay, baby?"

She nodded timidly.

"*Your* girl?"

Oh, it took effort to keep that honeyed, professional tone that set my bullshit detectors screaming bloody murder. He skipped right past the part where she was blatantly distressed. I kinda reveled in the shock in his eyes. Under that composure, I could see it. Every man has a breaking point, a fissure that ignites us and pushes us past rational thinking. I'd just stepped on his, and as he sucked down a breath, I wondered how hard I needed to press to get him to break. One swing. That's all I needed to level him and let Charlie file paperwork for a week.

"Yeah, *my* girl. Ain't that right, boys?"

Axel, looking a bit unhinged, all too pleased with the tension and ready to swing if I said go, nodded, stepping wide to cross his arms as Mav did the same, the three of us blocking his view of the town and the harbor. *Mav.* Goddammit, we liked to think of him as a full-grown man, but he was just a kid. If shit went sideways, I needed him to get her out of here so Axel and I could handle things until Charlie showed up.

"Yeah, buddy. Red came into town, and the two of you were destiny." Okay, so the smug satisfaction of Axel's I-told-you-so was a little irritating, but it fit the fucking script, so I'd let it slide. For now.

Dude didn't like the moniker, either. Sticking to that suave persona I didn't buy for a minute, he slapped on a smile. "Well, congratulations, then. Noel and I go *way back*." He tried to glare at her, tucked against my side with a hand on my chest, and I pulled her tighter against me, positioning my body between them. "Old friends. I thought she was my *fiancé*, but clearly I missed a memo. I'm Eric, by the way. Eric Connely."

Eric extended a hand I would absolutely not be taking. I smirked, quirking my head at the arm he kept expectantly poised between us, and then sizing him up nice and slowly, so no one with functioning vision could miss the point. Schooling my features into a who-invited-the-dumb-fuck expression, I glanced to Axel and then Noel, only to find she had closed her eyes against my chest and her hand was shaking where she'd balled it against me.

Absolutely. Fucking. Not.

Suddenly, all her vague answers were making bucket loads of sense I'd rather not think too hard about, simply because murder was illegal, even if they deserved it.

"Yes. Well. That's nice for you," I finally said dryly. "We've got plans today, so I hope you find your way back to the airport, *Eric*."

Finally, finding his balls and taking the damn hint, he awkwardly lowered his hand and straightened his already straight jacket. "You going fishing?"

"Just got back," I lied, improvising, and thanking every single poker match because neither of my brothers gave so much as a flinch to contradict what just came out of my mouth. Like hell would he get any ideas about her being alone.

"Oh, wow. Well, I hope your trip was...fruitful." His lip curled before he forced a smile back onto his face. "In a town like this, I'd love to know what constitutes as *plans?*" he asked, still masked in some syrupy, backhanded bullshit.

I pressed a kiss to Noel's head, brain raffling through my 'fuck off' cards. Oh man, she was going to knee me in the groin later, but this one should work. "We're actually moving her into my place."

"Jesus," Eric muttered, finally breaking character, grinding his teeth, eyes turning hard. *Do it, asshole. Fucking do it, I dare you. Do something, anything, that can justify me rearranging that pretty face.* "Awfully fast, don't you think, even for one of these little religious communities?"

"Whether it's fast or not is absolutely none of your business." Seeming to stir back to life, Noel lifted her chin, plastering on a tacky smile. I hated it. That wasn't my Skittles. Wasn't the embodied sunshine the town loved. It was fake. Practiced. "Sometimes, you just know when you find the one," she supplied happily, patting my chest for emphasis.

There it was. She spoke up and the vein in his temple visibly pulsated. Red crept up his neck. This was a control contest, and he was losing. *Do it, dipshit. Whatever dumbass, bullshit decision just ran through your pea-sized brain, do it.* He swallowed. Hard. But something in those dark blue eyes said he could see me baiting him, begging for the fight. A subtle smirk pulled at the corner of my mouth, and I let it linger as he spoke.

"Well. I'll see you around."

"Looking forward to it."

NEVER LETTING GO of Noel's hand, I stuck by her side as she locked up Grizzly Grind, shooing Kara home without bothering to close. Seeing as she about broke skin with how tightly she clung onto me, I didn't think she minded. And *I* didn't mind that one bit.

Once she was safely tucked inside my truck, the boys and I filed in. There was a beat of silence, and then chaos broke loose. Noel, Maverick, and Axel all spoke at once, nervous voices ricocheting off the cab walls. I was too busy counting backward, forcing controlled breaths in, and strangling my steering wheel like I might decide to snap it.

"I'm *moving in* with you!?"

"Yo. What the fuck was that? Your name is *Noel*?"

"Uhhh, can somebody tell me what the hell is going on? I'm always down to tussle, but I'd kinda like to know why before I smash some dude's face in."

"James?!" Axel barked, going silent when I held up a solitary finger.

"*Noel*—cute stuff—I think we all need some clarification on what just went down." Slowly, I opened my eyes and turned to face her as she stared back at me.

"*You first,*" she yelped back.

Relief swept through me at the snap in her tone. "*There you are,* sweet Jesus. What happened back there? I was afraid you'd cut out your tongue."

"Har-har," she mocked, fire coming back into her eyes. "Hilarious. I was trying not to piss myself!"

"Yes, I saw that."

Her eyes flew wide as she squeaked, "That I was trying not to *piss myself?!*"

"That you were scared shitless. *That prick* is the ex you didn't want to talk about?!"

"Can everybody take a chill pill?" Mav demanded. "Lower the volume, just a notch. This is a tiny space. Hold up, *why* were you scared of that little shit?" The way our baby brother could look down on anybody in the name of solidarity made the big brother in me proud.

"That's Eric," she squeaked, voice still higher than usual.

"We got that," I said, shifting from one side of my seat to the other.

"That's my ex-boyfriend and the reason I'm in Mistyvale in the first place. Can we please get back to the whole *we're dating* and moving in thing?!"

"I thought you were here to fill in for Brin while she's on leave," Mav said, skipping her questions. I made a mental note to slip him a crisp twenty because I didn't have a fucking clue how to navigate that situation. I'd just...done what felt right, said what came to me without particularly thinking through the consequences of keeping up the farce.

"I'm filling in for Brin because your big brother is a superhero and helped me get out of town with basically no notice."

"Because of the *shit*?" Axel asked, blinking. I shifted again, anxiety making sitting still physically painful.

"Slow down. Axel, Mav, shut up. *Noel*. Start from the top."

So she did. Noel told us her whole story. He was a subtle psycho—I guess El would probably call him a narcissist. The point in the story where he started verbally abusing her and distancing her from her support group was the point at which I slammed my truck into reverse and decided to get us home. Sitting still would cause questionable behavior on my part, and a fuck ton of paperwork for Charlie. I snatched my cell and hammered out a text at the light on the full Rhodes family thread.

JAMESON

Emergency family meeting. The Main House in ten.
Rhyett. Call me if you have wheels on the ground.

GRINDING my teeth at the awareness that this was the 'personal bullshit' he'd kept from me, I decided I very well might deck him when I saw him next. Being a dad didn't get him a free pass for being a class-A jackass. Men like Eric didn't take well to be challenged. They received their reputations being compromised even less. Which meant she'd been sitting here in danger and: A—I'd been an insensitive prick; and B—we didn't know she needed protection, and he didn't think to fucking tell me.

Juniper was waiting on the porch, looking twelve kinds of confused when we pulled up. For all she knew, me and the boys were out on the water already. Seasons were stupidly structured, and missing a set could be catastrophic to a bottom line by the end of the summer. *Me* calling the meeting and being the first one here? Yeah. She knew shit wasn't good. The moment my mother spotted Noel, her visible concern ratcheted up, and as she came down the stairs, she pulled her gray hair back into a bun.

"Sweetheart, what on earth is going on? You're supposed to be out on the water."

"Hey, Mom," I said, still accepting her hug. You never turn down a hug from Juniper Rhodes. Not even mad. They're like gold. And yes, my brothers say the same thing. But the woman embodied love and somehow transferred a bit of it when she wrapped up another human. Fucking magic. Breathing a little deeper with my mom in my arms, I sighed. "Plans changed. Noel—*Lizzy*—is in trouble. We all need to talk."

Her little concern furrow never left her brow. Not as she led us all upstairs, as the girls filed in behind us, not as tea was served, or as Milo came stomping inside pissed as a hornet.

"What the hell is going on?" He demanded as he slammed the front door. "Where the f—" he coughed when he saw Noel, "—*heck* did you three run off to? We were due on the water an hour ago."

I took a deep breath as Mom took him his cup of Earl Grey and turned back to me expectantly.

Elora came to sit beside Noel, setting their knees together in silent solidarity. "Guys, what's going on? You're scaring me."

"Same," Leighton said, tucking black curls behind her ear. They looked nice. She never styled it, and I wondered if it was left over from the wedding. "Are Rhyett and Brex okay?"

"Please tell me they're okay," Alice said, worrying her bottom lip.

"Everybody is fine. But we need a new Rhodes family game plan for Noel," I said, doing my best to be reassuring.

"*Who?*" Kaia questioned.

"Me." Everyone turned to face her as she rose to her feet and sucked down a breath. "I'm so sorry, you guys. I didn't mean to inconvenience anyone, and I never thought this would follow me clear up here, but I haven't been entirely forthcoming about what brought me to Mistyvale."

Thirty minutes later, Juniper and Elora both had arms around Noel's shoulders, hugging her close and whispering reassurances.

"You did the right thing," my mother said, lovingly tightening her grip on Noel.

Elora's wide eyes looked devastated, but I knew her well enough to see the anger beneath them as she repeated, "I'm so sorry."

"What about the restraining order?"

"He either isn't afraid of it or made it vanish along with my case," Noel said, rubbing at her temples. "I'll call my lawyer. Everything just happened so fast."

"Damn," Leighton murmured, shaking her head. "Is this one of those mafia, immortal—that's wrong—illusion?"

"Illuminati?" Kaia supplied helpfully.

"—yes, *Illuminati*, masons, higher upper families?"

"Apparently," Noel said, shaking her head. "They're all in politics or government of some sort."

"Red flag," Kaia said, blowing a breath between her lips. I laughed. The twins had always made me laugh, but the sound caught Noel's attention, a tiny smile immediately on her lips as those gorgeous brown eyes found mine. If I looked at her any longer, I was going to go to her, pull her onto my lap and never fucking let go. So, I walked around the couch, braced my hands on the back of it—anything to keep them occupied—and forced my eyes to my father. That'll sober you up real quick.

Infamous Captain Milo Rhodes sat with his knees wide, elbows braced atop them and his face resting on his hands, brow furrowed, expression stoic. He looked as grim as when the cannery announced unexpected price cuts.

"It would be hard, but I could leave one of the boys here. Mav, would—"

"I'll stay," I blurted. Every single pair of eyes slowly tracked over my direction and for the first time since Mom had found my porn stashed under the mattress as a junior high punk, I had absolutely no idea what in the hell to say. I looked over to Noel—my Skittles—and back to my father's solemn face. "It should be me if one of us stays behind."

Milo sucked on a tooth, eyeing me like a thousand-piece puzzle he was in no mood to solve. But I knew what had to be underlying that expression. This was *my year*. This was my year to take over and—

"That's insane," Noel snapped. If I wasn't kidding myself, she'd lost some of the color she'd gained back over the last hour. "Jameson, you're going to be captain next year. You're crucial out there, I'm sure."

"She's right," Dad harrumphed.

"I can stay. You'll hardly notice," Mav spoke at the same time, both of them chuckling as they looked at each other. Our father clasped a hand on Maverick's shoulder and sucked down a long breath.

"Look, your heart is in the right place, son, but I can't lose you out there. I'm counting on you this year. As for *Noel*," he emphasized her true name, obviously still tripped up on the change. The protective frustration written over his face spoke to the turmoil in his mind. There's nothing the man wouldn't do for the women in our family. He was obviously having the same thought as his eyes flicked to Noel and back to me. "She could stay here with your mother and sisters?"

"Of course!" Mom jumped at the opportunity to feel helpful. I loved her fucking heart. No hesitation. No questions. Ready to give her our home as a fortress. If anyone could scare the piss out of an entitled, limp-dick, no self-image bastard bathing in his ego, it was Juniper Rhodes. Tiny, and *positively terrifying.* "It's not unusual for wives and partners to bond together through the season," she added, obviously wanting her to not feel like an inconvenience. God, I loved my mother.

"Guys, this is *ridiculous.* I'm fine. Besides, what about Rhyett's?" Noel spoke up, chewing on her delicate lower lip, the anxious habit making me want to run a thumb along it. "I'm house-sitting. Of course, I hadn't realized the neighbor he'd told me I'd be looking out for would be Jameson, but I don't mind."

"We can come and stay with her," Elora said, straightening. "A few of us together—"

"Absolutely not," Axel and I snapped at once.

"Oh, piss off, I'm an excellent shot," Elora argued. "Certainly better than Axel—no offense, little brother." She was. Not that any of us would admit it, but my sisters were just as capable of defending themselves as my brothers. In a town where every hiking trail was home to a bear—or twelve—we'd all gotten real comfortable with forty-fives and bear spray.

"I'd rather you never had to find out if you can back up that theory," Axel argued.

"What about Max?"

Axel had just gone to open his mouth, but I perked up. Actually, I didn't mind that idea so much. "Max and Broderick could rotate?"

"Woah," Noel argued. "Look. I don't actually need babysitters. He has to protect that perfect public family image. He's not dumb enough to do anything. I appreciate you all wanting to look out for me, and I see where Rhyett gets that whole blonde *Clark Kent* thing, but I barely know Max, or even Broderick for that matter."

"That doesn't say a lot in your current situation, sweetie," Mom offered softly. "We're all unfamiliar faces. I know that's difficult."

"So was dealing with my family," Noel said with a nervous laugh. The twins both snickered, Kaia dipping down where she lay on the couch, covering her face with her blanket. "But that doesn't mean these men will just hop to and—*unnecessarily*—volunteer to babysit a woman they don't even really know."

"They will," our entire family answered as one, lighting her expression with surprise. Knowing giggles rotated through the girls. As if growing up with six brothers didn't make dating hard enough, adding Max and Broderick to the lineup had made it impossible for them, much to my satisfaction.

"You don't even want to check?"

"No point," I said, offering her a smile as I leaned back, crossing my arms, suddenly feeling much calmer about the entire prospect. "We know their answers."

THIRTEEN

NOEL

"Hold up, Jamie-boy, you're telling me you're out on the water, but we can't use the best room in your house? I call bullshit." Max, whom Jameson teasingly called Maxi-pad, was an impeccably dressed, ambiguously aged man somewhere between eighteen and thirty-five, with beautiful, round brown eyes. I wanted to guess he was somewhere between my age and Jameson's, but his skin was as smooth as a freaking baby's butt. I studied his forehead as he talked, trying to see if he'd had Botox. I'd have to ask him. He spoke with an authoritative, sexy baritone that made me guess he held sway in whatever work he did and dripped with a mouthwatering aftershave that spelled two things: superb taste and an excellent budget.

"Stay out of my shit," Jameson groaned, pinching the bridge of his nose where he laid his head on the back of his couch. After several rounds of debate, Team Rhodes concluded that legitimately moving me into Jameson's was the best way to ensure Eric stayed the hell off my case. Jameson's taste was notably more minimalistic than Rhyett's, and substantially more anally organized. Where Rhy left things cozy and lived in, Jameson had the bare-bones necessities and nearly empty walls. "You're making me regret this decision."

"Boo-freaking-hoo, you've gotta do what you've gotta do, and as long as I've got Wi-Fi and a coffee machine, I can work wherever. Plus, Noelly-benelli here looks like an excellent wing woman."

Giggling, I watched his frustration grow as he flipped his silky raven hair off his forehead again, blowing out an exasperated breath. "Dammit, Hadlee was right. She's always right. It's obnoxious."

"You're telling me," Jameson grumbled as my eyes ping-ponged between the two of them.

"Told me to get my hair done in Austin. Should have listened. Now I'm stuck in the tasteless tundra with overgrown bangs like a wannabe skater boy from the nineties."

Jameson opened one lazy eye to survey us, a cocky smirk that spelled trouble stretching over his face. "*I'll* cut it for you."

"Over my dead body," Max grumbled, scooping his duffle bag up and vanishing into the master bedroom, just off the living area. I laughed into my knees, where they were tucked against my chest.

"Get out of my room!" Jameson barked, returning to his temple massage. "Tell me when you're ready to pull a Britney, and I've got the setup for you."

"If I get to that point, for the love of god, just yeet me off the Moore's Cliffs," Max hollered back. I laughed and Jameson gave a dark chuckle that did something obnoxiously warm to my insides. There was a crash and clatter from somewhere in Max's vicinity and Jameson swore, rising off the couch with a groan.

"I got it," Elora said as the back door slammed shut, buzzing past him and dumping her backpack at his feet. It seemed that the Rhodes had a precise protocol for which family member handled what task during any kind of crisis, even something small they were blowing so far out of proportion it would get lost in the stratosphere. Jameson gave her an *umph* of approval before his eyes drifted back to me. When she vanished into his room as well, he nodded slowly, bringing a broad hand to rest against his mouth.

"You should have told me."

"What?" I balked. He'd been suspiciously quiet as the rest of his siblings buzzed about, planning and pretending my protests hadn't been vocalized, but I'd felt this conversation brewing between us, tension pumping into the air.

"We would have looked out for you. Would have known the moment his pretentious shoes hit the ground. This town is fucking small, and we've got friends everywhere—he never should have blindsided you like that."

"Look, Jameson, I appreciate what you're offering, but I don't need anyone looking after me."

"I beg to differ."

Rude. "What's that supposed to mean?"

"Like I need to explain myself."

"Clearly, you do." He rolled his eyes, and I glowered back.

"*Everyone* needs good people to watch their back." His words—his soft, pained expression—made my eyes burn. "You're hiding some slimy power player who's got it out for you?"

"Hiding *from* him, yes."

"Hiding him *from us*," he corrected gruffly. "You should have said something."

There were a million whys on my tongue as I tried not to think about how he'd felt so close to me last night. About what I'd done in that shower with him in mind. About how part of me was curious to know what he would actually feel like. And all the reasons I didn't want to bring this part of my life with me. But this was blatantly overboard.

"Honestly, with all due respect, I don't owe you anything."

"Bullshit."

"Excuse me?" My temper flared. Look, they were all showing up like angels, ready to seek revenge on my behalf, but I didn't owe *anybody* anything. At least, not before they all came charging in like a rogue drama queen army. That had been the point in starting over.

"You're Brexley's only fucking family, my brother brought you into our homes, our lives, so you're *my* fucking concern. End. Of. Story."

I blinked, his words hitting my chest in a way I absolutely didn't expect. How did anyone respond to something like that? Regardless of his intentions, there was just one minor problem. This was the first time we'd been the two of us since the confrontation on the sidewalk, and I had to point out the elephant in the room.

"Jameson, this will never work."

"What?"

"This, this *ploy*."

"Ploy?"

"Geez," I muttered, rubbing at my forehead as emotional overwhelm niggled at my mind. "This fake moving-in thing. I'm grateful for the assist out there, but it should have stopped where it started."

"You don't think people will believe we're dating?"

"*Do you?*" I balked. Absolutely not. We'd done nothing but drive each other crazy, aside from Jameson strutting his masculine excellence around like god's gift to women and reducing me into utter drooling stupidity.

"People will believe what I tell them to fucking believe."

The freaking ego on this one. "*Please*, we can't get through an hour without biting each other's heads off."

"Ahh, but at least we'd have a lot of hot makeup sex."

My head spun, images of his hand against my pussy as my muscles gave out in a steaming shower bombarding my senses. Images of his eyes heavy with lust as his body moved over mine. *Holy shit. Nope, nope, nope.* Scandalized by my rogue, horny imagination, heat flushed my face as my useless fingers hovered over my lips. Release with Jameson Rhodes sounded like a painted universe of explosions. Like two packets of hot sauce per taco. Like a pillow that was always cool and a lifetime supply of chocolate.

As my throat bobbed, Jameson smiled slowly, rolling his full bottom lip between his teeth, the expression laced with arrogance, before saying, "See? You'd even believe it. So, make it whatever you want, Skittles. If it'll piss him off more, we can be engaged. Or, maybe we don't pretend to be serious—you've only been here a handful of weeks. Maybe we're just fucking."

I wrinkled my nose. "*Blech.* Could you be any more crude?"

"Yes. Would you like that?"

"*Stop that.*"

"Or what, Skittles? Look, I'm just trying to lighten the mood. Shit's been particularly tense today. Laugh with me, now and then."

"I think you have that backward."

"Whatever helps you sleep at night."

"I still don't think this is a good idea. I'll just stay at Rhyett's. What's the difference?"

"The difference is that limp-dick-twat-waffle knows Rhyett is back in Florida and will think you're alone there, and I'd like to give him a reason for my face to star in his nightmares. Starting with the idea of me standing guard over you."

When I reclaimed the oxygen that came cackling out of my lungs when *limp-dick-twat-waffle* came out of Jameson Rhodes' mouth, I shook my head. "You hate me. Why on earth would you let me—*nay*, force me to—move into your house?"

"Look. You were going to be next door, anyway. If you need anything at Rhyett's, you have keys to both places. At least here, I can know you're safe. See it with my own two eyes. This *ploy*, as you call it, only needs to go on until that sleazeball is off the island. Which will be what? A few days before he knows he lost? Max has always hopped between our houses after long nights hanging out. It's the same with Broderick. They crash in my guest rooms more often than not. Nobody local will bat an eye at them being here."

"But I won't ever be alone," I said, repeating his explanation for the strategy.

"Exactly."

"And what if we have to sell it?"

"Sell what?"

"The house, Jameson. Don't you know it's a seller's market? Jesus, Rhodes, the fake relationship you dangled in front of Eric like a red flag with a bull."

He deadpanned, amusement sparkling in those intense eyes. *"Sometimes you just know?"*

"What?"

He chuckled. "Sometimes you just know when you've found the one. You think *I* waved a red flag? I thought he'd have an aneurysm. It was fucking brilliant. Almost clever enough to get me my hit."

My stomach twisted. Yeah, okay, that was stupid on my part, but God, it felt good to piss him off with three real men standing beside me. "Your...hit?" I asked, scowling at him.

"I just needed him to clock me once to wipe that smug look off his face for good. Fucker would be drinking out of a straw, and that was *before* I knew what he put you through."

"You sound like Alex."

"Another ex?" he questioned dryly.

I laughed, shaking my head. "Little brother. Always hated Eric. He's all bluster about this shit."

Jameson's rough fingers clamped around my chin, turning me to face him on the couch beside me. "I don't bluster."

Bursting out laughing, I tugged out of his grasp, hating the heat he sent dancing, hating the way the old Noel stirred in my chest.

"You think I'm kidding?"

"Men are all talk—"

"Well, I'm not. You're staying with me, Noel McShane, because out of all my brothers, I have always been the scary motherfucker. I didn't start fights, but I certainly ended them. I didn't start trouble, but it sure as shit came to a screeching halt when I entered a room. And it won't take him long in this town to realize exactly who he's dealing with."

Swallowing was suddenly impossible. Whispering to horses, taming a mountain lion, bending the air kind of impossible. I'd never had an actual alpha male. Toxic masculinity had been a slimy companion for the last few years, but this...protective, cautious, chivalrous, secretly teddy-bear-soft energy? That was new.

"You know, I read a lot of books, and this isn't how this works."

"What?" He chuckled before pursing his lips and looking at me like I'd just announced a plan to paint the house pink.

"In all those fake dating rom-coms, there's always a trade-off."

"Trade-off?" The words were disjointed, almost robotic, like he had to force them out one by one.

"What's in it for you?"

"Jesus, Skittles." Eyes slamming closed like it physically pained him, Jameson palmed his face. "What the fuck do you mean *what's in it for me?*"

"These deals always have to benefit both parties."

"Says who?"

"Every book *ever.*"

"You realize you read *fiction*, right?" It was almost comically cute how growly he got when he was annoyed.

"Obviously. Nonfiction is for nerds."

"There are so many comebacks, I physically can't choose."

"Piss off."

"You piss off. This isn't some sappy chick book. This is real life. With a real predator. Taking advantage of a shit fucking system."

"Right. Okay, so that's what *I'm* getting. Tick off the predator and make him think I'm not alone."

"Because you aren't."

I swallowed thickly, the sincerity in his eyes making me grateful that my ass was securely planted on the couch so my knees couldn't fail. Clearing my throat, I asked again, "What do you get out of this?"

"Hopefully, I avoid the aneurysm this conversation is threatening."

"I mean it, Jameson."

"So do I. Jesus, keep nagging and you'll be playing the grieving widow."

"We're *married* now?"

"If a ring pop is good enough for you, I've got an old one in the pantry."

The laugh that had been building bubbled up my throat. Jameson Rhodes was funny under that rain-induced surly attitude. "Come on, what needs do you have that I can fill?"

The panty-melting smirk he promptly wiped off his face could have incinerated me in an instant. *Bam.* Spontaneous combustion, right there on his couch. "I don't think this is that kind of arrangement."

"Eww."

"What did you expect?"

"Class-and-or-family reunion that you need a smoking hot girlfriend to show off at?"

"Like I would ever give a fuck what any of them thought. Next?"

"Uhhh, my skill sets consist of reading, making other people read, and yoga. Do you need help of the back-bend variety?"

One dark brow arched, and the man somehow swaggered, holding still. *Why did that look make my thighs tighten??* It seemed a challenge to swallow his ensuing amusement. "You're fucking serious."

"Surprisingly, yes."

"It can't just be a good deed because I fucking care about your safety."

"Nope. That's not how they work."

"Says who?!" He barked, clearly equal parts entertained and frustrated. But when I went to open my mouth, he grumbled, "Your stupid writers with their stupid stories, yeah, yeah. *Jesus.*" When Jameson's steely eyes found mine again, they slowly narrowed.

"*There it is.* What are you thinking?" When he said nothing, I pushed, "Come on, I can see those wheels turning. What can I give back to you?"

"Shut up for two seconds, woman, and let me think."

I laughed, but his glare halted the air in my throat. Zipping my lips and twisting an imaginary lock, I tossed him the invisible key.

"You're not going to let this go?" He glowered when I shook my head. "This is fucking ridiculous." My wide, expectantly blinking eyes made him groan, hands catching his forehead as it fell. "Fucking women, I swear to god, one of you will be the death of me." I stifled my laugh. Finally, he lifted his eyes to mine, some dawn of realization on his face. "Practice."

"What?" I balked, before remembering I was supposed to be quiet and clamping my hands over my mouth. Messing with Jameson was rapidly becoming one of my favorite pastimes.

"Look. I'm thirty-three-years-old, and Mom and Elora are frequently pointing out I haven't had a relationship since Stephanie. And honestly past breakfast, I don't have a clue what doing the boyfriend thing even looks like, so what if you're...a guinea pig?"

I deadpanned. "Very flattering."

"Well, I was trying to just do the right thing, and you forced me to pick a bargain."

"I didn't expect to be compared to a rodent."

"Come on, help me out."

"*Practice?* Like, teach you how to be a boyfriend." I pressed, curiosity winning out over the fleeting ding to my ego.

"Don't mock," he said, scowling as he shifted his weight.

I laughed, shaking my head. "I'm not. I just...didn't expect that."

"What did you expect?"

"Baked goods and folded socks?"

He laughed, grumbling, "Dammit, I should have thought of that."

"No, no, this is better. This way I get to take Eric down a notch—"

"I'm more excited about the '*making sure you're safe*' part," Jameson interjected.

"And you learn how to court a proper lady, which means I can be bossy."

His smirk betrayed his attempt to look annoyed as he squeezed his temples, and I found myself grinning as he grumbled, "Deeply regretting my life choices."

"We'll start with your general grouchy fuckery."

"*Fuckery?*" He asked, brows skyrocketing as a smirk pulled on his lips.

"You swear a lot. Women don't like that."

"Tough shi—" All it took was a raised brow for him to stop and furrow his face. "Damn. I do swear a lot. Look, I grew up at sea. Fight me."

I laughed. "Oooh, yes, I like this. Okay, Rhodes, you have a deal."

"Thank fu—" he cleared his throat, his general look of confusion bringing me way more pleasure than it should. "*God.* Thank God."

"So, how do we sell it?"

His smirk turned cocky as hell, and fuck me, it was gorgeous. He really was the perfect male specimen. "You afraid to sell the role, McShane?"

"No," I balked, shaking my head.

"Worried a little hand-holding or a kiss in public will dissolve your prim little panties?"

God, yes. "No, you perv. Jesus, Jameson, do you have a sex addiction or something? Seems to be all you can think about."

"What red-blooded man doesn't? What else? You worried if you stay here you'll fall in love with me?"

"In your dreams." *Yesyesyes.* Lord knew my willpower was pathetically lacking when it came to humans of the penis-wielding variety. Especially when everything about them spelled red freaking flag.

"Then this will work. He'll get pissed off and fly home with his tail between his legs. Why the hell do you always have to argue with me?"

Groaning, needing to dissolve the fantasies of that man and that obnoxious mouth on my eager skin running rampant in my mind, I bit back, "Because it's certainly more fun than agreeing with you."

That smirk grew until it teetered dangerously close to the cliff of Rhodes-grin-worthy. "Hmm, touché, Skittles."

"Guys, everything looks good outside!" One of the brothers' voices bellowed down the hallway, effectively ending our play. They all sounded eerily similar. "All the cameras are still working. Checked with your security system, and it's all reporting data." *Ahh, there it was*—Axel's voice crept closer and when he popped into the room, he was peeling orange gloves off his hands with Maverick in his usual place behind him.

"Same with Rhyett's," Maverick added, grinning goofily as he flashed me a wink. "Charlie and Bells' guys know the story."

"Yo!"

Axel turned as Broderick's voice reverberated off the entry hallway. This was like attempting to calm a panic attack in Grand Central Station.

"In the living room," Jameson said back. Broderick loped in a second later, dropping a backpack off one shoulder and duffle bag off the other. What in the hell kind of town built the kind of camaraderie where a man asked for help with some random woman with literally no notice, and two striking men would materialize by the end of the day?

"Where am I?"

"Den," Jameson said simply, but Broderick collapsed into the armchair beside the couch with a whoosh.

"It's been a day."

"Get your ass handed to you by teenagers again?" Jameson said with a smirk.

"They are relentless, I swear to god."

Axel laughed, shaking his head and stuffing the gloves in his back pocket. "I'm gonna throw on a pot of coffee before we get out of here." Because *they* had to leave. My stomach turned uneasily at the idea of the four remaining men I knew in this town being unreachable at sea. The family banked on this season above all the others combined and couldn't afford to lose an entire set—a day already detrimental enough.

"Hell, yes," Broderick said, allowing his head to loll on the couch, then hopping up and following Axel into the kitchen.

"Just a bunch of kids," Mav grumbled out one side of his mouth as he followed them before he started humming a tune. Jameson stared after them for a long while before looking back to me.

"You good?"

"Yeah. This is one big, grand overreaction, truth be told."

His scowl said he had an abundance of arguments dying to escape. "Better to be safe than sorry."

"Yeah," I agreed quietly. "I guess so."

He nodded, not saying anything for a long beat before wordlessly rising and heading towards the kitchen, where he seemed to walk into an invisible wall. A long-suffering sigh leaked from Jameson's lungs with all the enthusiasm of a tire around a nail. He looked over his shoulder and slowly, pointedly, turned around. Haunted blues locked on me.

"Hey, Noel?"

"Yes?"

"I've *never* hated you. That's the problem."

FOURTEEN

JAMESON

There were a million and one reasons I hadn't wanted to go to sea growing up. But a woman had certainly never been one of them. My stomach was in knots, wound up like a noose promising a swift, brutal end. No fanfare. Just an efficient snap. It was disproportionate to the time Noel had been in our life, and my naivety chose now to vanish, making me painfully aware of the attachment I had no right to be feeling. She was right. A soon-to-be politician wouldn't do something openly aggressive in a town with eyes everywhere and a propensity for nosy busybodies. We had no mafia thugs in tinted SUVs for him to hire on the island. The harbor was my territory, and *Team Rhodes* had fully rallied.

Everything logical told me it was fine. That *she* would be fine. But my anxiety had become a feral bear in my chest. Rhyett, the jackass, still wasn't answering his phone. And I was leaving a shit situation on my best friends' plates when it was me who'd volunteered and coerced her into rolling with it. Her insipid negotiations would likely be forgotten when I returned, as I highly doubted that greasy fuck would stick around long enough to test my claim. He didn't spell stupid despite a history showing an abysmal IQ. He'd been subtle when they were together, slowly sinking his claws in deeper and deeper until he crushed her. Which made me worry if he'd come clear up here, he wouldn't be so easy to shake off, and like his original attempt to bring her under his control, his play would be subtle. The smart ones didn't hit head-on—they slipped in from the side when you let your guard down.

Axel and Mav were hovering at the top of the emerald canopy-covered ramp down to the docks, trying to make their snooping slightly less obvious than setting up lawn chairs with binoculars. Noel, now equipped with bear spray and a direct number for Charlie, stood with her arms crossed in front of the Grizzly Grind.

Max and Elora cheerily hopped out of his slick Audi SUV, both of their computer bags hooked over their shoulders as they bypassed us and dipped inside the shop.

"Well," Noel said on a breath. "You certainly went all out with the theatrics, didn't you? I did always appreciate an award-winning performance."

"This is nothing. You should have seen us the first time Elora tried to bring home a jock."

She laughed. "God, I can't fathom putting up with you and Rhyett as big brothers."

"Max is, ironically, even more protective, if you'll believe that."

"He has that subtly-destroy-the-fabric-of-your-life vibe about him."

She wasn't wrong. Max could throw down as well as the rest of us, but he'd never been one for a physical confrontation. Preferring to outmaneuver opponents like a fox, he would make anyone wish they'd gone for the fistfight before he was done with them. Chuckling, I admitted, "You met the matured version."

She giggled. "I'm sure Eric will fuck off in no time, though I appreciate the assist." Something about Noel McShane swearing made me disproportionately happy, which she inevitably noticed, prompting her to demand, "What's happening to your face?"

"What? *Nothing.*"

"I saw your *teeth.*" When I just rolled my eyes, she laughed. "Careful, Jameson, keep grinning like that, you could get stuck that way."

"I like when you swear."

"What?!"

"It's cute."

"*Cute?*" she squeaked.

"You're so tiny—all those colors—it just clashes. *That's* cute."

"If you say so."

"I do." I tucked a dark red curl behind her ear, smiling down at her as her breath hitched. Fuck, I loved that sound. Loved knowing something so simple could steal her air. If nothing else positive developed out of this, at least the excuse to touch her when we were in public was a win. "Alright. You good here?" She nodded, the fair column of her neck working as she swallowed. That maroon jacket made her complexion look edible, like sweet cream and berries, just asking me to taste her. This was going to be impossible, and we hadn't even started.

"So..." Noel hedged.

"So?"

"How do we uh—do this?"

I laughed, mumbling, "Pretend you like me?" Threading our fingers together between us, I ignored my idiot brothers as they both smirked in tandem. I brought her hand up and pressed my lips to her knuckles, ignoring the insufferable need to do more, taste something, anything. The ruse was only necessary if that ex of hers reared his ugly face, and the woman was way too smart to indulge for any other reason. She'd made that perfectly clear. Finally mastering my impulses, I instructed, "Take care of yourself, Noel. We'll be back by Friday."

A light smattering of rain misted through the gray right as she nodded, painted lips pursed. Today's top was a fuchsia pink that matched her lipstick. I would have thought the color would clash with her hair, but to my dismay, it didn't. It was cute as hell. *She* was cute as hell. As Noel looked up at me with her adorable little features, that fair, freckled skin and just-fucked hair, energy crackling between us, my entire being seemed to demand I kiss her goodbye. Not because it would look real in front of whatever snoops had their faces smashed against the window panes facing Main Street, not because there were a dozen boats prepping to launch and the men would see and validate our scheme. It *should* have been for those reasons. But it wasn't. It was because I needed to know if she'd melt against me like I thought she would, because that subtle, sweet smell and hint of lemon had my mouth watering. And for that reason alone, I could never let myself indulge in that particular fantasy.

Gritting my teeth, I dropped her little hand and turned for my brothers without looking back.

The ramp to the docks was aluminum, our footsteps loud as they rumbled down the length of it. I could feel Mav and Axel staring into my back, and snarled, "Shut up, both of you."

Naturally, they both burst out laughing as we made a beeline, paces indicating exactly how much time we'd lost with the douche delay. Mav loped on past me when we hit the docks, shaking his head as he stuffed Bluetooth headphones into his ears. Axel stepped up beside me, obviously fighting the need to say something stupid.

"Should've kissed her."

Yep, there it was. "*You* should've kissed her. Weeks ago. None of us would be in this mess." Nevermind how the thought alone made my fists clench until I stuffed one in my pocket, the other wrapped tight around my jacket.

His scoff was equal parts disbelief and humor. "So, this is *my* fault?"

"Obviously." I waved to Captain Ramos, one of the oldest captains on the island, his sons both busy hoisting their groceries onto their deck like a human conveyor belt. The heavy thud of rubber rain boots on the ramp, now a good thirty yards behind us, barely caught my attention. The docks were always bustling. He waved back, his oldest son, Tony, bracing the box on a knee to do the same.

"You didn't *have* to swoop in there like that," Axel argued.

"What was I supposed to do, just leave her hanging?"

"Because pretending you're dating and moving in together was the most logical solution?"

Another wave for Captain McGrath, who dressed like a cartoon sailor with his red jacket and hat, tobacco pipe between his lips, which hid in a graying bush of facial hair. "Look, man, I didn't think."

"Obviously."

"You had a better idea?"

"Getting her the hell away from him and leaving it to Charlie would have been my first option."

"Knocking Eric's teeth down his throat was mine. You're welcome. This way, we still get to sail out today."

"I mean, I was certainly tempted," he agreed as we passed the *Rose*, whose family had been on the water for four generations, its name in honor of their original matriarch. It was in the slip beside the *Tide Turner*, where Kenny was untying and tossing the rope up to his uncle, Mike. Both men lifted their chins in acknowledgment as we strode by. "But I certainly wouldn't have opened my fat mouth with a lie."

"Fine," I ground out. "It was a dumb idea, but I didn't see you coming up with anything on your feet, so I did what I had to."

"James! *Wait!*" A breathless call caught my attention before Axel could argue, and I whirled, hands flexing as I spotted Noel running in her bumblebee rain boots. My brief flash of panic dissipated when I saw no one in her wake, instead landing on the smile on her face. Had somebody run Eric over? That would be oddly convenient. "Jameson!"

"Hey," I called back, aware that every man on the docks had paused, straightening to watch the adorable chaos pixie as she sprinted toward me. "Baby, what's up?" I'd only taken half a dozen steps back her way when she collided into me like a pint-sized freight train, leaping up and wrapping her arms around my neck. My hands automatically grabbed her legs, dropping the rain jacket I'd been clutching, prompting her to wrap them around my hips as I staggered to catch my balance.

And then she was kissing me with no heed to whether or not my feet were truly steady.

No woman had ever kissed *me* first. It was always my doing. Like I'd ever allow something so ridiculous. But Noel crushed her mouth to mine, her warm scent and flavor better than I'd even imagined. Goddammit, I needed to know what all of her tasted like. Needed to feel her under my hands.

Before I knew it, I was kissing her back as she clung to me koala-style. One palm stayed against her back, stroking up and down before ducking beneath that damn rain slicker, seeking desperate purchase. I wanted to slink beneath her shirt, graze over her skin, and feel those perfectly palm-sized breasts. The other threaded through her thick hair and I groaned at how her body fit mine. Those fuck-me curls were just as sexy against my fingers as they looked. Grappling for dominance, I moved into her, tongue dying to fuck that perfect mouth. To taste and claim. The little moan in her throat was enough to undo my resolve entirely.

Angry thoughts warned me this was a mistake, a terrible fucking idea, but I couldn't seem to give enough shits to listen as I wrapped my fingers tighter into her hair, twisting the short locks at her nape and angling her so I could devour her wholly. Somewhere in the distance, someone called my name, but I couldn't stop. Couldn't let go. Clung back to her with the force of every moment, every bickering match, every time I'd remembered the stolen image of her perfect, naked body. Clung to the fact that Noel was setting the damn pace, matching me move for move. The woman was nothing if not a perpetual surprise.

A ravenous fever spread through my chest as her chilled fingers wove into my hair, the mist the only thing keeping us from combusting right there on the docks. *Goddamn.* Every drop of blood evacuated the northern half of my body, desperate for the promised land. Someone wolf-whistled, but I didn't care.

Knew I *should've*. I wasn't one to give a shit about anybody's opinion, but I had never been big on PDA. Not even with Steph. But *Noel...*

I couldn't stop tasting her. Couldn't touch *enough* of her.

The familiar rumble of the boat's engine forced me to peel away, panting as I locked on those gorgeous, dark browns. For a beat, the same bewildered hunger stared back at me before she blinked, clearly thinking the same thing I was. *What the hell was* that?

Breathless, she smiled up at me as she slipped down my body, her cheery little mask snapping back into place before whispering, "Lesson number one: whilst about to be apart for more than a few hours, always say a proper, public goodbye."

I laughed, squeezing her ass as I smiled down at her, shaking my head. "Noted."

"Jameson!" My dad barked, impatience oozing from just my name.

"Coming!" I called over a shoulder. Her cheek was flushed against mine when I lowered my mouth to her ear. Some deep, primal satisfaction swelled in my chest when goosebumps trailed down her neck. "Will you think of that kiss when you get yourself off while I'm gone?"

She sucked down a scandalized breath, but there was mischief in her eyes, a twitch at the corner of her lips. "I *do not* do that."

Somehow, I highly doubted that. Noel might have gone through some shit, but nothing about the woman spelled 'prude'. She was confident, playful, and knew *exactly* what she'd just done. Chuckling darkly, I promised, "You will tonight."

With an eye roll, she drawled, "You seem awfully self-assured."

"*Jameson*! Let's *roll*!" Milo was officially getting pissed, his barked demand seething. In his defense, that took a decent amount of effort, so I likely deserved it. Didn't give enough shits to turn around, though. Not with Noel's soft, warm body pressed against mine, her hot palms still settled on my chest. Damn, she was little. What the fuck kind of psychopath could even think about hurting something so precious?

"You telling me that was just for show?"

She winked playfully. "Had to sell it."

Shaking my head, I breathed her in, not believing that breathless excuse for a second. At my age, I knew what a fake orgasm felt and sounded like—knew what fake attraction *looked* like. That sure as shit wasn't it. Although, if that had been the mission, she'd certainly accomplished it. Glancing around, I found half the surrounding crews divided between watching the free show and getting back to work. But the town would certainly buzz with our farewell.

I pressed a kiss to her forehead before whispering, "Keep telling yourself whatever helps you sleep at night. But I'll be thinking of that kiss while I fuck my fist this week." I stepped away with a wink, and knelt to grab my discarded jacket, straightening to find her standing there panting, face flushed, those painted lips parted, and round eyes full of promise. Oh, I was in the deepest kind of shit.

"*Jameson!*" Milo bellowed. I laughed, shaking my head at her and spotting Max where he stood as a half-decent sentinel—if I didn't account for the shit-eating grin on his face—in front of the shop across from the harbor. The boat rumbled, water sloshing against the wood as my dad lost the last of his fucks.

"Be safe out there," she said softly. I couldn't decide if her words made me go a little warm and fuzzy or if her concern had *me* concerned that she actually gave a shit. I'd never been one to play it... safe. Risks were part of the territory.

"See you soon, baby." Not wanting to swim, I turned to see the boat drifting out of the slip, my brothers both shirtless, grinning back at me with their hands on their hips. *Son of a bitch.* Taking the dock at a sprint, I leapt over the four feet Milo had managed to put between the end and the deck. I tossed the jacket over the rail as Axel and Mav both grabbed an arm, helping me over and steadying me as they laughed. I straightened, glancing back to where Noel was biting her lip to hide her smile. All three of us raised a hand in farewell, and she did the same.

"Admit it," Axel said, slapping a hand on my back. "You are *so* fucked."

FIFTEEN

NOEL

My entire body was still buzzing when I walked back into an empty Grizzly Grind, a big, doofy smile on my face. I was the goldendoodle of baristas. The *Napoleon Dynamite* of town idiots. Still, I blew out a breath, ignoring the incessant pulse in my lady region as I washed my hands and slipped back behind the counter, where I belonged. I took my time, thoroughly washing every inch of my hands, paying attention to the backs and between my fingers as my brain played and replayed that scene on the docks, if for no other reason than not knowing what I would say to my companions. If Aphrodite, Eros, and Saint Valentine all collaborated to craft a perfect kiss, it wouldn't touch the mind-melting experience that was locking lips with Jameson Rhodes. *Everything* was hot and bothered, my skin dying for more of his touch, mouth livid I'd taken him away.

Un. Fucking. Real.

It would take hours to unwind the horny goodness he'd solidified in my body in a matter of minutes. There weren't enough cold showers in the world to erase the feeling of his hand as it slipped under my jacket, hot against my back, or the way he stole my kiss and made it his own, dominating me right into submission. *Oh god*, the way his flavor settled on my tongue. Perhaps if I flung myself into the ocean, something between the drop and the chill could snap me out of it. I could serve three hundred cups of coffee and not erase the way he'd just marked my body without ever meaning to.

Alas, the universe has comically horrible timing and not a soul wandered in to demand unquantifiable quantities of caffeine, leaving me the lone target of Elora and Max as they both stared at me, brows kissing hairlines, eyes like expectant saucers.

It was Max who cleared his throat first. "Um. Noelie-bear? What in the hell did I just witness out there? You and our Jameson seemed to have quite the..."

"Moment," Elora supplied when he seemed to grapple for the word. Max nodded as she repeated, "*Quite* the moment."

Heat flushed my face as I glanced toward the door, hoping and praying for someone, *anyone*, to walk through and order sixty-two cups of coffee and a hot bagel to-go. Not a soul arrived. "Oh, um, that was just...uh...we were just practicing, you know? Make sure the town believes the rumors as they circulate."

"*Practicing*, huh?" Elora said, stifling her smile. "Well, I must say, it looked a bit too authentic, if you ask me."

"Which, I didn't." The paper to-go menus suddenly desperately needed shuffling, reorganizing, stacking, and ensuring the spines were aligned. Maybe I'd polish the windows next.

Ignoring my rebuttal, Max grinned as he agreed, "Ahh, yes, an Oscar-worthy fake kiss. I must have missed that category at the Academy Awards this year."

"Look, I might have gone a little off-script. It meant nothing. Just...selling it."

"Welp, you certainly sold me," he said, sipping his latte and looking twelve kinds of smug.

Elora chuckled, stirring more honey into her tea. "Looks like our *Noel* is caught up in a web of her own making."

"You two are enjoying this way too much." I rolled my eyes, cleaning the espresso machine and praying Kara would get her ass back from her very late lunch. "Maybe it was a wee lapse in judgment."

"Ahh, yes, the ol' lapse in judgment excuse. Classic. You're fooling no one, my friend," Max insisted, setting his cup down before opening his laptop. That blinding grin he'd worn outside was stretching back up his cheeks.

"I've never seen a real-life fake relationship play out—will they be a rom-com or sitcom?" Elora teased. Huffing, I turned back to retrieve more cake pops from the cabinets.

"Neither," I insisted. "The man can't stand me. As soon as Eric is off the island, this whole charade will be a funny joke you'll all tell at family reunions."

"Ahh, yes. The One Where Noelie Fake-Dry-Humped Uncle Jameson on The Dock."

"Okay, I did not *dry hump* him."

"I'd need a cigarette after a kiss like that," he rebutted, earning a stifled laugh from Elora as she hid her face inside the ceramic mug. Refusing to admit the heat climbing up my neck was inevitably the world's most humiliating shade of lobster red, I narrowed my eyes on Max.

"Also, was that just a *Friends* reference?"

"You know it."

"I knew I liked you."

"Even with our incessant pestering?"

"To be determined."

"Find me a man to climb on like a baby sloth, and I'll drop it."

"Wing-woman duties, activated." I did my best *I Dream of Jeannie* impression, crossing my arms and nodding once, which earned a laugh from both of them. Desperate to get the attention off the kiss that melted my brain out of my ears, I redirected to Elora. Two could play at that game. *Or, was it three?* I had no ammo on Max, so it had to be El. "First duty as active wing-woman: what in the hell is going on between you and Broderick?" To my simultaneous horror and satisfaction, Elora looked floored as she glanced around, as though a patron might have materialized without announcing themselves. Max grinned devilishly, and I locked on him as she shook her head. "Ooooh, give me the scoop."

"Oh man, this shit goes so far back."

"Shut up, Max," she hissed.

"No, no, keep talking, *Max*," I encouraged, fighting a laugh

"It's *nothing*," Elora argued.

"Nothing that anyone with eyeballs can ignore," Max said smugly, waggling his brows and making me cackle as I wiped down the counter, keeping my hands busy. He shoved his laptop away before steepling his fingers atop their table.

"Oh boy, here we go." Elora buried her pretty face in her palms, shaking her head. How was it possible to feel self-satisfied and bad for her at the same time? But hey, if my drama was fair game, so was hers.

"Those two have driven me crazy since we were in junior freaking high. Dancing around, retreating, competing in everything, bickering about *everything*."

"Oooh," I said, setting down the towel, "do tell."

"Keep talking and I tell her *everything* about Luca Moretti," Elora threatened, pointedly shutting her laptop and glowering at him across the table. My gaze flicked to Max, who was scowling back at her.

"You. Wouldn't."

"Find out," she challenged.

"Seventh grade Halloween dance."

I bounced over to Elora, hand freezing mid-towel-stroke and suddenly wishing I had a bag of popcorn instead. She quirked her head, smirking. This had to be good.

"Ninth grade homecoming *assembly*." I resisted the desire to *oooh* at whatever she had threatened back, but I had to watch Max as he leaned in his chair, spreading an arm over the back as his smile broadened.

"Playing dirty," he said, tone both scandalized and impressed. "Junior year prom."

"Excuse me, should I be accepting applications for a new best friend?" Elora blinked at me and I retreated to lean against the back counter, pointing at my chest. "Noel seems like buckets of fun."

"Then no speaking of he-who-shall-not-be-named."

"Fine."

"Fine," Max agreed, crossing his arms and leaning back in his chair. He scowled down at the buzzing vibration of his phone on the table, quick to snatch it up when 'Jorogumo Defense' popped up on his screen. Well, that was intriguing.

Elora smiled smugly, opening her laptop back up. I slowly continued wiping the counter down, both amused and interest utterly piqued.

THE WEEK WAS LONG. Partially because Eric, the manipulative bastard, was weaseling his way in and around town with the locals. Broderick had come home blustering that he was in *Rhyett's* bar, befriending the bartender and a few regulars. The following day, Max came home livid that he was hopping on one of the tour boats with a well-respected captain who was a friend to the Rhodes. But despite his attempt to undermine my little oasis here, I'd been... having fun. Elora and Max were constantly entangled in verbal sparring matches or playing one card game or another. Broderick was an expert at stirring up conversations that somehow wound deeper than anticipated.

Mostly, it was long because…I missed Jameson.

Was it possible to miss someone that drove you crazy? I missed the feel of him on that damn dock. *That's* what I missed. Which wasn't allowed. There was no missing the sensation of that man pressed against my mouth. In an impulsive moment of uncontainable curiosity and farfetched reach, it had been one helluva kiss to make this ploy work—which it had, as the town was already speculating over wedding dates—and infuriate Eric if he caught wind of it. Despite the ridiculous tension in my core, I had not brought myself any kind of relief, mostly just to spite the cocky bastard. Even worse, I couldn't stop imagining him using that kiss while he serviced himself. The visual resulted in a most unwelcome tightening in my belly.

WHEN MY PERIOD showed up *five* days early, I was at the Grizzly Grind. The weekly tsunami drill still scared the dickens out of me— seriously, that keening alarm would only be appropriate in *War of the Worlds*, but they let the thing scream at us every Wednesday afternoon—and I'd slipped to the bathroom as it blared, swearing when I discovered the horrific murder scene in my once adorable underwear, and suddenly thankful I was wearing black jeans. It seemed everything was out of order these days. But the second day brought with it an ungodly kind of cramping, like the hell I'd endured as a teenager, making for the second time in as many days I'd had to leave the shop to the girls unexpectedly. No way to learn like a substitute manager dropping you into the deep end.

Elora's grumpy face greeted me from the couch when I came in the door, a hot pad and bag of gummy worms both set on her belly with *How I Met Your Mother* playing on the television.

"The red tide get you too?" I griped, dropping my purse and kicking off both boots. Suddenly my early start made sense. She'd been up in my space all month and thrown off my cycle, dammit.

"The *what*?"

"Red tide. We get this nasty algae tide in Florida every summer that makes it impossible to breathe, rendering the beaches unusable. Brex and I decided it seemed a fitting name for Aunt Flo."

A subtle smirk crept up her face as she popped a handful of gummies in her mouth, chewing as she asked, *"Aunt Flo?"*

"Also known as shark week. *Don't get in the water.*"

"I'm sad I didn't get more time with Brexley. You two sound hilarious."

"Positively fabulous," I teased, heading straight for the guest room, where I stripped and swapped into pajamas, grabbing a pillow and my own hot pad from where I'd stashed it in the zipped compartment of my suitcase. "Care if I join you?"

She scrunched up her legs to make room at the end of the couch. "Welcome to Misery Island, where we love company."

Smiling until a wall of nausea rocked through me, I flopped down, reaching around to plug the cord in. Max emerged from the owner's suite, looking cautious as he edged around the room like he was attempting to blend into the wall.

"You're a terrible chameleon," I grumbled. He winced, freezing like a cartoon character that got caught snooping where they didn't belong.

"Not you too," he whined, shoulders slumping as he screwed up his face.

"Not me, *what?*"

"Red alert?" he grumbled, abandoning his placement and heading for the kitchen. I giggled and then winced as the cramps seized my thighs. My grandfather once told me that women only felt pain during birth and cycles because of the 'sin in the garden'. Usually, I didn't buy into those belief systems. But I'll tell you what, as agony threatened my ability to breathe, I resolved to pulling that bitch, Eve, out of the grave just so I could send her back myself, should the ability ever present itself.

"Yeah," I finally grumbled when the pain subsided enough to formulate words. Max rifled through something in the kitchen behind us. "You could say that."

"I will be hiding in Jameson's room unless I'm needed until the threat subsides."

"Chicken," Elora mumbled.

He raised a hand in farewell. "Guilty as charged."

We watched another two episodes after he retreated before the garage door opened and a very scruffy Jameson stepped inside, eyeing us from the mudroom. My belly clenched, and for a beat, it had nothing to do with menses. If he was handsome cleaned up in fresh clothes, then roughed up he was *impossibly hotter*. What was it about a rugged man with grime on his hands that made my ovaries sob? How I ever thought white collar was attractive was beyond me, because Jameson was all man, and in other circumstances, I'd be tempted to jump his bones.

"Hi," I whispered stupidly. There was absolutely no need to be mouse-like, for pity's sake. This whole dumb fake dating thing was his idea. I'd just...cranked the stove up to culinary inferno mode and justified my curiosity with the ruse. You know. Nothing to melt into the couch over. But as those steely eyes landed on me and I fought the need to incinerate at the memory of those gritty hands on my ass, the thought occurred that perhaps I could truly vanish if I went somewhere like...Siberia? Surely, Eric wouldn't follow me there, and then I could be dead to the world and—

"Hey," he said gruffly, clearing his throat and cutting off my spiral with one word.

"You're a day early," I noted, wishing it wasn't so obvious I was happy about it. Heart rate faster. Face aching with the smile that refused to be denied.

"Welcome home," Elora said, a bit sardonically. Her brother eyed the television and sighed when he spotted that telltale bar booth.

"Oh man, already!?" Jameson dropped his duffle bag at the hallway arch. "Christ, El, it usually takes a month for your witchy stuff to bring somebody down with you."

She flipped him the middle finger, and I grinned as he shucked his jacket off and hung it, neatly setting his boots on the rack before snatching the bag and disappearing into his room. I made a note to ask her what the hell his remark meant later. Did Elora regularly dictate the schedule of other women's cycles?

Jameson marched right past us a few minutes later and it took every muscle in my body to not sit bolt upright to gape at his freshly showered, shirtless form as he went into the kitchen.

Oh. My. God. Oh my god, *ohmygod!* I'd seen the photo of him playing football with his brothers, flannel hanging open to tease up his center, but the full thing was...wow. Just. *Wow.* A freaking spectacle to behold. The ninth wonder of the world. *Eighth?* Hell if I knew, it wasn't relevant anyway, and the point was Jameson Rhodes was downright *spectacular.* I'd wager he spent time at the gym beyond his life on the boat, and those glorious muscles had some of the most beautiful lines of ink I'd ever seen committed to a living being.

It was obvious what those years on the water had funded. The nautical-themed sleeve alone must have cost him more than my first car. Which was a shitty example because, let's be real, the thing should've been condemned. But those tattoos were exemplary. The old school ship sat on bucking waves that extended across his chest, giving way to a map and compass. An anchor tucked below his arm across his ribs. Don't even get me started on that perfect trail of hair just begging my fingers to stroke the pattern where it dipped below his...goddamn him, *gray sweats.* Cue the internal wolf-whistle.

"Close your mouth, you'll slobber on my feet," Elora quipped, grinning when I gave her a finger right back. A few minutes and several loud thuds, clinks, and creaks later, Jameson returned and tossed two bars of chocolate down on our respective stomachs before maneuvering two cups of tea out of the opposite hand, setting them on the gorgeous, rugged wood coffee table, atop custom burnt wood coasters with anchors branded on their center.

"What's that?" I asked, arching a brow.

He smirked. "You're welcome."

"Not quite what I said."

"Raspberry leaf tea for your cranky ass baby box."

That was the line that sent me laughing until I wheezed. His responding smile was heart-meltingly delicious as Jameson waved his hands, shooing us apart so we'd make room for him on the center cushion. Elora promptly set her legs over his, but he nudged them forward and lifted mine onto his lap. For a heartbeat, my nerves reminded me they were precariously close to his goods, but I forgot all about that, moaning as he started rubbing the sole of my foot. How was it possible to not know how freaking sore those things were until a too-sexy man was touching them? When I studied him, curiosity niggling in the back of my mind, he rolled his eyes.

"*Six* sisters and a mother who is only now going through menopause, and you think I'm not prepared for this shit?"

Something in my chest softened, even at his teasing tone. "You know, you're better at this than you think, Rhodes."

JAMESON

"SUN'S OUT! WAKE UP, BITCHES!"

"Go to hell, Max," I growled, jamming my eyelids tighter and wishing I could vanish. Or *he* could. Shit, it was my house, so him. Definitely *him.*

"Get up, Grouchy McGee. Come on, Noelie bean!" It was at that point that my body froze, as someone else stirred against me. *Oh, for the love of god.* The light soaring through open windows was blinding as I came to, intensely aware of the soft, warm, tiny female body pressed so perfectly against my side, tucked under my arm. *Goddammit.* We'd fallen asleep watching the same show Elora had played on a loop since the year she'd started her cycle in the first place.

I didn't *sleep* with women. I certainly wasn't *Barney Stinson*, but he had a few very valid points. Hell, it hadn't happened more than a handful of times, none of which had ended well, and all of whom I had never seen again after breakfast.

There would be no shooing her out of my house, no polite chit-chat punctuated by the delicious freedom of my front door clicking shut. No, Noel hummed contentedly, nuzzling into me and if I wasn't so busy trying to think of how to get out of this mess, I would have really fucking liked it. She...fit. That sounded stupid, even to me, but it was true. Her body fit against mine. I didn't remember laying down, and certainly didn't remember tucking her against me or cradling her head in my now numb-as-shit arm. But there she was. Her chaotic curls tickling my face. Breath hot on my chest above what I could only assume was a drool spot. It should have repulsed me, but oddly enough made me want to smile. She'd slept well, then. That was oddly satisfying. Did she feel safe with me?

Jesus, what the hell did I give a single flying fuck for. *Nope. Nope, nope, nope.*

Thank fuck, she seemed to have the same thought process dawning because Noel grumbled something unintelligible, followed by a distinct, "Oh my god!"

The little chaos pixie flailed off the couch, and I scrambled for her a beat too late. She fell on her ass and I swore as I followed her, toppling her over when I'd meant to stop her. Lucky to catch my body weight, I hovered above her for a beat, acutely aware of the morning wood now pressed against her tight belly.

"Jesus," I blustered, scrambling upright as giggles flew from her mouth. "*Why* are you *laughing?*" I demanded, but she started cackling, clutching at her belly. "Christ, are you okay?"

"Cannot believe...you just fell off the couch with me."

"Oh, for fucks sake," I said, rolling my eyes as I got to my feet.

Max arrived with mugs of coffee in hand—black, just like I liked it, because at least one person could pay attention in this house. For that alone, I'd ignore the smug-as-shit expression on his face.

"You could help me up, you know?" she said as she struggled to her feet.

"*Could*," I agreed, smirking as I sipped on my coffee. We were not a thing. We were not *becoming* a thing. That damn kiss on the docks meant nothing, and I'd shown her basic human decency last night. That's all. Because having an organ forcibly shove cups of fluid out of your body while causing a torso-wide Charlie horse sounded like hell, and girls got extra sensitive about shit like feeling unwanted, and I hated that. That. Was. All. Basic consideration.

But as she huffed, blowing tousled locks off her face, I caught that scent. *Her* scent. The one she'd left on my skin and leached into my clothes to torture me for the entire week. And suddenly I was back on the damn dock with her legs locked around my hips and those perfect pixie lips bending to my will. Acutely aware of the perpetual case of blue balls she'd so gloriously bestowed in that goodbye, I shook my head, turning for the kitchen.

"Jackass," she grumbled, accepting Max's cup of coffee.

She'd kissed me. *She* had kissed *me*. Unacceptable. Incredible. Edible. Absurdly inappropriate, given her age. And I fucking needed more. *Goddammit.*

"Get dressed, we're taking the jackass to hike."

"Max, I love you—" Well that was news to me, and he might've been into guys since we hit puberty, but that didn't stop the territorial twist in my stomach. Bullshit, of course, she wasn't actually fucking mine. "—but like hell am I *climbing* up a *mountain* like this." Noel gestured vaguely to the body I was ardently attempting *not* to look at.

Elora came gliding into the space, already in some athletic getup that showed more skin than I was strictly comfortable with. Sisters belonged in turtlenecks unless they'd found a man blessed by her brothers *and* her father. End of the fucking story. Not this strappy crop top shit. Men are sleazy as hell, and Elora, of all people, deserved a king who worshiped her, not some dog panting after her body.

"He's right, babe. You can't miss a day like this here. You'll thank us once you're out there."

"Not sure if you've been to Florida, but it's flat as hell," Noel pointed out before taking another long sip that apparently earned a sex-like moan that did unwelcome things to my circulatory system. "I'll slow you all down."

"We will not abandon you, my little cabbage." Max glanced my way and wrinkled his nose. "Well. Grouchy McGee might, but El and I will move slow with you. Just soak up some vitamin D. Get some fresh—not rainy—air."

"Fine," she said with a sigh and another wistful sip from her mug. "Damn, Maxipad, you make a good cuppa coffee."

Noelie-bean...Maxipad...little cabbage? What the hell had I come home to? How the fuck long were we on the boat? It was *my* bag of coffee she was praising. He'd just poured it in the filter and added water, not spent an hour deciding between samples at a roaster in Seattle before getting on a standing order so my chronically rotating guest list always had the best. *But whatever.* Annoyed—and bitter at myself for *being* annoyed—I moved for the kitchen to top off my depleted cup as Elora kept up her chipper chattering.

"If you don't have anything to wear, I've got extra and you're right about my size. Come on," she said, making grabby hands at my fake girlfriend. "Let's go before the clouds come back."

"LOOK! El, it's like a little fairy garden."

I'm not exaggerating when I tell you the best damn part of our hellish, eternally damp island was the way the sun lit up the forest. You know, when it dared to make an appearance. Everything was green here. Even the tree trunks were half consumed by emerald moss. Blankets of it hung from branches and coated the dirt. Noel had been exuberantly exploring her new surroundings like a six-year-old we surprised with a trip to Disney World. She gave off mad golden retriever energy, and I'd bitten back a smile more than once.

"Fiddlehead ferns!" Elora chirped back, skipping up beside her and grinning. El loved Mistyvale the most out of all of us kids. We might have all grown up here, but from the time she could talk, she romanticized everything. And I mean *everything*. We weren't going grocery shopping, we were *embarking on an adventure*. We didn't walk, we *explored*. That one time she fell in a puddle, she actually just learned what mud felt like beneath her clothes and decided it wasn't for her. But kudos to that kid in class who liked to bathe in it. More power to you, man.

I'd always assumed she was an oddity—one of her kind—but as

she knelt beside a beaming Noel to study the way the fiddleheads curled in on themselves in a tight little spiral, I realized Brin and I had been correct in assuming there were actually two of them. Go fucking figure.

"They're so cute. When they unfurl, they look like tiny little dancers." Elora gave an apt imitation of the way the leaves uncurled. "Faeries really would love them. I wonder if they have these in Ireland."

"You can eat 'em," I added as Elora yammered on about her deep adoration of the little greens.

"What?!" Noel gasped, turning to face me with comically wide eyes. My shrug was evidently unsatisfactory as that adorable face was turning scowl-like. Max, ever the hero, had to pipe in, for once in my favor.

"Nah, he's right, Noelie. As kids we'd all harvest them and cook them right up. Honestly, this place is a forager's paradise."

"Hunting and fishing are both abundant too." Judging by the wrinkle in her little freckled nose, she didn't much care for my addition. "I didn't say *you* had to do it."

"Good, thank you. Once it's dead and dismembered, it's easier to stomach eating something that was perfectly content, minding its business."

"Jesus," I said, fighting back my smile as I shook my head. Max's knowing attention chapped my hide, his smirk growing as he bypassed me, a hand on a mossy trunk for balance, and I pretended not to notice him. "Brutal."

"Am I wrong?" she said with a reserved giggle.

"S'pose not."

"Suppose," she scoffed, accepting my outstretched hand as she stepped over a log. "What do you *suppose*? I said it how it is."

"Yeah, you're right." Just hadn't heard anyone say it that way, that was all. Now I was losing the fight with my face, trying not to grant her a smile. Refusing to release control of my own faculties, I picked up the pace, continuing on down the trail.

"You'll have to learn something about me," she quipped, a bit breathlessly as she fought to catch up on those tiny legs of hers.

"What's that?"

"I'm always right."

Cute. Shooting my skepticism in her direction, I drawled, "That so?"

"Yes," she chirped, nodding vehemently. I wanted to slide a

knuckle down the smooth bridge of her nose as she lifted it into the air and push the little button on the end. *Attracted to a nose.* That was new, and Axel was right—I was fucked.

"Really."

"Yep, and the sooner you come to terms with that, the faster your life will—" Noel's taunt drifted off as we made it through the forest onto the open stretch of cliff. Her pink lips parted, eyes round in what I could only describe as wonder, and for a minute, I slowed down to see what she did. Just greening up, the island stretched out to an abrupt edge, black rock shooting down into the sea, where it crashed against craggy boulders. Black sand beaches strewn in yellow, maroon, and green seaweed and sun-bleached driftwood served as a perimeter to great stretches of cliff—more would be visible during a real low tide. Beyond the channel, more jagged mountains rose, some protruding limbs of Mistyvale, but others were additional islands altogether. The sky and sea both mirrored a pale gunmetal blue, colliding on the horizon on an unusually cloudless day, while the blessed sun glimmered across the subtle waves. Beautiful. The isles were beautiful.

But they didn't hold a candle to the way my Skittles' brown eyes were glistening with unshed tears or the way her delicate, freckled fingers came to hover against her lips as she caught her breath. I wanted to say something, to check on her, but the others beat me to it.

"Welcome to the real Alaska, Noelli-Benelli," Max said cheerily, slinging an arm over her shoulder and tightening my throat in one move. My sunbeam of a sister looped her arm around Noel's waist, leaving me the observer on the outside looking in.

"You're going to love summer," I whispered, surprised when her glassy eyes slid to mine as she turned over her shoulder.

SIXTEEN

NOEL

NOEL

The buzzies are drunkenly fornicating in the woods
like they stumbled into fae wine.

JOSIE

Um. Excuse me?

NOEL

I'm enduring bee heaven, which unfortunately equates
to allergy hell.

JOSIE

I'm going to need more words, hun.

NOEL

POLLEN. Pollen EVERYWHERE.

JOSIE

laughing emoji What?!

VALLIE

Please hold, catching up.

NOEL

It's insane. I thought Florida had bad allergies.

BREXLEY

Because we do. All year.

NOEL

Not like this. This is madness. MADNESS, I tell you.
This shit is EVERYWHERE. And whilst bees are
equipped with happy little bee butts and must be
absolutely belligerent, my sinuses are experiencing
something very different right now.

VALLIE

Awe, we love to see happy little bee butts. Wren is
learning beekeeping. Did I tell you that?

NOEL

No! Does she love it? Oh my Lanta, of course, she
loves it.

BREXLEY

Rhyett wants to know if it's the spruce trees.

NOEL

Hell if I know. But the haze is so thick over the trees it
looks thicker than smog. Or fog. Or smoke. It makes
Florida look like heaven.

BREXLEY

Psh. Receipts?

I grinned, pulling my cell up to snap a picture through the shop
window, overlooking the channel and the trees beyond, where a thick
yellow cloud had descended on Mistyvale. Sending it off, I watched
the dots appear and vanish twice before Vallie's came through.

VALLIE

Dude. Wtf is that.

NOEL

The last frontier.

JOSIE

It's like War of the Worlds.

NOEL

War of the BEES.

JOSIE

Have you actually seen fornicating bees, or are you
just assuming they're celebrating like it's 1999?

NOEL

I've yet to witness a bee orgy, but it's a healthy
assumption.

VALLIE

Okay, okay, enough bee butts. What the hell is going
on with you? Has Eric left yet?!

WINCING, I glanced at the time, and then to Kara where she was re-stocking tumblers on the wall a beat before Brexley's face popped up on my phone. I hadn't exactly been...*entirely* forthcoming with her when she and Rhyett got home from their trip. There'd been an incident in the airport that involved Brexley slipping on a tile floor and a very over-protective pair of adorable soon-to-be-parents insisting on derailing their flights to take her to the nearest urgent care to ensure nothing had impacted future baby Rhodes.

It seemed...selfishly unnecessary to add my stress to her stress. Especially when she was thousands of miles, and thousands of dollars, away from physically being able to do anything. And due to her compulsive need to protectively hover like a feral mother bear, I opted not to tell her that Eric had rolled into town.

"Hey Kara, I'm going to hop into the back. I'll be right out."

"You got it, boss!"

Max, laptop open in his favorite seat by the window, quirked his head. I shook mine, giving him what I hoped was a convincing thumbs up before ducking outside and sliding over the touch screen button, mustering my best smile in hopes of disarming her. Judging by the terrifying silence that greeted me, and the sheen of water over familiar sky-blue eyes, it wasn't particularly working.

"Hi, honey! How are you feeling?" I asked, too cheerily. *Sheesh, tone it down, Noel.* She looked closer to tears and my stomach bottomed out.

"What in God's name did Vallie mean by that?"

"What? They're beekeeping! Ain't it great?"

"Don't be a smartass, Noel. What aren't you telling me?"

I sighed, wishing I'd grabbed my latte on the way out the door just for something to do to stall. Wandering down the alleyway, my army of composure gradually congregated inside my chest, one ounce at a time.

"Noel, is Eric *there?!*"

When she didn't bother to break the ensuing silence, and my feet finally found the sidewalk that bordered the harbor, I blew out a heavy breath. "Yeah, babe. He is."

"How?!" She croaked. "We moved you thousands of miles away to a town nobody knows the name of unless they have family there."

"You know, I didn't bother asking. The man gets what he wants, evidently."

"Why are you being so calm about this?"

"Because I refuse to give him another ounce of my energy."

"Okay, I can admire that, but...babe, just come home. The whole point was to get you away from him."

"You think I don't know that? But...Brin deserves to bond with Giddy, so I'm not going anywhere."

"So you just—what?—indulge this fucked up game of his?"

Ew, god it sounded wretched when she said it like that. I wrinkled my nose. Slowly making my way down towards the dock, I said, "Look, Brex. He's a schmuck. But he'll get bored, he'll go home. All of this will be over."

"What is that douche nozzle even doing?"

"I don't know, he has to be bored out of his mind here. No midnight takeout–"

"I meant right now?" She said, anger setting her jaw tight, a stress v appearing between her eyes. "Like, what the hell was the point of going up there?"

"Convincing me to come back home, oddly enough." The metal ramp thundered under my rubber boots as I let gravity yank me down the path.

"Noel, he scares me. This whole thing—*getting the charge dropped,* spinning it to the media? He's scary, babe."

"Don't I know it."

"This isn't funny."

"I'm not trying to make it funny, but like hell am I going to drag my boots around afraid of him, either." Like I wasn't painfully aware the *what the fuck* scale in this situation was terrifyingly skewed in his favor. But I'd made the mistake of giving the man two years of my life, and way too many pieces of me, and I certainly wouldn't be giving up another. I told Rhyett I'd look after Grizzly Grind while Brin was recuperating and bonding with baby Wright, and I felt... settled here. Especially with Elora showing me the town, dragging me to yoga and up mountains and to coffee shops. She was like a walking Mistyvale Zagat guide.

"It's not safe—you being all alone up there."

"I'm not alone, hun. You saw to that."

"What's that mean?"

"Rhyett hasn't talked to anybody?" By *anybody*, I absolutely meant Jameson. Though I'm sure Axel or Elora or Broderick or any of my other self-appointed babysitters would have worked just as well. She shook her head, and I closed my eyes, dragging down a breath and praying for patience. Why in the hell hadn't they talked? Choosing my words carefully, I said, "I'm staying next door."

Her brow furrowed, expression shifting from fear to utter confusion. Honestly, same, girl, same.

"Wait, *Jameson's* next door? I'm assuming you're not over at the Jenkins'."

"Look at you, meeting all the neighbors and shit." Bringing my hand up to my heart, I sighed, "Makes me so proud."

"Noel," she scolded, earning a laugh.

"Yes, Brex, over at Jameson's."

Her silence was positively deafening.

"What?" I demanded.

"You're so screwed."

"What?" I balked, planting my free hand on my hip before realizing she couldn't see me.

"You two are like firecrackers—loud, proud, and inevitably explosive."

"Ew, graphic, Brex."

"And right on the money. How in the hell did that happen? Oh god, have you slept with him? Are all Rhodes men this well endow—"

"No! Jeez, jump to conclusions, much?"

"I've seen the man. I know your type. Ergo." She flourished her hand on the screen as if my clothes had hit the floor before their plane took off. I laughed, rounding the corner where the *Rhodes Away* proudly bobbed in its slip. "Oh my god, you're down on the docks right now."

"Rein it in, woman. Jesus. I work here, remember? We're just friends."

"Since when?"

"Since..." *He saw me naked, gave me a jar of rocks, then forced me to steal hand-me-downs?* Even I wouldn't believe it. Welp, it was time to rip the metaphorical band-aid off. "He pretended to be my boyfriend so he could get Eric to fuck off."

Her once-animated expression fell so blank I could have reflected sunlight off her face. If...you know, sunlight existed in Mistyvale for more than a day. And she was here. And—never mind, that's beside the point. Below her narrowed eyes, Brexley moved her fist in a circle as she made an obnoxious squeaking noise, miming an eraser.

"Roll that back. *What?*"

"Eric may have come into the coffee shop—"

"What?!" Her eyes flew wide in absolute horror.

"—and demanded time to talk—"

"Hell no. Like hell did my girl give him any of her time."

"—and even though I said no, he kinda drug me out on the sidewalk."

"Noel McShane, so help me god—"

"Anyway," I cut in dramatically, waving away her concern. "Jameson saw, and it pissed him off, and he went all *Clark Kent* ripping off his glasses and button-up and told Eric we were moving in together."

Her eyes rounded. "He took his shirt off?"

"No, dummy, Jesus. Stay with me. I meant he decided to play *Superman* and save me."

"See, I knew it. This is so fucked up. You needed saving." Head falling forward, she rubbed her spare hand across her forehead.

"I had it handled."

"Like you had Florida handled?"

"Hey!" I barked, suddenly defensive. She had no right to judge me. She didn't live it. "That's not fair."

"You know what I meant."

"Do I? Because it felt kinda judgey. Hey—*no*—you don't get to cry." My useless temper immediately disintegrated as tears welled in her eyes. What in the hell kind of resolve was that?

"Stupid first-trimester hormones. Ugh, this sucks! Ignore them, they're involuntary," she sniffled, wiping a tear off her cheek. "I swear to god. Listen. You know what I meant. He tricked everyone, Noel."

"Not everyone," I pointed out. "You and Rhyett never trusted him."

Brex sucked down a deep breath. "No. We didn't. But we didn't see what was happening either. I'm so sorry, Noel. I'm your best friend. I should have known—should have seen."

"Brex, this is not your fault."

"Please come home. Why don't you want to come home?"

Steel-blue eyes flashed in my vision and I shook my head, wishing the image would go with it. "I feel good here. And I made a commitment to not only Rhyett but Brinleigh. The shop is doing well —really well, actually—and I'm expanding onto the patio for the rare occasions the weather cooperates, and I've already made friends."

"It's *you*. You'll always make friends."

She had a point. "That's *not* the point. I like it here. I mean—it's wet and gray, and quiet, and we currently have more pollen than air particles, but it's beautiful and I've been dying to explore for years and—"

"Okay, okay," she put her hand up as she continued, "I relent. But what are you doing when Jameson is out fishing?"

"Elora, Broderick, the twins, and Max are all hanging around. Like I said, you made sure I wasn't alone."

Features softening, morphing into something between relief and warm, gooey heart eyes, she nodded. "Rhyett did, at least."

"I wouldn't have him without you, so it's still your doing."

Her little giggle wasn't enough to keep my attention from drifting over the boats bobbing softly in their slips. They were unusually quiet today, not a single Rhodes in sight. They must be up at the Main House. Sighing, hating how deeply disappointed I was, I headed back for the Grizzly Grind.

"So?" Brexley said, her voice simmering with anticipation. "What did grumpier *Clark Kent* do next?"

JAMESON

ELORA

Noel, Max, and I are heading down to the Birch Barrel

AXEL

Save me a spot

LEIGHTON

Nachos?

ELORA

Yes, and obviously.

KAIA

Hell yes, I have got to get out of this house. I'm losing my mind.

ALESSANDRA

Say less. Omw!

ELORA

James?

WITH A HEAVY SIGH, I lifted my eyes up to the snow-capped mountains beyond the channel. It didn't matter how many years the green rolling hills, towering peaks, or low ceilings of fog surrounded me. It was always like a deep breath. *Home.* This place would always be home.

I could see the Birch Barrel—Rhyett's bar—from my spot across the docks. My neighbor, Mrs. Anderson, needed a few more tools before her sink would drain properly again, and I'd just stepped out of Tommy's hardware when my pocket started buzzing me to death. And fuck me, the idea of a night out wasn't half bad.

Noel. Noel, in low light, with pleasant music in the air...

Stupid? Absolutely. But I'd never cared much for flaunting high intelligence when a good time hung in the balance. Plus, a follow-up for that damn kiss was long overdue.

JAMESON

Yeah, I'm in. Ten?

ELORA

Sounds good! See you then.

MAVERICK

Someone sneak me in?

KAIA

No way. You gotta serve your time, Mav.

MAVERICK

You all suck.

RHEYTT'S PLACE was a lot like its owner—expensive, classy, and strategic. Contemporary enough to pull in the younger demographic, but rustic enough to feel like old Alaska. He might have been a pain in my ass with all of his Dudley-do-right crap growing up, but my brother could build a fucking business better than anybody. We missed him around here...*I* missed him around here, despite being pissed he'd hidden the truth from me. Still too pissed to pick up the damn phone. He'd been calling relentlessly all day long, but I didn't trust my tongue to not tear into him.

Aside from business, you know what Rhyett was good at? Emotional bullshit. More aptly, *articulating* emotional bullshit. Me? Not so much.

The metal clang of my truck door punctuated a decision I would no doubt be describing as hair-brained in no time at all. Tools safely tucked away in the locked cab, I stuffed my hands in my pockets and started walking up toward the bar, cursing as my mind wandered in loops that all led to the same subject. Was she happy here? Was she comfortable with me? With this ridiculous ploy my fat mouth got us into? Should I tell her the damn truth—that I'd already resolved to ask her out before the dumb fuck showed up?

Would Shithead get out of her life anytime soon? Was I a horrible person for feeling bittersweet about that, simply because it would remove my excuse for being in her proximity? Because hell hadn't frozen over, which meant there was no way I deserved her without it.

For fuck's sake, it was the most emotion I'd waded through since Grandpops died. And I sure as shit had never waffled with my worthiness to be in a woman's life.

Opening a door into any establishment in Mistyvale was essentially like stepping out of that magic land behind the wardrobe. What was that movie called? *Narnia.* Yeah, that's it. The point is, the wall of warmth was so abrasive it made my skin ache as I entered the Birch Barrel. It was the usual clamor of laughter and voices, music from the jukebox-wired stereo system, and the sharp clatter of somebody breaking apart billiard balls. My hands flexed. I wasn't a hermit by any means, but I didn't have a propensity for chaos, either. A drink in my blood and a cue in my hand, and I'd feel right at home in no time.

At least, that's what I thought until my chest pulled on me like a homing beacon, only for my heart to take an unexpected nosedive. Axel—the golden child—braced his arms around Noel's little body, his long arms wrapped around her to 'guide' her shot with the cue, the Rhodes family anchor on his forearm flexing as she laughed. My blood ran like ice. What. The actual. Fuck? He was talking to her, cheek-to-cheek, as she laughed against him, her eyes sliding closed. I wanted to puke. Actually wanted to empty my stomach of bile. A beat behind nausea was a blind kind of rage, and I had to remind myself of several very important things.

One: Noel wasn't actually mine. Although, if we were talking about keeping up appearances, that dick head with his groin to her perky little ass certainly wasn't helping.

Two: The idea of anyone—much less my cocky little brother—touching her made me simultaneously violent and ill. Contrary to the debauched reputation I allowed to flourish around town purely for entertainment, I'd never been one to share and had no intention of finding out if that specific conquest would get me off.

Judging by the way my temper was screaming for retribution for a woman who, technically, owed me no allegiance, I realized I had my answer. Absolutely. Fucking. Not. Air hit my lungs like an ice bath, and I realized I'd forgotten to fucking inhale. *Great.* My basic autonomic systems were failing.

"Hey James, what can I get you, man?" It was Dan's voice behind the bar that made me aware I'd wandered over in my haze of territorial frustration. He had a rag tossed over his shoulder, eyes on me expectantly. "You alright?"

"Yeah, just..." I shook my head. "Tired," I finally answered.

"The usual?"

"Sure." Like I could give a shit with Axel high-fiving my girl after she sunk her shot right into the pocket. "Make it two." I didn't know what the hell her drink of choice would be, but she seemed like the kind of woman who would be enamored by learning the landscape. A local brew might be just up her alley, and with that bubbly little personality, meeting the women behind the flavor would light her the hell up. Dan came and went. Beers in hand, my feet led me to her side, teeth gritting as I reminded myself I couldn't actually deck my brother for touching the newest addition to our big-ass family *tribe.*

Noel sunk another ball and leapt backward with her arms raised in victory, cue stick precariously wielded with little regard to her surroundings, nearly hitting my dumbass brother. Not that I'd complain.

My irritation stuttered when that beaming face turned and landed on me.

"Hey!" she chirped, throwing her arms around me, ignoring the way my hands flew out, beers sloshing. Flabbergasted, I couldn't even give a damn, because she was still beaming when she peeled away. "Did you *see* that?!"

The ache of my cheeks made me aware I was mirroring her smile, looking down to where the booze had splashed on the floor. Taking a deep breath, I nodded. "Yep, sure did."

"Axel taught me how to play!"

"I see that," I said flatly, eyeing my brother as he beamed back at me with a wink. The little fucker. "Looked like a pro to me."

"Well, thank you very much. Are you going to put some money where your mouth is?"

I smirked. It would be physically impossible not to indulge her pride. Nodding, I said, "Yeah, baby, but I brought you something first." Something deeply primal loved the way her eyes flashed at the word *baby*. Had the shithead not given her any pet names? For fuck's sake. Without another word, I held out her pint, arguing with the smile threatening to take over my face as she accepted.

"What's this?"

"Local ale, thought you'd like to try a Mistyvale brewery."

"I didn't even know we had a brewery on the island!" She swished it around like some hoity-toity wine sampling. Why in God's name did I have it in my head that I could ever satisfy some high-maintenance city—

"Damn! That's good," she said excitedly, shifting the cue to her side, the handle now firmly planted on the ground so she could savor her next drink. Satisfaction heated my chest, and I wove my body between her and my brother.

"What the hell?" I hissed under my breath. His shit-eating grin was beyond aggravating.

"What?" Axel said, tone innocent even as his smirk said differently.

"Keep your hands off my girl, asshole."

"*Your* girl," he scoffed. "There's a thought. Besides, we keep things close."

"Not *that* close."

When he made to step back into her space, I shifted my weight to block him.

"Ease up, James."

"The town needs to believe we're together."

"Please," he drawled, tonguing at his front tooth. "You've had plenty of chances to do something. Mark my words, man. If you don't get your shit together, somebody else will."

"You two having a staring contest over there?" Noel quipped, and I turned back to find amusement over her face, a bit of froth on her cheek. Smirking, I leaned forward, raising a hand to wipe it away and smiling when she flushed, looking to her feet. "Uh—thanks, I didn't realize—"

Her words cut off as I stepped in close, wrapping a hand around her waist and opting to pretend my brother no longer existed. A delicate palm came to settle on my chest, and Axel lunged to catch the cue stick she'd abandoned. I chuckled.

"Hey," I said, lowering my voice.

"Hey," she parroted back, blinking up at me as her breath coasted over my neck. Her freckles were fucking adorable, and I realized the darkest of them made up a distinct jagged 'w' where the rest were light little sprinkles. Gently, I raised my free hand to cup the side of her face, and ran my thumb over her cheek, tracing them. "What's that for?" she breathed.

Chuckling, I said, "You have Cassiopeia on your cheek."

"What?" She giggled, leaning back enough to bring her beer up and take a sip, not breaking eye contact. Goddamn, she was gorgeous. "The vanity chick?"

"That's one way to put it."

"Never took you for a mythology guy. Hell, never took you as an astronomy guy." Her amusement was a palpable thing, and, honestly, I was just floored she knew the reference.

"Never asked."

She narrowed her eyes, pursing her lips as her head bobbed. "Touché, Rhodes."

"So?"

"So...what?" Noel quirked her head.

"How's the beer?" I clarified, stepping back, needing to either taste her again or distance us.

"So good! I like the citrus a lot. Reminds me of home."

"Wanna meet the mastermind behind it?"

"What? Hell yeah," she said, grinning as she brushed imaginary debris from my flannel. Ridiculous satisfaction swelled in my chest, knowing that she was electively touching me. "He here?"

"Yeah, *she* is. Come on." My gaze darted to Axel—who looked too damn happy—before grabbing her hand and leading her through the space until we got to Rosalie, where she was relaxed in a back booth. Bright white teeth gleamed as she saw us, and then she was on her feet.

"Hey James, who's your friend?"

"Hey Rose, this is Noel. Noel, this is Rosalie. She's the mastermind behind Arctic Zest."

"Oh! Cute name, I love that." Noel reached out a hand, beaming when Rose took it. "Nice to meet you—great stuff!"

"Thanks—twice! You new to town? I've never seen you around."

"Yeah, I've been here a few weeks."

"And this one already got his claws in you?" Rosalie jerked her thumb in my direction.

"Yep, just couldn't resist that charm," Noel said, blinking pointedly up at me and earning a laugh from our new companion. This might have been a mistake.

"Jameson?! *Charming*? Girl, I think you're confused. This man has the finesse of a brick through a window."

Noel burst out in unapologetic laughter, free hand rushing up to cover her mouth like she could contain it. "Oh, you have stories to tell, don't you?"

"For *days*."

Wiggling, Noel trilled, "Oh, do share with the class!"

"*Oh boy*," I muttered, tugging at the back of my neck. This was bound to be equal parts entertaining and humiliating. Not sure what the hell else I'd expected, I just shook my head.

Rose waved me away, vaguely toward the bar. "Be a doll and go fetch us a Northern Spice, and then come get comfy. It's going to be a long night."

SEVENTEEN

NOEL

To my absolute surprise and delight, Jameson had been brought to heel by a five-foot-one blonde with the world's biggest brown eyes. Rosalie was a curvy, early-thirties bombshell who oozed boss bitch energy, and I fucking loved it. For good reason, because she owned the local spa in town, along with shares in the coffee shop downtown and now, the brewery. *When* the woman slept was beyond me.

Looking simultaneously annoyed and amused, my grumpy fake boyfriend arrived back at the corner booth with a tray of sample-sized glasses, and I settled in for one hell of a night. She wore a graphic T with some kind of band logo tied at her waist and distressed high-top jeans over what looked like cowgirl boots. Her long blonde hair was neatly curled, and minimal makeup had been expertly applied.

When she told me she had stories about Jameson for days, she wasn't exaggerating. They'd been friends since childhood, and it seemed a great deal of his fuck-ups had been in Rosalie's presence, to my utter satisfaction. Mistyvale was...*small*.

"Anywhere With You" by Jake Owen came on the stereo right as Jameson skirted off to order nachos. The rest of the family was playing pool, or out on the dance floor, all seeming quite content with the hand they'd drawn. I was sufficiently buzzed and beyond content when Rosalie leaned forward, placing her hand over mine and leaning in so conspiratorially I had no choice but to follow suit.

"You know, I could never have gotten here without Jameson."

"What?" I asked, quirking my head.

"Well, at least it would have been a hell of a lot harder. He tried to gift me the startup cash for the spa." When my eyes widened, she nodded. "I know. That little curmudgeon is such a softie when it really boils down to it." Her words made me burst out laughing, earning a mischievous grin as she continued, "Claimed he'd been fishing since high school, was young, single, and childless, and tried to gift me twenty grand. I refused."

"Naturally."

"But he wore me down, allowed it to be an investment but refused to take more than two percent interest, and it couldn't accrue for the first five years."

"What?" I asked, bewilderment resting like carbonation bubbles in my chest. I turned to watch as he rested his corded forearms on the bar, waiting for Dan to make his way on over to order.

"Yep. I knew he was trying to help me get my feet under me, but still." She shook her head. "I give him shit because he likes it that way, and nothing makes him vanish faster than compliments or thank you's, but my wife and I could never have done this without him. When my son was little, he'd even watch him for me while I worked if he wasn't out on the water."

Something in my chest tightened as I watched him patiently wave an older gentleman in front of him in line at the bar, allowing him to order first.

"He can grumble and be a real Johnny Rain Cloud when he wants to, but when it comes down to it, he's a damn good man. We've partnered in a few other ventures after I paid him back. I insisted, of course, though he could have cared less. When Tara and I decided to go in on the brewery, I hadn't even had time to ask or present projections, and he was pulling out a checkbook, grumbling about how overdue we were for a local brew. Called it a *public service*," she said with a laugh. The adoration in her eyes was enough to make the best woman wobbly. "He called Rhyett, and within the hour, we had our first client."

I thought about how quickly he'd stepped in between me and a ticked-off Eric, and wondered what the man wouldn't do for the women in his life. Although Max and Broderick had both been forthcoming about how much of a defender Jameson had always been in their lives, too. So, maybe it was just who the man was at heart. My train of thought was cut off by the buzzing in my pocket. Shock lit up my chest when I spotted my siblings on a thread. I loved them both, but unlike the perpetually vibrating pockets of the Rhodes siblings, it was the first time I'd seen them pop in.

ALEX

Hey sis, how's the land of the midnight sun?

MADDIE

Find a sexy lumberjack to break you in half yet?

ALEX

Ew. Jesus, Mads.

WHEN MY EYES flicked from the screen to a spectacularly rugged, fresh-off-the-boat Jameson in his chronic flannel, I burst out laughing.

"Who's that?" Rosalie questioned, perking up expectantly as I shook my head.

"My siblings, oddly enough."

"Not close?"

"We're not *not* close, we just...suck at staying in touch. Even when we all lived in Tampa, I was lucky if we saw each other once a month outside family dinners. I certainly wasn't ever waking up to Alex brewing coffee in my kitchen."

Rosalie snorted, shaking her head. "Say sayonara to that peace and quiet now that you're a Rhodes. I expect you'll never eat a solitary breakfast again."

"You know, I've caught on to that," I said, laughing, but pulling my phone up so I wouldn't forget. "We're all just kind of...out of sight, out of mind people, you know?"

NOEL

No spine-snapping lumberjacks, I'm sad to report.

ALEX

Hey Siri, how do you remove yourself from a text
thread?

"THEY CAN BE A LOT." Laughing, I turned back to Rosalie as she said, "Believe me, I remember meeting them all the first time. That was pre-Finn, and even then," her brow hiked and she leaned back into the booth. "It was a lot. But goddamn, they know how to love big."

"You'd kind of have to," I declared, finding Elora where she danced with a man she'd already vehemently sworn disinterest in, and Alessandra and Axel schooling a couple of college-aged guys at the pool table. Her sharp intake of air drew my posture up straighter, eyes wandering but coming up empty. "What?"

"There's my Tara!" She pointed to a petite little lady with a pixie cut and a tiny sparkling stud in her nose. She was rocking expensive-looking yoga pants and cute slip-on tennis shoes. Once she'd properly introduced us, she leaned for a kiss that made me blush, and I excused myself, making my way across the bar as the music swapped to Thomas Rhett's "Die a Happy Man" and the dancers slowed down, some leaving the floor to grab fresh drinks.

"Hey," I said as I sidled up next to Jameson. "Where'd you go?"

"You were in good company."

"Aren't I now?"

"You tell me." Sweet baby cheeses, the man could liquefy stone with those eyes. I swore I saw a little smile play in them before he pursed his lips, shaking his head. "Certainly not my call to make."

"Hmm, I guess I'll just have to find out. Dance with me?"

He scoffed, shaking his head. "Don't dance, darlin'."

Darlin'. Good god, what kind of woman felt weak at the knees being called darlin', like some old cowboy movie? This girl, *that's who*. "Oh, come on, it's slow. Doesn't even take any skill. Just wiggle about."

"Wiggle. About."

I laughed, rolling my eyes. "Yes, you big gargoyle. Just move to the music."

"Seamen don't wiggle."

Seamen. *Semen*. Hah. Narrowing my eyes and giving him a cheeky little grin, I insisted, "Oh, I think they do."

"Did you just—"

"Maybe."

He huffed a sigh that vaguely resembled a laugh. "I have a better idea."

"Oh, really?" I challenged, lifting my chin.

He nodded, taking his time as he kept his eyes on mine, slowly draining his beer and setting it aside. "We'll get back to where this started."

Jameson lacing his fingers between mine was as close to an orgasm as I'd had since my damn shower escapade. The heat of him against my palm was so luxurious there weren't adequate words for it. That simple, delicious sensation turned my brain stupid as I obediently followed him over to the billiards tables, tongue suddenly heavy in my mouth. The man's ass was as delectable as the rest of him. His hands deftly hoisted a cue, swiping the chalk and dusting not only the tip but his fingers as well before handing it to me.

"Show me what you got, Skittles."

"Prepare to be dazzled." Narrowing my eyes playfully, I accepted the chalk, dusting my fingers like I'd seen both Axel and Jameson do, assuming it was to make the stick glide.

"*Dazzled*, huh?"

"Just wait until I unleash my triple spin and win." Stifling the satisfaction of getting that telltale lip twitch, I shifted to the wall to pick up my cue.

"Sounds more like a triple fluke and fail to me."

"*Psh*. You're going to eat those words, Jameson Rhodes."

His grumble sounded a lot like, "I'm going to eat *something*."

Mouth going dry, my eyes snapped to his right as a smirk spelling 'trouble' spread on his face. Clearing my throat, I rounded the table, set the white ball where I wanted it, and slowly bent down to line up the break. "Care to put some money where your mouth is?" I slid the stick back and forth between my fingers, making sure it could glide smoothly, acutely aware of his focus on the movement.

"Ten minutes with Axel, and you think you're a pool shark?"

I straightened, feigning puzzled thoughtfulness, before tsking my tongue. "Mmmm, I'm too happy to be pool sharky. More like...a pool dolphin? Agile, graceful—"

"And ready to make a *splash*?"

The smirk on that man's face was enough to dissolve the best woman's resolve. It took a great deal of effort to resist squeezing my thighs together to ease the tension between my legs. He'd never even touched me but could dictate my body with a look. *Trouble*. T-r-o-u-quadruple b-l-e. Clearing my throat and cursing the fact that the flush to my face was involuntary, I moved my focus to the table. Swallowing down my sudden anxiety, I took the turn, yelping excitedly when a striped ball rolled into the pocket.

"Lucky shot," he teased, bracing his hands atop the cue against his mouth. Angle properly adjusted, I shot again, this time narrowly missing. I made to straighten but bumped into a hard wall of man as his arms came around me, scruffy cheek rough against mine. "Here, it's really all in the wrist. Let me show you how to handle the stick."

An ounce of spit nearly lodged in my throat, and I smirked over my shoulder where his face hovered mere inches away. Jameson kept a rough beard, but the edges were precisely groomed, a little scab on his neckline where he'd clearly nicked himself.

"I assure you, I know how to handle a *stick*."

He chuckled darkly, tracing my cheek with the tip of his nose. "Then, you won't mind if I feel the way you move."

Breath shallow, the firm—*oh so firm*—heat of him pressed against my ass, I turned back to the table, refusing to gratify him by admitting he rattled me. His broad, calloused palm came to wrap around my braced hand.

"Here, shift just a little and you can really just slide right in." He adjusted my forefinger as I fought to remember what swallowing felt like, the press of him against my backside driving me into madness. Moving to my back hand, he squeezed me gently. "You're clutching it too tightly. Loosen up and use your wrist."

This. Motherfucker. Knew exactly what he was doing. Not about to be the first to fold, I arched into him, turning to stare him down and meeting smoldering steel-blues. His smile was soft but undeniable, my bravado vanishing the instant I saw it. Shifting my focus to the table, I started to move while trying to remember how to breathe. Jameson began tracing my cheekbone again, inhaling deeply, and every ounce of blood in my body headed for my nether regions. I took the shot and, despite the sudden hammer of my heart, sunk my ball.

"*Just* like that, baby." His praise coasted across my skin, my ribs constricting as heat bloomed against them. "This is where you belong, Skittles. If anybody gets to bend my woman over a table, it damn well better be *me*. There's no one in this town that would believe I'd let another man touch you like that and stick around to see if you were loyal. Axel's lucky he's my brother." He traced up my cheek again, my breath quickening in response.

"*Jealous*, Jameson?"

"Not a word in my vocabulary, sweet stuff."

"No?" I breathed, acutely aware of the smile it brought to his lips against my face.

"No."

Painstakingly, I straightened, turning in his hold as he shifted to pin my ass against the table. Jameson's distinct scent laced the air between us and my body screamed to kiss him again. To taste my fill.

I cleared my throat. "You know, you're not as intimidating as you think you are."

"And you're not as charming as you think *you* are."

"Everyone else seems to think so."

"That's the problem."

"Sounds an awful lot like jealousy to me." Running a hand down the hard plane of his chest and cursing the way every inch of me wanted to lean in for more, I smiled coyly. The idea of making a man like Jameson jealous was...empowering, to say the least. He wet his full lips, effectively gluing my focus to them for what he said next.

"Just communicating expectations. Isn't that part of the whole relationship thing?"

"You're obviously an excellent pupil. I think my work here is done." When his dimples betrayed his amusement, I couldn't restrain my smile anymore, the leash snapping like a cheap hair tie. "It was hardly a hug, Jameson," I said, patting his chest in what I hoped was a reassurance. "He was showing me how to take a shot."

"It's not about Axel."

"No?"

"It's about seeing you in someone else's arms." His voice tightened, jaw flexing. "Or smiling for another man and realizing how much I hate the idea of anyone else touching you."

My pulse was an erratic percussion solo, chest rising and falling in rapid succession, brushing up against him. Slowly, Jameson raised a hand to brush stray strands of hair off my face, electrifying my blood. His eyes darted behind me for a beat before his smirk broadened, oozing arrogance, and I hated that I liked it. Hated that I wanted to know exactly why he looked so confident.

"So you *are* jealous," I taunted, the words breathless. Eyes darkening, he rested his forehead against mine.

"Will you just—" his word was amputated by a harsh exhale, and then his lips were molten hot, crushing mine, stealing the air from my lungs, his warm, rough fingers scraping through my hair, gripping me tighter.

My world imploded.

Every movement was dangerously decadent, heady exhales exchanged as he kissed me like I belonged to him. Ravaging and claiming, while caging me against the table as his tongue plundered, demanding I yield to him. Fuck, I did. Gratefully, greedily, I complied, wishing he would pillage more than just my mouth. I finally had my answer. The Rhodes men *did* kiss like they needed everyone in the building to know who their women belonged to. Deepening the claiming with a swipe of his tongue, his touches turned sinfully sweet, and I melted into a pool of submission against his palm.

EIGHTEEN

JAMESON

Kissing Noel was...inevitable. I'd craved her since the moment she'd shown up with her explosion of out-of-place colors, but the draw had been suffocating since she'd practically attacked me on the dock. Unfortunately, the long-awaited heat in my body and the rush of sensations were overshadowed by the looming presence of Eric fucking Connely watching from the front of the bar.

I was going to kiss her, *regardless*. Was going to steal her breath, either way. But the moment I'd spotted the shithead behind her, I knew I had to make it fucking count. How anyone could hurt someone as precious as Noel, I would never comprehend. Hell, I barely knew her and would do anything to keep her safe and satiated. Women were to be worshipped and protected, not fucking manhandled into compliance. This one, in particular, was owed a karmic debt for the shit hand she'd been dealt with that prick.

So yeah, I might've played it up a notch, might have lowered myself to grip her thighs and lift her onto our billiards table. Might have made more of a statement by tossing the cue across it behind her. But the rest—the way she tasted, the way my entire body craved more of her as those lean legs locked around me, the need to touch and serve and fill her—that was all Noel. Brilliant, funny, beautiful Noel.

The electric current that ran between us? Out of this fucking world.

Goddamn. There were a hundred-and-one reasons I should have left her alone. One-hundred-and-one reasons she was better off without me, with someone younger. If I could have kept my ego in check, and mouth shut, she and Axel would have made a hell of a pair. But as sparks sizzled, the scent of her nearly overwhelming me, I no longer gave a damn about the 'should haves'. Because this woman had her talons so deeply embedded in my body that it was thrumming.

And I fucking wanted her.

Wanted her so badly that my sense of surroundings seemed to fade into static, the buzzing in my palms overwhelming as I ran one up her thigh and the other gripped her ribs. Not for the ploy. Not to keep her away from the coward in the corner—although that was still urgent. I wanted Noel McShane *for me*. Selfish. Stupid. But I'd sprinted past the point of caring.

The softest little moan slipped between her lips as I sucked the bottom one between my teeth, and she tightened her legs around my waist. My steadily growing erection gave a little pulse against her belly and she sucked down a breath. Why the fuck did I decide to finally kiss her *my way* in a crowded bar where absolutely nothing could be done about it?

A throat clearing pulled us from our stolen moment, my mind full of mouthwatering images of this fiery goddess splayed over my bed. Of what her bare curves would feel like pressed against my body. Noel panted against me for a beat, surprised brown eyes locking on mine and then we both peeled our foreheads apart. Her face fell the moment she spotted Eric, something like disappointed understanding slithering into her expression. I instinctively stepped between them, keeping her tucked behind me as she slid off the table to her feet.

"Can I *help* you?" I snarled, staring down a fuming coward playing brave as he crossed his arms.

We'd grown up tussling—a side effect of six brothers and many, many cousins—but I'd only ever started a fight once, when a jackass knocked Brinleigh's books out of her hands into a puddle in high school.

Never in my life had I wanted to break somebody's face in as passionately as I did this angry child in a man's body. He looked exactly like you'd expect an east coast politician's child to look— poised, prepared, preppy as shit. I wanted to see how cocky his smirk would be if I knocked a few of those too-pearly teeth out.

"You could start by restraining yourself in a public place and showing some sense of civility."

Chuckling darkly, I tilted my head, sizing him up. "You're not from around here, so I'll fill you in on a little Mistyvale culture. We don't give a shit about *civility*. And I have even fewer fucks to give about your opinion." I waved him away like a fly in a pasture but wasn't willing to give him my back. Seemed like just the kind of coward to hit a man from behind. Looping a hand behind me to grab Noel's, I pulled her up to my side so she could lead the way out of here, following immediately in her wake as she pulled me back towards Rosalie. Keep it public, keep us in a pool of witnesses. Good girl.

"Noel, you're coming home, baby. Please stop walking away from me. I miss you so much—*God*, please just talk to me." Her name on his lips made every inch of my skin crawl, violence itching in my palms. She cleared her throat, and I had to fight the desire to answer for her. Noel was a big girl. She could vocalize for herself, and if she seemed stuck, then I'd step in.

"Go home, Eric. You're wasting your breath."

"Don't say that, baby."

"I am *not* your baby," she snarled, whirling on him, hanging onto my arm like she knew I'd keep her safe. She didn't fight me when I kept my body between them. "You only have yourself to thank for that. So do us all a favor and go fuck yourself."

Pride swelled like a flame in my chest, and I smirked, lifting a brow and daring him to do something stupid. Damn, it was cute when she was mad, and even cuter when she flung a curse at the slimeball. My siblings were all heading in our direction, sensing trouble; eyes from around the bar seemed to perk up, seeking something juicy for the gossip mill. Hell, I spotted Max watching us with a furrowed brow, stepping out of his booth, ready to get her out of here, no doubt.

Eric straightened his back, his left eye twitching. "Is this seriously what you've reduced yourself to?"

When she just rolled her eyes and turned to leave, my nerves all bristled. His ego would not like her ignoring him one fucking bit.

"Whoring yourself around for a place to stay and a demeaning job? Always knew you were a pathetic little gold digger."

Noel stopped as abruptly as I did, but I jerked my chin forward when she turned to me, her perfect little mouth parted. Rosalie—*God bless her*—materialized right then, snaking her arm around Noel and tugging her away as I took my sweet time rounding on Eric. To his credit or stupidity, he didn't back down. Not even as I felt the girls retreat.

"Say that again," I challenged, smirking at his pretty, clean-shaven face. Several patrons evacuated their bar stools, the wooden feet screeching over the hard floor. Axel and Max both arrived on the scene as our sisters wove behind me, no doubt going after Noel. Axel placed a hand on my chest as Max raised his cell, the camera trained on Eric's face. Suppressing the need to snarl at my brother not to fucking hold me back, I just stared the bastard down. A unified front would go way farther. The dick weasel swallowed hard, ego warring with common sense as that fat fucking mouth opened and closed twice.

"Not so brave when your future constituents will be watching, are you?" Max said calmly, although I could see the way his fist clenched at his side.

"This is being blown out of proportion, gentlemen. Just having a friendly little chat with my fiancé."

"Last I checked, fiancés don't flee five-thousand miles away if they give a shit to hear you talk. Now, get out of my bar." I was about to offer to escort him out when a throat cleared and we all found Charlie and Bells in uniform. Bells had her hand on her taser, whereas Charlie's were both braced on his hips. Fuck, I loved this town.

"There a problem here, gentlemen?"

Eric blew out a defeated breath, plastering a practiced smile on his face as he shook his head. "No, sir. Just came in for a drink."

Axel adjusted his positioning so we stood shoulder to shoulder, cutting off his view of the girls, both of us jerking our heads towards the door. Charlie nodded. "Jameson is the acting proprietor of the Birch Barrel, and I believe I heard him ask you to leave."

"On my way out," Eric said, raising his hands in surrender. "See you around," he shot back to me as he turned for the door. It felt a lot like a promise.

"Looking forward to it," I drawled. *Motherfucker.* I'd be counting down the minutes. Charlie and Bells flanked him out. A collective breath seemed to wave through the onlookers, and I turned, craning my neck and scanning for red hair.

"You okay?" Axel demanded, voice still tense. Like anyone should ask about me right now.

"Where is she?"

"I don't know, I lost Rose in the crowd."

"Send Charlie back to the banquet room when he comes back, please."

"You got it."

"Thanks," I said gruffly, patting his shoulder as I wound my way back towards the party rooms.

"James?" Axel said, commanding my attention. I glanced back, finding his brow furrowed and muscles still taut. Ready. I *loved* my family. "Nothing stupid."

"Do I look like an amateur?"

He just chuckled, shaking his head.

I found the girls all consoling a livid Noel in the back room, where I'd known Rosalie would tuck them away. The perk of a small-town community was how we all knew each other and looked out for our own. And in her short weeks here, Noel had become ours. Not just mine, but Mistyvale's too. They'd guard her back. And I'd never been more grateful. She was holding strong; her chin raised, little hands clenching and flexing, arms crossing and uncrossing. But when her gaze landed on me, water brimmed in her eyes, the sight making anger jolt down my spine. Fucking hell, I should've beat the bastard's face in just for putting that kind of pain in her eyes. Consequences be damned.

"He's gone, baby," I reassured, squeezing between Elora and Tara, and wrapping her up in a hug. Relief flooded my system as she relaxed into my arms, setting her head on my chest. Every inch of me sang at the contact. At the way she fit against my frame. Trying to focus on that sensation instead of my need to track him down, I said, "Charlie saw him out. I'm going to talk to him about filing for the restraining order up here. Start the process over. This is bullshit."

"Thanks," she whispered, her little hand clutching my shirt tightly. "I'm *so* sorry."

"You have nothing to be sorry for." Fuck, I hated laws. We should settle some things Wild West style. The worst part of his spectacular timing was that I'd seen her register that I'd kissed her like that because he was here. And that wouldn't fucking do. Pressing my mouth to the crown of her head, I gave her a gentle squeeze, trying to think of what I could say, right as Charlie knocked on the door frame.

"James, you gonna give me an update?"

"Yeah, be right there," I said, pulling her forward to see her eyes. "You okay?"

She nodded, breathing, "Yeah, go. Thank you."

"We've got her," Elora soothed, offering Noel a glass of water as

Rosalie and Alice both sat beside her. Nodding, I backed up to talk to Charlie about how we could—*legally*—keep her safe so I didn't have to take it into my own hands. Because making my cousin read me my rights didn't mean jack shit if it kept her safe.

———

THE RIDE HOME from Birch Barrel was precariously silent, Noel staring out the rain-slicked window as towering trees blurred beyond. I wasn't sure if she was mad at me, hurt by his bullshit venom, or reliving her past. She'd talk if she wanted to. But I'd opened my mouth at least a dozen times, only to close it again before we pulled into the driveway. The engine cut off, leaving us sitting with only the tinny plunk of raindrops against the truck to fill the void. Finally, she reached for her handle and I mirrored the motion, not wanting to rush her, but not about to abandon her either. Noel had just pushed her door open, a wave of chilly air bursting into the cab when she softly spoke.

"Thank you for tonight."

"Of course," I said without hesitation.

"You didn't have to do that." She slid out onto her feet, turning to face me with a hand on the truck door.

"Stand up for you?" I asked, hopping out into the mud as icy droplets hit my skin. "Kind of the whole reason this started, isn't it?" The words tasted sour on my tongue because not even I was dense enough to believe that. I'd already resolved to say something—to *do* something—and try to earn her time before he ever stepped off that plane. I didn't *want* to want her. But I fucking did.

She shrugged a shoulder, looking anything but sure of herself. "Sure. I mean...putting on the show. You didn't have to sell it like that." Giving me a sad little smile, Noel closed the door with a creak and metallic slam, and headed through the rain towards the house, leaving me staring after her.

Putting...putting on the *show*? Fuck that. Why had I been such a colossal dumbass?

I was around the hood and headed her way in a heartbeat. Noel had just gotten the front door open when I caught up, flying across the porch in a rush. Her eyes widened in surprise when she turned, hand glued to the handle as I stepped in around her. Scooping her hand up in mine, I kicked the damn thing closed, and backed her up with my body until she was pinned against the wall. Threading my fingers through her hair, I angled her up and kissed her harder than I'd ever kissed anyone.

It was a collision, a conquest, a desperate attempt to show her how much I fucking needed her. It was raw, and some primal part of me was desperate to take her right there against the door. To show her this went so far beyond our bullshit little 'arrangement'.

A little moan filled my mouth as she responded, her hands coming up to tangle in my loose, damp curls, pulling me tighter against her like I wasn't already at risk of bruising her perfect little lips. She parted for me, my tongue reaching out to taste and take, my knee tucking between her thighs. Satisfaction roared through my chest when she stepped wider for me. Breath heaving, heart pounding, dick throbbing where it pressed against the confines of my zipper, I peeled our mouths apart, staring down into bewildered brown eyes.

"That was so you'd know it wasn't for the fucking show."

NOEL

JAMESON'S DESPERATE, bruising kisses halted only long enough for him to insinuate that this kiss was actually ours. No show. No pretense or ploy. Shock had barely skittered across my senses when he moved back in, and I ground my hips against his, hands scraping over his magnificent body, his clothes chilly and damp from the omnipresent rain.

He panted against my lips for a beat before growling, "I meant what I said tonight, Noel. Don't for a moment convince yourself that wasn't the God's honest truth."

I wanted to respond, wanted to question, but then his rough, glorious palm had angled my face up and away so he could graze my neck with his mouth like he wanted to eat me alive, spare hand roughly cupping at my breast. Words vanished. Thoughts muddled. Heat exploded, the inferno growing as he roughly tweaked my nipple. Suddenly, I was painfully aware I hadn't been shaving consistently since I got here. Could I muster the dignity to care? Absolutely not.

"Oh fuck," I breathed as he sucked on the delicate skin of my neck. Arching into him, our chests heaved together, hips grinding as desperate heat pooled between my legs. His hard cock was about to bust his jeans at this rate, every movement seeming to stoke his arousal. I wanted it to. Wanted to feel his silky smooth skin, to know how he moved, what he tasted like. My fingers scraped under his shirt, hoisting it up to strip the chilled, sticky fabric from his skin. Jameson's hands abandoned their perusal of my body, clamping down around my wrists.

Panting, he said, "If you start touching me like that, I won't be able to stop."

"Good," I breathed back. "Don't."

"Not *now*." He shook his head, confusion colliding with the wave of warmth in my throat. "The first time I fuck you, it won't be after you were thinking about *him*. The first time I fuck you, my name will be the *only* one on your mind—the only word you remember, the only thing you'll be able to scream. I won't have you confusing this with a sympathy fuck or a comfort fuck. I won't let that asshole tarnish what belongs to us." When I made to speak, his mouth came down hard and demanding, silencing my retort. Breathing hard, Jameson leaned back just enough to speak, his forehead resting against mine, his next words hot against my lips. "Because if I take you, I expect you to give me *everything*. Do you understand me?"

Head shaking, I breathed back, "No. I don't. Don't you *dare* stop."

He chuckled, the sound rumbling against my ribs. "Glad the feeling is mutual." Pressing my wrists—bound in *one* of his broad hands—to my chest, he braced himself on a forearm over my head and kissed me absolutely breathless. Once my mind was well and truly spinning, he abruptly, without warning, walked away, *smirking* as I balked at him.

"Night, Skittles."

"Motherfucker," I barked as he vanished around the corner, heaving down air as my pussy throbbed and stars spun behind my lids. His husky laugh trailed back to me a beat before I heard his bedroom door click closed.

Jameson Rhodes was an asshole. A damnably gorgeous, *sex-appeal god* of an asshole.

NINETEEN

NOEL

"Wake up, beautiful."

Blinking, entirely disoriented, I blearily took in the outline of a familiar face and gorgeous dark brown locks of hair. "*Whashapning?*"

His chuckle warmed my chest. "Come on. I wanna show you something."

"Time is it?" One eye was vehemently refusing to stay open.

"Just before six."

"*Why?*" I screwed up my face, jamming my other eye closed. It had been nearly impossible to fall asleep, worked up like I was. Finally, after one in the morning, I'd given up, wandered to the shower and desperately tried to relieve some of the pressure he'd wound so tightly in my core. Remembering exactly why I was so exhausted, I scowled at him, sitting upright. "Hey. You're an asshole, you know that?"

His laugh was sincere, smile blinding as he held out a cup of coffee. "Keep reminding me, it'll stick eventually. I brought a peace offering."

Yup, I was still gaping at that full-throttle grin. Snapping my mouth shut, I studied him for a moment, narrowing my eyes as he jostled the mug, contents sloshing. "Gonna take a lot more than that."

"Hard time sleeping?" He drawled smugly. My thighs clenched as memories of last night solidified. *Dammit.*

"Rat bastard," I mumbled, blowing on the steaming cup. Jameson chuckled darkly, the sound triggering very unwelcome sensations of desire and adoration I quite simply wasn't willing to acknowledge in the moment.

"I deserve that."

"Payback's a bitch, Rhodes."

"Looking forward to it. Now. Come on, get up."

"*Am* up."

"Out of bed," he amended, jerking his head towards the open door behind him.

"Early," I complained, scowling.

"You run a coffee shop," he pointed out dryly, amusement playing on his lips as he tossed one of his sweatshirts in my direction. In my sleep-numbed state, I hadn't even noticed it tucked beneath his arm. I would absolutely not be acknowledging how badly I wanted to bury my face in the fabric and inhale his scent.

"Keyword: *coffee*."

"In your hands, Skittles," he said, jerking his chin like an order. "Drink up."

Narrowing my eyes, I took down a long drag of hot, deliciously bitter liquid. "Better be good."

"You can beat me to death if it's not," he offered, his dark, scarred brow raising.

"Good enough for me." At least it was until he flung open the curtains and the blinding sun came rushing in to assault my eyes.

"Sun's out." He held up a hiking backpack before tossing it on the end of my bed. "Pack a bag, we'll be back tomorrow."

Nearly choking on the scalding liquid, I forced a swallow. "*Tomorrow!?*"

"Come on," he ordered, possessing the audacity to snap his fingers at me before I'd gotten down another single serving of caffeine. Man must've lost his mind. "Time is of the essence."

"What the hell am I packing for?"

"Camping. It's a Mistyvale rite of passage. Bring layers. I've got all the gear."

"I work tomorrow."

"*Afternoon.* I called Kara and told her I have to head out on the water tomorrow, so she's opening for you."

"Jesus."

"Is waiting at the top of the cliffs. Let's go. We're running out of time."

Before I could demand 'time for what', he was throwing open

drawers and ripping my clothes out of them. Startling forward, I demanded, "What the hell do you think you're doing?"

"Packing. At this rate, it will be two negligees and a couple lacy underthings with some heels. You prefer the impractical, don't you?" His smirk was infuriatingly adorable.

"Get out," I snarled, rushing for the dresser I'd *just* finally unpacked into when I realized Eric was evidently here to stay. Jameson headed for the door, grinning all too broadly. "Food," I grumbled.

"Already in the truck," he said firmly, smirking down at me. "For a barista, you're kinda feral in the morning." He laughed, the sound coming from deep in his chest as I chucked a pillow at his head, and then he was gone. Grumbling about insane people, I assembled a day's worth of clothes and pajamas, a few extra pairs of socks, and wrestled athletic wear onto my body. It took a beat in my groggy, half-asleep state to realize that was sincere excitement in his voice, his eagerness not in standing with his usual growly demeanor. Still bossy as hell, but in a cute way, like a kid on Christmas morning. Fine. I was officially mildly curious.

Chugging my coffee, I headed for the door.

"THIS IS the only time of year the tide is out far enough to see them," Jameson explained as we clambered over slick rocks between tide pools. We'd driven nearly an hour around the island to see the caves on the cliffside and the massive tide pools that bordered the ocean. The beach was at least one hundred yards of damp, wavy black sand, the waterline significantly receded. Streams of icy water carved mini-canyons through it in their fight to freedom. For what might have only been the second time since I arrived in Mistyvale, the sky was a gorgeous, open blue. God, I'd missed that. Something so simple. Try as I might to keep my attitude in check, the absence of the sun's caress and a blue sky had been eating at me.

This was heaven, the air still crisp, but the sun stretching out in the happiest of reunions, as waves distantly rolled against the sand and Jameson led the way across a beach only available for a few hours a day during the peak of the summer. He glanced back every few seconds, making sure I was still in his wake. Without fail, for the bigger steps or jumps, he'd turn, reaching out a hand until he knew I was steady.

"Elora told me a story about you guys climbing around out here on your own?"

He scoffed. "*All the time.* We spent a good chunk of the summer out here—we'd pack bags and walk all the way down the beach, hike the mountain, camp until the following morning, and walk back at low tide."

"It feels like a different world," I admitted, thinking back to my childhood outside of Tampa, where our fields were bisected by concrete.

"That's because it is," he agreed, turning to look at me expectantly.

Smiling softly, I explained, "We always lived off in the rural center of Florida so mom could have a little bit of land and a few horses. But with the abundance of venomous critters and modern-day dinosaurs, I can't fathom my parents allowing the three of us to run off and camp overnight unsupervised. Let alone trapped until the tide rolled out."

"Fair enough. I certainly wouldn't let my baby girl run around in the world of Florida Man."

I giggled, shaking my head in an attempt to stifle the effect of picturing Jameson as a dad. He would look damn good chasing around a little princess, and I had a sneaking suspicion he'd do it. He might grumble to his brothers, but from what I'd gathered, there weren't actually lines to what he'd do to keep his family happy. I was so screwed.

"It's really not that bad," I assured him.

"The headlines beg to differ."

"Yeah, well. I assumed you all were regularly mauled by bears or trampled by moose, and yet here you stand."

Shrugging, Jameson said, "We like the rumors—they keep people out of paradise."

"This is your paradise?" I asked, genuinely curious as he hopped over another stream, his smile broadening when I did the same without hesitating.

"Wide open land, quiet nights, mountains, and the sea. If you steer clear of the gossips, nobody really sticks their nose in your business. So, yeah. It is." Those sweet little dimples popped up as he asked, "What's yours?"

"Mmmm..." I trailed off, surprised when his hand came to settle against my back beneath the pack like a silent reassurance. Sucking down a breath, I admitted, "I don't know anymore, to be honest."

Jameson was quiet for a moment, the space filled by the song of the sea, until he pressed, "Gonna give me more than that?"

After emptying my lungs of every scrap of air only to refill them...twice, I said, "I guess...my future all hinged on Eric's for so long. His father's business. When he'd be old enough to campaign, what office he'd hold. I had the shop—but, even the Cracked Corset is more Brexley's baby than mine."

"What do you mean? Rhy makes it sound like that place is your kingdom."

"I mean...it is," I agreed, but my voice gave away the hesitation. Clarifying, I added, "We *made it* our oasis. Working with people is... my forte. I love it. Love getting them what they need. Love giving them a safe space to relax and explore. But that was Brexley's dream. I just ran with it because I love books, and bookish women, and the idea of a store niched to that demographic was fun. But, honestly, I just didn't have a plan of how in the hell to use my business degree until she asked me to get coffee and showed me the vacant space."

"Pretty epic that you just backed her play like that."

"That's what best friends do."

"Maybe."

"You'd back Broderick up, wouldn't you?" The sand shifted under my boots, and Jameson's hand slid towards my hip as he steadied me. Every iota of consciousness seemed to zero in on his touch, my brain scrambling to hear what he said.

"With the right proposition."

I choked on a laugh, earning a hiked brow. "Oh please. Brin and Paul. Mrs. Anderson. Rosalie and Tara. They all speak about you like their hero." They did. If he wasn't investing in single moms, or looking after corporate widows, he was fixing the neighbor's plumbing or replacing shingles on their roof. There wasn't anyone in town who didn't talk about Jameson with respect when he wasn't around to flip shit at. "Play it cool all you want, but your secret is out."

"My secret?" he asked skeptically.

"You've got a big ol' heart under all that muscle."

"Whatever you want to tell yourself. So...?"

"So?" I asked, smiling as he let the word linger.

"You know my zoo of a family. You haven't said much about yours."

"That's because we're a sixth of the size and much less entertaining."

"You said Alex is protective. He older?"

"Younger," I admitted, a pang of homesickness twisting in my gut. "But he hated Eric from the beginning. He acts tough—construction kid—but he's really just a sweetie."

"Just the two of you?"

Guilt shot through me, brow furrowing in frustration. How hadn't I ever talked about home? I guess home was precariously close to Eric, and that brought with it an entire mountain of painful baggage I wasn't ready to conquer just yet. "We have an older sister, Maddie. She's married with a kiddo."

"You're not close?"

"I...struggle to stay in touch. Out of sight, out of mind, I guess." I chewed on my bottom lip. "I love them, I'm just...we were never as close as you guys."

"Nobody is as close as my siblings. They drive me crazy. Can't take a shit in peace."

Bursting out laughing, I smiled over at him. The statement was crude—and no doubt true—but it was the way he looked at me that said he'd cracked a joke for my benefit. To lighten the conversation. I owed him for it.

"Not going to carry on that family tradition with a litter of your own?" My tone stayed mercifully light, but it was probably one of the more personal questions I'd dared to ask. His scoff was answer enough, but to my surprise, he slid his palm back to my lower back as he answered.

"I'm no Rhyett. I barely survived growing up in that chaos, so I'm not about to create my own. Maybe—*maybe*—I could do one boy, if I found a partner I could tolerate for more than a millisecond." Well, that was an interesting insight, my brows furrowing as I absorbed it. I shouldn't be curious about the depth of the statement, but Jameson must've heard the wheels churning against my skull, because he asked, "What about you? Want kids someday?"

"Well, I'm no Juniper," I parroted back in the same tone. "Although I always thought two or three would be nice." Blowing out a weighted breath, I amended, "If I ever found the right person."

"You will," he said, tone uncharacteristically soft. My head snapped up, turning to focus on him instead of the ground ahead. He smiled softly. "Only an idiot wouldn't see what you have to offer, Skittles. Even if it takes six shots of espresso to keep up with you."

A cataclysmic collision detonated in my belly, throat tightening, mouth going dry. I wanted to believe him. Really wanted to, but every insult slung my way tried to claw to the surface of my mind. Fighting to shove them away, I said, "You're not so bad yourself, Wolverine. An exemplary student, in my not-so-humble opinion. You'll make some woman very happy one day." But God, the idea of anyone else touching him made my skin crawl with disproportionate irritation.

"Maybe," he allowed simply, but the tone created little confidence.

Eager for a subject change, I asked, "Really gonna stick to that Skittles thing, are you?"

"It's certainly better than Red."

"What's wrong with Red?"

"It's topical, at best," he said plainly. "I love my brothers, but they don't know you like I do."

"Because *Skittles* says soul-deep connection?" I challenged, lips twitching.

"At least it's customized to you specifically. Rhyett had this crush in high school, and called her Freckles…" About ten minutes of easy sibling stories passed between us before we fell silent, eyes on the rocky beach. Part of what I enjoyed about Jameson was that he didn't feel the need to fill the quiet. When conversation trailed off, he allowed the rush of waves and hush of the wind to surround us. So many people were so afraid to be present that constant chatter was necessary. And yeah, I could be that way too, especially when nervous, but when I was comfortable with someone or in a group of trusted…

I trusted Jameson Rhodes. Wholeheartedly. The realization left me fighting the desire to gape at him again. Sand shifting beneath my feet, I continued on, enjoying the fact that he was just willing to *be*. Eventually I looked up from the slippery kelp-coated rocks to a cave in the shape of a—

"That's Keyhole Cavern."

I giggled, nodding, "Welp, that's fitting." Sandstone had eroded into a perfect antique-style keyhole rimmed in copper and kelp. "It looks like a secret passage to *Neverland* or something," I said, smiling.

"Honestly, Rhyett, Axel and I are lucky to be alive. We loved the caves so much, we'd march clear out here and play in them until the tide came in before sprinting back to the high ground. I'm not sure how we even made it back all those times."

"Obviously you're supposed to be here for something."

"Are you one of *those* people?"

Smirking, I asked, "*Those* people?"

"You know, the *fate* kind?" He questioned, the emphasis on the word, feeling like an illusion to Brexley when she attempted to dismiss Rhyett. "The zodiac, destiny, pre-ordained path people?"

"Pre-ordained path people? Say that three times fast."

"No thanks," he said back to me as he reached out a hand to trace his fingertips over the end of the rock wall. I could hear the smile in his voice.

"I'm not sure if I believe anything is pre-ordained," I admitted, thinking about faith, thinking about my life so far as I stepped over slick rocks, avoiding the barnacles on one. "We all make our choices, and live with the consequences, you know?"

"I agree. But you believe there's a purpose behind it all?"

"Obviously."

"You say like that's the end of it."

"Well, don't you?"

He shrugged, glancing back at me. "I'm not sure. Sometimes I think this is all there is."

"All there is?"

"Heaven, hell, life." Shaking his head, Jameson turned back for me after climbing up onto the side of a gradual incline. He extended a hand to hoist me up onto the mountainous climb.

"Sorry," I mumbled, accepting the offering gratefully, feeling anything but sure on my feet.

"You're fine. Take your time. This is unfamiliar territory for you. It's *my* backyard." When I smiled in answer, he nodded, turning back to the walk. "And I don't know. We're here. We live. We experience. We work. We die. Maybe that's it."

"Awfully pessimistic of you."

"I guess there's only one way to find out."

"In a rush to know?"

He snorted, dropping my hand and turning to lead up a softly worn trail through the grass and whimsical, delicate yellow buttercups that danced in the breeze. "Not particularly. I'm enjoying the journey."

"You don't always give that impression."

"I'm wounded," he said mirthfully, hand to his chest. "Look. Most things and people are a pain in my ass. They exhaust me. It doesn't mean I don't love them, I just...I love this too. Crave *this*. The..."

When his words wandered off, looking up the mountainside, I supplied, "*Freedom?*"

"Yeah. That too. I guess it's the peace of it."

"Mistyvale certainly doesn't lack in that."

"No," he said on a huff. "We certainly don't." The terrain shifted then, the climb requiring more focus on my part and helpful assists on his. Companionable silence settled between us again, only the heavy sound of exerted breathing mingling with the song of the forest. There was nothing that quiet in Florida. Our beaches were busy. Our springs were busy. Peace was a commodity rarely granted unless you could brave the creatures of the Everglades, and then it came with a side of deep paranoia. Florida would always—*always*—be home for me, and I loved growing up there, but if the critters weren't after you, the bacteria and parasites were.

Jameson led me through the woods, following a gentle trail of prior feet, pausing occasionally to make sure I was okay, or offering a water break. When we finally reached the summit, breath ragged from exertion, he turned and nodded.

"Nicely done. Just a few more feet." When he stopped, I nearly collided with him, my legs trembling under my weight after the hours of work. Jerking my gaze from my feet to the horizon, the oxygen rushed from my lungs as I took in the view. The signature emerald Mistyvale mountains funneled together to a crystal blue lake in what had to be a volcanic crater. Beyond them, we could just make out one channel slicing between green islands. Hot damn, this place was breathtakingly beautiful. Just like the rugged man looking so at ease as he swung his pack off his shoulder. "Home sweet home," he said under his breath.

*J*AMESON

TO NOEL'S CREDIT, it took most people at least a full summer of consistent hiking to conquer the trail I'd just drug her up with no remorse. It was delightful that she did it without a single complaint, that overly optimistic attitude of hers coming in handy. We could have camped anywhere along the trail, but she just kept cruising, her eyes full of that wonder that did things to my gut. Whenever I'd glance at her, she smiled softly as she panted for air. Like every tree, moss-covered rock, and stream were fascinating. Maybe after all those years stuck between endless cities, it *was* fascinating.

Tarp in place, tent laid out, I was sliding the poles into place when she quietly excused herself. Oddly at home for someone who hadn't actually grown up camping in these mountains. After the last few hours of endless trekking, I assumed she just needed to find a good tree to hide behind, and continued to set up camp. Unpacking my Bluetooth speaker, I started Rhyett and my 'Good ol' Days' playlist, nodding to the rhythm of the Rolling Stones' "Beast Of Burden" as I slid the pieces together like one gigantic puzzle. The wind picked up a bit more than I liked, whistling through the pine branches as I whispered the lyrics to myself.

Before we started hiking, I'd made sure Noel practiced pulling her bear spray off the hook, but that didn't ease my nerves at her wandering off on her own. When the fuck did I become a nervous man? *Christ.* Shaking my head, I kept my hands busy, quickly hammering stakes into the earth and popping our temporary shelter up with practiced motions. This tent and I had been *through* it together. Years of sanctuary found beneath the sound of rain on the tarp. Adventures and sunsets, and near run-ins with bears I was lucky to scrape out of.

The sleeping bags were still clipped to Noel's bag, so I'd just straightened to look for her when I heard her yelp crack through the woods. I didn't think. Didn't hesitate. Just checked that my firearm was safe in the holster and fucking bolted as fast as my feet could carry me in the direction she'd headed.

"Noel!?" I bellowed. "Noel?!" My feet slowed as I heard...*laughter?*

"Over here," she called back, her voice a twist between misery and amusement. What the fuck was going on? Heart still in my throat, I froze as I rounded an enormous spruce tree and found her wide eyes set over a grimace. Eyes frantically scraping over her for injuries, I hesitated, wincing as I took in her soaked clothing and scraped palms.

"You're drenched."

"Uh...yeah."

"Not in the way I like my women to be."

She wrinkled her little nose, then burst out laughing, unable to feign disapproval. *Yeah. I might be in love with this girl.*

Jesus H. Christ, where the hell did that come from?

Hands stiffly held off of her body, she shook them off. Splatters of water landed back on the bank by the steady creek I assumed she failed to cross successfully. Her pants and sweatshirt were both soaked through, and to my immense trepidation, so were the sleeping bags. *Welp. Things just got interesting.*

She seemed to have the same realization, grimacing. "Oh god, I'm so sorry." I was shaking my head, trying to bite back my mirth at the sight of her mud-splattered clothing, when she kept going. "I didn't mean to, I just slipped, but the bags—"

"*Will dry*, Skittles. Take a breath."

Still shaking the water out of her sleeves, she made her way towards me, big brown eyes heavy with shame. "I swear it was an accident. *I'm so sorry.* Here you thought of everything, and I went and—"

The moment she was within arms' reach, I snagged her around the back of the neck, bringing her face to mine and shutting her up with a kiss that quickly sent blood racing straight to my dick. Her icy hands slipping beneath my shirt acted like an accelerant on the inferno of my feral fucking need for her. But first... "It was an accident. We'll figure it out."

"I swear I'm so—"

Crushing her lips with mine, I shook my head. Jesus, she was being so damn hard on herself. "So help me, if you don't stop apologizing for being fucking human, I might lose it. Did you intentionally dunk our supplies?" When she blinked up at me, shaking her head, I added, "Then you did nothing wrong, baby."

Eyes softening, she smiled gently, a relieved little breath escaping from her.

"What?" I questioned, sensing something unsaid.

"I like it when you call me that."

By the time we reached camp, she was shivering, her teeth chattering together. Still, she beamed at the view and then ogled the tent, disbelief in her voice as she demanded, "In the time it took me to piddle and fall in a puddle, you set up camp?!"

"Piddle?" I said, unable to resist the smile. Her eye roll was worth it. "*Puddle*?" I demanded, blinking at her verbiage regarding the steadily flowing creek she'd fallen victim to.

Looking adorably annoyed, she huffed, "Stream. *Tiny river.* Whatever. Point is, that was fast."

"I've only done it a thousand times, no big deal." Shifting around her, I scooped the backpack off her shoulders, impressed she'd hefted the damn thing clear up here. I'd fully expected to lug both bags up at some point.

"So, where are *you* sleeping?" she quipped, grinning when I glared at her.

"Afraid of your roommate?"

"No," she said, scoffing.

"I'm not making a move, baby. You have—well, *had*—your own sleeping bag. Regardless, Juniper raised a perfect gentleman." Her smirk said she knew I was anything but. But I meant it. She was safe. I'd never been the kind of man that would pressure a woman into anything. And I'd sure as shit never needed to. Not that I wouldn't chomp at the bit if she offered herself to me.

I knelt to take apart her pack, trying not to wince when I found the sleep rolls entirely saturated, the bag itself discouragingly damp. It was supposed to be water resistant, but we were about to find out. "Ahh, shit," I mumbled under my breath, unclipping the sleeping bags and unzipping the top layer.

"I'm—"

"Don't finish that sentence."

"*Sorry,*" she winced. I glared up at her as I pulled out her sopping clothes. I pursed my lips to keep from laughing. That was about right. With a long-suffering sigh, I stood up, shifted for my pack, and pulled out a rope.

"Here," I said, tossing her one end as I walked away with the other.

"Um...are you going to hang me for treason?"

Rolling my eyes, I glared back at her. "*Tie it to the tree*, Noel."

"You're leaving me for the wolves, aren't you?" She shifted towards the closest trunk.

"We don't really have wolves here."

"*Bears*, then. You're leaving me for the bears. Going to soak me in honey and leave me out for bait."

"I assure you, if I'm pouring honey on your skin, it's for a very different reason."

Heat flashed in her eyes, nearly halting her shivers before she convulsed again. Fuck, I loved the way arousal looked on Noel McShane. Savored the fact that a playful taunt could elicit it. I did not, however, like how cold looked. Despite her shivers, she managed to tie her end up, and I did the same, crafting a makeshift clothing line. I laid her drenched set of clothes over the rope, and she wordlessly followed suit, unzipping the sleeping bags and hanging them down the center of the line. She was still laying out soaked blankets and clothing pieces when I walked past her to gather firewood, hesitating at the last piece she pulled from her bag. A lacey, hot pink thing that made her blush as she strung it up. Brows no doubt in my hairline, I quirked my head, tonguing at a canine to avoid smiling.

"You, uh...you brought the negligee?"

Her gaze found her feet, and her fair cheeks turned a delicious shade of near strawberry pink. I wanted to eat her for dinner. Clearing her throat, Noel mumbled, "Mmm...not sure how that snuck in there."

Swallowing my laugh, I walked away while shaking my head, making it to the tree line before the chuckle won the battle. By the time I returned, the wind had picked up speed, not boding well for my little Floridian companion. Wordlessly, I eyed her damp clothes as I built the fire.

"Not to be *that* guy, but you've got to get out of those."

"I'm fine," she insisted, but the clench in her jaw said otherwise. On our best end-of-June days, we'd hit sixty degrees, and with the wind chill, it was dramatically cooler. "We can't just go back?"

"I mean, if you want to hike over mountains just as steep as we came up for the rest of the day. But the easy path is gone by now and won't be back until low tide tomorrow morning."

"Well, crap."

"You can wear mine," I offered. "I've got a pair of sweats in my bag. Get changed and come sit by the fire. I'll make some coffee."

"Are you um—" When I glared at her, she swallowed, grinning nervously as she amended, "Thanks."

"You got it. Hustle. You'll catch your death."

Fire finally roaring enough to satisfy me, I'd just set down our second log 'bench' and poured the French press into tin mugs when Noel finally snuck out of the tent, drowning in my sweats and hoodie. Goddamn, why was that so fucking cute? She'd cuffed the pants, cinched the waist to hold them on her hips, and had the sleeves rolled up. It still hung off her. My damn chest heated.

I planted my ass on the ground, leaning against the log, and stretching my contentedly exhausted legs out to warm up my boots. The mountains and I had always had a deep love affair, but for the first time in my life, something else overshadowed their peace.

She flitted over to the clothing line, hanging up her outfit from earlier to dry before turning to face me, skin still a beautiful peachy flush. Nervously, she clasped her hands, giving me an apologetic smile as she wandered over.

"Thanks." Noel swallowed hard, pouring herself onto the ground beside me. "*Again.* Thanks again."

I nodded, wetting my lips but holding my tongue as I held out a steaming tin cup. Fuck, I wanted to peel those baggy clothes right off her lean little body. Clearing my throat, I turned to the view, motioning to it with my coffee as I braced on the opposite elbow.

"Welcome to paradise."

"HAH! YOU *SUCK*! I WIN!" Noel taunted as she did her victory dance. She'd been kicking my ass at cards for the better half of the afternoon. Coffee with a generous pour of Bailey's, an afternoon fire and no shortage of sunshine had been the best recovery for our camping day, thank fuck. It would have been horrible if she'd been miserable the whole time. Maybe she wasn't the most graceful winner, but she was entertaining as hell.

"Still won't play a real game," I countered. She refused to play poker, which was my game of choice. It turned out that games of luck were right up her alley, where strategy and confidence were mine.

"Psh. Does anything about this face say, 'lies well'?"

"It's not about lying, Skittles."

"Bluffing is just a euphemism for lying, *Wolverine.*" She'd just finished flinging the nickname at me like an insult when "American Girl" by Tom Petty and the Heartbreakers came on the playlist. Immediately perking up, Noel started singing along. Her talent wasn't professional by any means—basically just talking, but with more volume—but it was cute as shit as she jumped to her feet and started to dance. It had been years since I'd ever watched a woman contentedly make a fool of herself, and all I could think was...*that's my girl.*

Only...she wasn't. Not really. Not yet, at least. "*What* are you doing?" I said, taunting her as I shook my head. She just sang louder, her voice taking on a slightly more melodic tone like she'd bothered with effort, wiggling her hips from side to side, my gray sweats looking precariously close to abandoning their post. "Rhyett told me Brex loves oldies. Didn't realize that applied to both of you."

She sat down looking flushed, curls a little frizzy. "Oh man, we grew up together on these songs."

Panting for breath, she grinned up at the blue sky before laying back into the buttercups. She fit there with her fireweed pink earrings, surrounded by little yellow blooms, no more substantial than weeds, deep in the Alaskan woods. "I think I enjoy camping," she declared before shrugging. "I mean, all things considered."

"I enjoy you being here camping with me."

Fuck me, when she smiled, the hum of the mountain stopped to watch.

TWENTY

NOEL

Jameson had thought of everything. Well, everything except for his klutz of a fake-maybe-not-fake girlfriend falling into a damn creek and ruining half of his best-laid plans. He'd been so gracious about it; my mind was still suspended, waiting for him to snap or lose his shit over the snacks that weren't sealed up or the fact that the blankets had also been drenched in a thirty-second time frame.

Beyond that, though, there were packs of food for dinner, extra snacks that had survived the plunge, and he'd even packed two of Rosalie's beer bottles, wrapped in his clothes to sustain the hike. Bellies full and fire crackling, we were both leaning against our respective logs, ales nearly empty, stargazing from the top of the world. The chill of evening was setting in as Alaska's eerie eternal blue light slowly faded into darkness. It must've been after midnight —the speaker having died a while ago. We'd ushered in nightfall with slowly exchanged stories. He might have been more concisely put together than my meandering bunny trails through topics, but Jameson was at peace out here; shockingly eager to share tale for tale.

"I can't imagine living anywhere else," he admitted. "Mistyvale is home. But I don't know if I could do it without some travel."

"Adventure is a necessary commodity."

"Especially when your options are as limited as ours are."

"Where to?" I asked, curiosity ruling my day.

"Usually somewhere warm, often mountains or canyons or both. I *clearly* like to hike."

His sardonic statement made me snort—not exactly flattering, but the amused arch of his eyebrows was pretty cute. "Favorite place to visit?"

"Zion," he answered without hesitation. "You could explore Southern Utah for months and never run out of trails, but there's something about the red rock that makes it feel like another planet."

"I've never been," I admitted sheepishly. "Never really traveled much after high school."

"Stick with me, and we'll inevitably remedy that. It's in our blood."

"Descend from gypsies?" I joked.

"Yes," he said without missing a beat. I chuckled, but when his brows winged up, my mouth popped open. "Don't look so surprised," he said, chuckling. "Wandering souls on all sides. Nomads and voyagers make up our bloodlines, right up to the Alutiiq here on the island. I blame the blood for our need to travel." He smirked as he looked me up and down. "You're inevitably Celtic?"

Rolling my eyes and primping my hair, I dryly asked, "*What on earth* gave you that idea?" Yes, there were other cultures that shared my red hair and abundance of freckles, but it wasn't hard to guess. If my appearance didn't give it away, the last name certainly did.

When at last Jameson stood—at the end of a story about him and Axel during a particularly close call crab fishing—he walked over to take my bottle, grouping it with his own before offering me his other hand. I stumbled into his chest as I gained my balance, and he smirked down at me. Though subtle, his smiles were stunning. Addicting. I reveled in this one, our bodies too close to avoid the sparks in the air between us. My breath sped up in time with my pulse, because if I kissed him again, I wasn't sure I could stop. Not anymore. Everything in my body was buzzing, begging to feel him, to see what those powerful hands and cocky words could do if I submitted to them.

Craving Jameson was...different. There was something...*primal*...about how desperately my body needed to feel his. It had been years since I had felt the fluttering rollercoaster of new relationship jitters, and while this wasn't supposed to mean anything, his words last night, and that kiss, made it clear the physical draw wasn't at all one-sided. But this was temporary. Eric would get the fucking clue—hopefully, while I vanished entirely from town—and Jameson would keep fishing, and Brin would eventually want her spot back, which would leave me...somewhere. Somewhere else. Swallowing hard, I looked to my feet, remembering how to breathe and moving to say we should get some sleep when he cleared his throat.

"We've got an early day. We should—err—get some rest." His jaw tightened. Something playing in his eyes that sent more heat churning in my core. Like he was also fighting an internal battle.

"Yeah, great." It was *not* great. What part of me wanted to *rest?* Not a single inch. Not even my icy fingers. Still, I followed his lead as he motioned to our tent, the fire reduced to a pool of fiercely undulating orange coals. It had been absolutely perfect for s'mores. Which we had thoroughly taken advantage of, so I couldn't use that as an excuse to stay up with him any later. The lingering sugary burn of melted marshmallows was still on my tongue.

Heart fluctuating from my stomach to my throat like a caffeinated yoyo, I stepped inside, grimacing at his makeshift bed rolls, sans blankets. That was my bad, so I couldn't very well have the gall to complain.

For the first time, the silence was filled with intention, nothing peaceful about it as the hum of the zipper closed us in. Kneeling on one mat, I glanced back to see him shirking off his hoodie, the fabric of his t-shirt clinging to the thick fleece, peeling it away from those delectable abs.

Sweet.

Baby.

Cheeses.

The man was unreal gorgeous every day, but there, in the gentle blue light of Alaskan night? My pussy throbbed, mouth filling with saliva like I was on my knees for a very different damn reason.

Holy fuck, to feel him in my mouth, thick and long, his fingers in my hair. I'd always loved sex. Loved having it, loved reading about it. Which was why Eric being generally repulsed by anything beyond the basic shit, had been spectacularly hard. How many times can missionary be fun? I thought perhaps his taste would change over time, or that my desire might lessen with age. Neither had happened.

So, as thick fingers ran up the length of his torso to snag his shirt and yank it back into place, I forced myself to swallow. The men in books all melted for their women if she enjoyed blowing him, but... would Jameson?

"Why are you looking at me like that?"

His words snapped me out of it, mouth popping open, only for me to jam it shut, swallowing hard. "Sorry, I just got lost in my head."

His smirk insinuated he knew exactly where my head had been. Or at least which dangerous neighborhood she'd wandered into. When Jameson laid down on the mat mere feet from mine, he laced his hands behind his head, shifting exactly twice before going still.

"I suppose you're used to sleeping in all kinds of tough spots?" I said, needing to fill the void or cross the damn line. Unprepared for the latter, I landed on small talk. He shrugged his shoulders, not bothering to open his eyes.

"The mountain doesn't try to buck me into the upper bunk, so it's not so bad."

I laughed at that image before saying, "Definitely pictured you on top."

So, so slowly, he turned and opened his eyes to glare at me. "That so?"

Nodding and feigning innocent eyes, I explained, "I've always been afraid of a bunk bed collapsing on me."

He chuckled, shaking his head, not believing my bullshit for a moment. "Fuck, you like to get a man's heart rate up."

That wasn't actually what I'd wanted to get up, but sure, go off, man. Grinning, I turned to stare up at the glow of the tarp, forcing myself to bite my tongue and not vocalize every desperate thought in my head. My cheeks hurt. *Actually* ached like I'd bruised them smiling today.

"Goodnight, Noel," he rasped.

Exhaling in an impatient—bordering on desperate—huff, I said, "Night."

WHEN I WAS AROUND EIGHT, my parents decided gymnastics would be good for me. My pediatrician had suggested it to combat my clumsiness. Three nights a week, they drove me into the city to a cute purple gym that smelled like foam blocks, with tall ceilings and a Russian instructor who looked exactly like Keira Knightley in a bun and shimmering leggings. Try as I might, I could not get my body to cooperate with willingly diving towards the ground headfirst and trusting my hands to catch me.

It turns out back handsprings were easier than sleeping on a hard mat without layers in the freezing mountains beside a man I wanted to taste. Hell, I wanted to save a horse and ride Jameson until morning. I wanted him to destroy me for all other men, because he was just that kind of silent promise of absolute female devastation. If I could walk back across the beach by low tide, we'd done it wrong. That was how desperately I wanted to cross the damn gap between us.

Hours might have gone by before the cold won our battle and I shivered so intensely my muscles were cramping. I'd just started forcing down breaths as deeply as I could when plastic creaked behind me, and just as suddenly, his broad, solid arms snaked around my waist, pulling me against him. My ribs halted as his heat bled into me, soft belly curving around my ass. Oh. Dear. Fuck. Jameson Rhodes was a cuddler. Not only was he a cuddler, but his muscles were rock solid against my back, those thick legs tucking against mine, breath on my neck sending goosebumps down the length of my body.

"You okay?" he asked, voice so cracked with sleep it was adorable.

That was the cue that finally sent my lungs working. "Had a temporary encounter with oxygen deficiency. All good now."

He huffed a quiet laugh and then nuzzled into my neck. Momentarily frozen in disbelief, I swallowed, aware it was absolutely audible, and then tentatively wrapped my hands around his muscular arms. Humming contentedly, Jameson tightened his grip, snaking a thigh between mine and sending my heart into overdrive. To my utter delight, the man was a living, breathing space heater, his body warmth leaching into every inch of my skin like a godsend.

"You're freezing," he mumbled into my neck. Slowly, he rubbed a pattern up and down my arms, a sleepy attempt at friction through the sweatshirt. That didn't stop my core from heating, anticipation tightening the muscles as I breathed in his mouth-watering scent. Fuck, I wanted to drink him in. It was his abruptly halted movement that made me aware I was arching into him, ass pressed to his *very* firm groin, body melding into his touch as my head fell back onto his shoulder.

"*Noel,*" he growled, no longer so sleepy. The predatory edge in his voice sent goosebumps dancing down my skin. I simply shifted harder against him, intertwining our fingers where he'd snuck his arm beneath me. Grinding my ass down his erection, a soft whimper left my lips. "Noel," he warned again, but I didn't stop, instead turning over my shoulder to meet his gaze, where he'd just propped up on a forearm. I bit my lip, watching as he attempted to either ignite me or make sense of me with those hard, shadowed eyes—I was fine with either. Spontaneous combustion would be a welcome reprieve from the desire threatening to burst through my body. My desperate nipples were attempting to erect a two-tower circus tent through his loaned hoodie.

"Baby, don't start something you don't want me to finish."

"Who says I don't want you to finish?" I took the hand he'd settled over my chest and slid his palm down to my breast, his eyes closing as the air rushed from us both. My heart performed the drum solo of the century, and it took every ounce of focus to say, "That would kind of be the point, wouldn't it?"

"*Fuck*," he rasped, grinding against my ass as his hand flew to the hem of my shirt, diving beneath it as the other one looped up to grab my throat, guiding my face up so he could kiss up the side of my neck. Jameson's skin on my bare breast was fucking orgasmic. *Unreal* incredible. Melted butter on fresh-baked sourdough toast, triple layer chocolate cake in a raspberry drizzle, and the world's sauciest lasagna *incredible*. Every inch of my body was suddenly on alert, buzzing in an attempt to draw his attention next.

"If you say I can have you, I'm not going to be able to stop. I can't resist this anymore." He gave my breast a little squeeze, pinching the hard nipple between his fingers as he ground his thick erection against my ass again. I wanted to squeak in disbelief, wanted to melt against him entirely. It was a surprise when my mouth still formed coherent words.

"It's a damn good thing you don't have to, then."

Eyes darkening, Jameson claimed me, immediately dominating the kiss with his tongue, shifting his braced hand to support my head so he could devour me thoroughly. Like he'd known twisting at this angle was already uncomfortable.

Everything was burning. Churning and tightening. His hand abandoned its place on my breast, diving beneath the loose sweats and earning a low groan from his chest when he found me bare.

"Fuck me," He muttered, rubbing his palm over my freshly shaved, silky smooth sex. Because, whether or not I'd admit it aloud, I was actually prepared this time. "So damn soft. You bare for *me*, beautiful?" When I nodded against him, he blew out a heavy breath punctuated by five words that set my blood alight. "*Such* a good fucking girl."

Praise kink? Certainly hadn't realized I had one, but holy mother of god, that sure as hell activated it. His words had wet heat pooling faster than I could fathom, those rough fingers smoothly sliding through my slick center only to expertly circle back to my clit. Breath catching in my throat, he sighed as he stimulated that bundle of nerves, demolishing my body in a matter of seconds. Jameson Rhodes was the kind of man that would melt women and shamelessly return them to their loved ones in a liquid state contained in a damn mason jar. Or at least, that's how it felt as he worked me, expertly stimulating me with practiced motions before sliding a thick finger into my center, the knuckle of another finger playing against the tight ring of muscle behind it.

"*Goddamn* baby, I fucking knew it."

"What?" I breathed, the air coming out in a rush. *Dammit, shut up, Noel. Don't ask questions–Jameson is touching you. What else matters?*

"You're *perfect*. So wet for me." Free hand diving beneath the neckline of his loaned hoodie, he grabbed a breast, squeezing and tweaking as his mouth came down on mine—hard. Knuckle against my ass, a finger deep inside me, and his thumb applying pressure to my clit, Jameson ruled my fucking body. And he did it with one damn hand. Every synapse fired off, determined to bow to the conqueror of Noel-land. Trembling, panting, sweating, my head fell back against his chest, and he held me there, gliding his palm from my breast to wrap around my neck. The touch intensified every other sensation, blood thrumming.

Stars popped into my vision as the spring in my core tightened with his ruthless, demanding motions. Shifting his mouth to my ear, he whispered, "You going to come for me, Noel? Going to be my good girl and come all over my hand?"

Well, hello, Mr. Rhodes, pack me up and call me your plaything, because at this rate, I'm about to be putty in your palm. My brain hyper-fixated on one piece of that filthy sentence, doing internal backflips and hollering '*yahoo*' at the claiming praise. *His* good girl. Oh, god, I knew I shouldn't love the sound of that, but my entire body begged to differ. I *wanted* to be his. *Wanted* for him to want me like that. Beyond that, I wanted to please him. More desperately than I could even make sense of.

"Yes," I breathed, a throaty moan escaping as his movements intensified, fingers pinching and rolling my nipple until it almost hurt. But fuck, if it wasn't the most delicious kind of pain, sending fervent desire flooding through my veins. Jameson Rhodes was conducting a symphony of sensations across my skin, and he hadn't even pulled out his cock yet. What in the hell had I been missing all this time?

"Damn, Noel. You have me so worked up. If I let you come, will you return the favor, baby?" Whimpering, I nodded frantically, desperate for that promised release. Desperate to see how he wanted to be served. Fuck, I'd known he'd be good—let's be real, Jameson oozed sex-god levels of testosterone—but I hadn't realized the command he'd have over my body. The longer he worked, the harder the waves hit. Pleasure rocked through me, rolling in sync with his demanding movements. But every time sweet release glittered within my grasp, his motions would ease up, leaving me tiptoeing that edge before he'd nip or kiss or suck at my neck and resume his tireless ministrations.

When I thought I couldn't take it anymore, whimpering as I rolled my hips against him, he kissed up my jaw, and groaned, "I want this cunt *soaking* wet when I finally slide inside you. *Come for me*, Noel."

I did. *God*, I did. Maybe it was the expert curl of those thick fingers against my walls, or just the electrifying sensation of my name on his tongue after filthy words. Long and hard, he ripped wave after wave of agonizing release from me, a satisfied moan rumbling deep in his chest as my orgasm clamped around his fingers, arousal seeping down his hand. Darkness encroached on my vision, eyes rolling back as stars glittered in them. Too much. Too much, and not nearly enough. I needed *him*. Not that my brain could form a sentence as he ripped the last of my senses out of me.

Dear. *God*. What on earth was it about such a good man having such a filthy mouth that drop-kicked me right over the edge?

He didn't relent, didn't lessen the pressure or merciless rhythm until I went limp in his arms, coated in a thin sheen of sweat, and panting as my head lolled back onto his shoulder. Chuckling, he slowly slipped out of me, startling me breathless when he gave my pussy a little clap. Jameson stiffly rolled onto his back, pulling me tight against him as we caught our breath and he flexed his arousal-slicked hand, stretching it out. When I finally summoned the strength to look at him, stunning masculine satisfaction curved his lips, even his closed eyes somehow content.

"Thank you," I whisper-panted against his chest. When he just curled me tighter against him and kissed my crown, I shook my head. "Nobody has...ever put me first like that." His fingers halted where they'd been trailing up and down my arm. "*Jameson?*"

TWENTY-ONE

JAMESON

Anger threatened the reign arousal had on my body, vision blurring for a second as her words settled in. "What do you mean, beautiful? Nobody's let you come first?"

"Hell, nobody has made me come that hard." If it could have, my ego would have purred. "Lost my vision for a second there."

Satisfaction was a living entity in my blood, but my mind was still stuck on what she'd said before. "Well, I can't say I'm mad about that. They took care of you, though?" Her shrug was fucking answer enough.

"I've gotten pretty handy at taking care of myself," she chirped, like there wasn't anything wrong with that statement.

I wanted to puke and knock Eric's teeth in all at once. If I hadn't already known what a piece of shit he was, that would have had me asking questions. Selfish lovers were poor excuses for men. "Not anymore, baby. The only time I want you taking care of yourself is if I'm *watching,* or out at sea." When it felt like she was about to protest, I clamped my hand back around her pussy, applying just enough pressure to her clit to steal her breath again. "As long as we're doing this, your pleasure belongs to me. Do you understand? If you're hungry, baby, it's not your job to give yourself what you need. That's on me."

"Jame—"

Her protest turned into a whimper of pleasure as I shifted against her, dipping my finger back inside her hot, slick entrance. "Lazy lovers piss me off. It's not hard to make your body sing. And

I've wanted to show you pleasure like this since you stepped on my island."

When my movements ceased, she gave a breathy little laugh. "Had a funny way of showing it to start with."

"Didn't say I *wanted* to want you."

"How charming," she muttered, but I held her tighter when she inched away.

"Does it matter? I can't fucking fight this anymore, baby. You've been teasing me with those damn scrappy little tops for weeks."

"Thought you hated them."

"I hate that anyone else gets to think about you like this when you're wearing them."

She chuckled softly. "Territorial bastard, are you?"

I grinned, pressing against her clit and loving the way she melted against me. Willingly at my mercy. Knew that sharp tongue would have an off switch somewhere. "I know *exactly* who I'm holding. If we're doing this, it's just us, baby. I can't half-ass anything."

"Full asses only," she panted, grinding her backside into me as I chuckled.

"I like the sound of that," I said, lacing the words with every ounce of need she'd built into me as I dipped two fingers back into her, her body writhing against mine.

"Oh, sweet fuck," she squeaked, her inability to draw a full breath satisfying every primal part of my body.

Slipping my fingers out and dragging her arousal over the tight rim of her asshole, I promised, "It would be." Airless humor danced from her lips, and a satisfied smile inched across my face. The static crackle of her nerves made my chest ache. We all like to play pretend like we're civilized, somehow superior creatures, when in reality, all we are are animals. Just as ravenous as the next.

"As tempting as that is," I drawled, dragging my hand back until I could palm her perfect little ass. "I've been dreaming about your smart mouth wrapped around my dick for fucking *weeks*."

Somehow her hard inhale sounded happy, but then she was turning in my arms, eyes sparkling. My palm slid around to her ass, and I grabbed a perfect, chilly handful, pulling her tighter against me as her gaze flicked between my eyes. And then she was kissing me. Her kisses were always gentler than mine, subtle need begging for my attention—and judging by the effect my words had, my approval —as she nipped and sucked, tongue coasting along the rim of my bottom lip. When Noel pulled away, I had to swallow my disappointment, but my loss was short-lived as she positioned herself above me, straddling my hips.

"You wanna ride me, baby?"

"Hell yes," she breathed, chest still heaving as her eyes scraped over me. Finally, the evaluation was shameless, like she'd finally given herself permission to want this. Hell, had I? Thoughts for a different time, as her smile gave way to breathy words. "But first, I promised to return the favor."

With her straddling me, my hoodie skimming her thighs, I no longer had the patience. Yeah, she'd feel fantastic, but the need to seat myself inside her, to show her what it felt like to be mine, demanded I *move*. Take control of the situation. Buzzing palms slipping beneath the hoodie to grip her waist, I promised, "Your wet cunt sliding down my cock would certainly get the job done."

She grinned, the expression bashful as she bit that lower lip, trying to hide her satisfaction. Like nobody had talked to her that way before. I knew exactly what kind of books she sold in that store, and there was no way my words were new to her.

Still, Noel smirked as she drawled, "Such a dirty mouth, Mr. Rhodes."

"Did I *offend* you?" She shook her head, and I jerked my chin, urging her to do something. *Anything*. Because the anticipation was driving me to madness, palms aching, cock throbbing. "Didn't think so."

With a coy smile on her face, Noel worked her way down my body, hands tearing my shirt up so she could scrape her nails over my abs. I hissed as red lines sprung to life, but then she was looping her fingers in my pants and boxers in one go, sliding them down. I lifted my hips up so she could shimmy them over my ass and down my thighs. When my heavy cock bobbed free, her breath hitched, eyes flashing with what I could only call hunger. She glanced at my face as if looking for approval. With a slight nod of my chin, she slid down my legs and wrapped her hand around my dick, fingers not quite connecting around the girth.

A groan rumbled in my chest. Of course, her touch was fucking fire. When she closed her mouth down over the head of my cock, it took every ounce of control not to blow my load right then and there. "*Fuuuuck*, baby."

Grinding my teeth, I shifted against the mat, hands scrambling to tangle in something but coming to her curls instead, wrapping them around a fist. She moaned. The goddess, with my cock edging towards her throat, *moaned* as I tightened my grip, and *fuck. Me.* The sound threatened to snap my restraint. Movements as harsh and demanding as mine had been, Noel took me into her throat until I felt the muscles tighten. She hummed as tears rimmed her eyes, bobbing smoothly down the length. I loosened my fist and threaded my fingers into those curls I loved so damn much, easing her back a bit. Something primal flashed in her eyes as she fought my hold, bobbing up and down, using her hand to grip the base and keep from choking. She almost seemed to enjoy pushing her limits. Relaxing against the mat, I soaked up each sexy slide and demanding suck, the sensation of her tongue over my slit, and I don't know what the hell she did next, but the pressure was *unbelievable.* A familiar tug pulled at my spine and I grabbed either side of her face, pulling her free with a little pop.

Panting, skin coated in a thin layer of sweat, I pulled her up to me, tasting the salt of my pre-cum on her lips. "*Fuuuck,* baby," I breathed against her. A satisfied breath rushed from her, and then I was shifting, wrapping my hands around her torso and lowering her onto the mat so I could tear those damn sweats off. She giggled as I slipped her feet free, but the sound cut off with a gasp when I spread her wide and dove in for my feast. Fingers tangled in my hair, Noel panted my name and I savored the sound of it as I licked straight up her center, stealing the traces of her release.

"Holy shit, holy shit, *holy shit,*" she breathed, tightening her hold on me.

"Fuck me, you taste so good." Her moan was answer enough as I slid a finger inside her, licking and sucking, nipping at her clit, my composure teetering as she pressed herself into my mouth. "That's right, baby, take what you want."

"You," she finally gasped. "Jameson, I need *you!*"

Music to my damn ears. Sliding my knees between her thighs, I sat up, frantically looking around and snatching my jeans from the ground so I could fish a condom out of my wallet.

"Such a good little Boy Scout," she teased as I pulled the foil wrapper free.

"Put it on me," I ordered, ignoring the bait and handing her the rubber. Her mouth popped open, eyes flashing with something I couldn't place. She did, immediately leaning up to sheath my dick inside it. The moment she'd rolled it up to the base, her hand slid down around to cup my balls, running her fingers along the backside. I groaned as the heat of her sent a wave of need crashing against me.

If I didn't get her wrapped around me, I was likely to implode. "Hell, baby."

A pleased little laugh slipped through her lips, and then I tore my hoodie from her frame, hocking it aside before laying her on her back. Her red curls fanned out around her shoulders as those gorgeous brown pools found my eyes.

"You're fucking exquisite," I growled, eyes scraping over her long, tight ribcage and pale pink nipples. At war with myself, it took a beat to debate between sucking one in my mouth or getting inside her, but the jerk of my cock decided for me. Bracing her feet against my shoulders, I barked, "Hold on to me." She did. Such a good fucking girl. She pushed her heels against my upper chest, hands wrapping around my wrists where I was clutching her thighs, pulling me into her. I lined myself up without dropping my hold on her delicious, lean legs, and slowly sunk into her, one glorious inch at a time, until my balls met her perky ass.

Her lungs filled with a rush of air, swollen lips parting on a desperate cry. "*Jameson!*"

I'd never fucked in the woods. Never been so far out of town, there wasn't a chance of anybody hearing. There was something unbelievable about it being just us. Just the two of us and the mountain as she cried my name for the heavens to hear.

Just like I'd promised her she would.

"Holy shit–" she sucked down air "–*so* full." Noel took every damn inch like she was made for me.

"Oh, fuck," I panted as I slowly shifted, already fighting the familiar tightening in my balls. "You take me so good, baby." *Like hell* was I not going to give my Noel one hell of a show. But it might require my entire lineup of emergency distractions—baseball, hockey, drought, famine. Anything to not fixate on the red-headed goddess, arching in a soundless scream as her head fell back. The column of her neck worked as she swallowed, then gasped. Perky nipples peaked in the chill air as her legs trembled. *Goddamn*, I needed to suck on one of those.

We'd been climbing towards this peak from the moment she'd stepped foot on the island. From the moment I'd pulled into the Mistyvale harbor and found her in the Grizzly Grind. Every chaste caress, every joke, every snarky remark on both our parts had built toward this moment. *This moment* as her body surrendered, wrapping tighter and tighter around me, her beautiful bare breasts heaving as she tried to suck down breath between my desperate thrusts. I couldn't get deep enough. Couldn't join her hard enough. With each snap of my hips, her hot, tight, soaked channel threatened to milk me for every ounce of need I'd built up since before I'd seen her through that window. *My* hot, tight, soaked channel. Because *she* was mine. I'd known it. Known it, and fought it like my life depended on it. Known it, and been an absolute prick because I didn't fucking want to.

I'd make it up to her. Spend my life making her cry my name just like this, my skin smarting where her nails threatened to break it. Make sure she was safe and provided for, and chasing whatever adorable, inevitably unhinged, brilliant dream her gorgeous heart could concoct. Watching her writhe beneath me, coming undone at my touch. Those precious pink lips parted on a desperate gasp and my cock twitched as I remembered exactly what they'd just felt like. What she'd *looked* like, blinking up at me through tears, like she desperately wanted to suck me until I poured down her throat. A man could get used to that.

The yank on my spine and telltale tightening in my balls had me gritting my teeth. I groaned, "I'm *close*, baby."

"Me too," she whimpered as she met my thrust, eyes frantic before they slammed closed again.

"You are so fucking beautiful. I've wanted you since I *saw* you."

"Good, now shut up and fuck me."

I chuckled darkly, breathing, "Yes, ma'am," as I did just that. Jack hammering into her, I gave her everything I had, breathing as desperate and demanding as my movements, skin slicked with sweat.

"More," she begged, one hand scrambling for purchase as the other snaked between us. I swatted her hand away, taking up a steady rhythm against her clit. The moment my fingers applied pressure, she cried, "*Oh shit*, Jameson!"

"That's right, baby. Let go. Give it to me."

"*Oh god*," she cried.

"*Give it to me, baby.*"

"Please!" The sound of her begging was enough to drive me mad.

My movements grew more urgent, thrusts erratic as I deepened them, trying to hit that elusive spot. "Come all over my cock," I gritted through my teeth, barely holding back my release. My abs flexed tight with every single snap of my hips, arms shaking with the effort as I demanded every slick ounce of her pleasure. Tight breasts bouncing with each movement, I studied the desperate lines of her taut muscles, her adorable little face. The perfect O of her lips.

"Come for me, baby." When Noel's orgasm clamped down, her head thrown back in a cry of ecstasy and nails digging into my arms where she held me, I followed her right the hell over the edge, shouting her name for the mountain to hear.

Half laying over her and half on the chilled mat, we caught our breath, sucking down desperate gulps as our smiles filled the space. Arm hanging heavy across her, she gently stroked lines up and down my sweaty back, and I inhaled the sexed-up scent of her. Fuck, she was mouth-watering. Could I ever get enough? Her breathless voice cut my train of thought, a smile lacing every syllable.

"Well...that's one way to warm a girl up."

I WOKE up with the heavy warmth of Noel's sleeping body draped over mine. Heaven. She'd brought me heaven on top of the world. We'd had a marathon of sex last night, trading orgasms like legal tender. A sex-a-thon, if you will. I could still taste her cum on my lips, smell us in the air, intertwining with her lemon shampoo and the spruce of the chilled mountain. The tickle of her curls across my chest made me smile, and for a moment, I just soaked her in, wishing we could stay up here forever, just the two of us away from the world. But the tide wouldn't wait for us, so, with a sigh, I squeezed her tight, tucked her in beneath my hoody, then got dressed and snuck outside to make breakfast.

By the time Noel emerged, glorious sex hair in a halo around her pretty little face, I'd poured steaming cups of coffee into the camping tins, had the fire happily flickering, and bacon and eggs set on tin plates beside bread and butter. Her smile was so adorable it threatened to destroy me. We cuddled up on the mountaintop for as long as I could practically justify before breaking down camp in a rush and heading back to the trail.

"WAIT, so what's this stop for?" She demanded as we pulled in outside my cousin Jake's house. Jake fished too, but he also ran the local print shop and made all the local jerseys and team swag.

"Gotta pick up the football jerseys."

"Because...you coach high school football."

"Stop acting so surprised."

Her giggle was infectious, and I bit my tongue to keep from grinning like a moron. She'd made me repeat myself a dozen times when my position came up during a story on our mountain.

"Who coaches when you're gone?"

"Broderick."

"And if *he's* gone?" Broderick was getting ready to leave for a conference in Nevada, and I was kinda pleased she'd noted it. Was obviously comfortable with my friends.

"Anthony, the history teacher, subs on the rare occasion both of us are out of town."

"Wow."

Shaking my head, I leaned for the door, hopping out of the truck, and making a beeline for Jake's garage. He was already expecting us, so by the second knock, he'd flung the door open, arms wide for a hug. Jake and Charlie both had sandy blonde hair, but the same steel-blue eyes as our dads. His complexion leaned more towards olive than ours, which we'd always been a bit jealous of. I hugged him back before turning and introducing him to Noel.

"Wow, it's nice to finally meet you. Glad James didn't make you up."

"Flesh and blood, I'm afraid," she said, grinning as she rocked on her heels with anxiety.

"Well, I'm sorry to say I only have a few minutes, and then I gotta head out for boat prep, just like James."

"You're on the *Rhodes Away* too?"

Jake and I chuckled, exchanging knowing glances. "Uh, for all our sakes, it's best if we keep family and business separate. Uncle Milo and I don't always communicate well." That was an understatement. They loved each other to death on solid land but might beat each other to death at sea. It was the weirdest paradox, deeply rooted in a clash of dominant egos.

"Fair enough," she said, smiling. No questions asked.

"You gonna swing by and see Sterling and Junebug?" I asked. Jake was the coolest uncle on the planet—Charlie's kids told me all the time. They were five and nine, and loved very few things more than their time at the beach with their uncles or sneaky ride-alongs in their dad's cruiser.

"We did breakfast this morning."

"Good," I said, nodding. "I'll get my hugs before we head out."

"Good luck this run."

"You too, man."

Jake slid over three enormous boxes. Noel and I hefted out the first two, but as icy rain was pelting down, I insisted she stay warm and cozy inside the truck cab. When I made it back to him, he gave me a long whistle.

"Damn. You weren't exaggerating. She's a looker."

"A fucking siren is what she is."

"She doing okay? Charlie told me about Friday night."

"Yeah," I said, realizing through all our chats on our hike and on the mountaintop, she hadn't said shit about Eric and what went down at the Birch Barrel. I selfishly hadn't wanted to darken our day by bringing it up. "She'll be alright. Better once we can get this fucker out of her life."

"He'll do everything he can, you know?"

"Yeah. I do." Charlie was a damn good man, and a damn good cop, to boot. There's a sentence I'd never thought I'd say. But if anybody deserved to shine their Sheriff's badge, it was Charlie Rhodes. If anybody could come up with a solution to keep her safe and push it through court, it was him. We hugged before I snatched the last box and headed back for the truck.

Our next stop was the supply store, grabbing groceries and a few tools for me to pack back onto the boat. Noel insisted on coming with me, since she worked on the harbor anyway. It wasn't until I was dropping her off at Grizzly Grind that I realized I might not see her again before I left, and my stomach took a bloody nosedive. I'd never wanted to bail on a season as much as I did now. Maybe Rhyett was right. Because the idea of having to reenact walking her up to the door and holding her against my chest, trying to memorize the feel of her body against mine and the scent of her hair, like I could take a part of her with me onto the water, was terrifying. How had Dad done it all those years?

"Will you be back this week?" She asked hopefully, sneaking onto her tiptoes to steal another kiss as my blood thrummed for more. One night was not enough. I needed this woman like I'd needed the sea for the last eighteen years. Only, the idea of not coming home to her made me sick. What the hell was happening to me?

I forced my shoulder to shrug. "Could be three days, could be twelve. We don't really know until we get out there."

"Damn."

"That sums it up."

"You good sticking to the plan?" We'd talked through all our precautions. She had Charlie on speed dial, and Broderick, El, and

Max were all planning to stay at the house again while I was gone. Hopefully, Charlie and Bells could run Eric out of town in the meantime. She sighed, jaw tight for a second before she nodded.

"Yeah. I'm just…I'm going to miss you, you big grouch."

Chuckling, I rested my forehead against hers. "Thanks for running boring errands with me."

"Thanks for warming me up."

Grin broadening, I leaned forward to nip at her neck, loving the way she giggled and tried to flee until I snatched her up. Noel fit me perfectly. My palm easily encompassed her waist, the ivory globes of her breasts were just enough for a handful, and that ass. God, just the thought of it had me wanting to eat her out right there on the damn sidewalk. She was turning me into a psycho-exhibitionist. Because regular exhibitionists had rules and shit.

Kissing her deeply, I savored her scent, the give of her lips beneath my own. "You can expect a repeat as soon as I'm off the damn boat."

"I'll hold you to that."

Goodbyes were awful. There was nothing *good* about them. Swallowing hard, I nodded, leaning down to give her one last long kiss before turning for my truck and pulling away from the curb. I tried not to look back at her as I flipped a U-turn back into town, but my eyes refused to cooperate. Chest constricting, I recoiled from the mirror because…she looked like she was crying. And the idea of that might very well kill me.

TWENTY-TWO

NOEL

"What in God's name is in the water up there?" Brex said, eyes wide.

Giggling, I dabbed the blending sponge across my face, turning my attention back to the mirror as Vallie let out a low whistle on my phone screen. I'd just filled the girls in on the explosive, life-altering experience that was Jameson Rhodes' definition of 'camping'.

"What do you mean?" I asked, blending in the concealer beneath my eyes. The upside to a half-a-dozen orgasms with the hottest man on the island was the contented way my muscles were all relaxed. The downside—aside from the delicious ache in my core—was we'd gotten very little in the way of sleep last night. And it showed.

"I mean..." Her hesitation pulled my attention back to where I'd rigged a stand for my phone on top of a tampon box and the mirror. "Rhyett is an ass man, too. And the *praise*?"

"Oh, sweet baby cheeses," I said, melting. "He got all feral and possessive. I've never been someone's *good girl* before. I wasn't mad about it."

"Hell, the first time Rhyett said that, I thought I'd die."

"What is it about these men?!"

Josie released a pained little whimper, collapsing into her hands to cover her face. "*Ugh*, you two, I'm going to die single, aren't I?" The image of her late husband flashed in my eyes, but before the pain of Blaze's absence could rock me too deeply, she mumbled, "Can you save me one of those brothers? I'm not picky."

I cackled before snapping my mouth shut and clapping my hands over it. Val was still snickering as Brex waggled her brows and asked, "Just, you know, *vaguely* 'one of them'?"

"Oh, shut up," Josie said, giggling as her cheeks pinked. Blaze might have started her football obsession, but it had grown to be its own monster. The irony of her tracking stats for none other than Paxton freaking Rhodes for years before Rhyett wandered into The Three Leaf would never get old.

"Josie and Paxton, sitting in a tree—" I teased, her eye roll transforming my childlike antics into another peal of laughter. My cheeks were aching, just getting to see them all again. There'd never been a time I was this grateful for technology.

"*Please.* I'm sure half of Chicago has flung themselves at his feet."

"Nothing like experience to perfect a skill set," I said, trying to swallow my giggles. Jos just wrinkled her nose, but her blush was totally worth it.

"I wonder if all the Rhodes brothers are about the peaches," Vallie contemplated. She was only half watching us, the majority of her attention on her laptop as she typed away. She looked beautiful as always, her goddess braids half spun back into a messy bun, a crimson top popping against her warm sepia skin, and a black blazer adding just the perfect dash of professional. Personally, I'd probably liquify if I walked in and had to argue my case against a woman like that.

"Not exactly a tasteful way to ask that," Josie said, choking on her laugh right as I snickered.

"Why yes, fake-boyfriend I actually kinda *really* like. Do all your brothers indulge in ravenous, decadent sex?"

Cackling, Brex just shook her head, and I went back to blending my foundation as she said, "That just sounds like you're looking for an orgy."

"I mean, if you were gonna indulge in your darkest fantasies, that gene pool would be the one to do it in." Val's smirk was all trouble, but then she scowled at her laptop. "Love you guys, but I gotta go. Just had a deposition move up, and I gotta pick up some documents to get ready."

"Wait, don't they have to give you notice?"

She slammed the laptop closed and bent to slide it into her backpack. "Not Judge Carson. Bastard."

"Good luck," Josie chirped, tucking a frizzy, dark curl behind her ear.

"Yeah, good luck!" I echoed.

"You keep us all posted on the lumberjack," Vallie ordered.

Rolling my eyes at the description, I flashed her a smile before chirping, "Love you."

They all echoed it back before Vallie's screen vanished, the images rearranging to show me Josie and Brex. "So, what's going on with you two? Back door play aside."

Wrinkling her nose, Josie shook her head. "None of that for me. It's still the great drought of the twenty-first century. Brex, how are you feeling?"

"Good, actually! Supposedly, morning sickness can hit at any time during the first trimester, but so far, it's been pretty easy, all things considered."

"Good, babe, I'm so glad."

"Yeah," I added lamely, swapping my sponge for mascara. Returning my eyes to the mirror, I asked, "Any ideas on names?"

"No, we want to wait until we know what we're having."

"You mean *you* want to wait until *you* know what you're having," I corrected, earning a snort of amusement from Josie and a scowl so palpable I felt it through the screen from Brex. Glancing in her direction, I snickered when I confirmed what I already knew.

"Yeah, 'cause Rhy is cool as a cucumber," Josie added.

"Fine. Yes. *I* want to know what we're having before *I* fall in love with a name." Rhyett called for her right then, Royal barking enthusiastically enough that it had to be time for—"Hey, guys, Rhy just got home and it's time to walk the dog, but I'll check in later, okay?"

"Love you," Josie and I said in unison, grinning as Brex did the same. A pang of jealousy twisted in my stomach as I realized how much I missed my cat, Chloe. I knew they were taking good care of her, but her sweet little face flashed in my eyes and I cursed the fact that I had to swallow back tears. Would it be pathetic to video chat with my cat? Maybe. Was I beyond asking? Nope.

Brex vanished a beat later, leaving me and Jos hanging out as I lined my brows. "So, how are the kids?" I asked, missing their sweet faces something fierce. I'd never been away from them for this long— had been there when Jos got married, when they brought Gemma home for the first time. Hell, I'd been at the hospital with her for her delivery with Kyler. But I'd specifically avoided any kind of travel after Blaze died in the line of duty, leaving Jos a single mama with a folded flag encased in her apartment where her best friend *should* be. This was the longest I'd been away from her, too.

"Gem's getting big—just finished spring soccer, which she loved—and is mostly excited to start school this fall. Kyler is learning his alphabet, and despite mommy's adamant attempts, still prefers peeing in my potted plants to the toilet."

Chuckling, heart aching, I shook my head. "Miss you, babe."

"You too. *So* much. Eric hasn't caused any more trouble?"

I winced, piling all my cosmetics back in the case as a sigh leaked from my ribs. "He's being...odd. Settling in like he's here to fucking stay. But, no. It's almost worse, you know?"

"Because you're waiting on pins and needles?"

"Exactly."

"Always wondering what the hell he's about to do."

"Yes!"

"Effectively, he has you walking on eggshells despite not being with him, the sneaky fucker."

"My sentiments as well. On that note...are you still in touch with Shamra?"

Mouth popping open, Josie furrowed her brow, and I hated myself for asking this of her. But with Eric lurking, I needed to formulate a plan—and a backup plan, for that matter—in case he decided to take this whole situation nuclear. Shamra was the friend Blaze had died for. His best friend's little sister was a badass in her own right. We'd all met her a few dozen times at barbeques and gatherings, then spent evenings laughing, leading up to the wedding.

Blaze saw the threat before she did, and those instincts took over before she could react. At least, that's how the other survivors told his story.

"Um..." she cleared her throat. "She's still Kyler and Gemma's godmother, so *yeah*, we see her. That came out of nowhere. Why are you asking?"

"I have...an idea on getting Eric out of the picture, but I don't really want to talk about it."

"Plausible deniability?"

"Something like that," I admitted with a grimace, the wince mirrored back at me on her features. "Can you please send me her number? I want to run an idea by her." The text popped up above our video chat a heartbeat after she grabbed her phone. "Thanks!"

"What's Jameson think?" She asked before yawning. It might

have been mid-afternoon for me, but it was getting late on her side of the country.

"I don't really talk to him about all of it."

"Why the hell not?" She scowled at me, the confusion wrinkling her brow.

"I'm just trying to focus on the good stuff, you know? I can't change him, so I'm just putting my energy into what I have control of. Which is currently my work and rekindling the old Noel. A sexual awakening is just an unexpected benefit."

"Look, babe." Josie had always been the sweetest, most gentle-hearted of our friends from college. Where Brex got hyper-sensitive, and Vallie could be unintentionally condescending with an IQ that likely lapped mine in elementary school, Josie...got it. Got *life*. The tough shit. Being a widow in her twenties, with two kids depending on her to keep a roof over their heads and food in their bellies, only softened her heart more. It was only the fact that it was *her* speaking that kept my defenses low. "I'm all for not giving him any more of your *energy* or power or what have you. And by all means, enjoy the ever-loving hell out of a sexy man who looks at you like a snack. However, you also need to offload some of that weight on your shoulders. And I'd bet he'd carry it with you. Good men need to be needed."

"He's been supportive. Hell, they all are."

"Obviously."

"I have things under control." Okay, that was laughable. There was nothing about any of this that felt like it was under my control.

"Just...think about it. He's gone out of his way to take you on, to protect you, to make sure you feel safe. Men don't extend effort if they don't care. Remember when I dated Garret?"

Ugh. Men suck. What kind of idiot took so much as one look at a woman like Josie and didn't see how freaking undeniably brilliant she was? Garret made her work way too hard for way too little, in my not-so-humble opinion. After Blaze, none of us would tolerate that shit for a heartbeat.

"Douche canoe. Yeah. I remember."

"You told me that *if he wanted to*, he fucking would. Not to waste my time on a man who wouldn't invest his time in me. I'm paying that forward right now."

"Jos, it's all *fake*."

"Bull. Nothing about any of this sounds fake."

My throat worked to swallow. Because she was right. Nothing

about Jameson felt fake when we were together. Not the way he protected me, not the way he spoke or touched or made sure I was safe and *satisfied*. Not the obnoxiously dangerous, glowy ache in my chest as I thought about him. Forcing a smile onto my face, I teased, "I mean, the orgasms certainly weren't."

"*Yes, yes,* I'm thrilled for you, despite the fact that I'm withering on the vine and out of batteries. Stop deflecting. *Maybe* the pretense of why he drug you into his house was fabricated to nullify an immediate threat to the peace. But you two had chemistry before Eric showed up."

"If by 'chemistry' you mean 'drove each other crazy'?"

Nonplussed, she rolled her round brown eyes, her deadpan telling me she didn't find me particularly cute today. "The dance between desire and detestation is delicate. You two tangoed into lust, at the very least, a long time ago."

"Can you blame me?"

"Absolutely not. The genes in that family are fucking ridiculous. But, Noel. Can you listen to me for a minute? Seriously. I know humor is your defense mechanism of choice, but just hear me out." When I just swallowed, eyes locked on the tiny Josie balanced on a tampon box on my counter, she continued. "Jameson is investing *his time* in *you*. Hell, he's investing his friends' and family's time in you. He does it because *he wants to.*"

"Hero complex," I mumbled softly, but my throat felt suddenly swollen.

"Maybe. But maybe you've forgotten what it feels like to have someone value you above their own interests. Maybe it's time you remember what that looks like."

JOSIE'S WORDS played on an endless loop that could rival the *It's a Small World* song, so I opted to walk to the main house for Rhodes family dinner rather than drive over. Giving myself a minute to clear my head. The guys lived in a small subdivision about two blocks away from their parents, the stretch of town connected by a curving black sand beach. It was that rocky coastline my soul craved. The beaches in Mistyvale didn't deliver the same sense of serenity as those I'd grown up on, but something about salt and sea seemed to soothe my nerves, even if it was freezing and vaguely damp, even when the sun came out. The surrounding woods glowed gold and green as the evening sun glittered through the damp branches. Countless black stones crunched under my boots as the waves softly lapped against the island, but my eyes caught on the two lone figures about a hundred yards down the bay.

Awareness tingled in my limbs, and anticipation wound tight in my center before I realized why her words finally faded. *Jameson.* Some sense of him brought a smile to my face as I closed the distance, my heart flipping as I realized he was still on the island. He knelt beside a little boy wearing hunters' orange rain gear, with dark black hair, their hands sifting through the rocky sand. A gray beanie hugged over that hair I'd luxuriated in all morning. A rain slicker tugged tight over his broad shoulders. When I was about thirty yards out, Jameson paused, catching me in his periphery and offering a crooked, sexy smile before refocusing on the little guy beside him. As I got closer, I realized I'd seen him once before, balancing on Axel's lap at Brex and Rhyett's reception dinner. The pieces clicked together as he smiled up at Jameson, a familiar dimple in his cheek just below those trademark Rhodes gray-blues.

Hell, if I didn't know better, he could have passed for Jameson's. That thought brought an unwelcome rush of green to my vision and I swallowed it down, watching as preciously chubby little cherub fingers dropped stones into Jameson's awaiting hand. My lungs stumbled over a breath. Not stones—*sea glass.* They were sifting around for sea glass. Hedging another few steps in, I spotted teals and ambers, greens and pinks, all collecting together, carefully cherished like precious gems in his broad palm. My mind spun with a sensation like a caffeine rush as it hit me with the image of my bedside table adorned with an enormous jar full of them. Had he found some of those with him?

"Hi," the little guy chirped. "*I know you!* You're—uh, you're, *uh...*"

"Sterling, this is my friend, Noel." Jameson stood as he introduced us, straightening to his full, glorious height as warmth bloomed in my chest. "Red, meet Charlie's youngest, Sterling."

I bent to shake Sterling's adorably outstretched hand at his eye level. "It's very nice to meet you."

"You're sisters with Auntie Brex!?"

I giggled, squatting down as Jameson ruffled his shiny black hair. "Yeah, you could say that."

"Well, are you, or *aren't you*? Because that's what daddy said. He said you and Brex were sisters, and that's why you gave her to Unca' Rhyett."

I flicked my gaze up to Jameson, whose lips were curled in gentle amusement, before meeting those little gray eyes again. They weren't as blue as the Rhodes siblings, a sprinkling of amber pulling him toward hazel, although the uncanny resemblance remained. "Yes, I would say we're sisters. In every way that counts."

"What's that mean?"

Kicking myself for not just saying yes, and leaving it be, I glanced again to that gentle smile and back. Jameson seemed equally intrigued about where I was going with this and amused with my predicament.

"Well, we grew up together, but we're not *technically* blood sisters. But she's been my best friend for as long as I can remember, and we love each other very much. Sometimes more than I love my own siblings, if I'm honest."

Jameson spoke up, offering, "You know how Uncle Broderick *isn't technically* your daddy's brother, bud?"

"Yeah." His nod was reserved, eyes serious as he looked between the two of us expectantly. Jameson soldiered right along.

"He's still your uncle, right?"

"Yeah."

"Uncle Broderick is family we *chose* a long time ago, buddy, just like Uncle Max and Auntie Bells."

Sterling narrowed those gray eyes on me for a moment before seeming satisfied. "You wanna see a starfish!?" He blurted out, turning before he had his answer. Chuckling, we watched him bound off down the beach. Jameson eyed me for a minute, warmth seeping from the expression before following in his tiny footsteps. Wordlessly, he held out his free hand in my direction, my heart faltering as I stepped up to accept the offering.

Warm and rough, tiny flecks of black sand clinging to thick fingers, his calloused palm melded around mine as we crunched our way after Sterling. When he said nothing, I asked, "How old is he?"

"Five."

"You're just hanging with him?"

"Yeah," he said, voice soft but matter-of-fact.

"I thought you guys were heading out on the water today?"

"Later."

"You happy to see me?"

"Course."

I shook my head, a smirk stretching up my cheeks. "You've reverted to monosyllabic conversations, I see?"

A tug on my hand punctuated his soft chuckle, followed by another when I didn't immediately heed it. Before I could even steady myself, he'd intertwined our arms behind my back, his free hand sliding up to spear through my hair, lips coming down on mine with enough intensity to rob every scrap of oxygen from my bloodstream.

When he traced my bottom lip, I opened for him, and Jameson swooped in, not hesitating to deepen the kiss. Heat spread through my body, desperate to taste every inch of this man, to lick up the hard lines of his abs, to memorize the sweat-slicked pattern of his tattoos beneath my fingers. At last, remembering how to breathe, I soaked up his glorious musk and wished more than anything I could have more.

A million and one questions buzzed through my brain. *How long were they in the harbor for? When was he going to be back? Why had they stayed?* Did his knees feel as vulnerable to collapse as mine did, or could he stabilize us both? Judging by the way he slid his palm down the length of my back to cup my ass, he must've been more stable than I was.

"Found one!!" a little voice declared, cutting off our wordless reunion. Blinking and a bit disoriented, I looked around when Jameson pulled back, satisfaction written over the subtle lines of a smile. Sterling grinned up at us, unphased by our embrace. I couldn't decide if I loved that or hated it. Did he just see enough love in his life to think little of it, or was he just used to Uncle Jameson sucking face? Should I care either way, so long as it was currently mine he wanted to taste?

This didn't mean anything. *Couldn't* mean anything. It was supposed to be temporary. But nothing about his hand on my ass, or the possessive way he tucked me into his side, felt temporary. Nothing in that *damn kiss* felt temporary. Nothing in the way my soul seemed to reach for him did, either. Insane. This was insane. One night in a tent, and my thoughts were all a muddled mess of lust and...nope. Not going there.

Clearing my throat and my thoughts, I smacked on my best attempt at a smile.

"Wow!" I said, mustering every ounce of remaining espresso in my veins to scrounge up some enthusiasm as Sterling showed off an enormous pale pink starfish, at least the size of Jameson's hand. A high-pitched whistle brought all three of us to attention, and I spotted Axel perched on the top step of the staircase to the Rhodes' house. He waved us over before turning back and heading inside.

"Dinner time," Sterling said before sprinting for the small, moss-coated cliff face. I was about to follow in his wake, mind spinning with that greeting, when Jameson tugged my hip against his. Holy shit, that smolder could turn me molten hot in point-four seconds or fewer. Those previous million questions threatened the control I had on my lips, but only one snuck through.

"What are we doing, Jameson? There's nobody here."

"There was nobody on the summit, either." Thank God for that, because I think I screamed his name until my voice gave out. That panty-melting smirk spread over his face, like he was reminiscing, too. *That was so you'd know it wasn't for the fucking show.* His snarled words after he'd decimated my logic in his foyer reverberated in my skull, my emotions a mess of uncertainty and messed up desire.

"So...?" I hedged nervously.

"I told you before."

"You're going to have to expand for me." When his lips came down on mine again, I kissed him back for all of a heartbeat before laughing against him. "Well, I *know* you can do *that.*"

Forehead resting against mine, Jameson sighed. Low and hungry, he softly said, "Of course, I'm happy to see you, Skittles. I'm just... grappling with how to do this."

"*Fake-date* me? I told you this would never work. It never works. And sex just makes everything confusing. At no point in history, fictional or otherwise, has a fake-dating relationship ever—"

My words were silenced with a bruising kiss, his hands gripping my body, sliding up to cup my face before he let out a breath against my lips. "Can you just—give me a minute? I don't do this touchy-feely shit, okay?"

Trying and failing to resist the urge to laugh, I earned a crisp clap to my ass, followed by an endearing squeeze as he grinned at me. He nipped kisses up my neckline, making me burst into laughter, and arch away from him only to find myself trapped in the cage of his arms. As he buried his face against my neck, I couldn't say I was particularly mad about it. Beyond the demanding draw to Jameson, there was a kind of...security that cocooned me when I was with him. A girl should feel safe in her man's arms, and a pang of ache ran through me at the alienness of the sensation. It shouldn't mean anything that I knew I was safe there. Anger shadowed along the edge of my mind—anger that I'd thought so little of myself to tolerate that kind of uncertain hell for so long.

But as he pressed his lips against my neck, scruff smarting against the tender skin, my body settled against him, and arousal swallowed my apprehension. His next words only fanned that flame.

"You gotta let me hear myself think, or I'll have to find a better use for that mouth," he promised as his words sent a fever through my center. I wanted that. Wanted *him*. One night was not nearly enough. "If we're going to pull this off, you're going to have to let me process every now and then."

And just like that, my stomach sank. All illusions of something between us dashed on the black sand beneath our feet. 'Going to pull this off'. So, it *was* fake; we were just enjoying the benefits of it? What exactly did that mean? And why was his first declaration still tightening my core despite the uncertainty assaulting my veins? Sensing my sudden trepidation, perhaps psychically aware my pulse was suddenly thrumming against my skin, he dropped his gaze to lock on mine.

"Shit, that came out wrong. Look, baby, you make me want to be better—to figure this shit out—but it's going to take me a minute. I've...avoided doing any of this for so long." No stranger to an endless string of excuses, I started to extricate myself from his grip. Jameson brought his forehead to mine, cradling either side of my face in sudden desperation and stealing my breath with his next declaration. "*Wait*, Noel. You don't owe me anything, but please just...be patient with me. It took every scrap of strength to drive away from you at Grizzly Grind today. Watching you in my rearview was one of the hardest things I've ever done. *Of course*, I'm happy to see you. I just... don't know how to get myself to leave you twice in one day." When he kissed me this time, his dominance stole my breath until I forgot my own damn name.

***

SOMEHOW, neither of us burst into flames sitting sandwiched between Rhodes on opposite sides of the dinner table. Jameson's earlier declaration had been followed by a kiss so desperate it left me breathless, hands roaming until Axel and Sterling were back on the stairs bellowing for us to come to dinner. But the arousal he'd sent sprinting into my bloodstream refused to be tamed. My anxious anticipation funneled into my leg, which bounced compulsively beneath it. At least, right until Elora's eyes flicked between my rapidly tapping heel and up to my face.

"Shut up," I breathed as she swallowed her laughter, smirking around the rim of her wineglass.

"Got somewhere better to be?" she teased.

"No," I said, clearing my throat. "Just jittery—too much of the new fresh brew today."

"I think you're brewing a lot more than coffee these days," she muttered under her breath.

I snickered, spearing the last bite of steak off my plate and popping it in my mouth. She wasn't wrong. The heat of his eyes on my face brought blood to my cheeks, the brewing temptation only rising hotter between us. One night *wasn't* enough. Hell, I wasn't stupid enough to think two would be. And maybe it was confusing as hell—his words and actions in direct contradiction to this little 'arrangement' to keep Eric at bay. But as the others chattered around us, my blood thrummed relentlessly, my body purring in his presence and not really giving two shits if it was real or not. Either way, I needed more of him. It was just a matter of deciding if the pleasure would be worth the inevitable heartbreak.

When dessert replaced our dinner plates, I averted my eyes, feeling like I was about to wither under his relentless focus, his foot finding mine under the table. Days away from turning twenty-six, and I was playing footsie at dinner, wishing it didn't send nerves flapping in my stomach. The moment a respectable amount of cobbler had been vacuumed off my plate, I cleared my throat.

"Juniper, Milo, thank you so much for having me. I've got to turn in early—I open tomorrow."

Elora grinned wickedly at her plate, but I kicked her shin before she could open her mouth. I wasn't lying, despite that not being why I wanted to sprint out the front door.

To my surprise, it was Broderick's sly smile and smooth baritone that cut the tension. "Wouldn't want to cut in on *bedtime*, Red."

I leaned down to give him a hug—pinching his arm and earning a low chuckle—before making the rounds as Juniper chirped, "Thank you so much for making it, sweetie!"

"Yeah, I'm gonna miss you, Noel!" Alice said, reminding me it was Alice's bon voyage party that had demanded all of our presence here in the first place. And here I was, worried about sneaking off with her brother. Selfish. Horrible way to start a friendship, Noel.

"You go down there and kick some ass, Miss Rhodes," I said,

shifting to hug her as she stood from her seat. I was fairly convinced there'd never been a family quite as welcoming as the Rhodes. One season up here, and they took me in like one of their own.

"Don't let him give you too much trouble," she said, smirking like she knew more than she ought to as her gaze flicked to Jameson. He promptly collared her, ruffling her pretty, long brown hair before tucking her against him for a tight hug. "You taking off, too?"

"Yeah, I'll get Skittles home and settled before we head out on the water."

"Sure you will," Broderick grumbled, kicking back in his chair with his fingers laced behind his head in a rare sign of cockiness. But it was to Jameson that my focus returned. Eyes dark with promise, he held out a hand. I couldn't accept it fast enough.

TWENTY-THREE

JAMESON

The front door smacked loudly against the hallway, but I couldn't bring myself to give a shit. My hands were too preoccupied stripping the jacket off Noel's lean frame, lips colliding with the desperation of an unwanted goodbye. *This woman.*

I was no stranger to lust, no stranger to desire, but this was… different. Electric. Like she was a physical need as her hands dipped below my shirt. Noel bit into my bottom lip as I slammed the door closed, giggling when I groaned.

"These fucking flannels," she muttered, fumbling with the buttons. I laughed, bowing my head against hers as her shaky fingers worked to unhook each tiny piece. Her words reminded me of that first day in the coffee shop. "Always knew I hated these for a good reason."

Her breathy laugh was a balm to my chest I certainly hadn't known I fucking needed. Not heeding her yelp of frustration as I slid my palms up her side, I tossed her shirt to the ground, moving for her jeans as she returned to her efforts.

Milo expected me on the dock in thirty minutes, and over my dead body would we not use every single one of them. I was just shimmying denim over that perfect, tight little ass when she finally freed the last button, yanking the sleeves off before diving under the t-shirt beneath it. Up and over my head, the fabric joined the collection in the entryway, shortly followed by both our pants somewhere in the living room. Noel laughed as I fought off her skinny jeans and she clung to my shoulders for balance.

"No more of these," I growled. "Fast clothes, only."

"Deal," she breathed back.

"C'mere," I ordered as I scooped her up, wrapping her legs around my waist. She dug her fingers into my hair, locking our mouths together as I carried her further into the house, hands roaming her sinful body as her legs tightened on my hips.

"Dresses, skirts, yoga pants."

"What?" I scoffed, chuckling against her lips.

"Fast clothes. *Fuckable* clothes. No panties."

"Hell, baby, tell me about 'em later." She giggled as I sucked her lower lip between mine. When I peeled apart, I muttered, "Need you on my bed this time."

"Yes, sir," she agreed, moving back in to devour me as fiercely as I needed to take her.

I'd had good sex. Loads of it, actually. Curvy girls, athletic girls, kinky girls, missionary girls. Nobody—and I mean *nobody*—had ever lit my body up like this spitfire siren. Hearing those two little words leave her precious lips pulled on every animal instinct buried inside my body. Hands roaming, mouths memorizing each other, we clumsily reached my bedroom. I laid her out and reached for the nightstand in the same motion, finding a condom without abandoning her lips.

Noel dropping her legs from my hips and spreading them wide so I could sheath myself in her drenched, hot center, was a kind of nirvana I'd never known existed. If I had, I would have gone hunting for it so much sooner.

"Fuck," she breathed, dropping her head against the bed as her eyes slid closed. "*Fuck*, you feel so good. Too good. *Ridiculously* good." If she could still talk this much, I clearly wasn't doing a *good enough* job yet.

Smirking as I slowly pulled out and rocked back in against her, I said, "Still love it when you swear."

Laughing, Noel barked, "*That's* what you're thinking about?!"

"Among other things."

I stole her breath then, snapping my hips forward to hit that spot in the back that had her coming undone in seconds. "What kind...of other things?" She panted as her hands clawed against my bare back.

Shaking my head in amusement, I demanded, "C'mere, baby." Eyes heavy with lust, she handed me her wrists so I could pull her upright. A little whimper escaped her as our bodies slipped apart, replaced with a gasp as I flipped her onto all fours. Grabbing two perfect palmfuls of her ass, I groaned. She was pale and perky, that mouthwatering body arching against me as I slid my cock back into her.

"Oh, god," she breathed as I seated myself fully. Arms sliding out ahead of her, Noel stretched out, lengthening the lines of her gorgeous torso, arching her ass up towards me.

"I was *thinking* that you're perfect...and so fucking precious that I can't believe you let me touch you like this." I slid my hands across her smooth hips, not sure what to hang onto, enamored with every inch of speckled, ivory skin. Desire ratcheted up with every thrust, every touch. "That you take my cock *so* fucking well," I said, slamming home to emphasize my point as she gasped for air. "That I want to devour every inch of you," *thrust*, "and no matter how many of your nights I get to steal, it won't be enough." *Thrust.*

"Jameson," she breathed, the heady sound of my name enough to threaten my composure. Clenching my teeth, I increased my intensity, relishing the little cries of pleasure each thrust pulled from her. "*Jameson*," she chanted again.

"That's right, baby. *Just* my name. From here on out, *only* my name." Fuck, I wanted that. Wanted that more than I could even wrap my head around. Then she was nodding, breathlessly mouthing something. I eased the pressure enough to grant her a gasp of air, only for my balls to tighten on the word she exhaled.

"Yes."

Oh, fuck me.

Yes? Yes, *just my name*? Goddamn, I loved the sound of that. Returning to a punishing pace, hands gripping her hips as I fought to stay in control, I rasped, "Good. Say it again."

"*Yes*, Jameson!" Noel cried out, dropping her head into her hands as that telltale flex of her walls pulled me in deeper, harder, more determined. Her body was somehow fighting me and welcoming me all at once.

I'd thought one of us would cave during dinner. Thought she'd escape to the back hallway where I'd shove her inside my old bedroom and take her there. Her restraint was astounding. Infuriating. Every moment of need had built up like a dam about to burst. When she cried out my name again, she pulled me right over the edge with her, and I came so hard that stars popped into my vision.

Noel collapsed against the mattress, and I followed, not ready to peel away from her. Not ready to lose the feeling of her ass curved into me, or the sound of her desperate breaths, lighting my world on fire just by existing there in my arms. Rotating onto our sides and spooning her against me, this deep sense of peace seemed to settle between us, and for the first time in my life, I felt like I was exactly where I needed to be, exactly when I needed to be there.

Fear was quick to nip at its heels. This was supposed to be temporary. There was no way this little sunbeam would settle forever in a place like Mistyvale. And there was no way for me to walk away from this town—this family—without dishonoring everything the men before me had fought so tirelessly for. Hell, I'd never even wanted to be the kind of man that thought about this shit.

Yet...I held her. Held her, and realized that, for better or worse, I was past the point of no return. Soaked up her sexed-up scent—the smell of *us* filling my room. When her breathing deepened to that of sleep, my chest went warm. She'd fallen asleep in my arms again. As if she knew she was safe; she understood how much I cared for her and could relax into that. Gingerly, I slipped out of her, tucking the blanket up and over her where she was languid against my bed. I couldn't leave her. Couldn't walk away from the goddess sleeping in my sanctuary. Unfortunately, the sound of my front door opening begged to differ.

"Jameson—"

"Shhh!" I hissed, watching to make sure Axel's fat mouth hadn't ruined her sleep. Sighing, I darted to my bathroom to clean up, ducked back into the room, dressed in fresh clothes, and grabbed my jacket off the chair in the corner.

"We're late," he whisper-yelled down the hallway.

"Come any further back here, and we'll be a lot later," I threatened. Tucked in or not, this view was *mine*. I wasn't about to share it with my damn brother. I set her alarm, my note promising to be home soon beside it. Throat thick, I leaned down to press a kiss to her forehead, whispering, "Gotta go, baby."

A traitorous ache planted between my ribs as I walked out, storming past Axel for the front door. Max was waiting against the banister of my porch.

"Told you not to interrupt," he gloated to Axel, who looked sheepish as he ducked his head and headed for the truck. But it was Max I nearly clotheslined, grabbing his collar to demand his attention.

"He doesn't get near her—understand?"

"Yeah, buddy. We got her, okay?"

"El and Broderick have that damn conference."

"I know."

"It's not fair for me to put this on you—"

"But you *need me*. I swear, I got her, man."

Nodding, fighting the draw to fuck my responsibilities and stay with her, I tongued at a canine. Max set a hand on my shoulder, giving it a squeeze.

"Hey. You know there's nothing I wouldn't do for this family."

"Yeah." I looked up to where Axel was waiting expectantly in the driver's side of my truck, revving the engine. "Her birthday's Wednesday."

"I remember."

"I left money and instructions on the counter." The knowledge I likely wouldn't make it back in time pissed me off to no end. But Rhodes knew nothing if not how to party, and like hell would I miss making sure she knew it mattered to me. Poetry and prose had never been my forte, but I could at least show her this. Show her *she* mattered to me.

"Thanks, Max."

"Get outta here, you big worry wart. I've got her."

WE CAUGHT sixty-thousand pounds of reds in just over forty-eight hours, and never in my life had I been so grateful my dad was exactly who he was. By Tuesday night, we headed back in to deliver. Six hours to go until I could wrap Noel up in my arms. Six hours until I could bury my face in her hair and beg to get back in her bed to give her the best damn birthday sex of her life.

"What's with you and Noel these days?" Mav asked, as if he knew what I was thinking about, sidling up next to me as I watched the water fly past us. There was nothing in any direction, just the open navy of a calm sea and the sun blaring down at us. Dying to have eyes on the shoreline, on the promise of home, I kept my focus on the horizon despite logic reminding me we were hours from being able to spot it. "I just mean, it seemed like things were...escalating there."

"Mind your business, kid."

He chuckled as Axel joined us, crossing his arms over his chest. "When it was Rhyett's business, you had no problem telling the whole family about it."

"That was different," I practically growled.

"Like hell it was," he said, barking a laugh.

"Not *her.*"

"What?" Mav asked, turning to lean his ass against the railing, clearly just as unadvisedly comfortable on the water as the rest of us.

"It wasn't Noel."

"Because Brex didn't deserve the privacy?" Axel demanded, apparently in the mood to poke the bear.

"Course she did. But they started out as some cheap one-night stand. It's not like either of them took it seriously in the beginning, either. Haven't said shit since he decided she was *more.*"

"Soo...you're saying that there *is* something there?" Mav hedged, fishing for more details than he was entitled to.

"Don't know."

"Yes, you do," Axel challenged. "Sounded like you were gonna kill me when I came to get you Sunday night. That means something."

"Don't know," I said again, shrugging my shoulder.

"Jesus, you're frustrating," Axel grumbled, shaking his head. "Leave it, Mav. The caveman doesn't know how to communicate." Mav did not, in fact, decide to leave it.

"Come on, man, I'm just curious. Everybody is. You like her. Beyond the sex."

"*Of course,* I like her. How could I *not?* Ten minutes with the woman and *Scrooge* himself would fill stockings." That's what the world needed. More light, like Noel. More people who took something simple, like how a local took their coffee, and made it special. Annoyingly optimistic, just like my big brother, but when it was her...it just...hit differently. Maybe she was naïve, but she made me want to be better. To do better. "And *the sex* is none of your goddamn business."

His face fell, and I had a sinking suspicion it had nothing to do with my snarled warning. Uncharacteristic worry played over his features. Finally, our baby brother cleared his throat. "Don't wait to tell her, Jameson. I just...I have this feeling about her, alright? That's why I'm prying."

I turned to scowl at him, demanding, "What kind of feeling?"

"The good kind."

"Be more cryptic," I drawled sarcastically. "It's really helping."

"Look who's talking," Axel jabbed as Maverick smirked.

"The...meant-to-be-family kind of feeling."

"Jesus, man. That's a stretch." No. It wasn't. I'd already wanted her. But the idea of something happening to her had cemented it in my brain. Noel was mine. Was always supposed to be mine. I'd been a fling kind of guy because they'd been fling kinds of girls. She... *wasn't.*

Noel McShane was the real deal. The timing couldn't have been more spectacularly horrible. But it was what it was. "We're just getting to know each other."

Maverick shook his head, face going uncharacteristically serious. "I don't think so. Don't fuck this up. That's all I'm saying."

"Noted." Like I wasn't wrestling with exactly that. My girl thought this was for show. Thought this was to ward off Eric. I needed to get my ass off the damn water and make sure she knew otherwise.

WE'D JUST PULLED up to the dock when I leapt for it, bristling when Kenny jumped off the *Tide Turner* with his eyes on me. *Everything* bristled. *That* didn't look good.

"Hey, man, I've got somewhere to be," I said by way of greeting. I didn't very well care what the hell was going on in town or with Kenny. I just wanted to get home. Because two days away were two days too damn many. Fuck, we weren't even technically together—just screwing—and I was acting like a lovesick puppy.

"What's going on with you, man?"

"What do you mean?" I snapped, not particularly caring for his clipped tone.

"You and the barista? What's the deal?"

"Christ, *this again*? Doesn't anybody have anything better to do than stick their nose in my personal life?"

Kenny's expression pinched, but then he quickened his step to keep stride with me. "Word around town is you stole McShane from Eric Connely? I know you like to push limits, but I never thought you'd stoop to that."

"Fucking *excuse me*?" I snarled, coming to a dead stop and balling my fists at my side as he nearly collided with me. Trying not to waylay a man I'd grown up with, I glared down light blue eyes as he blinked in apparent confusion at my reaction.

"Look, man. It's not technically any of my business. But I've known you for a long damn time, and if I was about to fuck up my entire reputation, I know you'd be the first one to say something. So that's what I'm doing, alright?" He took a deep breath as my head settled into an eerie calm. The kind of calm on the water that gives you goosebumps because it always precedes a storm. When I didn't respond, he saw fit to continue. "The harbor has been buzzing. Tell me you didn't *steal* an engaged woman, Rhodes. That doesn't sound like you—I've been telling everybody I didn't buy it."

"The fuck I did," I snapped. "And you're right. It's *not* any of your damn business. I've never known you to buy into the rumor mill."

"I wouldn't usually. Look, James, I'm sorry to even push the issue. But people are kinda ruffled after that standoff at Birch Barrel last week. Your *cousin* escorting a senator's kid out in uniform. He says you're keeping her from him. And then there's this," he added, concern furrowing his brow as he pulled a crumpled-up newspaper out of his coat pocket and handed it to me. The sound of my family marching our way across the wood didn't ease the nerves settling in my stomach as Kenny focused on me expectantly. Begrudgingly, I looked down at the paper, unfolding it and reading the headline as my blood boiled.

Florida Senator's Son Graces Mistyvale with a Generous Donation to Local College, Igniting Excitement and Gratitude in the Community!

The black-and-white photo below showed Eric beside the town mayor, shaking hands and smiling at the camera. An American golden boy, incarnated.

"What the fuck?" I growled, brows knitting together as I read over the article to follow. Evidently, he'd seen fit to befriend not only our mayor but a local fishing legend—the second image in the article showed him aboard a prized legacy vessel with as much esteem as the *Rhodes Away*. The new business building on campus would bear *his* goddamn name.

Clever motherfucker. Goddamn, he would really do anything just to rattle her cage, wouldn't he?

"He also donated to the children's hospital and has been volunteering down at the shelter for the last week. Some locals were down at Luca's and started asking him what in the hell brought him clear up here. He claims his fiancé came here on vacation to help Rhyett with the shop while Brin was on leave, and you stole her from him." I leveled him with a glare that begged him to fuck around and find out, and his confusion deepened. "I *told them* it had to be bullshit. Told him you weren't that kind of man. And Lizzy—or *Noel,* whatever her name actually is—didn't seem like the kind of broad that would run out on her engagement."

"Thanks for the heads up," I said, planting the paper against his chest as I sidestepped him.

"You gonna fill me in?"

"Nope."

"What are you gonna do?"

"Gotta go figure that out. This damn town is starved for entertainment." I heard the crumple of paper, and rumble of footsteps, and then Axel was in step beside me, eyes scraping over the damn headline.

"Sneaky motherfucker."

"Yeah," I grunted as anger and panic grappled for purchase.

"What the hell is going on?" Mav demanded. To my surprise, Milo was just behind us.

Shaking my head, I said, "He can't get her back, so he's gonna make it his mission to take away her sanctuary. *That's what.*"

"You didn't steal her away," Axel snarled, handing Mav the paper. So they'd clearly heard that much of the conversation. "Our family dates back *generations* on this island. He can't honestly think he'll turn them against us, can he? Plus, she fled five thousand miles to escape him. Nobody's gonna believe that shit."

"Kenny nearly did."

"Kenny's good on the boat, but dumb as rocks," Milo mumbled, accepting the paper as Mav passed it over. I choked on my laugh. Dad never flung insults, his words striking me in the chest.

"He can't have her, so he's gonna position himself in *our town* and try to ruin her reputation? Seriously?" My youngest brother's tone was laced with the same venom pumping through my veins and promising retribution. But I had no idea how to respond to this shit. No tact for PR, where this dick weasel was obviously fluent in it. "Is it the seventeen hundreds again?"

"Can everybody just *shut up* for a minute? I need to think—need to make sure Noel is okay." I didn't have to think for long, because my girl was stepping out of the Grizzly Grind, spotting us on the docks and making a beeline in my direction.

It was time to think a hell of a lot faster.

TWENTY-FOUR

NOEL

"I'm so sorry!" I blurted, the moment he was within earshot. His confusion painted across that beautiful, scruffy face, brows nearly connecting as he scowled at me. I'd been crying for two days. The day Jameson left, the first insults were flung my way. Never directly, but not quiet enough for me to miss them as the gossips not-so-subtly skirted out the shop door.

The second, the picture Alice sent us of her new apartment was overshadowed when the damn paper printed an article about the *virtuous* Eric Connely gracing the island in the 'trip of a lifetime', falling in love with the locals, and generously bestowing his plentiful resources.

By this morning, half the town was buzzing with the chatter of their very own 'wayward son' coercing me to abandon my 'future husband', plying me with booze and a scandalous love affair.

This. This is what Eric was good at. Playing people like damn fiddles until the circumstances fell in his favor. He'd been so subtle, ducking back off our radar and making his way through the town.

If he couldn't rattle Jameson—*duh, the man was a rock*—he would rattle me. Rattle his family. Come after us personally, in a town too small to avoid the talk. Or the damage words could inflict on a family business. Jameson shook his head as I all but ran in his direction.

"What in the hell do you have to be sorry about?"

"Dragging you into this. Putting your family on his radar. I—"

"Have *nothing* to apologize for." His words were more a demand than reassurance as he widened his stride to scoop me up against him in a heartbeat. For the first time since I'd fallen asleep in his arms, I *breathed*. Max had done his best to comfort me, but it wasn't the same. Wasn't this promise that I wouldn't be alone in this. The promise of safety I found here, against Jameson, soaking up his sweaty, sea-laced scent. Dangerous feelings I wasn't even about to address stirred in my gut. He hadn't even made it off the dock before I saw Kenny corner him. Kenny, who hadn't been in for his morning mocha breve since the rumor mill started churning. Kenny, who so easily fell into the trap.

"The town has seen worse scandals than an affair. I assure you, they'll get over it," Milo said, though his tone was solemn as Jameson lowered me onto my feet. "Might take a few months, but they'll move on the next time one of our girls falls for a Coastie," he grumbled. That hint of local rivalry between the Coast Guard and fishing families had been particularly entertaining, but I didn't have time to think too deeply about it at the moment.

Jameson widened his stance to bring our faces closer, stooping to look me in the eye as his chilled hands scooped up to cradle my face. "Let's get home. We can discuss all this somewhere *idiots* can't overhear." He pressed a punishing kiss to my mouth, and my soul seemed to settle.

NOBODY in the family was remotely surprised that this was Eric's strategy. In fact, it was kind of a brilliant spin if I thought about it. Back home, he'd gone after my reputation, using his family's clout to cover up the charges. He was portraying the doting, grace-filled fiancé—*oh yeah*, that bit was fun. Did he propose? Yep. Did I say no? Yep. Was that what sent him flying off his hinges in the first place? Yep.—willing to take me back after my *treachery*.

This was a B-grade film script, at best. The fact that people were believing any of it should have surprised me more than it did. But the rumor mill is a bizarre paradox where headlines equate to facts, and old money holds merit over authentic testimony and documented evidence.

Juniper graciously filled our bellies with hot tea and warmed up leftover mashed potatoes and roast chicken. I kinda wondered if she was *Mary Poppins* in disguise, all of her doting maternal tendencies warming my heart. Suddenly, I missed my own mother, the thought short-lived as theories continued circulating the table.

"Okay, so how do we retaliate?" Maverick asked, his anger palpable as he threatened to vibrate his leg until it forcibly resigned from duty.

"Or do we retaliate at all?" Milo countered calmly. "I already texted some captains—McGrath, Brown, and Jones—and they'll meet me at Birch Barrel. I'll clear the air with the patriarchs in town, and the truth should circulate quickly once they take the information back to their wives. And by *truth,* I mean Noel ran away and into Jameson's arms when he offered her safety." Right. Because Milo Rhodes wasn't the kind of man to lie to other good men. Even for us. So, whatever this thing was between us had to be honest.

"So, we basically do damage control?" Leighton questioned. Their parents exchanged a long glance before nodding.

"It's a small town. Word will get around, and if the two of you are in this together, they'll sense that, too." Juniper added. Just like that, my nerves lessened. Jameson had been eerily level-headed as his siblings batted ideas and irritation around in equal measure, his fingers firmly intertwined in mine as he seemed to chew over their words. The lethal edge to his gaze as it drilled into the table, however, was enough to set my anxiety on alert. He'd already been mad, but watching our names get dragged through the mud might just be enough to push him right over the edge and take shit into his own hands. As we walked out of the main house, I couldn't help but wonder, could a good local family name override a nationally respected one?

We made the car ride home in silence, both of us deep in our own heads. I should've seen this play coming, but I'd let them all get blindsided by it. I needed to talk to Brex, or maybe Josie. *Mmm, definitely Josie,* as she was less likely to panic and more likely to stay level when I needed her to. Something about that single mom life keeping her feet firmly planted in the face of stress. However, Vallie absolutely needed to be brought into the fold. But that could wait —*had to wait,* as she was likely in bed at this time of evening.

In true Jameson fashion, he rushed around the truck to open my door and help me down, pressing a soft kiss to my forehead when I found my feet. Leading the way up and into the house with a pinched spot between his brows, he remained chillingly silent, and I wasn't sure if he was mad or in his head, my stomach winding tighter all the while.

One arm crossed under the other, literally bracing his chin in some deep trance of contemplation, he wandered into the house, kicking off his boots without relaxing his face. He was still in his dirty boat clothes, having taken me to consult the calvary the moment he made it home. As that full bottom lip vanished between his teeth, my trepidation won out.

"James?" I asked softly. His face relaxed a bit for the first time as his gaze found mine. I swallowed hard, shifting my weight from one side to the other. "I really am sorry."

Anger or hurt, or some blended braid of the two flashed in his eyes. But before I could continue, he closed the distance, scooping my face into his palms and threading thick fingers into my hair. It was second nature, the way he tilted me up to him, his lips claiming mine. It differed from that first night on the mountain. These kisses were consuming, like he was siphoning off a bit of himself to infuse his strength into me in exchange for a piece of mine. Like the rainstorm of Jameson Rhodes was wrapping me up, concealing me, hiding me away from the world in his shadows as I offered him just a taste of Florida sun. I reveled in it. The man's silent intensity somehow made me feel safe as the heat of desire stirred to life and crawled through my veins.

Hips grinding into mine, Jameson pulled back, keeping our foreheads connected as we shared a breath. "Please."

"Please?" I questioned, blinking as I panted against him. He shook his head infinitesimally. The movement was so small I would have missed it if he hadn't bowed against my forehead.

"Please stop doing that. Please stop apologizing."

"But I'm—"

"Taking ownership of a grown man's actions. You didn't *make him* come here. Didn't invite him or make him play the rumor mill like a teenage girl. You being here doesn't justify his mental games. You have a right to be happy, Noel. You have a right to chase whatever the fuck lights your soul on fire and own every goddamned inch of it. No matter what that looks like. Just...please stop apologizing for existing—for being human. You owe us nothing."

"You don't owe me anything, either."

"Oh, baby. Don't you get it? I owe you *my life*, if that's what you need to be safe, free, and happy. But I can't deal with you beating yourself up for something you had no part in." Words like a flame in my chest, he held my gaze for one second more before bringing his mouth to mine with a bruising intensity. Parting my lips, I invited him in, and Jameson deepened the kiss without hesitation, swapping breaths as we savored the taste of each other.

I needed him. Needed him to touch me, his skin against mine. Wanted to see if I could get him to melt under my mouth. Gradually, the kiss eased in intensity, and we caught our breath as my hands wandered under his black t-shirt, desperate for the heat of him. Without warning, Jameson bent to scoop my legs out from under me, his lips twitching when a little yelp escaped my throat. Kissing the crown of my head, he carried me like a bride over the threshold, bringing me into his room and chuckling as my hands found his belt the moment he set me down.

A gentle nip of my lip was enough to bring my eyes to his, a tiny flick of his head slowing my movements. Jameson wiggled out of his jeans, yanking his shirt off to reveal his spectacular frame, sending that torturous heat rushing through my core, mouth filling with saliva, like that's exactly what I'd been waiting for. Maybe it was. I wanted him in my mouth, to suck him deep and relish the feeling of him getting hard against my tongue.

His head shake was nearly imperceptible, but I heeded the unspoken request as he backed up to his walk-in shower. Gaze locked on mine, Jameson leaned in and started the water before jerking his chin in my direction. Tentatively, I reached for the hem of my shirt, and when his smile confirmed that's what he wanted, lifted it up and over my head. A surprised little gasp caught in my throat when I popped free of the fabric to find he'd closed the distance. Urgent reverence filled the way he coasted that broad palm over my side before the other joined in to slide up my back and unclip the pink bra.

This was...*different*. Everything about this felt different. My lungs spun into overdrive, core churning as expectation wound every inch of my body tight like a coil. Heart hammering so hard the whoosh of it played in my ears, I hadn't realized I was shaking until Jameson looped his fingers into mine. Dark eyes scraping over my free breasts and down the length of my torso, the man looked every inch the predator he could be. And I'd never in my life felt safer. Never felt more wanted.

"So fucking perfect," he whispered, voice low with a kind of promise I was dying to see him make good on. Broad, calloused palms coasted over my sides, slipping beneath my panties as mine returned the gesture. Fabric pooling at our feet, we both shifted back and forth to free ourselves from the garments. When his hands settled just below my breasts, he wrapped his fingers around them, coming to flick my nipples, lips twitching a beat before my head fell back, pussy pulsing with need. The man had said *three* freaking words—THREE—and had every inch of my body and soul wound taught and ready for him to take anything he wanted.

"You have the most beautiful tits, baby. Do you know how crazy they drive me?"

"What?" I barked a laugh, glancing down at my itty bitty titties. Some women were curvy, and some were pear-shaped or athletic, or triangular. I'd been bestowed with the glorious, goddess-like curves of a Q-Tip. Nobody, not even desperate Brad Fisher, had complimented my pale, size A-minus boobs. Jameson lit a flame across my skin as he sucked one hard nipple into his mouth, a groan teasing from the depth of his chest, destroying my composure like the conqueror he was. Arousal became a persistent attack against the confines of my veins.

When he straightened, Jameson tugged my fingers as he backed into the shower. Swallowing down my nerves, I followed, my hand trailing him until I could cup his thick erection, eyes sliding shut at the silky soft skin and firm promise of unspeakable pleasure. An involuntary shiver raked down my spine as hot water cascaded over my muscles, sluicing off the long brunette curls settling over his forehead. Steel-blue eyes smoldered down at me as that little dimple teased the stubbled flesh of his cheek.

Maintaining his vows to the Buddhist monks, Jameson wordlessly brought his hands up my sides, pulling me against him. The heady combination of his touch and the hot water pouring over my sides was enough to drive me to madness.

"Please," I whispered, needing him to finally take the edge off this magma boiling me alive. "*Please*, Jameson."

"Say it again." His voice was a tight, desperate rasp, chest heavy as he studied me intently.

"*Jameson*–" I breathed, his name truncated as he claimed my mouth again, this time with the intensity of a starving man. With a huff, he pulled away just as abruptly, turning and soaping down in record time, pulling a laugh from my throat. I expected him to return, to come back and pick up where he'd left me. So, when he flicked his chin at me, confusion buried in my chest. Right up until that smirking bastard tugged me into him, and slowly, leisurely, ran his soapy hands over every inch of my chest and back as though he had all the time imaginable.

Heady pants filled the space between us and Jameson bowed our foreheads together again, whispering, "You deserve the *world*, Noel McShane. Never forget that."

TWENTY-FIVE

JAMESON

Noel—the sunspot—McShane didn't want to go out for her birthday. With my ridiculous town going feral for fresh gossip, I couldn't blame her. While normally I'd push the issue for her sake, she'd leisurely stripped down to her birthday suit before I'd even gotten out of bed for the day and slowly lowered that perfect pussy onto my morning wood, erasing all thoughts of protest. We spent the entire day taking turns between eating the endless rounds of takeout we ordered, ringing orgasms from our bodies with explosive, startling efficiency, playing cards, and watching movies on a loop. To my immense satisfaction, we spent the bulk of her birthday naked, save for when I had to slip into basketball shorts to answer the door when my siblings graciously delivered our meals. Sometimes, having a million of us had its benefits. Especially on an island that lacked the amenities of the twenty-first century.

The next day brought with it a necessary but unexpected stress: telling her family about us. While I watched her animatedly talking on a video chat, I pulled my phone free and shot a text off to Rhy, remembering what his morning entailed.

JAMESON

How's Brex?

RHYETT

Nervous, but excited.

> JAMESON
>
> The appointment went well, then?

RHYETT

My bride has a very cute picture of what appears to
be a black and white gummy bear glued to her hands.

> JAMESON
>
> Lol good news, man. Thanks for the update.

RHYETT

Thanks for checking in. How's Noel?

> JAMESON
>
> On the phone with her mom. She's telling them we're
> dating.

RHYETT

How's it going?

> JAMESON
>
> They seem…concerned.

RHYETT

Fair. I would be too, if my daughter was dating
someone like you. *winking emoji*

> JAMESON
>
> Fuck off.

RHYETT

But for real, lying to loved ones aside, how is she?

> JAMESON
>
> I've been feeling for her this week—she's homesick.

RHYETT

Your birthday surprise this weekend should help.
Anything else we can do? Christmas in Florida feels
like a long way to wait if she's low.

I LEFT his last message on read. Partially because I was transfixed as
she paced back and forth across my back porch, and partially because
I was still pissed he'd hidden her situation from me when I would've
been…well, less of a prick, if I'd known what was on her plate.
Knowing I needed his help didn't ease the irritation at the fact.

Noel had texted her sister, Maddie, to tell her she was seeing
someone. Her mother had all three of them on a video chat so fast my

head spun as she skirted outside. It seemed…tense. To say the least. I couldn't blame them.

Their sister/daughter fled five thousand miles away to escape an abuser, only to 'fall into bed with some guy', and then said ex rematerialized like the phantom psycho stalker he was. I'd already have my ass on a seat on the way to the airport if I were Alex.

We'd decided—together—that we wouldn't tell her mother this was fake. Or that it had started out that way. Because who the hell knew what it was now? Neither of us was eager to broach the subject.

According to her daughter, Frankie McShane was many amazing things, but a liar wasn't one of them. Should she have the opportunity to spread the news of our relationship on her side of the country, with her connections to the Connely family, it would be best if she one hundred percent believed I was in love with her daughter. Fuck, I was beginning to believe the same thing.

Fast. *Too fast.* That word hadn't even been uttered internally since Steffy. It sure as shit shouldn't be traipsing across my mind now.

When she at last tossed her phone to the cushioned patio couch, I huffed a breath and made a beeline for her. Noel returned to her pacing, even as I stepped outside and made my way to a chair. The third time she walked by me, my hands jutted out to snatch her waist. Her air whooshed out as she complied, melting against my hands and pouring herself over my lap.

"They mad?"

"Not…*mad*, exactly," she said, eyes sliding closed as she leaned her forehead into mine. "Concerned, I think, more than anything."

"That's understandable. They don't know me. Did it help that Brex does?"

My girl nodded. "At least, for Maddie and mom. Alex threatened your imminent demise and promised to call my dad."

A snort escaped before I stifled it. "Well. If Eric finally meets an untimely death, then I'll get mildly concerned."

She grinned at that, shaking her head as life sparkled in those gorgeous brown irises. The relief was fleeting though, worry pinching her brows as she admitted, "I hate lying to them."

"I know."

"Maddie seemed suspicious," Noel said with a grimace.

"She say something?"

Shaking her head, loose red curls bobbed as she explained, "Nah, she just got really quiet. It was the way she looked at me, like I was up to something or in trouble."

When she chewed on her lip, I reached up to push the strands off her face, and she leaned into my palm against her skin. Noel McShane melting into my touch would never fucking get old. "Give it time, baby. It only makes sense that they're scared for you after everything he just put you through. Now, some new guy they've never met comes on the scene. I'd be skeptical in their shoes. You'll talk soon, I'm sure."

"Yeah," she sighed. "Yeah, you're right." Closing her eyes, her shoulders melted away from her neck as I stroked my thumb over her cheekbone.

Looking to help her relax, I asked, "Your parents are still together?"

"They got together in college," she said, her smile audible. "Had their thirtieth wedding anniversary last year."

"Tell me about them." So she did, her body gradually relaxing as I stroked the length of her back in what I hoped was a soothing circle. I'd never been more grateful for the scraps of bright fabric she called suitable attire. I was fairly convinced she wore them *for me* these days.

"Daddy was kind of wild when he was younger. You'd never know it now," she continued after ten minutes or so. "Anybody with eyes can spot Arthur the accountant the moment he walks in a room."

My phone buzzed, and I glanced at the message, rolling my eyes and mumbling, "Asshole," when I spotted the image. Noel, naturally, perked up, ruled by her curiosity.

"Who's the asshole?"

"Broderick."

She giggled before narrowing her eyes. "Somehow, I just can't picture that man deserving that particular moniker. I'm going to require persuading."

"Oh, trust me," I said with a sigh, tapping in the passcode so I could open the images he sent me. "He is."

"*Puppies?!*" My phone transferred hands so fast that I felt like a cartoon that had to spin its face back on right. Chuckling, I peered over the top of it as she swiped through the photos. Fluffy little teddy bear retriever faces staring back at her. "They're so cute!"

"Furry little fuckers. I've always loved retrievers the most."

"Knew there was a soft heart somewhere in there," she teased, flashing one of the smiles that incinerated my intelligence faster than the others. "Look at their 'wil faces!" she cooed.

"I'd call that one William, and that one Thatcher," I said, pointing at the two that looked like they'd have the most copper in their faces when they grew up. It had been years since my lifestyle afforded a pet, and damn, did I miss it. Recognition dawned on that pretty little face, lips falling open and eyes rounding before she planted a kiss on my forehead.

"Wait," she breathed against my skin. "Like *A Knight's Tale?*"

"Obviously."

"Don't *obviously* me. There could be another *William Thatcher.*"

Smirking, I hiked up a brow. "You dare disparage the name?"

"Never," she gasped, feigning outrage before bursting out laughing. "But for real, that's my favorite movie. Of all time. I have the damn thing memorized."

"Well, ain't that something?" My smile grew involuntarily. Goddamn, this girl made me happy.

"Yours too?" She asked, hopeful enough that I wasn't about to dash them. How the fuck did a man pick a favorite movie? That wasn't actually a feasible task, was it?

"Something like that."

Her smile gave way to curiosity, gaze flicking to the screen and back to my face. "Although I fail to see how Broderick is an asshole."

"He sent me a link to a *litter of puppies.*"

"Blasphemous bastard." She giggled, shaking her head. "Care to fill me in?"

"I love dogs."

A maniacal laugh bubbled up her throat before she clamped her hand down over her mouth. "Yes. Good. So you *do* have a soul somewhere in there."

My pinch to her thigh wasn't hard—just enough to get her attention—but she squealed and lunged backward like she'd dismounted my lap in favor of her ass on the patio. I threw my arms around her, my growl earning a squeal of laughter as I pressed kisses up her collar. "I can't have a fucking dog," I grumbled against her skin. "Much less a *puppy.*"

"Why?" She blinked, her confusion somehow adorable and simultaneously ridiculous.

"I fish for a living."

Brow furrowed, she scowled down at the photos. "So? Is that... against the rules or something?"

Rolling my eyes, I explained the obvious. "Who the hell would take care of it? Potty train it? I'm never home."

"Oh," she said, her face falling. She looked back at the screen, face twisting in contemplation. "I mean, I'm not sure Chloe would approve once she's up here, but I'm home. I helped Brex train Royal. If you want one—or two—you should get one. You deserve to have a buddy. Or buddies." Surprise lit my soul on fire right as her eyes widened. The implications of her words struck us both, her lips popping open.

"Generous offer," I said softly, tucking her obstinate curls behind her ear again as she slowly blew the air from her lungs, melting over me and wrapping her hands behind my back. Maybe she was hiding that edible blush in her cheeks, or maybe she just needed the reassurance that her future casting hadn't entirely terrified me.

Quite the opposite. While my internal alarms should have been screaming to run for the damn hills...I felt oddly at peace. *Too* at peace for logic to be content. Chewing that reaction over would take more time than we likely had. My hands buzzed with the need to touch and claim as I ran my palms over her thighs, the strip of exposed skin below her shirt. Right as I was thinking I could get used to the feel of her body wrapped around mine—my unobstructed view of the mountains through the fog making the moment feel eerily idyllic—my front door banged open, my brother's voice bouncing off the walls. Right on cue.

"*Yo!* Do you have coffee? I'm out."

Closing my eyes, I sighed dramatically. "Axel, you know if you bothered to shop, you wouldn't have to steal my shit all the time."

"I did shop. Town was out, too."

"Fucking island," I grumbled as a smirking Noel slunk off my lap, a trace of pink still in her skin. Throttling my brother suddenly became an actual possibility. "Barge must have skipped us this week."

"They can do that?" She asked, shock lacing her voice as she stretched, popping her back. Her exposed abs were just begging for my fucking tongue to run across them.

Axel was a *jackass*.

"Yeah," I sighed. "When the storms are too bad, they won't risk the jaunt out here."

"So...what happens if you run out of supplies?"

"Tough shit and phone a friend...or, *brother*, in Axel's case."

"That doesn't seem very...safe."

I snorted, shaking my head. "Last winter, we got hit back-to-back with storms. Couldn't find a scrap of dairy for ten days. Coffee becomes a damn currency. Never realized as a kid that those weeks on beans and rice were rations."

"Oh, hey, Red!" Axel said as he popped his head outside, cheery and oblivious to the fact that I had very different plans for my afternoon off. "Throwin' on a pot—you guys want some?"

I was about to bark *no*, tell him to take the bag and get out, when Noel said, "I could go for a cup! I guess I better check in with Grizzly Grind and make sure we have what we need for the week."

The glare I sent my brother had him grinning back at me for a beat before the two of them vanished inside. Groaning, I set my head against the back of the chair, begrudging the fog as it crept over my lawn, gradually blotting out the view. So much for half a day with my girl.

When we all split ways, I couldn't shake the trepidation in my gut at the mere idea of being away from her. The boys reassured me, of course, that we'd steal her for guys' night, but I couldn't shake the feeling that we should have just stayed home.

TWENTY-SIX

NOEL

"This is *insane*, Brex," I said, slamming the truck door as I slid into the driver's seat and worked to keep my phone at face level while adjusting my purse. We'd been video chatting for the last thirty minutes as I wandered the island searching for supplies for the shop.

"You checked all three stores?" She asked, wide-eyed.

"Not only did I check, I had the stock boys check. They're fresh out of all dairy. Full stop. The whole damn town. I could fly to a village, but I somehow suspect my prospects would be worse."

"How much do you have left?"

I mentally calculated, wincing. "About enough for the next two days, but after that, it'll be black coffee only."

"Wild."

Phone safely secured in the dashboard cradle, I palmed at my face. We'd already brought each other up to speed on baby appointments, the updated name list, and my harrowing chronicles of surviving my family's reaction to my 'dating' while I'd driven to my final fruitless destination. She'd smirked a little too cockily during the 'I volunteered to train a puppy since I'm home' conversation. Still, I'd had to run into the last store, effectively scapegoating the reality of that ridiculous offer.

As I sat in the parking lot, looking up at the towering mountain range, I had to admit this place had its perks. Supply issues aside, it was *breathtaking* here. Was that enough to give up the convenience of Tampa in the long run?

"Well, I better get to work," I said with a sigh. "Take in what I could get my hands on."

"Isn't it poker night?"

I laughed at the fact that she knew that. The culprit was obvious. "Is Rhyett jonesing?"

"He misses them more after seeing them, I think."

"Well, that's not so funny," I said sympathetically. Currently more homesick than I cared to admit, I sighed. "Yeah, the boys are all getting together. Broderick flew back into town this morning, so he'll be there. Jameson invited me, but I close the shop tonight."

"You stay safe in the storm, okay?"

Rolling my eyes, I said, "It's Mistyvale, Brex. It's literally just rain."

She didn't miss a beat before instructing, "Don't float away."

THE GRIZZLY GRIND was a ghost town. Dusting both sides of the blinds, polishing the pastry case, glass cleaner on the stainless appliances level of ghost town. By three o'clock, I'd sent Kara home, confident if we got a brief rush, I'd conquer it myself. Another two hours of silence passed—which I filled with my current romantic suspense read—before the front door opened, and Jameson's neighbor, Mrs. Anderson, popped in.

"Brrr," she said, shaking her hair out. "It's freezing out there. Eerie too. When are you closed, sweetheart?"

"Not for another hour," I said, doing my best attempt to smile, although it felt like my face had forgotten how to move. "You see Jameson today?"

"Oh yes, he came by to reattach that door that kept falling off the hinges. Bless him."

That sentiment reactivated my cheeks, a genuine smile creeping up as I said, "Good, it's been bugging him. What can I get for you?"

"Just the usual."

"London Fog is particularly fitting for the day," I noted. We dove into our usual chatter as I brewed her tea and steamed milk, but my eyes kept glancing sidelong towards the window, her description sinking under my skin. *Eerie too.* Fog was always creepy, but my skin pricked as I realized I'd made a mistake. Because for the first time since Eric showed up on the island, I was in a private space, alone.

Silly, that thought. He hadn't made any physical advances since he got here, and Jameson would be playing right down the street at

Jake's house. I'd just wander over to him instead of going home if I was still anxious after work. Glaring at the five-hundred-page thriller that had no doubt planted the anxiety in my chest, I slid the hardback back into my bag. Enough of that for the day.

A few more patrons came in after Mrs. Anderson bid me *adieu*, but they were all in the mood for black coffee or tea, nothing to take my mind off the oddity of the day for more than thirty seconds, unfortunately. I'd just polished away the last water stain on the espresso machine, tossing the rag in the hamper and snatching my purse from under the counter when the tsunami siren started screaming. Startling out of my skin, I glanced at the clock on the wall, even though I knew it was well after two p.m. and certainly not Wednesday.

Oh, dear god. Stomach suddenly in my throat, I fumbled with my bag, searching for my phone as my eyes flew towards the harbor as it bobbed and swayed with the subtle tide. Siren whooping louder when I opened the door, I blinked down at my phone screen, finally noting the enormous notification icon telling me I was in 'immediate danger'.

I'd lived on the water my entire life and never heard an alarm like that. Certainly hadn't ever prepared for the water trying to take back its land. Despite the weekly alarms, I realized I'd never asked any of the Rhodes what the protocol was in the very unlikely event that the real thing ever...happened.

Jameson's name flashed on my screen, a picture I'd snapped that day on the mountaintop now filling my phone. His voice eased my pounding heart.

"Hey baby, you okay?"

"Yeah," I said, sighing as I clung to every syllable of that delicious, steady timbre. "Where are you?" I pinned the phone between my shoulder and ear, fighting to lock the door and cursing the fact that my hands were shaking.

"We're on our way. Listen...Are you listening to me?"

"Yes, sir," I said, hating how quickly my voice weakened when I was uncertain.

"That's my girl. Okay. These happen *all the time*. It's probably nothing—just an earthquake somewhere close enough for them to worry. So, I don't want you to panic."

Swallowing hard, I nodded before catching myself. "Kay."

His little huff of amusement warmed my chest a beat before he skeptically said, "You're panicking."

"I'm not rocking in circles or anything, if that's what you mean."

Lock finally slipping into place, I freed my keys as he said, "You parked on the harbor?"

"Yeah."

"Good girl, I'll be right there."

"What about poker night?" I asked, fumbling with the clunky keyring to find Rhyett's truck fob.

"Jake's house is at sea level, so we'll move to Charlie's. But we'll come ride with you, alright?"

Nodding, I sighed before realizing for the second time in as many seconds that he couldn't actually see me. "Yeah. Good. Okay."

"I know it sounds scary, but honestly, Skittles, it's probably no big deal. *Breathe*, okay?"

"Yeah," I agreed, trying to force my body to relax. "Yeah. Okay."

"You want me to stay on with you?"

Yes. Steeling my spine, I insisted, "No. No, I'm okay. I'll go get the car started. Just hurry, okay?"

"We're comin' Red!" I heard Axel say before laughing in the background. His ease was somehow even more disarming, and I sucked down my first deep breath in what felt like forever.

"See you soon, baby."

I nearly told him I loved him. Just like that, it almost walked off my tongue before my eyes widened in shock. Because when in God's name did *that* happen? But everything in my body knew the truth of it. Somewhere along the way, our roles blurred, and I fell for him hook, line, and sinker.

If Jameson was here, I'd be okay. If Jameson was with me, I was safe. Even from a monster wave—he'd somehow know what to do, where to go. Seemed to have a plan already. Panic washed through me but for a very different reason. Swallowing that insane near-slip, I finally responded.

"See you soon."

Fob in hand, I turned towards the harbor, only for a scream to tear from my chest.

Lurking against the building was Eric. He was sucking on a canine, blatantly displeased. The siren roared, filling the air around us as my pulse hammered a death knell against my ears.

"I don't have time for you right now," I said simply, moving to walk past him. Eric halted me with a hand around my bicep. "Don't touch me," I ground between my teeth, glaring at him before looking around. Cars whirred on by, the neighboring parking lots emptying the last of their patrons. I wanted to scream, but fear of being the crazy woman he'd undoubtedly made me out to be wrapped a noose around my neck.

"Baby, we have to get to high ground. You're not safe here."

"*You're* not safe here," I bit back. "Jameson is coming to pick me up, and we're headed to see his family."

He ground his teeth. "You're really going to keep up with that?"

"With *what*?" I bit out, jerking my arm away from him and putting a step between us.

"The whole fisherman bit. It's a smoke screen, isn't it?"

"Smoke screen?" I balked, arching a brow and looking him up and down like the madman he was. Beautiful. Polished. *A lie*—all of it was a lie. A well-constructed, professionally styled front.

"Not even *you* move that fast," he sneered, lip curling as he turned to match my stride.

"*Not even me*? What the hell does that mean? You know what— never mind. I don't care," I said pointedly, shaking my head as I clicked the button on the fob and the truck's engine roared to life. Twenty yards. I just needed to make it twenty yards to jump in and hit the lock button. "Get to high ground, Eric."

"I'll get to high ground *with you*, sweetheart."

"Are you kidding me?!" I stopped dead in the middle of the street, alarms blaring from all sides as my heart thundered and a clammy sheen of sweat coated my palms.

"No, I'm not kidding," he said, affronted as he blinked in apparent confusion. Like he honestly expected I would go anywhere with him. "We can drive up to the college. I have a new friend—a professor—who will let us wait this out in his classroom."

"Don't fucking *sweetheart* me," I bit back. "I'm not your fucking sweetheart."

"Babe, look, I know you're mad."

"I'm not your *babe,* either. I'm not your anything. Go wait it out with your friend at the college. I'm expected somewhere."

Eric's hand wrapped around my wrist, yanking me back to him as I yelped. Scowling up at him, I shoved a hand against his chest, but he just gripped my other hand tighter. Not willing to give him the satisfaction of knowing how much it hurt, I snarled, "You're still the same damn coward in the same shitty suits. I said *don't touch me.*" Slamming my heel onto his foot, I yanked away as he hissed in pain, but the next thing I knew, he'd shoved me forward, my knees singing with the impact of the pavement and hands stinging as I caught myself, purse skittering across the concrete. Somewhere beyond the sirens, I could have sworn I heard my name.

Making to scramble upright, he cut me off, wrapping his hand through my hair, scalp screaming with just as much enthusiasm as the sirens blaring above us. The buzz of the cars filling the road towards the evac route blurred into the distance, every single nerve ending seeming to focus in on where he threatened to tear the hair from my head.

Breath hot against my neck, he bent to snarl in my ear. "Stop being such a disrespectful bitch, and fucking *talk to me*. I can't even believe how ungrateful you are. After everything *I did for you*—the money I gave you, the roof I put over your head—you can't even give me five damn minutes to tell you how sorry I am for what happened in Florida. You never would have lived that well on your own. Or have you forgotten where you *came from?*" My eyes burned in pain as that betrayal washed through me all over again. Heart threatening to slam through my ribs, I fought for breath, sobs clawing at my chest. *Never again*. That's what I'd promised myself. That I'd never be back in this position, that I'd build a new life.

Getting rid of ghosts was much more complicated than I'd anticipated.

"It wasn't supposed to go like this. I wanted to *apologize*. To tell you that you were right. But you just *love* pushing my buttons, don't you?" Eric barked, yanking my head back to him. I glared at him as best I could, words failing me as my chest heaved. The echo of footsteps cut between the blaring screech of the tsunami speakers. My mind focused on the sound of his breath beside me. Eyes and throat. That's all I knew about self-defense, and I'd gathered those from badass heroines in books, not practical application. Could I move fast enough? Strike true enough or hard enough to make an escape? "You do this to yourself, you know? Always know exactly what to say to piss me off, you disrespectful—"

Eric's words abruptly cut off, and I screamed as his grip on my hair yanked me back a beat before releasing. There was a scuffle across the pavement, the sound swallowed by the keening siren and a clatter of pissed-off, distinctly male voices.

I barely caught myself above the asphalt, and then all chaos broke out. Head spinning, I was vaguely aware powerful arms were heaving me off the street and whirling me behind a towering male body. Maverick's young, flushed, and terrified face lowered to mine, his big, warm palms swallowing both sides of my cheeks, turning me this way and that, his frantic eyes scouring over every inch of me until he seemed certain I was in one piece.

"Oh, thank fuck," he breathed, suddenly crushing me against him as shouts and curses clamored behind his lanky frame. Panting against his broad, gangly chest, I swallowed the relieved sob in my chest as his arms tightened around me. *Safe.* I was safe. When Mav shakily turned back over a shoulder, my eyes went wide as I spotted my now-bloody ex pinned against the harbor fence.

And my Jameson with his broad hand around his throat.

TWENTY-SEVEN

JAMESON

My fist slammed into him so many times I'd not bothered to count, but it didn't fucking matter because he was still fighting back. Eric landed a blow to my kidney and another to my ribs before I tackled him, ramming my shoulder into his gut and driving him back into the fence, wishing I could've tossed him into the water instead. I was so far beyond feeling any pain if he'd inflicted it, my anger a living, breathing thing wielding my limbs like a damn puppet.

There aren't motherfucking words adequate enough to sum up the lethal, primal fury that swept through my veins when I watched him kick her to the ground. Noel. *My Noel*, scrambling on her hands and knees as he came after her.

Blood spattered my face, but I just cocked my arm back again as I thundered, "You sick motherfucker!" *Smash.* "Waste of breath." *Dodge.* "Worthless piece of shit." *Crack.* That one did it, blood rushing from his nose as he staggered back with a curse, and I lunged, pinning him to the chain link fence by the throat before slamming my fist into his face again....and again, and again.

"*James!*" Axel set a hand on my shoulder when Eric's knees threatened to buckle under the last strike. At least my brother was smart enough to not step between us. He'd helped me rip him off her as Mav dove in to scoop her away. Anger still lacing his tone, he barked, "You can't *kill him.*"

"*Bullshit*, I can't."

"Not *here*," he bit out over the blare of that goddamned alarm. Fuck me. He'd attacked her in broad damn daylight, but I couldn't fucking finish it? Bullshit. Eric had stopped resisting, but his eyes were still open as blood painted his swelling face. There was a grown man's tooth somewhere on the foggy street and it sure as hell wasn't mine. I'd almost regained enough control to step away, to let this monster stagger free. But then the fucker *smiled* and spat blood at my feet. His words were broken pants and rattles, but they were audible through the gap in the siren.

"Little bitch opens her legs for you, and you're willing to go to prison?"

"Oh fuck," Axel said, but he released his hold on me as I landed an uppercut to Eric's gut. His groan of pain was music to my fucking ears as he doubled over. The next landed blow—this one to the side of his head, snapping his face back into the harbor fence—transformed that smug expression into what I could only describe as fear, and he finally fought to guard his face.

Dumb, masochistic psychopath. A little late for that, in my not-so-humble opinion.

Strong arms wrapped around my chest, yanking me backward as Eric fell to his knees.

"Listen to me," I snarled, fighting as my brothers pulled me away. "Let me fucking go!" I barked, ripping my arms free.

"James," Broderick warned, keeping his hand on my back.

"I've got it," I rasped, lungs igniting with each breath, moving to tower over Eric, unwilling to turn my back to eye my brothers. Resisting the urge to snap his fucking neck as unchecked vengeance shuddered through me, I lowered my voice so it was just for him. "I'm going to give you one chance to not fuck this up for yourself, so I suggest you shut the fuck up and listen, you piece of shit." He made to stagger to his feet, but I shoved him into the metal again, cursing the goddamned tsunami alarm as my ears rang, adrenaline amplifying it. Air now fire against my ribs, I snarled, *"Stay down."* When he glared at me, I met his stare, wiping my sleeve across my bloody face, immensely pleased by his silence. By the shadow of fear in his eyes. "You lost her. Don't you fucking fool yourself into thinking you ever deserved her. She found a man who knows *exactly* what he's holding." The metal clang of the fence ringing out cut the air as I hoisted him by the collar and slammed him back into it. Breath steadier, I got as close to his face as I could. "Mark my words. If you ever so much as threaten her again, you'll find yourself in a crab pot watching the light disappear while the last scrap of air leaks from your pathetic lungs," I said, taunting him, satisfied as anger

flashed in those hollow navy eyes. I smirked down at him. "While you wonder where it all went wrong–spoiler alert, you slimy prick–*this* is that moment. You can decide to get the fuck off my island and leave her alone, or this is the moment everything goes wrong for you, and I swear to God, my face will be the last thing you ever fucking see. Am. I. Clear?"

I wondered what the hell kind of drugs he had to be on, as the fact that he had the grit left in his body to protest was staggering. Blood leaking down his lip, he ground out, "She's my—"

"Nothing," I snapped. "She's *your* nothing."

"There are witnesses," he hissed, glossy eyes darting sidelong like any of the men at my back might side with him. Bullshit. This was the poker night crew. Nobody had seen shit.

"And people go missing on the water all the fucking time. Trust me when I tell you there isn't a human on the planet that will give a shit if you're one of them."

"Is she worth throwing your life away for?!" He shouted, blood spattering my face. I didn't flinch, just sneered back at him.

"You tell me—you just did."

"You threatened a senator's—"

"I don't give a fuck who's spawn you are. You say my girl's name again, you face your maker. End of fucking story."

He sneered, lip curling. "This isn't fucking over. Prison—"

"Means jack shit if I fall asleep at night knowing you're at the bottom of the ocean, and she's free to live her life without looking over her shoulder." A little voice crept up in my chest that said that was the boldest damn bluff of my life. Would I serve life in prison if it kept her safe? Yeah. No shit. But for the first time in my monotonous existence, there was something worth living for. And I wanted to live *with her,* not throw it away. Noel had somehow planted her claws so deep in my chest, I wasn't sure I could surgically remove the hold she had on me. Not that he'd ever know that. "Besides, nobody saw shit in this fog. Ain't that right, boys?" I tossed the last bit over my shoulder, smiling as they answered.

"Nah, man, visibility is for crap. I was just evacuating when we bumped into each other," Broderick said smoothly.

"That new guy went missing? Must've fallen off a boat. Dumbass didn't listen to his captain, I guess. *Shame,*" Max added.

Jaw set, point proven, I stared him down until Charlie's voice broke the sizzling energy. "James, let him go, man."

Sucking down air, I released him, slowly backing a step away.

"Such a good little lapdog," Eric panted over a laugh. I lunged forward, cracking my forearm into the side of his head and looming over him as he collapsed like a sack of wheat.

"Fucking psychopath," I ground between clenched teeth.

"*Jesus*," Charlie muttered as he sidled up next to us. He canted his head at Eric's pathetic blood-spattered form. Looking up at the rest of us, he demanded, "*For the record*, he passed out when James still had him against the fence, alright?"

"Holy fuck," Jake said, loping up beside me and releasing a sigh I think we'd all been collectively holding.

"Feel better?" Axel quirked, and I shrugged, shaking out my screaming hand. Broken, for sure. Worth it.

"A bit," I allowed as Charlie knelt and checked Eric's pulse. "He deserved worse." My mind was suddenly numb as I whirled, searching for red hair and alabaster skin. "Where is she?"

Eyes scanning, I found Mav still holding her against his lanky form, her eyes wide and on me. He'd done good—put some distance between them and the brawl. Minutes, *if that*, had passed since he knocked her off her feet. But it felt like a damn lifetime. Noel flung herself away from my brother to close the distance, throwing her arms around my neck as she burst into tears against my chest. An agonizing ache bloomed as my heart splintered into unrecoverable pieces. I should've killed him. Should've ended this. Seeming to see the train of thought in my eyes, Mav shook his head, lids heavy as he watched her cling to me. I wrapped her up. Inhaling her sweet scent, I soothed her, running my hand over her back.

"Shhh, baby, I'm right here. I've got you. You're safe."

"He just came out of—" The sob that broke her voice fractured my resolve to leave him breathing. I glared at my cousin where he watched me like I was a rattlesnake, waiting to strike. He wasn't wrong. "—nowhere."

"I know, baby, I know. Are you okay? What hurts?"

Her shaking hand came to settle against her scalp, and then she shook her head. "I'm okay."

"That's my girl." But as I raised my hand to rub calming lines down her head, I spotted my shaky fingers, already swelling, discolored, and painted in blood. I wasn't any goddamn better than the monster she'd been running from. Just as fucking feral when it came down to it. And she deserved so much more.

NOEL

IT SEEMED like an entire lifetime passed as we answered questions. Jameson never left my side, keeping me tucked against his ribs right until the EMTs insisted on an exam, to which he reluctantly agreed. Charlie had moved us all to higher ground before the responding officers conducted their interviews, the blaring roar of the tsunami sirens adding chaos to an evening more hellscape than resolution. Because it was just starting over again. I knew it in my gut—if Vallie and her firm of urban legal heroes couldn't keep Eric behind bars, how on earth could a small-town judicial system?

They couldn't. That was the reality of it. A leaden sense of helplessness sunk into my bones. Because the only thing that made this different was Charlie bearing witness through the fog. But he'd been yards behind Jameson, catching up only once he and Axel had torn Eric away. I needed to call Blaze's friend back—the time to pull metaphorical punches was over.

Jameson. He'd...gone feral for me. There wasn't really another way to say it. Eric opened his fat mouth during his one shot at a reprieve, and if it hadn't been for Charlie, Broderick, and Axel, I was fairly certain he would have beaten him to death. I couldn't say I'd be sad about it, except for the mark that would leave on Jameson's soul. The idea of him getting into trouble for defending me made bile climb up my throat. While he'd stayed fastened to my side, he avoided my eyes through the entire investigation, answering Bells' questions robotically, no doubt in his own kind of shock.

By the time the tsunami alarm stopped keening and they gave us the all-clear to go home, my mind had...gone numb. Hollow silence rang in my ears. While I was relieved all the Rhodes' homes were no longer under threat, I wasn't sure I could face them all. Not after this. Not after their boys had thrown themselves into physical danger. Not after my cowardice put Jameson at risk for legal repercussions. Because there would be repercussions. Eric had set us up perfectly for his actions to be suspect. So easily spun. All I could do was pray that the Rhodes name held true in Mistyvale—that Milo's meetings with the captains would lay enough groundwork that the rumor mill and media wouldn't clamp on to the opportunity to shred his name. Their family's name.

"Hey," his low voice rumbled through the truck cab, and I could feel Jameson's eyes on me. "You okay?"

"Tired," I offered by way of explanation, terrified if I opened my mouth, every fear and anxiety would come pouring through it until we both drowned.

Jameson had defended me tonight. He'd thrown himself into a situation that could have resulted in his injury without hesitating, and if I'd had any strength to stay in my hometown and hold my ground, he never would have had to. Nodding in understanding, he slipped out of the cab. I hadn't even realized we'd gotten home. Wordlessly, he opened my door, helped me out, and guided me into the house. I didn't break the silence as I made my way straight for the guest room, stripping off my jacket and wincing as my back ached.

Numbly, I fumbled through the motions and got into the shower, as if that would wash it all away. Make the swirl of thoughts vanish in the suds, stripping away sweat, grime, and years of regret. When the steady stream of tears turned to a sob, it was only thirty seconds before Jameson opened the bathroom door.

For the first time, I was internally begging him to say *something*. He remained stoic, brow pinched, jaw set, and eyes evaluative as he slowly unbuttoned his flannel. Those beautiful, broad hands were both bandaged, the right one bruised beyond the white wrap the EMTs had applied over where he'd split the skin. Guilt twisted through me, my swallow hard, as he worked his shirt free and set it neatly against the counter. I wanted to send him away, to burst into apologies, but I couldn't. Couldn't muster words as he tossed the fabric aside and stepped under the steaming stream of water.

In the same level of silence, Jameson moved in behind me until our bodies were flush under the heat. There was nothing erotic about his cock against my ass or the firm wall of muscle wrapping around my back. But my soul seemed to melt as he freed the showerhead and slowly washed the sweat from my skin. Strong fingers turned gentle as he ran suds through my hair, then coated it in conditioner. Traced them along my collarbone, pressing the ghost of kisses down my neck through the steady water, melting my shoulders down my back.

He dried me off, led me back to his dark room, to *his* bed, immediately cradling his broad body around mine. To my complete shock, my eyes drifted closed, knowing I was safe in his arms.

TWENTY-EIGHT

JAMESON

"You alright?" Broderick asked the moment I stepped outside. I assumed my brothers were responsible for the full pot of fresh coffee on my counter, and I pulled in a deep breath as I took my first sip. He and Axel were both rocking on my porch chairs.

I slid out of bed around five in the morning, eyes aching and dry from the hours I'd spent just watching her sleep. How she could watch me behave like a damn animal, letting my temper drive me to the cusp of murder in an open street and then sleep in those same arms was beyond me. But I savored every damn second, just waiting for her to wake up and come to her senses.

Nodding, I sipped my coffee. Millions of words rushed through my head—most of them angry, a few bitter that I hadn't just gotten rid of him when I had my shot, but mostly...scared. "I'm going to lose her over this."

"What?" Axel barked right as Broderick spoke up, straightening from his place on the white rocking chair.

"Why would you jump to that conclusion?"

The scalding liquid burned going down, but I savored it. Buying myself time. Reminding me I was alive. "She fled five thousand miles to avoid ending up with a monster. Only for mine to rear its head."

"My man," Broderick scolded, rising in the same motion. "This is not the same thing."

"Kinda relieved you're worried about that and not prison time," Axel added, shoulders sagging.

I shrugged. "Bells would've pulled me in if Charlie didn't have the balls to do it and they had any grounds to stand on."

"Agreed," Broderick interjected. "I think it was cut-and-dry defense. He fought back. You just finished it, like you always do."

Nodding, I blew a heavy breath out. "The girls working damage control?"

"They've even got Max doing...whatever he does. And Mav and Milo working the rumor mill," Axel said, also rising. Small-town gossip trains could be toxic as fuck, or your greatest asset. In this case, I was beyond grateful our family was enormous, and my siblings had hit the ground running. The girls released the truth of our story to every friend and petty Betty they could think of. El even typed up the release for the Gazette and sent it to one of their writers, who she'd befriended clear the hell back in elementary school. Whatever favor she called in had evidently been significant enough for her to trash the story they'd drafted initially in favor of Elora's.

Our parents pleaded my case wherever they could. And the sun wasn't even warm yet. We avoided the gossips of town like the plague, but in this case, the fact that a Rhodes hadn't given them a juicy story in years would hopefully mean they'd chomp at the bit to sprinkle last night's drama all over town, the way we wanted the narrative told. It wasn't until Broderick set his coffee down on the side table so that he could open his arms up that I realized the gnawing in my gut was fucking *terror*.

Holy shit, I'd never, not once in my life, felt fear like this. Surely, I'd scared her to fucking death, only shock keeping her anchored in my arms last night. She'd come to her senses. Or Eric's family would do what they do best, and Charlie's guys would slap cuffs on me tonight, and I'd lose the chance to tell her everything bombarding my head.

In my mere weeks with Noel, she'd shown me what life could really be. Stiffly accepting his hug, I said, "Love you, man."

"You too. Glad you're okay. You've gotta breathe through this, James. Don't jump to conclusions." His words brought a smirk to my face. Those evaluative brown eyes hadn't left me the entire time Axel filled me in, and evidently, my genuine concern stayed etched on my face. Between Broderick and Rhyett, there was no hiding anything. "I highly suspect her thoughts aren't anywhere near your own, but what do I know?"

More than I was willing to admit. Few humans in my life could dive as deep into the human psyche as Broderick Allan. Rival only to perhaps Elora, who had blown up my phone until one in the morning, incapable of taking the hint but unwilling to invade Noel's sanctuary. Lucky for me. If it had just been me in this house, there was no doubt in my mind she would've let herself in the garage door. Followed by the rest of them. Nodding as though his words resonated, I pulled back, taking another sip of coffee as I looked to the forest that bordered our little strip of homes.

"She okay?" Axel asked after a long silence, save for the steady sip of black coffee. The same gray fog hung pendulously in the air, gradually rolling through the trees.

"*Physically?* Yeah. We got there before he could hurt her too much. But...she didn't say a word all night."

They both grimaced, knowing enough of her to recognize that wasn't good. My Skittles was a perpetual chatterbox. The rumble of a familiar SUV rolling onto the gravel drive jerked all three of our heads up. Juniper's sleek black car inched down my driveway, and I sighed, setting down my cup.

"We'll hang tight," Axel reassured. "Make sure she's alright."

Nodding, I headed for my mother.

After a wordless hug that threatened to shatter my composure, Juniper nodded toward her rig, and I silently complied, sliding into the passenger seat as she reclaimed the driver's side. I hadn't bothered to question her intention or where we were headed, just trusted that there was a reason she was alone. When her long, bare nails tapped at her phone and "Simple Man" by Lynyrd Skynyrd came on the speakers, my eyes slid closed, burning despite myself. In Juniper's world, those lyrics had qualified as a lullaby. And while she had six sons—not one—the words had been her go-to, filling the house through our childhood. So softly it was nearly inaudible, she began singing the lyrics.

I rested my head on my seat, feeling the road bend and curve beneath our tires. Blind or not, I knew where she was bringing me about three minutes in. With the whirr of the bridge to our favorite neighboring island under rubber, I finally peeled my eyes open, but it was my mother that I watched. Her face was relaxed as she guided us to our favorite walk for lazy, thoughtful days. The place she brought me when it was just the two of us, sneaking away from the constant noise of our house. Stepping out to the trail head, I was somehow reduced to the teenage boy she'd brought here after his first heartbreak. She leaned against her car to remove her boots and I did the same. Barefoot, we wandered through the emerald glow of towering pines and spruce, the chill and stab of the earth and rocks hard against my feet. She was always quick to accept my outstretched hand to steady her over streams or logs and up the tiny footbridges.

When at last the trees gave way to open meadows that abruptly fell into the sea, she sighed, settling in the tall grass and wildflowers. She patted the ground beside her, the lyrics still ringing in my memory as I joined her. There we sat as the sun finally burned through the fog, the clouds gradually rolling toward the mountains behind us.

"Are you satisfied?" She finally asked, leaning nonchalantly on her hands. I scoffed, drawing a breath that burned my lungs.

Tonguing at a molar, I nodded, but the words that escaped contradicted the sentiment. "Should've killed him for touching her."

"But...?" she hedged.

"Didn't want to throw away my chance for a life with her."

"What's your heart say?"

Throat tight, I watched the water meet the cliffs below, attempting to steady my breathing. "I know it's madness, mom...but I love her."

"I know," she said without hesitating.

Scowling, I turned to study her as she smiled back at me, skin crinkling around her eyes with every smile, every near-death experience the twelve of us put her through. "*How?*"

"You're many things, my sweet boy, but subtle isn't one of them. You've loved three women in your life. But she's the only one that deserves it."

"We just started out. Just *started* to get to know each other."

"But you would have thrown your life away for her last night."

"He's a piece of shit—"

"It's not about him. It's not even about *them*."

"I don't follow."

"Oh, my sweet boy." She sighed, lifting a hand to stroke my jaw like I was still her little five-year-old and not a full grown man that nearly beat someone to death, the evidence over the bruised mess of my hands. "You didn't hesitate to risk your own neck for her last night."

"Would've defended my siblings, or Brin, or—"

"Anyone who couldn't defend themselves. Sure. You're telling me that's what this is?" A solitary blonde brow arched towards her braided hair. "This was personal."

My chest ached, and I refocused on the water crashing below us as sunlight gradually fought free to wrap around us. "I can't describe it, but she's *mine*, Mom. I've known it for a while now."

"Does she?"

"No."

The corner of her lips quirked. "She should."

"I'm...I'm going to lose her, aren't I?" Just saying it aloud lanced pain through my chest.

"If that's your decision," she said, casually shrugging a shoulder like we weren't discussing my entire future.

"*My* decision?"

"Well, will you let her in or push her away?"

Brow furrowed, I turned back to look at her, but she just lifted her chin, basking in the emerging sunshine. "I'm no different from him."

Mom barked out a laugh before leveling me with a glare that said I was twelve kinds of stupid.

"You *weren't there*," I said defensively. "I fucking lost it, Mom. I thought I'd beat him to death right there on the docks. *Wanted* to. He laid his hands on her and I fucking snapped."

"And you believe that makes you and him the same?"

"A good man—a simple man—doesn't lose control out of anger." I shook my head. "I've never mastered mine. She deserves to feel safe. To know she's not in danger."

She pursed her lips, narrowing her eyes on me. "And you believe you're a danger to her."

"God, no," I blanched, recoiling from the idea of ever hurting her.

"And you don't think she knows that? Knows the difference?"

Throat thick, I watched the matriarch of our big, chaotic family chewing over her words before I admitted, "I don't know. How could she not be afraid of a man like that? A man that nearly kills another in broad damn daylight."

"Because there's an enormous difference between masculine energy that uses his strength to control and manipulate, and a man that uses his strength to honor and defend, as the universe intended. Which are you?"

"I sure as shit wanted to control *him*."

She laughed, the sound disproportionately light for the situation. "Well, I don't think there's a soul that's had the honor of witnessing Noel that wouldn't share that sentiment." She tucked a stray strand of hair behind her ear as the wind picked up around us. "You're being as obstinate as a mule, Jameson. Dig deep, baby. Listen to your heart—what's she saying?" She sighed, shaking her head. "Sometimes I wonder if we didn't speak your burdens into being when we named you."

"What's wrong with Jameson?"

"Your *middle name*, darling."

"Oh," I laughed. *Jameson Atlas Rhodes*. "Always wished I could be a titan."

"Yes, I'm aware," she said with a long-suffering sigh. "It's the burden he carries that concerns me. You cannot bear the weight of the world. As much as I know you wish you could save everyone. What you did last night was brave, if you ask me. You brothers all recounted it—Maverick in *great* detail. You took her on as your own the instant you knew she was in need."

"May have had an ulterior motive," I admitted. "Just wanted her to let me touch her when I hadn't earned the right to."

She gave me a belly laugh that brought a smile to my own face. "Well, fair as that may be, I don't believe for a minute your drive to protect didn't step in there as well."

"Fair."

"Can you see the difference?"

"Between the two of us?" I clarified. When she nodded, I returned my focus to the water, contemplating the last several weeks. My gaze dropped to my hands, to the ugly, livid bruises across my fingers. I could never—not in any lifetime—hurt Noel. Or anyone who didn't really fucking deserve it. Meeting Mom's gaze, I slowly nodded.

"Then go get her before it's too late."

Throat thick, I nodded. I just had one stop to make first.

TWENTY-NINE

NOEL

Waking up to an empty room was a cold slap in the face. Was it… over, then? Our little charade? Our brief glimpse at something more? Had it all been in my head? I should go home, draw Eric's attention back away from the Rhodes, keep the fight in my own damn backyard. Should've stood my ground.

The little Noel who'd never given up, no matter how far into the back of my brain I shoved her, seemed to clear her throat. Raised a hand, like she needed permission to speak.

They say when you die that your life replays in an elaborate slideshow of highs and lows. What nobody talks about is the way grief, transition, or uncertainty can orchestrate the same experience. Jameson's face through that window, me clumsily spilling coffee down his jeans, a jar of sea glass, the earth-shattering sensation of kissing him on the docks. My soul echoed the low rumble of his laughter when I said something outrageous, painted a picture of the primal hunger in his eyes when he came…

Jameson played like a film reel in my head.

And that little Noel—the one that clung to dangerous things like hope—told me I had imagined nothing. Blinking the ache from my eyes, I peeled myself from his bed. Best to pray she was right, but prepare myself for what it would look like if she wasn't.

My first action item had been to layer coverup over the rings under my eyes, then paint on makeup fit for a wedding to hide the fact that I was currently dead inside. I got dressed and packed up my things. The little Noel stomped her foot and muttered epithets while logic argued that Jameson had moved me in here to protect me and if our ruse was moot...well, I'd just be in the way. He was just being protective, and I'd gotten sucked into the magnificent undertow of touches and laughter. Lost track of the purpose along the way, even as he warned me he didn't do relationships and told me smart girls knew better. But...

Whatever had started this...I loved him. I *loved* him...and he'd gotten hurt because of *me*.

He hadn't said a word last night, my chest aching with the burden I'd brought to his doorstep. A burden that belonged with me.

The zipper of my suitcase had just purred closed when the energy shifted, and I felt the burn of his gaze caress my neck. Tears threatened to spill over when he came to wrap his arms around me, his front to my back, like nothing had changed. He stiffened the moment his chin settled on my shoulder.

"What are you doing?" Jameson's voice came out like I had raked him over hot coals. My eyes slid shut, and I shook my head.

"I'm sorry for everything, Jameson. I never should have pulled you into this."

"I think you're forgetting how that went down," he whispered, pressing a kiss to my temple.

Some twisted combination of a sob and a hiccup escaped my lips. "You know what I mean. I shouldn't have let you get involved in my mess."

"Your mess became mine the night I saw you through Rhyett's window."

My heart twisted right as his hands settled over my own. He slid them up my arms until he could turn me to face him. I couldn't look at him. Couldn't meet his eyes, because this was never supposed to mean this much—I wasn't supposed to stay. Certainly wasn't supposed to fall in love with the man. Because if he didn't love me back...

No. I would be fine. If I'd mastered anything these last few years, it was the art of being fine. This was always supposed to be temporary, always for a brief stint, while we got rid of Eric, and if I was honest, I'd been missing home for a while. Missed my friends, my beaches, my cat—

As if on cue, something pressed between my calves and I gasped, shock forcing my eyes wide as I jerked my head down to—

"Chloe?!" I yelped, practically choking on air as I took in her telltale copper markings and dark ears. Frantically flicking my gaze to

Jameson, I found that delicious, smug arrogance hidden beneath his concern. His words finally broke through the wall of anxiety and clicked into place. "How?!" I squeaked as the tears broke free of their dam, rolling down my face. Nearly collapsing beside her, I opened my arms and Chloe, meowing like her life depended on it, climbed up into my lap to nuzzle into my chest.

"You were homesick," he said by way of explanation, slowly lowering to join me on the carpet, gingerly stretching out his long legs. A wince escaped him and I grimaced, loathing that he was sore or injured. I should have prevented it. Somehow. Come up with a solution before he had to step in again.

Forcing down the shame that threatened to spill over, I asked, "But...*how?*"

"I called Rhyett a while back and arranged it. She'll miss her morning mouse hunt, but I don't think she'll begrudge not being chased by Royal every day. Dog's fucking weird. Adopts rabbits, but Chloe was fair game." Jameson was *babbling*. The man didn't babble, but his scrambling for an explanation was as oddly touching as the gesture that led to it.

"You...I can't believe you did this for me." My mouth dried out, his soft smile only deepening the ache in my chest. *Real. This is real. I'm not crazy—he's in this too.* Little Noel did an internal victory dance, complete with blown raspberries. "Before—*before* everything with Eric."

"Well, I'm touched you think I'm capable of miracles, Skittles. But yeah. It was before last night." He reached out a broad palm to stroke down her slick, striped fur. After a few moments of tearful cuddles, he said, "Tell me why your bags are packed."

"I—" a sob broke my words, and I buried my face in Chloe's neck, half-crying, half-giggling as she squirmed until she was comfortable, her deep purr returning. "I didn't think you'd want me staying here now that everything is over." Even as I said it, the words felt stupid, like weighted marbles in my mouth.

He brought me Chloe.

"Everything is...over?" His voice went deep and something like danger vibrated off him. But it was the pain on his face that made my ribs halt mid-inhale. "You're going to have to clarify because where I'm standing, we *just* got our fresh start."

"Jameson," I scolded, ignoring the heat his words planted in my chest.

"Noel," he drawled, mirroring my indignation.

"You moved me in here to keep me safe. Eric is in custody, ergo —" I spun my wrist, flourishing my hand for emphasis.

"Oh, fuck him," he rumbled. "This isn't about him. Don't insult me by pretending you don't know that." When I made to protest, he held up a hand, shaking his head. "The asshole gave me a shady excuse to get to touch you, *at best*. Wasn't sure how the hell to win you over otherwise."

Face warm, eyes stinging, I smiled up at him. I didn't believe that for an instant, not when I pictured his livid face when he pulled me against him that day outside Grizzly Grind, and certainly not when I eyed his bruised hands. Those secret, protective superhero instincts of his ruled those choices. "Is that what you're telling yourself?"

"Maybe," he said, a facsimile of a smile curving his cheeks as he stroked his big fingers down Chloe's head. She nuzzled into his great, broad palm, and I scoffed as she purred louder. "What?" He asked, smirking as he canted his head.

"She hates men."

"If you're applying that term to Eric, I'm insulted at the comparison."

That made me burst out laughing. For the first time, the sound of his name didn't make my insides tangle. "My apologies."

"She hates toxic *cowards*, is what you meant."

"You could say that," I allowed. A heavy silence began to pendulum between us expectantly. It took a beat for him to draw in a heavy breath.

"So...will you...stay?" Something like panic slid into his eyes, chest rising rapidly enough to betray the facade of calm. My chest threatened to cave in at the sight of his pain. *Real. This is real.* "With me," he rasped, as though I needed the clarification.

Vision blurring, I met his intense gaze. Those steel-blues searing with focus that could melt me to his floor. For once in my life, words failed me, leaving me to give him a watery nod as my ribs constricted.

Before I knew what was happening, Chloe had been displaced as he lifted me from my spot on the floor and brought me to straddle his lap. His big hand came to settle against my back, the other cradling my face to make me look at him.

"Thank fuck," he breathed before his lips came down like molten lava in the kiss to end all kisses. Oxygen fled the premises, tension seeming to melt from those broad shoulders.

Head spinning when we finally came up for air, I admitted, "I thought I would be way too much for you in the long run."

"What?" He huffed, the chagrin making me smile.

"I'm just...I guess I'm used to being too much for everyone in my life. Too much energy. Too much *color*," I said pointedly, trying to keep my tone light despite the way the confession tore at my soul. We were cutting down to the bone, here. The things I didn't even say to Brex or Jos. Because the reality was, I worked so hard to make other people smile and feel seen because I knew what it felt like to never be accepted at my full power...to grapple with decades of rejection. "I mean, Vallie keeps up if I caffeinate her adequately, but my siblings and everyone else—" we both knew whose name nearly spilled off my tongue. "Even Brex, more often than not. When you and I first met—"

"I said some stupid shit," he cut in. "Look, baby, you scared the daylights out of me."

"*I* scared *you*?" I asked incredulously, memorizing the lines of him as he stroked his thumbs over my face, still cradling me to him.

"Christ, baby, *yeah*." That glorious jaw clenched and unclenched, the furrow between his brows begging to be smoothed out by a thumb or my lips. "I wasn't supposed to fall for *anyone*, Skittles. Certainly not a spitfire eight years younger than me who could hand me my ass in ten seconds flat."

I choked on a laugh, sliding my hands around to settle on his broad shoulders as he continued. My brain took a second to catch up as it wrapped around the words 'fall for'.

"You're not too much. You've *never been* too much. You're exactly what the world needs. And even if you were, there's nothing you could do that could ever justify being treated like *that*. Do you understand me?" When my eyes fell, he gently wrapped my hair into a fist to tilt me up, keeping his other hand where he cradled my cheek, forcing me to look at him. "His violence and lack of control is a reflection of *his* weak character, not you. Don't you ever tell yourself otherwise."

Throat thick, I admitted, "I thought he loved me enough to get better."

"*That's* not love, baby." The dangerous blade in his graveled tone was somehow soothing. Maybe it was the lengths he'd already gone to in protecting me. Maybe it was the vulnerability in his eyes as he studied mine for something I couldn't place. Nobody else had ever felt...safe enough...to lay these pieces of my bruised heart bare. Not until Jameson.

"No," I finally agreed. He waited patiently as I composed my thoughts. The unspoken truth I'd lived with all this time in stubborn solitude. When his tolerance for the silence evidently waned, his rough hand gently squeezed the back of my neck in silent prompting. "I thought I could help him, you know?" The naïve reality planted an ache in my chest I couldn't articulate. "Knew he had some issues. But...I didn't mean to make him break like that."

"Baby, it was never your job to fix him, and the way he treated you was never—*never*—your fault. That's on *him*, not you." His rough thumb traced over my cheekbone, thick fingers weaving between strands of my hair as a bird called somewhere beyond the window. Jameson's eyes softened as he studied me, his bottom lip rolling between his teeth. When he spoke, his voice was softer, cocooning around my senses and silencing the outside world, like we'd ensconced ourselves in our own little bubble. "A wise woman recently reminded me that real men protect and serve. Cowards use their strength to control."

"A wise woman?" I said, sniffling as his words settled in my chest. He was right. I knew he was right. Had known it all the whole time, somehow thinking I could fix things along the way. Ignorantly believing he could change for me. That I was enough for Eric to heal, to stop drinking, to let me help him glue his broken pieces back together.

"I *might've* been in a panic, worried you'd think Eric and I were the same breed of monster." Horror roiled in my stomach, because never in my worst nightmares had Jameson ever been grouped in with *him*. What he did for me last night was terrifying, but it was terrifying because I could have lost him, not because I ever feared he could hurt me. When my mouth popped open, he set a gentle thumb against my lips, lowering his eyes to meet mine reassuringly. "Juniper *may* have talked some sense into me this morning."

So, that's where he'd gone. He wasn't running *from me*. He was talking all of this out with his mom. Honestly, the strategy had merit, and maybe if I tried that from time to time, I wouldn't feel so bottled up inside. Finally pouring the words out for Jameson had already been exhausting. So I just mumbled, "*An angel*, that woman."

"She'd pay you to say that in public."

I laughed, burying my face against his shoulder and locking my arms around his neck like I could stay there forever. Jameson rubbed soothing circles up and down my back, resting his own against my neck, breathing me in as I did the same. Finally, I asked, "You mean all of that?"

"I'd swear it on my life."

"Good," I said simply, moving in for a kiss. As Jameson met me, movement for precious movement, my mind rolled through everything that happened. He'd brought my fur baby here, a piece of home now in Mistyvale. Which meant...Jameson had been thinking about me being here long-term for more than twenty-four hours.

He'd asked me to stay. Gratitude heated my chest, that dangerous glowy sensation I refused to acknowledge solidifying into an irrefutable reality. It made no sense—was blatantly ill-advised, given the cataclysmic timing. But I couldn't change it, not even if I wanted to.

I was in love with Jameson Rhodes.

Tender touches turned more urgent as the truth of that settled in my soul, and for the first time, I didn't push the thought away as our fingers grappled for purchase. Because there was no part of this kiss that belonged to anything beyond *us*. I'd just slipped my hands beneath his T-shirt when he peeled away, serrated breaths sawing between us.

"Wait," he panted, urgent hands stroking the hair away from my face as he rasped the word again. "Wait."

My stomach churned uneasily. "Okay?" I breathed back. Nipples hard with arousal—effectively negating the point of my bra as they attempted to cut through it—heat pooling between my legs where his hardening erection strained against his jeans. Our chests grazed, and we steadied ourselves, my eyes locked on steel-blues. The suffocating desire to feel him inside me collided with the anxiety at what needed to be said. There was too much going on, and anything more might just kill me.

He studied me as I did the same to him. The anticipation had nerves tying knots in my gut, an oily feeling under my skin threatening my composure. When, at last, he spoke, my world tilted on its axis.

"I love you," he said slowly, deliberately. "I am *in love*...with you. And I know that it's madness. We've only known each other for a few months. But...do you remember the day this started—you said sometimes you just...know?" I nodded, remembering the salvation of his arm around me and the comforting, subtle thump of his pulse as I buried my face against his chest, knowing I was safe with him. "*I know...*You're it for me, baby—"

It was my turn to cut him off, my kiss pilfering his words away as my heart sprinted off the starting line, threatening to compose the most off-key musical he'd ever seen.

"Baby," he breathed between kisses. "Did you hear me?"

I laughed, the sound somewhere in the neighborhood of hysteria. "Yeah, *Wolverine*," I teased, loving the way his smile cracked against my lips, fingers tightening where he held me. "I heard you." The next kiss was more urgent as my hands dove beneath his shirt, pulling him into me. "I love you, too. And it fucking terrifies me because it's too fast—"

"*So* fast," he agreed, chuckling darkly.

"—but I do."

"I'm so fucking glad to hear you say that," he admitted before claiming my lips again. One, two, three desperate kisses nearly bruised me. His shirt hit the floor, mine just behind it, and then our hands were working belts free like our lives depended on it, bodies bending in ridiculous floor-bound acrobatics to strip our jeans through breathless laughs of relief and ravenous touches. My bra hit the ground with comical desperation, and then he was laying me down across the carpet, both of us incapable of peeling apart long enough to exert the effort required to reach the bed.

"So fucking beautiful," Jameson said on a guttural exhalation. He sucked a bare breast into his mouth right as my hand found the firm length of his shaft, thumb brushing over the bead of pre-cum on the swollen crown. I sighed as he circled my pebbled flesh with his tongue, pleasure and desire heating my center. As far as cocks go, Jameson's was fucking spectacular. I needed it. Needed *him*.

"I love you," I repeated, smiling this time as I rolled my hand over the length of him.

Jameson groaned, the sound vibrating where his mouth was again covering my nipple. He gave me a hot, decadent suck as his hands wiggled my panties free, fingers immediately parting my lips and dragging my arousal over my clit.

"Always so soaked for me." The words were practically purred as he started stimulating that sensitive bud of nerves. "Say it again," he rasped before returning to lavish my jealous breast in equal strokes of hungry affection.

"I love you," I gasped as his fingers found my center.

Smiling as he popped off my needy nipple, Jameson pressed kisses down the length of my chest and belly, working his way to my throbbing pussy, my head falling back as he reached his goal. Giving my clit a hard suck, he buried his face in my center, my hands frantically weaving in his hair like that might keep me anchored here.

"*Mine*," he breathed before diving back in, licking from my entrance to my clitoris—his finger gently pumped, just enough tantalizing sensation to drive me crazy. "This pussy is mine. This body, this heart, this mind, is mine. Do you understand me, baby?"

"Yours," I agreed breathlessly. His eyes darkened, satisfaction sparking in them as he returned to his work, adding a second thick finger, the delicious, aching stretch robbing my breath. I bucked against his face as his fingers curled, hitting that glorious, elusive spot. Good god, the man knew how to fuck—whether it was his fingers, tongue, or cock, he wielded them all with devastating accuracy. Pleasure built like a manic pressure as he worked. My arch against the floor was cut short by his free hand planting against my ribs like he'd pin me there until I had no choice but to come undone beneath him.

"I love you," I gasped again, the words prompting him to suck my clit more fervently, fingers increasing their demand against my walls. My mind spun incessantly, pleasure gradually vibrating through my body until my walls clamped around his hand so violently I was surprised he could keep curling against them. Release tore free like a hurricane, wave after wave rolling through my body. Jameson didn't stop, didn't ease up, merely slowed his movements enough to draw the pleasure out in expert motions. I moaned his name, toes curling as my hands gripped his thick hair. When my orgasm finally ebbed away, pleasure tiptoeing toward too much sensation, legs shaking, he gently slipped free.

"*Suck*, baby," he demanded, bringing his fingers to my lips. The heat of his words somehow penetrated the buzzing fog that had filled my mind. "I want you to taste how fucking perfect you are."

His dirty words shot to my center, and I did as he asked, gently closing my lips around him and sucking hard, tasting the tang of my pleasure.

"That's my good girl." My thighs clenched around his hips, which earned a wry smile. "You like that," he noted. I nodded, sucking hard as my lips popped off his fingers.

Snatching his wrist before he could retreat, I pressed soft kisses to each bruised knuckle, eyes locked on his as something in them deepened.

"Worth it," he reassured softly.

"Thank you," I breathed back. "For everything, Jameson. Now, come here," I demanded breathlessly, finally releasing him, wrapping my hands around his biteable ass, tracing my fingers around the ridge of his hip until they could wrap around his hard cock. He smiled, that crooked one that made his dimples pop out. The real Jameson. The one reserved for me. "I need you," I breathed as I eyed the length of him. He rocked forward until I could sit up and wrap my lips around his silky smooth dick. *Fuck me*, he was thick today. *Thick and perfect.* Eyes slipping shut, I traced the line of his slit, scooping up the salty bead of pre-cum and savoring the taste of him.

"Baby," he groaned, bracing a hand on the floor above me, his head falling as he slowly thrust into my mouth. I moaned as he swelled against me. "You like my cock in your mouth?" I nodded as much as I could manage, jaw burning with the effort to take him deeper. "*Fuck*, baby, I could get used to this."

Relaxing my throat, I sucked him in until I gagged as he hit the back. Tears stung my eyes as lust collided with my love for this man. Wrapping a hand around the base of his thick shaft, I brought the other to toy with his balls as he fucked my mouth.

"*Fuuuck*, Noel." That. Right there. God, if I could just hear him say my name like that every single damn day, life would be well-lived. Pride lit my chest up like a damn jack-o'-lantern, and I pressed my tongue against the bottom of him as I tried to take every last inch. "Good girl, *fuck*, you're such a good girl. Swallow me, baby." When he rolled his hips forward, I gagged on his length again, but my hands flew up to grab his ass as he attempted to retreat. No. No way. I wanted every damn inch of him. "*Noel*," he rasped. "Fuck, you suck my cock so well." I nodded around him, as though the motion could show him how badly I wanted this. Wanted him. Wanted to claim him the way he claimed me. The added sensation seemed too much, his eyes slamming shut. "You *own me*, Noel," he said gruffly. Something white-hot and overwhelming hit my chest, having much less to do with the carnal inferno of hormones raging through me, and everything to do with the raw vulnerability in those gravelly words. It was only three hard pulls later that Jameson tore his decadent dick from me, hands cradling my face before scraping to my waist and flipping me over.

A gasp slipped through my lips as I landed on my stomach, his muscular arm hooking beneath my waist as I scrambled onto my hands. His hard, wet crown pressed against my entrance in the next heartbeat, sliding through my arousal to press against my clit, a moan pouring from me with each rotation. "I want you bare so badly, baby."

Logically, I knew we should have this conversation when we were level-headed, when the heat of the moment and desperate declarations didn't erase sense from the table. But I didn't care. *Couldn't* care as everything in my body screamed to feel him, to let him fill me.

"I'm yours," I breathed, arching against him as I turned over a shoulder. Eyes flaring, Jameson's chest seemed to halt. He spit on his hand, working his length before gliding up my pussy.

Every ounce of sense left my body as he speared into me in one forceful thrust. Gasping, I arched against him and Jameson froze, letting my body catch up to the sudden intrusion, stretching around him as he slowly rocked his hips before increasing intensity. The bare connection was unspeakably satisfying, both of us pausing as the sensations overtook us.

"Oh *fuck*," he breathed, arm tightening around my waist, rough fingers digging into my hip. "Fuck, baby, your cunt feels so fucking good. So. Damn. Tight."

"You're so thick," I mewled, as his next thrust stole every ounce of oxygen, pleasure winding my center impossibly tauter. He was. He filled me to capacity and beyond, ecstasy blending with an immaculate ache as my limits fractured beneath his demanding pace. A broad, rough palm clapped against my ass a beat before scraping down the length of my spine and wrapping in my hair. He held steady before spearing through the loose tendrils until his hand slid down my nape, circling my throat. Jameson guided my face back, head turning, desperate for a peek at him as he decimated every nerve ending, every synapse in my mind in overdrive at the sensations he tore from my body. The world pre-Jameson ceased to exist, as though he erased it with each relentless thrust.

A groan rumbled in his chest, and I found those steel-blues over my shoulder as the arch in my spine gave him the angle he'd evidently sought. The intensity of his focus was enough to lure even the strongest-willed woman into submission, hunger, and desperate need permeating every rigid line of him. That's all I had time to see, the new angle taking him impossibly deeper, the pleasure nearly buckling me entirely, grateful I could collapse against the floor so freely. Arms shaking, I bowed my head into my hands as his hips snapped forward in merciless thrusts again and again, hand trailing around until he could palm my breast, rolling the hard nipple between his fingers. My breasts ached, suddenly heavy with need.

"Jameson," I breathed, unable to muster any more volume under the force of his strokes. "Please," I begged, although I wasn't entirely sure what I was asking of him. When he slid himself free, I couldn't even protest, because, in the next breath, I was flat on my back. His weight settling over me was absolutely hedonistic, his lips slamming into mine. Jameson hitched my knee up, sliding his cock back home as our gazes locked.

Desperate kisses and roaming hands were overshadowed by the way he looked like he might die if he couldn't have this—have *me*. I had to agree, nervous that I'd disintegrate into nothing if he didn't finish what we'd started. His eyes locked on mine, as though he was determined to peer into my very depths. Breathless pants gave way to moans of ecstasy, Jameson releasing harsh grunts of effort as he took up an animalistic pace.

There was nothing formal about this, nothing fake or uncertain.

This was a claiming.

This was the two of us coming clean, connecting in the most base and simultaneously the most spiritual kind of conquest as the reality of what we'd found—what we were in the process of creating—crashed through us. Sex had never been accompanied by the soul-deep devastation that overwhelmed me as I watched Jameson's focus on my face as he ravaged me entirely. When my head lolled backward, eyes rolling until they had to shut, he growled back at me.

"No, baby, not today. Eyes on me, Noel." Fighting the lust-hooded satisfaction, I forced my lids open, snapping my gaze back to his face. The intensity of those steel-blues ignited something primal in me as he stared straight into my soul. "Good girl. Watch me fuck you, baby." Mouth popping open, I stared at where our bodies collided, his pace only slightly less ruthless as he, too, took the time to admire where we joined. "You're *mine*, baby," he said, tone heavy and reverent, like I was something sacred to be worshiped by the man braced above me. "Fuck, I'll never get enough of you."

"Me either."

"Come, *Noel*. Show me who you belong to."

Damn, no pressure. I laughed breathlessly, mouth falling open as I devoured the sight of his body against mine. Of this courageous man I loved more than life, who bore angry purple bruises across his ribs and lean abs from the fearless way he'd defended *me*.

"I love you," I said with a desperate exhale. His eyes flared, hips cracking forward impossibly harder.

"I love *you*. Now, *come*, beautiful."

When his relentless efforts at last conducted the perfect combination of sensations, the ensuing orgasm shattered my very being. Every inch of me—hair to tiptoes—succumbed to his demands before liquefying with pleasure. Neither of us could summon the strength to move, our sweaty naked bodies pooling together on the floor.

Drifting in and out of sleep, we just relished being together for what felt like a lifetime. Vaguely, I registered that my back and knees were smarting with what could only be rug burn, but I couldn't even summon a solitary fuck to give. They could be raw for all I cared. The ecstasy was worth it.

It wasn't until Jameson's phone vibrated for the third consecutive time that he sighed, finally sliding out of me to snatch his cell from where it had hit the floor.

Brow furrowed, he glanced from his cell to my face, concern lining his expression as he answered, "Yo, Charlie, what's up?" The beat of silence was punctuated by Jameson's eyes sliding shut in apparent resignation, free hand coming to yank against the back of his neck. "Son of a bitch. Yeah, man, thanks for the head's up." Every ounce of lust-hazed bliss drained from my body as the blood evacuated my face. Jameson scrambled to yank his shirt on as he barked into the phone, "Give me an hour."

THIRTY

JAMESON

A misdemeanor. The son of a bitch—or his father's high-paid attorneys—somehow talked the felony assault charges down to a *misdemeanor* and negotiated his release and return to Florida. They had dropped the stalking charge altogether under the guise of a coincidence that his trip coincided with hers. Evidently attacking an innocent woman in broad daylight was something to be laughed at in cigar lounges, so commonplace it couldn't be prioritized.

My blood was boiling as I drove up to Mistyvale's tiny airstrip, a private jet taxiing around the back of it. My skin lit up with the desire to decimate the damn thing, hands struggling not to snap my wheel as I watched until it parked and the steps lowered to the tarmac.

Axel's truck whipped into the spot beside mine, kicking up a spray of dirt and gravel. He, Max, Maverick, and our dad all hopped out as my feet hit the black stones. In a town this small, it was only ninety seconds before the county jail van pulled up to the gate, security ushering them through.

A towering man in a suit stepped off the private plane, bringing every inch of my body to attention, hair standing on end as I got my first glimpse at who could *only* be Eric's father. *My new fucking problem.* Teeth grinding, there was nothing we could do as they released Eric from the van and ushered him into the plane, Max's shutter blinking rapid fire as we observed from a distance. Arms crossed, about to crack a molar, my body all but vibrated with anger, and I watched as he vanished into the aircraft. Should've fucking killed him. At least, then, she'd be safe when this all went down.

Broderick and Elora appeared in his car right as the damn thing taxied.

"You alright?" Broderick asked, a heaviness in his tone I'd never heard before. I nodded, refusing to remove my eyes from the door Eric had disappeared behind, even as they came to stand on either side of our pissed-off lineup.

"Does she know?" Elora asked, voice soft as we all stared down the slick black tail of the thing as it made its way to the end of the runway.

"Which part?" I growled. There was only one *she* in question.

"All of it?"

"Knows he's leaving."

"*James,*" she said, aghast, breath hitching in evident horror. I could practically feel her focus as it assaulted my profile.

"*Don't.*" I hadn't had the heart to tell her more than that. Didn't want her added grief on my conscience. Because I knew. I *knew* what Noel's face would look like if I admitted Eric's family was pressing assault charges. Bogus bullshit. No doubt assuming they could outspend our little island family to bury the threat. Like hell would I go down without a fight. And like hell would the truth not win in my own damn town.

"What's the plan?" Milo asked, voice rough with a pain I could only imagine a father would hold for a son in my predicament.

"Turn myself into Charlie and Bells."

"Fuck this," Broderick, of all people, growled as he ran an angry hand over his short hair, kicking at the gravel, sending it skittering against the chain-link fence with a metallic clatter. The hanging mist felt even more ominous as his chronically maintained composure broke, despite the spots of sunlight. It felt like the world was trying to tell me the darkness would eventually scatter for something better, but we weren't quite there yet. "This is fucking bullshit."

"Love you too, man," I said, smirking. There was nothing in the world that ate Broderick alive quite like injustice.

"I fucking mean it. That fucker is fucking with our fucking family and it's fucking *bullshit*." Broderick *rarely* swore. It was even more rare than Noel—his propensity for doctorate-level dictation winning out unless he was seeing red.

"Well. You certainly demonstrated the variety of the word," El said, fighting a laugh. "Now, what's our plan?"

"I head to Charlie. You guys come up with a way to flip the script —rattle this motherfucker's cage for once. We meet back at the big house. Charlie was already calling in old Judge Cullen."

"Good. Rob is headed down now," my dad said calmly as the roar of the engines filled the space. Broderick's father, Rob, had been our family attorney for decades, not that we'd needed one for more than writing wills and chilling on a retainer for a moment such as this.

We stood in stoic silence as we watched the Connelys leave our island, taking the deafening whir with them, a line of middle fingers saluting them as they took off. I lamely prayed the damn thing would go down over the ocean, knowing it would never be that easy, before glancing at my watch and cursing under my breath.

"I gotta roll. Charlie bought me time, but I gotta get there before somebody gets dispatched to the house."

"We'll come with you. Take the truck," Axel offered, but Elora snaked her way through them to throw her arms around my neck. When she pulled back, her face was ghostly pale and deadly serious. Short curls tucked behind her ears, I studied her determined jaw and stiff shoulders.

"James, I want to respect your choices here, but I think you should tell her. Give her a chance to say what she needs to say," Elora coaxed, as I turned to face them all. She was right. I knew she was right. But the idea of seeing her cry—*over me*—was enough to bring me to my knees.

"El, I can't. Just don't."

"She deserves—"

"More than I can ever give her. But I've got to walk in there with my head tall, not groveling at her feet. I can't do this if I have to see her hurting. Please. Just." Pain lanced through her expression, tears brimming in those usually bright eyes for a beat before she threw her arms around my neck again, a shudder rolling through her. Well, fuck, if I had to watch her break too, I might cave anyway. "I'll be home tonight. It's early. Cullen is heading down, and Rob is on it. Which reminds me..." Gingerly, I freed myself, passing her to Broderick as he opened his arms. I fished the envelope out of my back pocket, unfolding it as I passed it to Milo. "This should be plenty for bail, and then some."

"Son, your mother and I can help you—"

"You will not be paying for *my* choices. End of fucking story." He nodded, seeming to understand that I needed to do this my way.

Needed to take care of this on my own. "Thank you," I replied gruffly, before pulling them each into a hug.

AS AXEL'S truck pulled into the police station beside me, my chest constricted. Every inch of my body vibrated with adrenaline, colliding with the desire to hold her, to feel her lips on mine. Fear riddled my spine. She was going to hate me for this. I knew it. Knew it, but couldn't be man enough to watch her break with me as Charlie came out of the precinct, jaw set and twelve kinds of misery carved into his stiff features.

"Be careful, son," Dad said softly, shaking his head as he stared down the entire building. "There are many ways to destroy someone. But targeting their loved ones is undoubtedly the most effective." Boy, like I didn't fucking know it.

"Well," I breathed, glancing sidelong at Milo. "This is going to suck."

Noel

JAMESON

I love you Noel. Please trust me.

THE LAST MESSAGE I'd received was taunting me from where it still sat open on my screen like a fucking condolence card. A reminder that something was very wrong, and nobody was answering my damn calls. Like a death in the family, a heavy blanket had settled over the house. I'd responded. Hell, I'd responded *three* times as terror crushed my windpipe when he didn't answer my calls.

Neither did Broderick, Axel, El, or Max, for that matter. I'd gone as far as calling the twins and Mav, before pacing myself into a frenzy when Jameson still hadn't come back by dinnertime. Not that the bile scaling my throat would allow me to even think about making food. He should've been back. He was supposed to be making sure Eric got on his damn plane and off the island, but the clock in the foyer had ticked me into madness as the sun made its arc behind the spotty cloud coverage.

When I finally caved and called Rhyett, only hearing his voice via the answering machine, I slammed my feet into rain boots and stomped towards the door. Everything in my body said something had gone very, very wrong. It might have been unhinged, but Christ himself could've walked through the front entryway and not been able to convince me otherwise. When the door smashed into the hall wall with enough force to rattle the lone picture frame in the entryway, I came to a dead stop, finding Elora on the front stoop with her head in her hands, and Broderick sitting beside her with his arm around her shoulders, his head resting against her.

"What happened?" my voice cracked out the two weak words. El's face was tear-streaked when they both turned to face me. Before she could say something, the rumble of rubber on gravel snapped all our heads forward, and relief galloped through my veins at the sight of that silver truck. I sprinted forward, relief coursing through me as Jameson flew out of the front seat, engine still rumbling where he'd abandoned the vehicle in park. He met me with every ounce of urgency as I threw myself around him. I needed to climb this man like a tree. And for a beat, as his mouth took mine, I forgot they'd all been radio silent, forgot the hours of fear that had just consumed my day as our bodies demanded a proper greeting.

Feet settled on the driveway, I came up short when he went to cradle my face and my eyes snagged on the black across his thumb. Stomach bottoming out, I snatched his wrist, pulling his hand down as his eyes slid shut in resignation. I splayed his palm open in one of mine, heart leaping into a full sprint as I took in the ink on his fingers. Ink like...fingerprints.

My body stiffened in his arms, chest cracking wide open as realization dawned.

"*Jameson?*"

*J*AMESON

THERE IT WAS. The inevitable hurt, betrayal, and disbelief I'd so desperately wanted to avoid. All the emotions painted across that beautiful pixie face. At least this way, we were home. At least I didn't have to put on some bullshit front and could just be...*her* Jameson.

"Baby," I said calmly, although no bone in my body could echo the sentiment. "I can explain."

"You fucking better," she snapped, fear consuming the irises I loved so much, chest heaving.

"We'll, *uh*, just be going," Broderick said gently, as he and El made for his car. For as much as they drove each other to madness, I was so grateful he'd been by her side today. They might not admit it, but their friendship was equal parts respect and endless debates. He knew as well as I did, my sister could break when there were problems she couldn't fix, and I'd always been terrified she wouldn't remember how to put herself together again. Broderick was a master at keeping people centered. The glare Noel leveled their direction told me they'd stuck to my plan, and she knew they'd held out on her, betrayal radiating from the tight hold of her shoulders and set of her jaw. El's eyes watered as they fell to her feet, and she reluctantly followed Broderick as he drug her away.

She *loved* Noel.

Probably more than anyone shy of Rhyett, the two of them had connected over these last months, and guilt ate at my stomach at the idea of driving a rift between them over El's undying loyalty to her family.

To me.

Fuck.

"Wait," Noel snapped her fingers, halting Broderick and El a foot away from his sedan, both of them shifting nervously on their feet. "You both stay." She whirled on me, ire in her eyes, my stomach sinking.

"*Baby.*"

"Don't," she snapped, pulling away as I reached for her. "Don't touch me. *Explain.*"

I stepped back, the agony twisted with terror threading through her voice as good as any physical blow. It would've been better if she'd hit me. Crossing my arms to keep myself from going to her to do exactly that, I assured her, "I'm okay. *We're* okay."

"But we're not going to be...*are we?*" she said, blinking back against the water threatening to spill down her cheeks. Fuck, I couldn't live with myself if that hint of fear became the real thing. If I couldn't pull off what I thought I could, and she suffered more for it.

If there was the slightest inclination that he was going to win this thing, I'd fucking kill him. Make it worth it.

"Rob and I have no doubts we'll win the case, Skittles. Evidence is overwhelmingly on our side." Okay, about ninety percent certainty, but that was pretty damn close. "It's just money and an aggravating amount of time he'll get from me."

"Who the hell is Rob?"

Fair question. Keeping my tone steadier than my pulse, I said, "Broderick's dad. He's our family attorney." Broderick gave a little wave, his expression more grimace than smile, obviously uncomfortable being dragged into this.

That seemed to appease her for a second before she scowled. "How bad is it? I need to call Vallie."

"Yeah, we should probably do that," I agreed simply. "It's a bogus assault charge. It won't hold up. It's my word versus his and—"

"He's a Connely," she said flatly, leveling me with a glare that dripped in a pain I couldn't understand. "They do whatever the fuck they want to do."

"I have eye-witnesses," I pointed out, rocking on my feet in an effort to not reach for her again. "All of them will vouch for me. Including a sheriff. There's no way that he's going to win, baby."

"You don't understand," she said, her chin wobbling as she blinked up at me. *There* she was. My brave girl. It was the tremble in her lip that threatened to undo me altogether. I needed to kiss the worry off her face to ease her fear.

But I couldn't.

Couldn't touch her unless she allowed it.

Couldn't promise her something I had no technical control over.

"He'll destroy us, Jameson." She could barely get the words through her lips, the tremor in her jaw giving away the depth of her fear. "When people cross their family, they *decimate* them. They don't leave enough of them to recover."

"Not me, baby. Not *us*. This family can't break—we'd never allow a coward like that to break *shit*. And you're not facing them alone. Not anymore."

"Don't you get it?!" She demanded, throwing her hands up. "He won't stop. *They* won't stop. And as well-intentioned as you all are, none of us have the resources that they do. Men like Eric do what they want; the people around them be damned. Do you know what went through my head today?! When you didn't come home."

The way she glared up at me left no room for error, so I just answered honestly, shame bubbling like oil in my gut. "No, baby. But I can imagine."

"*Can you?*" Her tears came then. "Because against all odds, I *found you*, Jameson. When I was at my lowest. When the world would have me—when *he* would have me—think I was alone and helpless against the big bad wolf banging on my door...I found you. And I...I can't do this without you. I *can't*. I can't imagine a life where you're not by my side. *Against all odds*, I moved five thousand miles from home—ran like a coward—and the world, universe, God, or whatever deity is looking over us, let me run right into *your* arms." Her voice cracked, the dam breaking into a steady flow as she shook her head. "You should have told me. I should have been allowed to at least go with you. Should have been able to *hold you*," her voice broke again, and she shook her head, blowing an angry breath out as she wiped at her eyes, jamming her fingers against the corners like she could contain her tears. "What if it was *our last chance?* How could you fucking take that from me—take *us* from me without even giving me a moment to *say goodbye?*"

Her sob decimated me, my composure breaking. Unable to help myself any longer, I shifted forward, scooping her little face up between my palms, lifting her chin as I demanded, "*Look at me.*" When she just jammed her eyes closed, lower lip trembling, I repeated myself. "I said look at me. Good girl. Listen here, Noel McShane, you're one of us now. And they might be loud, overwhelming as hell, and obnoxious at times, but they're not about to let this little shit hurt one of their own any more than he has. And they're *certainly* not going to let you face this alone."

"You're cocky."

"I'm *dedicated*," I corrected before swiping her lips between mine. Only backing up enough to talk, I said, "Worst-case scenario, my family would have had your back."

"I'm..." Her voice trailed off, cracking when she finished, "Tired. So damn tired, Jameson. Soul deep, exhausted from years of his bullshit."

"I know, baby," the words choked out of me, palms buzzing with the need to fix this for her. And for a moment, I thought about the role she played—in this town, in my family—always lifting people up, making customers smile, or feeling seen when *I* knew she'd actually been distracted. Noel buried her grief in the joy of those around her, solving her friends' problems and ignoring her own. But that didn't mean it wasn't there.

"You're the one good thing I have in my life right now." Those delicate fingers slid their way up to trace along my cheekbone, like she was working on memorizing my face. That ache did it—yanking her against me, my lips came down on hers, desperate to take away the weight on her shoulders. "You should've *told me*," she said between my stolen kiss and heartbreaking whimper. My chest fractured, jaw ticking as I sucked down a breath. The worst part was *I'd* fucking done this. I'd hurt her like this. And there wasn't a way to fix it. Either way—either decision I'd made—I was going to break something beautiful again.

"If we're doing this, the honesty goes both fucking ways, Jameson. You don't get to demand it from me and then hide something like turning yourself in to be *arrested*."

"I know. I *know, baby.* You're right. That wasn't fair. It was fucking shitty. I'm not going to try and justify it. I just..." Heart heavy with the distrust etched across the face I loved so much, I gathered the gumption to admit, "I'm not man enough to walk in there and do what needed to be done if you were breaking like this in front of me. I could never have left you like this. Never have left you crying outside that damn building and turned my back on you. It would've torn me in two. Maybe that makes me chicken shit. But I can't say I'm sorry because I'd do it again."

"What if they didn't let you come home?" She smacked her petite palms against my chest, punctuating the demand. "Did you *think* of that?"

Heart aching, shoulders drooping, I shook my head, honestly saying, "No, baby. No, I didn't." The horror that flashed across her features made me hate myself, and I rushed to explain, "Because the idea of not going home to you would have *killed me.* I trusted Judge Cullen, trusted Rob and Charlie to advocate, just like they did."

A breathy little scoff escaped her chest. "Got yourself a whole team, don't you?"

"Yeah, baby," I breathed, tucking a curl behind her ear. "Together, *we'll* beat this. I *know* we'll win. If I wasn't so confident, if there was any doubt in my body, I would tell you that. We'll get him. The whole family is digging up new angles. Now, come inside with me. Please."

"A lie of omission is still a lie, Jameson. I've done relationships built on deceit. Remember?"

"I know," I rasped, terror slicing through me as anger etched across her face. She soldiered on.

"And despite how ours started, I won't do it again. Please. Just… promise me. No more lies."

"*No more lies,*" I agreed, before leaning down and kissing her breathless, letting our bodies sink together, all the while sending up a silent prayer that I could make good on that promise. A throat cleared, and I knew Broderick was dying to excuse himself.

"Good," she said, peeling away. She turned to face our uncomfortable companions. "Now, somebody call Max. I need his help."

Noel

ENOUGH WAS FUCKING ENOUGH. Rage, so visceral my bones were vibrating, consumed every inch of my body. The selfish prick could call me names, insult my family, and try to steal my fire, but I would never let him get away with going after Jameson. I didn't give a shit if it was his idea or his damn demon of a father's. Jameson was *mine*. End. Of.

I'd been ranting about justice for the better half of the last hour as four sets of eyeballs tracked my movements.

"…If he's going to dominate in the courtroom, let's take the fight to him outside it. Fuck legal. Fuck strategy. We take this straight to the court of public motherfucking opinion," I snarled as Max plugged the USB I'd handed him into his computer, wide brown eyes cautiously tracking my livid pacing from one side of the room to the other. They blinked when his focus zeroed in on the file now open on his screen. Elora did the same thing from his side. Her lips were sealed as my diatribe finally ended. Like a concrete statue, Broderick sat unmoving in his chair in the corner, Axel leaning against the wall just behind him, just as motionless. He'd been here in under five minutes after Jameson texted him. I'd have to thank him when I wasn't seeing red someday.

"*Holy shit,*" Max said cheerily, leaning back to cross his arms as a sound more scoff than laugh burst through his lips. Jameson leaned in, only to stiffen. I knew what he was looking at. My bruises from the car accident and the day I showed up on Rhyett's step. My stomach turned like a bucking ship at sea. I'd never shown him those. Never shown anyone those. The way his knuckles went white where his fist rested on his thigh made me question my resolve to do it now, but I cleared my throat instead. Holding my ground. As Max casually scrolled through the file of damning evidence, I remembered the sinking feeling in my gut as I'd snapped pictures of shady-looking parking garage handoffs, not wanting to believe my own eyes. There were blatant candid shots with lowlifes and known felons.

Josie's late husband, Blaze, had friends in high places, and my play with Shamra paid off when she secured the last few pieces I'd needed without even hesitating. Hell, she seemed to enjoy herself, dusting the rust off those old reconnaissance skills.

"You got the videos off the hardware store cameras?" Jameson's eyes flicked to mine. I nodded.

"Yup. And the harbor and Grizzly Grind. Charlie pulled them both for evidence."

Jameson's smile twitched wider, understanding settling in. "Don't need a warrant when you can just ask the owners."

"Exactly," I said, smiling. "Turns out Mrs. Anderson, Captain McGrath, and your brother had no qualms about handing over what we needed."

"I mean. I'd cut 'em off before you knock his lights out," Max said, shaking his head. "But the point is pretty damn clear. You can see his face from the harbor cameras."

"Baby, you've just been sitting on all this the whole time?"

"Some of it," I admitted. "Charlie got the videos this afternoon. Some of it a friend sent over after last night, after things went sideways."

"A *friend?*" Jameson scowled up at me, nervous or jealous; I wasn't sure which. Either way, I smiled at the protective posture of his stiff shoulders and tense jaw. The flexing tendons in his arms.

"You remember when I told you about Blaze?" When Jameson and Max both nodded, I said, "What none of us talk about is that he lost his best friend in his second to last deployment. He'd promised to protect his sister, Shamra. Which is..."

When the words choked me, Jameson sucked down a breath, the pieces obviously clicking together as his face fell. "How he died." He scrubbed a palm over his face, aggrieved by the loss of a man he'd never met. I loved his big, broody, beautiful heart.

I nodded, my chest aching at the shadow of that funeral, the echo of those shots fired off in his honor. "Brothers, forever. He couldn't let him down. She's retired special ops now."

"*Pheeeeew,*" Max released the sound on a long exhale, like a deflating mylar balloon, as his fingers continued scrolling. "You're scary, Noelie-bear."

"Hell hath no fury," Jameson muttered, kicking an ankle up on his knee as he leaned back into the couch to evaluate me with a new scrutiny.

"But why the hell didn't you use this before?" Axel demanded, his blatant irritation finally breaking his monk-like silence.

A fire lit against my eyes, and I cursed the damn sting as they fell to my feet. Just like that, my rage simmered, memories of beach days full of laughter, sparkling gowns fanned out as I spun on dance floors, and bouquets on the counter aching where they still lived like ghosts in my chest.

The pain must have fractured my mask, because Jameson sucked down a breath before saying, "You didn't want to hurt him back. Didn't want him to get locked up and have that live on your conscience?"

The stupidity of my reality cracked through my center. Nobody had ever seen through me so clearly. "*I* was the one that stayed. *I* was the one dumb enough to think he'd change. The idea of the old Eric still being somewhere in there and trapping him in a cell...I felt like a monster. I thought if I left, if I filled my time, it would all just go away."

"*Baby*," Jameson soothed, but I could hear the pity in his voice as he snatched my hand and pulled me to him. I *loathed* being pitied. Even if it was him. Seeming to sense it, his voice leveled, "You could never, ever be a monster. These are his actions. You're just deciding not to lie for him anymore. Let him live with his choices."

I sniffled but nodded. "I know that you're right. I know it, but..."

"Something still aches to admit the cause is lost," Elora spoke up softly. "I get it."

"Why is this different? What changed?" Broderick asked gruffly, that ever-evaluative laser focus on me. Jameson's hand came to cup the back of my neck, thumb running a soothing line up and down the length of my spine.

When I didn't immediately respond, Elora did it for me, settling her hand on my knee with a reassuring squeeze. Her words were matter-of-fact as she said, "He came after Jameson this time."

Lips pursed, I nodded softly. Fuck with me—fine, I brought that on myself out of stubborn naivety, but fuck with my...my soul person? That was a very different game. One he was going to regret deciding to play.

The weight of our reality settled in Jameson's eyes a beat before he asked, "So, why did you ask for Max?"

"Jorogumo," I said simply, straightening and shifting towards Max as his eyes widened. The others all flicked their gazes between the two of us as a slow, amused smile cracked Max's handsome face. He flicked his dark bangs off his forehead.

"Um...gesundheit?" Axel teased, finally straightening off the wall, but I kept my focus on Max, whose expression was flickering in rapid succession between shock and bewildered entertainment.

"You clever little thing," Max muttered coyly, shaking his head as he dropped his eyes to the computer and began tapping in a rapid clacking of keys. "How'd you put it together?" There wasn't an ounce of doubt in his tone. He knew *exactly* what I knew, and it seemed he was already putting in the groundwork.

"The coffee shop—the first day you and El played babysitter."

"The day you dry-humped Jameson on the docks," he clarified with a sly smile.

Rolling my eyes, I corrected, "The day I *kissed* Jameson, yes. *You* got a call. I saw the screen."

"Um...is anybody going to translate for me?" Jameson grumbled, not bothering to conceal his annoyance, hand sliding down to clamp onto my shoulder to emphasize the words.

"Jorogumo is a prominent piece of Japanese folklore," Broderick explained. "Known as the binding bride, or sometimes spider woman —she's described as a lethal shapeshifter."

"Right," I affirmed. "She's known for luring men in with her beauty and then shifting into her true monster form." When every face expectantly turned to me under furrowed brows, I sighed. "Look, I liked manga in high school, okay?"

"I'm not connecting the dots," Axel admitted, looking frustrated.

"Max's 'mystery' job?" I added air quotes for good measure, both irritated and amused that nobody had bothered to pay better attention. "The tech work, the conference calls—he's an executive in a cyber defense company that lures criminals into their web before they destroy them, or they destroy themselves. It's called Jorogumo Defense."

If a breeze had blown through our living room, all four of them might have fallen out of their seats, judging by the minimal blood supply left to color their faces.

"And if he's willing, he's going to take this drive and do whatever the hell he would do with it if they had assigned him to take down

Connely Corp. My contact added a file in there you can use if his dad tries to retaliate."

Max's grin was maniacal, and I absolutely freaking loved it. "Why throw fists when you can throw his entire future?"

JAMESON

NOEL AND MAX made for a terrifying team.

In addition to defending against corporate espionage, our family bonus brother used his propensity for technological conquests to lure predators into government-cooperative webs, like some sort of cyber-vigilante. The man crashed at my place—draped over my couch like a rag doll, with his mouth wide open in ode to the Venus Fly Trap after one too many glasses of expensive Chardonnay—on a weekly damn basis. He turned salmon-pink if anyone uttered the name of his high school crush, Luca Moretti. Ate tacos like they were a primary food group, cried whenever El or Hadlee played *You've Got Mail*, baked cookies for Juniper *every* Mother's Day, rarely lost a bet on who would win a football game...and nonchalantly destroyed the lives of evil men for a living.

I would never look at his slick, expensive button-ups or collection of colognes the same. Especially not after he announced to the room that he'd actually been compiling his own file on Eric from the day he'd snagged his voice and face on his phone in Birch Barrel.

Between his findings and Noel's, and whatever freaky tech sabotage allowed him to drop anonymous tips to both authorities and the media, we were all piled on my couch watching Eric's swollen, purple and yellow face under a barrage of camera flashes as the feds escorted him to a cruiser in cuffs for the second time in twice as many days.

"Christ, you've got a badass right hook," Max muttered, lips upturned in satisfaction as we got our first clear shot at the damage.

"Damn straight," Axel said, knocking his shoulder into mine, where we sat on the couch.

"That's my man," Noel whispered, pinching my waist as she nuzzled tighter against my other side.

The best part? No matter what happened from here, she was

right. He might have been able to put the system in his greasy pocket. But *the people?* That's where the true power lies.

That was a battle not even the Connely Empire could win.

There was no coming back from being shoved into a glass house.

Max could live in my master bedroom for the rest of our damn lives, happily raiding my pantry stocked with his favorite liquors, and I'd never be able to pay him back for what he did for my girl.

Nightly sex-a-thons gave way to sinfully sweet cuddles dripping in an intimacy I'd never known, tentative new habits solidifying into the comfort of a reliable routine. Jameson dragged me along to the gym enough times that it felt like a second home, the lanky lines of the body I'd known gradually filling with just a hint of proud muscle.

The tumult of questions volleyed between us gradually vanished, and we welcomed in their place coffee made just the way we liked it and clothes sharing a closet in a chronically casual disarray neither of us cared enough to fix. Desperate kisses gradually transitioned into the familiar ease of something deeper as summer days gave way to the bitter chill of autumn. The salmon season ended, bringing with it a brief reprieve for Milo, Jameson, and his brothers before they geared up for cod. Brin started working back into the schedule at Grizzly Grind, effectively freeing most of my mental space. Rhyett would keep a spot for me, but using up time somewhere I could no longer add real value seemed a waste of resources on all fronts.

October came and went in a blur of oranges and reds, once green branches blushing with embarrassment at their impending nakedness. I was straightening the arrangement of miniature pumpkins on our counter on my last day in the shop, when a familiar focus caressed my neck, and relief coursed through me. Tomorrow was the last court appearance in Jameson's case, and his rough touch across my stomach as he came up behind me sent ease through my nervous center. So far, it looked like his legal team really had the damn thing in the bag. The radio silence from Eric after his final arrest solidified a blessed reprieve in the scheme of things. Small victories, but victories all the same. Leaning back into his hard chest, I breathed in that familiar musk.

"Missed you," I said, setting my head against him. Warm, soft lips pressed against my temple, and I sighed contentedly.

"You too, baby," he breathed back, comforting little tickles inching down my shoulder where his breath caressed a lazy line across the skin. "You about done here?"

Turning in his arms, I peered up at the man who flipped my world on its axis and breathed in his steady presence. After that initial shit show, Jameson hadn't shown a lick of nerves around *any* of it. With Eric in federal custody thousands of miles away, and life settling into our own new sense of normal, he'd barely acknowledged the bullshit my psycho ex stirred up while he was here.

"Yeah. I've got your coffee on the counter, and I think there are a couple of candles to set out, but then I'm good to go."

"Good. How do you feel?"

The question was obviously pertaining to my last day as a barista as I leapt off the cliff of comfort into the paralyzing free-fall of the unknown, but I let a slow, coy smile creep up my cheeks. "A little sore. Couldn't walk right this morning, but a few hours sitting with cold soda cans between my legs did the trick."

A solitary dark brow winged up like I'd snagged it on a fishhook, and he tongued at a canine, which I identified as his best suppressant against his own sense of humor. I burst out laughing, breaking his honest smile out as he smacked my ass, drawling, "Very classy."

"Always," I said with a wink. Sighing under his unwavering scrutiny and the little pinch against my tricep, I admitted, "Honestly...I'm nervous about still not having a plan. But...we'll figure it out after we survive tomorrow."

"Yeah," he said, grinning before he reunited our foreheads, tracing gentle little bunny kisses over my nose. "*We* will."

Jameson

NOT GUILTY ON ALL COUNTS. Those words through Judge Cullen's lips lit a fire of vindication in my chest, and it took every ounce of self-restraint not to leap into the air and shout *fuck yeah* as the gavel came down. My eyes met Max's in the back row, and he nodded in solidarity, his computer open, doing God-knows-what while he listened. Broderick gave me a solid thumbs up, and I shook Rob's hand like a dignified adult. But once we were on our feet, it was those brown doe-eyes that consumed every ounce of my being, and the instant I was free of the partition between court and civilians, she practically sprinted into my wide-open arms, colliding with me with just as much enthusiasm as we had that first day on the docks. Sans very public lip lock and koala hug, of course. My stomach knotted when I released her to find tears streaming down her delicate cheeks, eyes glassy as she opened her mouth twice before slamming it shut. I wiped my thumbs across her alabaster skin, soaking them up.

"We did it, baby," I said softly, fingers finding hers and threading together. A little sob hiccuped through her a beat before she nodded.

"We did it."

EPILOGUE

JAMESON

The week after Thanksgiving, my parents left for their first winter in Florida, and the remaining siblings breathed a collective sigh of relief. The twins and Mav were suddenly the sole occupants of the big house, all of them more than a little weirded out at the prospect. Noel's parents and brother, Alex—who I'd actually really hit it off with—left forty-eight hours later, leaving our small town feeling impossibly smaller.

The bite of winter had chapped my face in the four days we'd been on the water. Axel, Mav, and I brought on Caius, one of our endless roster of cousins, as our fourth crewman for the cod season, all of us thanking everything holy the snow held off long enough for us to train him in and make some damn money before the truly miserable conditions hit. My new vantage from the wheelhouse was...humbling, to say the least, knowing that three Rhodes generations had carved through these waters so I could do it so freely.

I pulled out my phone once I'd parked the truck in our drive, guilt weighing on my shoulders. We'd been so busy with all of our own bullshit, I'd barely talked to Alice since she left.

JAMESON

Hey sis, how's SoCal?

ALESSANDRA

Great! Enjoying the mild weather. You surviving cod?

JAMESON

Not too bad so far.

ALESSANDRA

Good! That makes me happy.

JAMESON

How's the new gig?

ALESSANDRA

Fine.

JAMESON

Just fine?

ALESSANDRA

Eh. Yeah. The job is great—I'm good at it.

JAMESON

But…?

ALESSANDRA

My boss is a dick.

I SNORTED, shaking my head as I tapped out a reply.

JAMESON

Bummer. Can you go around him?

ALESSANDRA

Nope.

He's the owner.

WINCING, I hopped out of the truck, walking around the nose as I typed my response.

JAMESON

Welp. Uhh, good luck with that.

ALESSANDRA

LOL very sage advice there, BIG brother. No pointers?

JAMESON

Get a new job?

ALESSANDRA

And let him win?! Absolutely not.

I WAS STILL SHAKING my head as I slid my phone into my back pocket and made my way to the front door. The house was warm with orange light when I stepped inside, something sweet and vaguely reminiscent of apple cider filled the air, and Noel had some swanky, jazzy Christmas music softly playing over the speakers, giving the whole thing a Norman Rockwell vibe nobody sane could have predicted I'd enjoy as much as I did. Go figure.

"Baby!" I barked, slipping from my boots and wondering where the hell she'd run off to. The kitchen was empty, nerves echoing in my center at her continued silence. As I rounded into the dining room, I found her standing expectantly, worrying that little bottom lip as she swayed her hips back and forth. She set the table for two, the nice plates and gold placemats her mother gave us, out on either side of a roast chicken, mashed potatoes, and steamed carrots.

"Welcome home," she said sweetly, my heart skipping a fucking beat as I closed the distance to pull her against me. Noel melded into my frame like someone had carved her from it, the echo of old fear washing away as our bodies collided, doing all the talking they needed to without saying a damn word.

Home. We were home. Something buzzed in the energy between us, an electric anticipation. Pulling back to peer down at her, I canted my head, and she smiled nervously, biting that bottom lip again.

"What's that look for?"

"I think...I think I figured it out."

"Gonna have to give me more than that," I said, studying her focus, something in my soul igniting at the energy vibrating off her.

"My...next step. I think I figured it out."

Sucking down a breath, I offered her a smile, before pulling the chair nearest her out, as that was the gentlemanly thing to do. "So, we *are* celebrating," I insinuated. She sat, grinning timidly, before she nodded and I took my spot across from her. My Skittles was nervous, but there was a confidence underlying the motion that made me sit a little straighter as I swiped the open wine bottle and poured us both glasses. "Whenever you're ready," I said, motioning to the table expectantly.

"I may or may not have to go back to school," she hedged cautiously. I chuckled.

"Alright," I said, smirking at Noel squirming in her seat, anxiety palpably vibrating off her tight shoulders. "You're cute when you're nervous."

"*You're* cute when *you're* nervous," she scoffed, rolling her eyes. With a little harrumph, she straightened her spine, steeling herself like I might reject this plan of hers. A sudden wave of anxiety hit my system. What if she was leaving? What if going back to school meant *leaving* Mistyvale? "I want to start a foundation that helps women get out of unsafe situations. And before you point it out, I know there are hundreds all over the country. But I want ours to be different."

Intrigue brought my forearms to the table, bracing myself, proud as hell as she stood her ground. "Go on."

"I want the nonprofit to help them get legal protection, and safe, affordable housing, and liaise between law enforcement and lawyers with them, so it's not so intimidating. I want to host yoga, and self-defense classes, and have a workplace wardrobe closet they can utilize to land a job that ensures actual financial independence—for a lot of them, it will be the first time they've felt that." She shifted in her seat, straightening that tight little dress I was ardently trying not to think about. "To expand on that, I want to offer personal branding and business development classes, bring in volunteers to teach and take headshots—equip them with the skill sets and confidence to get out, *and* feel safe doing so."

With eleven siblings, I'd felt the rush of pride countless times in my life. But nothing had ever compared to the way my body thrummed now. She wasn't my little Skittles anymore. She was a fucking phoenix, about to rise from the ashes of her old life, and she was all fucking mine.

"You need an investor? You know a grumpy old man with a passion for startups," I said with a wink.

Before the words had even left my mouth, she was grinning and shaking her head, red curls bobbing where they now danced to her collar bone. "No. Thank you, though. I'll secure donations myself."

"You know I'm here if you need me."

"I know," she said, nodding. "But I can't teach them how to build their life in a way they can't duplicate. And as much as I love your heart, you're the one and only Jameson Rhodes in this world."

"Well, Miss McShane, if I didn't know better, I'd say that was a compliment," I said teasingly, remembering those first combative days when she'd arrived on the island.

Her smile sent a familiar ray of sunshine straight into my heart. "Oh, Mr. Rhodes, it might've just been."

OBNOXIOUS, incessant bouncing on my shoulder woke me from a dead sleep, and I blinked into the soft gray gloom of our room. Chloe contentedly stretched out along my side, happily oblivious to her psychotic owner, who was grinning down at me expectantly.

"Come on!" she stage-whispered with no regard to the fact that our cat and I would prefer to rest uninterrupted.

"What?" I mumbled.

"Come. *On!*" She pushed my shoulder again for emphasis with each word, as though that explained everything. "Get. Up."

"Middle of the night—" I grumbled, her lips silencing my protest before she sprung from the bed with more enthusiasm than her feline friend ever showed. "Baby what's—"

"Stop grumbling and *come on!*"

A groan rumbled in my chest, but I rolled my numb-as-shit frame over, glaring at the red four-o'clock on the nightstand. "Our flight's not for six hours."

"Psh," she scoffed, latching onto my bare arm and dragging my ass off the bed. "This isn't about *the flight*," she muttered, still yanking me through the room as Chloe gave a lazy flick of her tail, one eye open a beat before she exposed her tubby little belly and returned to her glorious slumber. Great. I was jealous of a damn cat.

"*Baby*," I complained as she got us to the front door and hurled my winter jacket at me, not bothering to explain as she dove into her cute little snow boots. "Freaking chaos pixie, I swear to God."

She giggled as my eyes dropped to her shoes. *Heels* on *snow boots* —what kind of cosmic joke was that? It didn't matter that they were sexy as hell, or made her legs look two miles long, they weren't fucking practical. Hurrying to keep pace, I followed my Skittles out into the subtle crunch of our first snow of the season, the world aglow with the soft white of a blustering winter night.

Noel led me right into the middle of the damn street before bouncing on her toes, blinking expectantly as she beamed at me through the biting wind.

I stared back at her, entirely perplexed and no less sure as she hurled her arms around me, the fur of her hood stuck in my mouth as she squealed happily into my shoulder.

"Um..." When she lifted her face to the sky to collect fat crystalline flakes on her bare lashes and freckled nose, it finally hit me. "This is your first snow."

She turned her face—the perfect picture of winter with her rosy cheeks and now-decorated lashes—back in my direction and beamed. My heart swelled. And despite how desperately I wanted to go climb back under our warm covers, I couldn't miss this.

Not her first taste of frozen sky water.

Not her first snow angel.

I was certainly going to be her first snowball fight, even if the hour *was* ungodly.

Because Noel McShane was my world. And I would damn well do whatever it took to see her happy.

Thank you for reading!

WANT MORE JAMESON AND NOEL? I have a bonus epilogue, *A Christmas Proposal* for you. Plus, find out who's story comes next! You can grab your copy here: https://BookHip.com/XLMXTNA

CAN'T GET ENOUGH of the Rhodes family? Join us on the Grayshell Unhinged Patreon for exclusive bonus scenes + Character art (SFW and NSFW) + sneak peeks at my current WIP. You can join HERE.

WHAT COMES NEXT?

Order *Finding A Way Back Home*, the third Nomadic Rhodes book HERE! (Releasing 4/18/24)

E-Book Pre-order: https://a.co/d/aln3641

Signed paperback + swag Pre-Order: https://shorturl.at/ikEG2

AFTERWORD

Dear reader,

Jameson and Noel were born from a few things: my love of the sea, obsession with coffee, secret desire to chop off my hair (thanks, Noel, it's kinda rockin'), and my absolute obsession with the brooding, misunderstood, reluctant hero that can't help but fall for sunshine on wheels. Especially—*especially*—when they get off on the wrong foot, and drive each other kinda crazy.

I absolutely adore these two, and writing their slow burn was way too much fun, despite much revising that required unhealthily copious amounts of caffeine to finish

Fun fact! We actually spent three months in an Alaskan fishing town while I wrote *Brewing*, and having survived a summer there, I can confirm I named my island appropriately haha. While we were there, I managed the cutest little coffee shop right off the water, and while I did not receive Noel-sized gifts (I blame the fact that I'm introverted, and not a 5'3" sunbeam in hot pink), I know baristas that did. I don't think my 'method writing' has ever been taken to quite that extreme before, but I think it shows in Noel, which I love.

If you also loved their grumpy sunshine dynamic, I would be eternally honored if you gush online a little. (Honestly, though, those posts make me weep, and I tuck them away so the hard days don't win. You guys are my *why*.)

Thank you so much for reading.

PS. In all seriousness though, if you're staying in an unhealthy situation, please, please, please, don't wait for a Jameson or a Max to swoop in wearing grayscale flannel or gorgeous designer slacks to save you. I've unfortunately been witness to the after effects of the real thing too many times. When I started Noel's story, I had no idea that someone I love very much would end up in a spookily similar situation, and suddenly this book took on a whole new tone. It was unbelievably important to me that I showed that even the most incredible women sometimes still have work to do, and that ultimately, they have to save themselves.

Please get help. Get out. Reach out to your local women and children's shelter, or the national domestic abuse hotline, and consult professionals. Too many Noels are no longer in this world because they couldn't see a way out.

You're loved.

You're worth it.

Know there are people out there who will fight for you. You deserve to feel safe, valued and seen.

Hugging you from the road-xoxo, SJB

ACKNOWLEDGMENTS

First and foremost, I will always be eternally grateful for my amazing readers! I know every author says they have amazing readers, but honestly, mine are the best. Whether you're new to the party, or have been around since I first shared my vision for my fantasy series, you guys are why I do this. The beautiful posts, reviews, tags, and DMs when you relate to a character, scene or story make it all worth it. Love you forever.

MY HUBBY, thank you for everything you do to keep me (and our house) running. It takes one hell of a man to keep the ship afloat when your partner is buried in pages for days at a time. A little piece of you ends up in every hero I write, but I think Jameson got a few. Love you, stud.

HEATHER, my darling, my life preserver/right hand/sounding board/cheerleader/infinite supplier of tough love and virtual hugs, this book would not be what it is without you. Thank you for everything that you do. I couldn't do this without you.

JESSICA, my fellow logophile and dry humor enthusiast! Thank you for being a fucking kick ass critique partner, lamenter of all things indie, and lover of my fictional babies. Thank you for seeing what I see and always fighting to illuminate the vision. I'm so grateful our corners of the internet collided when they did.

KATE, my platonic soul mate, thank you for breathing life into this story, for loving me always and encouraging me endlessly. Thanks for having my back, and loving my growly, ex-threatening fisherman right out the gate. Stick your toes in the sand for me. Xoxo

HALAIA, My muse, my inspiration, my supplier of quick witticisms and hilarious one liners. Thank you for showing me the parts of our

'Mistyvale' that you love. You are in every book I write, but especially in this one. I see you in all the beautiful moments on these pages.

LILI, can I bite your nose? Cheers to late night writing marathons, panicked phone calls, and countless, "You can do it. What if..." conversations. You're my ride or die, baby. Thanks for being the voice I can always count on, and the smile I know I'll see when I need one.

HAILEY, my light in the dark, my unending inspiration. Thank you for showing me how to do the damn thing, and believing in me, always, even though I write smut lol

DADDY, I'm shocked you read this, but not really. Thank you for your unyielding support of all things Sydne. To infinity...

SHANNON, my dear, you are magical at converting babbling into beautiful covers. Thank you for two gorgeous options for this bad boy.

To all of my amazing indie author friends. Ya'll. I could never have gotten this far on my own. Bella, Jessica, and the 'writer chat' goblins, you guys have given me so much encouragement these last weeks, I don't know if I would have made it without you.

ABOUT THE AUTHOR

Sydne Barnett is a lover of spunky, badass heroines, and heroes that embrace their wild. She's an avid reader, never turns down a good cup of coffee, loves hiking with her hubby, and lives for finding their next adventure.

If she's not writing, you can probably find her behind her camera, swimming, or curled up with a homemade pastry, watching Friends, HYMYM, or Gilmore Girls.

Raised in the Treasure Valley, Idaho, Sydne has a love for one-light towns, and winding backroads, but refusing to ignore her soul's call for adventure, she hit the road with her family, and now they call the world their home.

Let's connect!

Reader's Group: https://www.facebook.com/groups/grayshellbabes

Tiktok: https://www.tiktok.com/@barnettbooktalk

Instagram: https://www.instagram.com/barnettbooktalk/

Newsletter: https://shorturl.at/acJS7

Patreon: https://www.patreon.com/GrayshellUnhinged

Nomadic Rhodes

South of The Skyway (Book 1)

Finding A Way Back Home (Book 3)

Romantic High Fantasy as S.J. Barnett

Commanding Flame And Shield (Grayshell rising, book one)

Commanding Earth And Shadow (Grayshell Rising, Book Two)